RELICS

Previously published Worldwide Mystery title by
MARY ANNA EVANS

ARTIFACTS

To those who taught me to read and write.
To all who understand the power of words.
To everyone who ever shared with me a story that they loved.

Recycling programs
for this product may
not exist in your area.

Relics

A Worldwide Mystery/May 2015

First published by Poisoned Pen Press

ISBN-13: 978-0-373-26943-3

Copyright © 2005 by Mary Anna Evans

Printed in U.S.A.

RELICS

MARY ANNA EVANS

W🌐RLDWIDE®

TORONTO • NEW YORK • LONDON
AMSTERDAM • PARIS • SYDNEY • HAMBURG
STOCKHOLM • ATHENS • TOKYO • MILAN
MADRID • WARSAW • BUDAPEST • AUCKLAND

Acknowledgments

I'd like to thank everyone who reviewed *Relics* in manuscript form: Michael Garmon, Rachel Garmon, David Evans, Suzanne Quin, Carl Quin, Lillian Sellers, David Reiser, Leonard Beeghley, Mary Anna Hovey, Kelly Bergdoll, Diane Howard, Jerry Steinberg, the staff of the Mississippi Writing/Thinking Institute, the teachers and staff of Brentwood School and, especially, Assistant Chief William Davis of the City of Montgomery Fire Department, who ensured that Fire Marshal Strahan behaved as a firefighter should. I'd also like to thank Dr. Liana Lupas of the American Bible Society for her expertise, which greatly enhanced Miss Dovey's song. Historical astronomy expertise was provided by the knowledgeable denizens of the HASTRO-L Internet discussion group. For communications questions, I relied on Thomas Farley, whose website, privateline.com, was particularly helpful, and Mark G. van der Hoek, a senior RF Engineer with a global consulting firm. Mark, a twenty-year veteran of the communications industry, went the extra mile in helping me keep the details of the Sujosa's communications woes plausible. These people caught errors of the grammatical, logical, psychological and ecological sort. All errors that remain are mine.

I owe Jenny Hanahan, Donis A. Casey, and my daughter Amanda a debt of gratitude for the use of their names. They bear no resemblance to the fictional characters named for them, although I do like those three characters a great deal and was glad to give them such lovely names.

Writing is both an art and a business, and I am grateful to everyone who has helped me improve my art and learn my business: Anne Hawkins, my agent; Robert Rosenwald and Barbara Peters, my publishers; Ellen Larson, my editor; the fine folks at Poisoned Pen Press—Jen Semon, Marilyn Pizzo, Monty Montee, Michelle Tanner and Nan Beams; and my publicist, Judy Spagnola. And, finally, my eternal gratitude goes out to the booksellers who get my books out to readers, and to the readers who enjoy them.

PROLOGUE

COLUMBUS COULD NOT have known how many people he would lead from the Old World to the New. The oceans were so wide and the new lands were so wild. At first, he—and the explorers who followed him—saw these lands only as obstacles barring the way to the spicy riches of the East. But then they learned of El Dorado. Many lives were spent in quest of a city with rooftops burning gold in the light of the setting sun.

In the end, the wealth of the Americas proved greater even than a fantasy city of gold. There was indeed gold in this New World, ready to be sifted from the ground or, more conveniently, stolen from the native kings. There were riches also to be had in the slave labor of those kings and their subjects. When the Old World tasted chocolate and maize and tomatoes and sweet, deadly tobacco smoke, still more fortunes were made. The wealthiest civilization the world has ever seen was built on the riches Columbus stumbled on by accident.

Not so long after Columbus' fateful journey, a ship found harbor in the Gulf of Mexico. Its weary passengers gathered their belongings and began walking north, given the will to go on by the elusive dream of fortune. But they found no gold or silver, no wealth or prosperity. In the river valley where they stopped at last, there was only land—black earth and colored clay—but that was treasure enough.

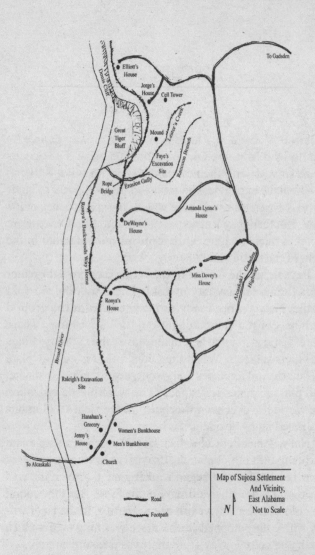

Map of Sujosa Settlement
And Vicinity,
East Alabama
Not to Scale

N

Road
Footpath

ONE

FAYE LONGCHAMP WAS born on the first floor of a Tallahassee hospital built at an elevation of fifty-five feet above sea level. In the thirty-six years since then, she had never set foot on a taller hill. Her cherished home, a tumbledown antebellum plantation house called Joyeuse, was built for her great-great-grandfather by his slaves—some of whom were also her ancestors. It sat firmly on an island with a maximum elevation of seventeen feet, and few of its inhabitants ever strayed far from their coastal paradise. Faye herself had never, before today, left the low-lying Florida Panhandle. If the term "flatlander" was ever true of anybody, it was surely true of Faye.

This was the reason the gaping ravines that yawned along the Alabama roadside made her clutch the steering wheel of her twenty-five-year-old Pontiac in white-knuckled terror. When her tires rolled too close to the edge of the worn pavement, crumbles of asphalt slid down slopes that looked vertical to Faye's flatlander eyes. And her tires rolled too close to the edge of the pavement with frightening regularity, because her barge-sized car was not built to maneuver hairpin turns. Faye had not expected Alabama to look like this. She made a mental note to never, ever venture into Colorado.

"Where are the guard rails?" she muttered. "How can

they possibly build a road like this without guard rails? This is America. Somebody might get sued."

Joe Wolf Mantooth sat in the passenger seat. Sometimes, the view out his window encompassed nothing but autumn-hued trees and a clear, meandering stream. Other times, the same window revealed a dizzying drop into the depths of a roadside precipice, but Joe always looked as relaxed as an old man after a good dinner. This was an accomplishment of sorts for a twenty-six-year-old.

"Want me to drive, Faye?"

Faye wanted to blurt out, "Are you kidding? You don't even have a driver's license," but Joe didn't deserve her rudeness. Instead, she said, "I can handle it."

She wished she could tear her eyes off the road, because her peripheral vision was picking up glimpses of loveliness. Russet-hued sumacs stood flaming among persimmons and sweet gums that simply couldn't decide what color they wanted to be. Their yellow and orange and purple leaves trembled like bits of glass in a kaleidoscope, framed by the laurel oak's constant green. All her life, Faye had heard people raving about autumn leaves. Until now, she'd never understood what the fuss was about.

The trees on Joyeuse Island were predominantly palms and live oaks, with an occasional dogwood planted by some ancestor who enjoyed white flowers at Easter time. Live oaks got their name because they carried their green leaves through every season. Palm trees held onto their fronds until they turned brown and fell off. The dogwoods tried to put on a show, but Joyeuse's short autumns made sure that each red leaf lasted about a day before it browned and dropped to the dirt.

Here in the southernmost reaches of the Appalachians, Faye was seeing autumn in all its glory for the first time, but enjoying it would have required her to take her attention away from the narrow, winding roadway. Convinced that doing so would bring certain death, she firmly insisted that the fluttering leaves stay in her peripheral vision.

Joe leaned back against the headrest and closed his eyes. His rhythmic breathing was the only sound in the car except for Faye's occasional cursing of the civil engineer who designed the deathtrap roadway beneath her tires.

The ever-darkening sky wasn't helping matters. Faye glanced at her watch. Sunset was still an hour away, but the sun was far on the other side of a mountain clad in autumnal clothing, and the trees' garish colors weren't bright enough to light the pavement ahead of her. She flipped on her headlights and goosed the accelerator.

Faye was eager to reach her destination for reasons that had nothing to do with the oncoming darkness or the treacherous road. Her new job as archaeologist for the NIH-funded Sujosa Genetic History and Rural Assistance Project—commonly called simply the Rural Assistance Project—excited her personally, as well as professionally. Here was her chance to do some important science, and to make a difference in the world, too.

As Faye had discovered while preparing for the job, the Sujosa had lived in an isolated valley in these hills since God was in kindergarten, and they held their secrets well. Their dark brown skin and Caucasian features suggested that they had arrived in Alabama sometime after 1492, but fringe theorists liked to argue that they might have beaten Columbus to the New World. Extreme fringe theorists thought they were one of the Lost Tribes of Israel.

Everyone agreed that they were settled in Alabama by Revolutionary times, because the word "Sujosa" appeared in several written documents of the era. Other documentary evidence proved that they had, at times, been deprived of the right to vote and own land, simply because their skin wasn't white enough. First by law and then by custom, they'd been forced to worship separately from their white neighbors. Their children had been segregated into their own school until as recently as 1978, even after black children were finally admitted to white schools.

In fact, no one had ever given a tinker's dam about the Sujosa—until a local doctor noticed that they didn't get AIDS, even when they'd been exposed many times. When the issue of *Health* that carried Dr. Brent Harbison's article hit the mailbox of the National Institutes of Health, the powerful and wealthy eye of the United States of America turned, for the first time, toward some of its weakest and poorest citizens.

The result was the Rural Assistance Project, whereby the NIH hoped to isolate the genetic basis for the Sujosa's formidable immune systems, and give a hand to the Sujosa settlement at the same time. The NIH wanted to know where in Europe or Africa or Asia (or, for that matter, Antarctica) these people originally lived, and where they got their inherited ability to fend off disease. A geneticist, a linguist, an oral historian, and assorted technicians would work with Faye to dig up the Sujosa's past, while an education specialist and a physician would work to help the land-poor Sujosa's future.

The project was an archaeologist's dream. And there could be no job more personally intriguing for a dark-skinned, Caucasian-featured archaeologist like Faye.

Faye glanced at Joe, who appeared to be sleeping, and smiled. It had taken quite a bit of wangling to get him on board the project as her assistant. Governmental agencies tended to be finicky about things like high school diplomas, and Joe didn't have one. His paycheck would be absurdly small, compared to his value to the team, but sometimes money wasn't the most important thing. She turned her eyes back to the road.

It couldn't be far to the settlement now. She passed through Alcaskaki, the last town before the bridge, and saw that there wasn't much to see—just a few city blocks of downtown surrounded by wood-frame houses and farmland. On the far outskirts of Alcaskaki, the farmland petered out and a ravine opened up on the left-hand side of the road. To her right sprawled the county high school, a dusty collection of institutional buildings clustered protectively around a monumental football stadium. A bare handful of cars remained in the parking lot, its students having fled for the day.

Leaves, grown tired of living, dropped from the dimly lit branches above, through the bright cones of her headlights, and onto the roadbed—red, yellow, orange, purple, and gold. As she drove over them, her tires stirred them into the air again.

The object dropped out of the trees ahead, like a panther after prey. She threw the wheel violently to the left, and the car obeyed by veering hard, then skidding on the gravel scattered over the roadway's crumbling pavement.

There was no time to study the thing as she passed under it. She retained only the image of someone dangling limp and blue-faced. Perched above was someone else, swathed in a hooded jacket. Beneath the hood, a dark face was lit by blue-green eyes the color of the luminous gulf waters around her island home. Then both faces faded out of sight, and she was fighting to regain control, thinking only of the deep chasm to her left. She heard the sound of shoes dragging over the roof of her car.

The Bonneville's brakes squealed as they fought against the momentum the old car had earned through its sheer bulk. It might stop sliding toward the ravine's sheer flank, and it might not, but the answer was a matter of physics. She and Joe were simply along for the ride.

THE CAR SKIDDED to a stop—dangerously near the edge of the ravine, but not in it. Dust rose around its tires as Faye jerked her door open and ran back along the road.

"What happened?" Joe said, running after her. His longer legs negated her head start and he was abreast of her within seconds. "Faye! Are you okay?"

"I think somebody's hurt." She pointed down the road.

Joe put on a burst of speed and reached the dangling form first, grasping it under its arms and lifting it to release the rope's tension.

"It's okay, Faye. Nobody's hurt."

"How can that be?" Then she saw what he held in his hands. Bottled-up fear turned to rage and she slapped the lifeless head as hard as she could. It was a papier-mâché dummy of a horned man wearing nothing but a banner that said, "Devils Go Home!"

"Somebody worked hard on this," Joe said, bending its articulated joints with the appreciation of a fellow craftsman.

Faye wasn't interested in the artistic quality of a prank that had nearly sent her and Joe to their deaths. She looked up into the tree, and into the darkening woods. There was no one there.

She pulled her father's pocketknife out of her pocket and cut the devil's rope. "I'm taking this with me so it doesn't kill somebody. We have to track down the idiot who made it."

"Nobody's hurt, Faye," Joe said again, as she hurled the loose-limbed devil into the Pontiac's back seat. "That's what counts. Let's go."

Faye took a deep breath and blew it out slow. Joe was right. When it came to the important things, like life and death and nature and spiritual stuff, he usually was. He seemed to have an esoteric Creek spiritual practice to suit every possible crisis of the soul. Faye's expertise lay in practicalities, like paying the bills. When she got out of graduate school and finished renovating her two-hundred year-old house and started putting some money aside re retirement, that's when she'd have time to meditate on the meaning of human existence. In the meantime, she had Joe to take care of things like that for her.

"Yeah," she echoed. "Nobody's hurt, and that's what counts." She cranked her old car and pointed it toward the Sujosa settlement. She would have enough on her plate as it was without tracking down mysterious kids in hooded jackets. She was about to take on a job for which she was barely qualified, joining a team of seasoned professionals a month into the game. While somehow managing not to fall off these god-awful hills.

No pressure there. No pressure at all.

TWO

As THEY CROSSED the Broad River bridge and entered the Sujosa settlement, autumn passed and winter settled in. The higher elevation surely contributed to the colder weather, and so did the brisk wind whipping along the river valley, but Faye couldn't shake her impression that there had been a change in season during the short drive. She reached into her tote bag and pulled out a black cardigan to wrap herself in.

The Sujosa settlement clustered on the riverbank, around a flat spot of ground that housed a church and a building bearing a sign that said, "Hanahan's Grocery and Sundries." A few houses were visible along roads that wound up the hills on either side of the church and store. They were scattered at intervals that suggested each was associated with several acres of land. Garden plots, left fallow by the fall harvest and marked only by bare soil and a few collard plants with enough guts to face winter, lay behind each one.

Following the directions she'd learned by heart, Faye drove past a tall, narrow house that gave a dignified air to the flanks of the hill to her right. It proudly sported mint-green asbestos siding, evidence that its owners had enjoyed a period of prosperity sometime during the mid-twentieth century. Dr. Andrews Raleigh, the project leader, had written to her explaining that it served as the bunkhouse for the men working on the project.

She parked the car in front of the smaller women's bunk-house nestled at the base of the same hill. A small, squa

building with a tall, peaked roof, it was the purest example
of a four-square Georgian vernacular house that Faye had
ever seen. Whoever had built it had enjoyed as much status
as a poor community like this one could confer.

Faye turned to Joe as they got out of the car. "I guess I'm
staying here. You're back at the green house, if you want
to go check it out."

Joe nodded, and Faye headed up the steps. After a short
hesitation, she went inside, surprising a statuesque brunette
apparently on the way out. Setting down a large metal briefcase, the woman extended a hand.

"You must be Faye Longchamp. I'm Carmen Martinez."
She carried herself with a confidence that lent glamour to
her tee-shirt and stylishly cut jeans. "I'm doing the oral
histories."

"Pleased to meet you," said Faye.

Oral historian. That was a job for someone who enjoyed going door-to-door, sitting in rocking chairs and trying to coerce old folks into telling her their tales. At first
glance, Faye wasn't sure Carmen was the right person for
the job. People tend to trust people like themselves, and
Faye doubted that flamboyant Carmen had much in common with folks who'd hardly left their remote settlement
in—how long? Nobody knew.

"I'll show you your room," said Carmen. "You're across
the hall from me, and Laurel is next to you." As Faye followed Carmen on the brief tour of the house, she thought
about the task before her. The Sujosa were thought to be a
tri-racial isolate group like the Melungeons of Appalachia
or the Redbones of Louisiana. Common wisdom held that
these relic populations were remnants of colonial America:
the products of intermarriage among Native Americans,
Africans imported as slaves, and Europeans who had imported themselves.

But other origin legends flourished. Some Melungeons

believed that their ancestors included Turks who reached
the Americas as servants or slaves on European sailing vessels. Some people thought the Sujosa descended from Portuguese sailors shipwrecked in the Gulf of Mexico. Cynical
observers saw such tales as efforts to explain away the fact
of dark skin without claiming the stigma of African descent. Nobody had ever known the origins of these groups
for certain, and nobody had much cared, until now.

After a tour of the bedrooms, bathroom, and kitchen,
Carmen led her back to the parlor. "You'll want to come
to our regular Friday team meeting tonight. We meet in
the church at seven-thirty. It'll be a good chance to get
you up to speed."

Faye wrapped one side of her unbuttoned cardigan over
the other. Carmen seemed plenty comfortable in her short-
sleeved tee-shirt, which made Faye feel like a wimp.

"I understand that Dr. Raleigh went ahead and began
excavating while he was waiting for me to be approved for
the position."

Carmen sighed. "I don't know why the bureaucrats sat
on your application while the rest of us were out here getting started. Raleigh should have done something."

"It wasn't his fault," Faye cut in, not anxious to start
ragging on her principal investigator before she even met
him. "I was a last-minute hire. He had a lead archaeologist in place—my research advisor, Dr. Magda Stockard-
McKenzie—but her health took a turn for the worse. It's
not easy being pregnant at 45."

"Better her than me," Carmen said, "although my *abuela*
keeps telling me that I need to start making babies before
she's too old to warp them with her Cuban ghost stories."

Faye couldn't make out a single wrinkle in Carmen's
olive skin. "Tell your grandmother that I said you've got
time."

"Yeah, maybe, but my *abuela* doesn't think she'll live to

see the day. Of course, the last time I was home, I caught her on a ladder washing her second-story windows. She'll outlive us all. But you don't want to hear my family stories. You want to unpack your car, then go check out your site."

Faye had never before been invited to put professional obsessiveness over social niceties. She was going to like it here.

Responding to the sound of footsteps crossing the porch, Carmen reached for the door, saying, "That'll be our roomie, Laurel. She's the education specialist hired to tutor the Sujosa children. You'll like her." Raising her voice so she could be heard outside, she said, "Hold on! I'm coming," then flung open the door.

Joe stood framed in the doorway with Faye's laptop hanging from one massive shoulder and her suitcase dangling from the other. His black ponytail was caught up in the suitcase strap, but he couldn't free it without setting down the fully loaded portable file box that he gripped with both hands. Joe's brawny frame was perfectly relaxed under a load that, combined, weighed more than Faye herself, but the lavender taffeta toiletry bag hanging from his wrist succeeded in making him look uncomfortable in a way that his other burdens could not. It contrasted fetchingly with his green eyes.

"I see that you don't actually *need* to unpack your car." Carmen had the slightly dazed expression that afflicted most women upon their first good look at Joe, but she was still capable of speech. Faye chalked up a point in her favor. The woman had all the earmarks of a worthy friend.

"Since you don't have to unpack, you'll have time to eat. They don't cook much at the men's bunkhouse, so your friend…" She lifted an eyebrow at Faye.

"My assistant. His name is Joe."

"…so Joe can eat here with you and me. I'll open another can of soup."

A can of soup. Faye was glad Joe's face was hidden as he leaned over to put the laptop down. He didn't consider canned soup to be actual food. It was obvious who would be assuming the unpaid role of project cook, and it wouldn't be Faye. Or Can-opener Carmen, either.

FAYE WAS LYING belly-down in the dirt, looking deep into a mud hole. She was trying to find some evidence that a professional archaeologist was involved in making this mess. So far, she was having no luck. She was thinking something along the lines of *The NIH should sue Dr. Raleigh for malpractice,* but she wasn't in the habit of talking to herself, so she didn't say it out loud. This was a good thing. While her head had been hanging down below the ground surface, Raleigh had walked up behind her.

"Ms. Longchamp—I hope you're happy with the start I've made in your absence." Dr. Raleigh, department chair at the Tuscaloosa university running the Rural Assistance Project, was a short, stout man with a swagger. Faye could forgive him for being short, since that wasn't his fault. She could even forgive him for being stout, which might not have been his fault. But she couldn't forgive the swagger, because she knew that it was wholly within his control.

Faye was conscious of the mud on the palms of her hand and the toes of her boots. A great brown blotch of mud adorned her chest and, if she closed one eye, she could see the grimy smear across the bridge of her nose. While she would have preferred to look and smell sweeter when she met her supervisor, mud was an archaeologist's occupational hazard.

Still, it wasn't embarrassment over her appearance that put her at a loss for words. It was that she had not yet recovered from the shock of discovering, within her first hour at the site, that Raleigh had made an undeniable wreck of her work before she'd even arrived.

She'd once heard Magda, her research advisor and friend, refer to Andrews Raleigh as a "self-satisfied bag of detritus," but she'd never heard her question the man's professional competence. In the chill twilight, seeing the mud hole that he considered a professional-quality excavation, she wondered how Magda could have given Raleigh so much credit.

Instead of neatly excavated units with precisely vertical sides, square corners, and flat floors, she'd found dozens of muddy holes and a single large pit that looked like a buffalo wallow.

"You and your crew have certainly moved a lot of dirt," she said cautiously. "I'm looking forward to managing such a hardworking team. What made you choose this site for your first excavation?"

"If I've chosen well, and I think I have, you'll find what you need right here and there will be no need for any other excavations. I chose this site because aerial photos show that the area was historically used as a garbage dump. When you review the historical documents, you'll see that I'm right. What better place to construct a history of the Sujosa, who we know have lived here for centuries?"

Faye, who had reviewed every available historical document on the Sujosa while chomping at the bit to begin work, was unimpressed by his logic. The spot where she was standing had indeed been a garbage dump—beginning in the 1940s. There was no reason to think that any information about the Sujosa's first three hundred years in Alabama was going to be found there, and it was a waste of project money to dig for it. But her first meeting with Raleigh wasn't the time to tell him so.

"I'm looking forward to getting started tomorrow."

"Not tomorrow. It's Saturday, and your crew's off. A lot of the team leaves the settlement for the weekend, anyway. You can get started Monday, but come to the meeting tonight. It will be a good chance to show you the ropes."

Faye nodded, still trying to grasp that Raleigh had wasted a full month on a bunch of mud holes, and that he had no sense that she was dying to get to work. He seemed to expect her to say something, so she manufactured a diplomatic response.

"I can see that this is going to be a challenge."

THREE

THE CHURCH WAS tiny, and, unlike most congregations, the members were gathered toward the front of the sanctuary. The first pew looked to be filled with folks whose names ended in "Ph.D." The half dozen or so technicians and support staff, Joe towering among them, lounged in the second row, where they could be seen but certainly not heard. With the exception of Faye and Joe, everyone in the room was white. Big surprise.

Plopping in the front row—a mere doctoral student amongst full professors—her soiled clothes won her a comfortable amount of breathing room. The gentlemen on either side of her each pulled a few inches away, hoping she'd keep her mud to herself. She hadn't had time to change clothes because she'd rushed back to the bunkhouse after meeting Raleigh and placed a panicked call to Magda.

"What am I going to do? The whole time I'm waiting for approval, Raleigh's out here screwing up the work—he's not even excavating in a rational place. He's the principal investigator. How do I tell him I've got to start over from scratch because he doesn't know what in hell he's doing?"

"You don't tell him. Our department chair is his best friend. If you challenge Raleigh's authority, he'll pull strings down here in Tallahassee. You'll get the dissertation committee from hell. Then you'll rot in graduate school." Two months of around-the-clock nausea had softened the harsh edges of Magda's speaking voice, but pregnancy hadn't affected her hard-nosed and practical approach to academia. "Raleigh knows all there is to know about Hispano-Moresque ceramics, but he does his best work in the basement of a museum. He probably hasn't done a lick of field archaeology since he left school. So here's what you're gonna do. You're gonna spend a week or so pretending to finish up his work, then you're gonna look around for another site to excavate and—surprise!—decide to work in the spot where you planned to be all along." And with that Faye had to be content.

Raleigh entered from the rear of the church's sanctuary, like an evangelist coming to reap the souls of the lost. "Welcome to our project team, Ms. Longchamp," he began. "We're glad to have you with us." Without allowing Faye to respond, he turned to a thin man of about forty-five, whose pale skin contrasted with a dark and carefully groomed mustache and goatee.

"Perhaps Dr. Bingham can begin with a summary of his progress on determining the Sujosa's genetic makeup."

The thin man nodded and flipped through his notes. "Yes. Yes, blood samples have been collected from a more-than-adequate cross-section of the Sujosa community. The lab results will be available in a few weeks. I've got a physical anthropology student tracking the occurrence of distinguishing Sujosa traits, such as the unpigmented areas of hair and light-colored eyes. My informal observations indicate that traits common to the Sujosa are associated with stronger-than-average immune systems, but it'll take some time to run the statistics. Our team is in the process of building on Dr. Harbison's genealogical work—"

He looked up from his notes. "Let me go on record as saying that Brent's work was very thorough." He glanced at his neighbor, who Faye realized must be Dr. Harbison himself, a handsome man in his mid-thirties. He was lean and tan, and his dark hair had been streaked blonde at the hairdresser in a style that was currently fashionable among

fraternity boys. He looked like a walking, talking version of
Ken, Barbie's male appendage, but Faye reflected that his
head must be filled with more than plastic, given the fame
he had earned from his work with the Sujosa.

Dr. Harbison nodded to acknowledge the compliment.
Dr. Bingham ducked his head nervously toward the notes
he didn't need. "Since he's a medical doctor and not trained
in genealogical research methods, I've assigned a student
to verify the family relationships that he established. We're
still looking into written documentation—birth certificates,
wills, deeds, court records, and such—in an effort to ex-
pand on his excellent work. Like Dr. Harbison, we have
run into what genealogists call a 'brick wall' in the mid-
nineteenth century. Oral history goes back another hundred
years before that, but the county courthouse in Alcaskaki
burned in 1851, taking all its written records with it. We
are currently looking for other sources that might give us
tangible evidence of the Sujosa's history."

He paused and looked at Dr. Raleigh as if he expected
a response.

Dr. Raleigh, who was not generous with eye contact,
continued pacing across the front of the church, his eyes
lowered and his chin tucked toward his chest, as if he were
deep in an important thought. "Dr. Amory? What can you
tell us about the linguistics portion of the project?" he said
without looking up.

The slick-smooth salt-and-pepper hair, combed back
from a receding hairline, was as precise as Dr. Amory's
reputation declared him to be. If a conclusion could not be
confirmed and reconfirmed, Hal Amory would not jump to
it. "As I've said before, the Sujosa left their place or places
of origin a very long time ago. They speak perfectly idio-
matic English with an accent that's indistinguishable from
the speech of non-Sujosa residents of the nearest town,
Alcaskaki. I spent the first two weeks of the project in

Jenny Hanahan's grocery store, recording samples of the speech of her Sujosa and non-Sujosa customers, as well as great chunks of conversation generated by Jenny herself. I've had the recordings transcribed and am analyzing them for unusual speech patterns, but my instincts say I won't find any. If you close your eyes and listen to the Sujosa speak, you could be anywhere in east central Alabama."

Faye took advantage of the pause in Dr. Amory's report, "While you were at the grocery store, did you notice anything about their food choices? Does the grocery stock foods or spices that are unusual for the area—foods that might be traceable to another culture?"

Dr. Raleigh graced her with his attention. "Ms. Longchamp. Dr. Amory is a linguist. If the project had needed a home economist, I would have written one into the grant proposal."

He flicked his eyes back toward Dr. Amory, who continued: "The word 'Sujosa' itself is the only term of linguistic significance that I've identified to date. Though the 'j' is pronounced as in "jelly," American-style, I feel certain that it derives from the Portuguese word, *sujo*, which means 'dirt' or 'dirty.'"

"Do you see this as a possible indication of Portuguese ancestry?" Dr. Raleigh asked.

"Quite the contrary," Dr. Amory said, "I should think that it contradicts the notion of a Portuguese origin for the Sujosa. Would you call yourself 'dirty'?"

Faye saw that Dr. Raleigh did not like being the subject of that particular rhetorical question.

"In my opinion," Dr. Amory concluded, "at some time in their history, the Sujosa lived near Portuguese-speakers who labeled them 'dirty,' and the name stuck."

Since it clearly bothered Dr. Raleigh, Faye offered her opinion. "There's precedent for that. Consider the Creek Nation, who lived in this area long before the Europeans got here. Their original name for themselves, the Muskogee, has been supplanted by an English word applied to them simply because they preferred to build their villages beside creeks. They've gone to a great deal of effort to keep the original name they gave themselves—and the culture that went with it—alive. Their name could easily have been lost to history, as the Sujosa's origins have been."

Ignoring Faye, Dr. Raleigh turned to Carmen. "Dr. Martinez, have you gleaned any pertinent information from your oral history interviews yet?"

Carmen stood. "A good number, maybe seventy-five percent, of the Sujosa I've approached so far were willing to be interviewed. I've gotten some interesting stories, but the amount of historical information they can provide is limited. We must remember that, though they may be economically disadvantaged, these are still twenty-first-century Americans. Like a lot of present-day Americans, they're just not very interested in the past. I've—"

"You have no progress to report?" Dr. Raleigh interrupted. "None of your interviews have yielded anything of value?"

"As I was saying. I've located one important source. Mrs. Dovey Murdock, a widow in her nineties, knows everything there is to know about the Sujosa and their history. She has agreed to give me her time, because she's afraid that a big part of the Sujosa's heritage will die with her. I am in hopes of hearing the story behind the hog-stealing Stewarts."

"I'll bite," Faye said. "There must be a good story there." Carmen shot her a smile. "According to Miss Dovey— that's what she likes to be called—there's a family of Stewarts in the settlement who spell their name with a 'w' in the middle, and there also is a family of Stuarts who spell their name with a 'u'. Both families descend from a common ancestor, but one set of cousins fell out with the other about a hundred years ago over a missing hog, destined for greatness at the county fair. Somebody—it isn't clear who—changed the spelling of their name to disassociate themselves from the criminals, but nobody in the settlement agrees on which family spawned the thieves. Thus, to this day, the Stuarts who spell their name with a 'u' refer to the other branch of the family as the 'hog-stealing Stewarts,' and, obviously, the Stewarts who spell their name with a 'w' have harsh words for the relatives, whom they also call the 'hog-stealing Stuarts.'"

Dr. Bingham stroked his goatee. He delivered the obvious question—"Who stole the hog?"—with a perfectly deadpan face.

Carmen said, "Miss Dovey knows, but so far she won't say. She says telling the story now would only hurt people who never laid a hand on anybody else's hog."

Dr. Amory's mouth was twitching. This evidence of a sense of humor made Faye like him better.

"And precisely how does this relate to the hypothesis of the federal grant that is paying all our salaries?" Dr. Raleigh had not yet demonstrated evidence of a lighter side.

When Carmen wasn't messing with the minds of over-serious scientists, she was all business. "I've made recordings of Miss Dovey singing songs about tremendous sailing ships and sailors who lived at sea for years on end. She knows stories about young women who were kidnapped to serve as 'companions' to sailors lonely for female company. Finding the truth in Miss Dovey's tales is like decoding a staticky radio signal. The truth is buried in there somewhere, but we won't know what it is until we filter out the noise. I have a few more interviews I want to do, but starting Monday, I will stop the general population interviews and devote all my efforts to untangling Miss Dovey's songs and stories."

"Had you the slightest intention of clearing this change in approach with me?"

Carmen would have taken a step back, if the pew hadn't been in her way. "I didn't see this as a change, more as a focusing of the approach we were already using. As far as clearing the change with you—that's what I thought I was doing right now."

Dr. Raleigh stopped pacing and lifted his chin off his chest. His wide-legged stance made him look more like a fly-weight boxer than a man of learning. "Well, I don't approve the change. You can't abandon the door-to-door canvassing of the settlement. It will compromise the project. For one thing, how do you know that there's not another Miss Dovey in the next house, one with even more informative stories than this one?"

"The settlement isn't that big. I've asked everyone I interviewed if they had elderly relatives who might remember old family stories and folk tales. They said—"

"But you just said that fully one-quarter of the Sujosa refused to speak with you. And you haven't tried everyone yet, have you? You don't really know who's lurking behind those last few doors, do you?"

"No, Dr. Raleigh."

"Then finish the survey as it was mapped out at the outset of this project before you make the unprofessional decision—without authorization—to prematurely narrow it to one person."

Carmen sat down, and Raleigh turned to Brent Harbison. "Anything from you, Brent?"

"Nope," said the doctor. To Faye's surprise, Raleigh accepted his rather succinct answer. Faye interpreted Raleigh's unwillingness to push him further as an indication of Brent Harbison's high status on the team and with NIH. She wondered how Raleigh felt about that.

"Very well," said Raleigh, and after a few words about

the following week's schedule, he dismissed the meeting.
Faye filed out with everyone else. The fact that Raleigh had
not given a progress report on the archaeological work had
not escaped her attention.

FOUR

FAYE AND JOE spent most of Saturday morning at Raleigh's excavation, which, if possible, looked even worse in the clear light of day. Never had she seen a less promising or more battered site, but she was determined to do the professional thing and devote the day to conducting a thorough review. Until, that is, she discovered that the work shed was locked, and that no one knew who had the key. Raleigh, of course, had taken off for the weekend, so she couldn't ask him. Late in the morning, she decided there was nothing more she could accomplish without staff or information, so she sent Joe off with one of the technicians to purchase supplies in Alcaskaki, and turned to setting up her office.

Faye's office was in a former storage room in the back of Hanahan's Grocery. She had to share it with Carmen, but, other problems aside, she was as excited as a six-year-old with brand-new school supplies. She spent a happy hour transferring her research materials into her very own filing cabinet and organizing her new aluminum briefcase.

Faye was proud of her color-coded files, but she loved her briefcase best. Hard use in the field might someday dent its smooth flanks or dull its silvery shine, but it would survive abuse that would shred an ordinary leather or canvas model. Faye knew, because she had shredded a few briefcases in her day.

She had unrolled her maps of the Sujosa settlement and the surrounding area and was thumbtacking them to the walls when Carmen appeared and settled down to write up her latest round of interviews. The two women worked quietly, side by side, for an hour or two. Then, when a conversation eventually started, it arose naturally from their work. Faye felt that this spoke well for their future as officemates and housemates, since she herself had never been good at idle chit-chat.

"I looked up words that sounded like 'Sujosa' on the Internet as soon as I got this project," Faye said as she slid her last file folder into place.

"Yeah, me too," Carmen said. "How long did it take you to find out that *sujo* meant 'dirty' in Portuguese?"

"Ten minutes," Faye said. "How 'bout you?"

"About that long. And yet that's the only progress Dr. Amory's made on his part of the project in a whole month. Do you think he's serious when he says he's been lounging around Jenny Hanahan's store all this time?"

"Maybe he has a crush on her," Faye said. "How long will it take you to finish the door-to-door survey and get back to Miss Dovey? It sounds to me like she's your best bet."

"Raleigh is an idiot." Carmen opened her briefcase—an aluminum model like Faye's, but bigger—and yanked out a fat binder, holding it high like a trophy. "Check this out—I just finished transcribing every interview I've done to date, and there's a lot more of Miss Dovey in this file than our asshole director needs to know about right now. I'll finish the interviews he wants me to do, then I'll spring these on him, pretending I just finished them. He'll never know how much data I collected without his approval."

With a conspiratorial grin, she waved the binder. "Miss Dovey's been getting up at dawn to feed the chickens for eighty-five years now. Guess where I've been having breakfast seven days a week for the past two weeks?"

"I thought the team didn't work on Saturdays," Faye said, reaching for the binder.

"When I'm on a field assignment, I work when I have to. I've never seen a budget for site work yet that gave a realistic total of the time required to do a project right. Raleigh's dig team has been working from eight to five with an hour off for lunch, five days a week, for a month. I don't know how you're going to finish the archaeological survey, considering all the time he's wasted."

Faye, flipping through the transcripts, reflected that Carmen didn't know the half of it. "Is that ethical, letting an interviewee feed you breakfast?"

"It's worse than that. I bribe her," Carmen said. "She still keeps chickens, so she's fried me some of the freshest eggs I ever tasted, but she's got no cash to buy things she can't raise herself, now that her husband's gone. When I come walking up every morning carrying a package of bacon, she meets me on the porch, already talking. 'What kind of questions you got for Miss Dovey today?' she wants to know. And you should see her kitchen. She's got an electric pump on her well now, but the old hand pump is still right there by her sink. And she never moved her wood-burning cook stove out of the house when she upgraded to LP. It just sits there like a museum piece."

"Like the kitchen in our bunkhouse," Faye said. "It's a real antique."

"Yeah, but Miss Dovey's kitchen feels—I don't know, it feels alive. She and her husband grew and slaughtered all their food for over fifty years, and they preserved it and cooked it in that room. She has a wooden table he built her, just to knead bread on. He made it low, so she could lean over and put her back into her work. She's had to let a lot of the gardening and canning go since he died, and I think her diet has suffered for it, but that kitchen has her life's history in it."

Faye couldn't help herself. "I do believe Dr. Raleigh has a home economist on his team after all."

Carmen rolled her desk chair over closer to Faye's, so she could smack her on the head with a brimming file folder.

"Seriously, Carmen," Faye went on, "this is a treasure trove. You're absolutely right—you may have already gotten some critical information from Miss Dovey, but when will you find time to do the digging it'll take to uncover it?"

"Here's an extra copy." Carmen handed her a second binder. "You want to read it? I'm not going to get any more work done on these notes until I've finished Dr. Raleigh's precious door-to-door survey."

Faye was impressed by the generosity of an academic willing to part with primary data. "You think I work all the time, too?"

"It's still Saturday, isn't it?"

"Busted," Faye said. "Okay, I'll read your interviews. I've done about all I can on the archaeology side today."

"Good, you can come with me on my afternoon round of interviews."

"Me?" Faye was honestly taken aback. "I don't do interviews—I dig in the dirt. I'd be in the way. Wouldn't I?"

"Not at all. It'll give you a chance to get a feel for the place. And unlike Dr. Raleigh, I don't think it's productive to pigeonhole a talented staff. I have no doubt you can help me in my work. Later, maybe I can help you in yours. That's how real professionals operate."

Faye held out a hand, and Carmen gave her a quick, deal-sealing shake. With a colleague like Carmen, things just might work out well, after all.

DESPITE FAYE'S INITIAL concerns, she found that Carmen's easy charm had worked its magic on the Sujosa. Wherever she went, whoever she passed as they wandered through the settlement, she called them by name and asked after their children and their pets, and they responded warmly. Faye, they more or less ignored, but Carmen, they loved.

Faye didn't mind being on the sidelines. The walk gave her archaeologist's brain a chance to look around and enjoy the contrast between old and new, between now and long ago. Actually, she was using the words "new" and "now" rather loosely. She doubted that a new home had been built in the Sujosa settlement during her lifetime—and she was pushing thirty-six. Some of the houses had to be way over a hundred years old, but the people who inhabited them weren't fossils. They were vibrant and lively, if poor, products of the twenty-first century who just happened to live in very old houses. She wondered what the odds were that any of them would let her excavate in their own backyards. They could be treading on treasures every time they walked out to water the petunias.

Eventually, Carmen led her to the front porch of the Smiley home, their first stop. It seemed to Faye that the Smileys were taking an inordinate amount of time to answer the knock on their front door. But Carmen filled in the down time ruminating on why she enjoyed her career as an oral historian.

"It's not even like work," she said, and Faye could hear an echo of Carmen's Cuban roots in the exotic twist she gave every vowel. "In my family, we'd sit together on Sunday afternoons, just talking, and my *abuela* told me such stories. And sometimes, when I was lucky, *her* mother, God rest her soul, would tell me stories, too. What if she had died without passing them on? And now I get paid to collect stories from—"

The Smileys' door finally opened, and a woman who Faye judged to be about her own age stepped into the doorway, filling the open space.

Carmen stuck out her hand. "I'm Carmen Martinez and this is Faye Longchamp. We're here to—"

The woman enveloped Carmen's hand in her larger one,

shook it once, and withdrew it, saying, "I'm Ronya Smiley. I know who you are."

Ronya Smiley was thick-waisted, broad-shouldered, and close to six feet tall. Her intelligent blue eyes were set into a face the color of a brown paper bag, and their expression was not welcoming.

"Then you know I'd like the chance to sit and talk awhile," said Carmen.

"I'm real busy today." Ronya crossed her arms.

A reedy little voice piped up. "Mama, mama, come see what I built with my blocks!"

Ronya turned her head, but didn't move from the door. "Mama will be there in a minute, Zack. Just as soon as these two nice ladies leave." She raised her eyebrows at Faye and Carmen, as if to say, "It's time for you two nice ladies to take a hint and get the hell out."

But Carmen only smiled. "Perhaps later in the afternoon?"

"Leo works in the limerock mine all week. Saturdays are the only time we have as a family. You ladies have a good evening." Ronya stepped back from the door, preparing to push it shut. Zack, a bright-faced four-year-old, rushed up and threw his arms around her powerful thigh, saying, "Mama, come see! I'm building a spaceship that'll take us to Mars!"

"Then perhaps another day?" Carmen asked, and Faye admired her dogged persistence.

Mrs. Smiley finally nodded, albeit grudgingly. "I'm supposed to sit with Kiki Montrose next Friday afternoon. Ain't nothing to do but just sit there while she sleeps. Come talk to me then."

The door closed and they could hear the sound of a deadbolt sliding into place.

"Good going!" Faye said, punching Carmen on the arm. Carmen shrugged off the compliment. "Some of the Sujosa are never going to cooperate with this study, and nobody can make them, but people do like to talk about themselves. If people see that I'm really truly interested in what they have to say, they usually respond."

Stepping off the porch, she set down her silver-toned briefcase and began writing in a notebook. When, five minutes later, Carmen was still at it, Faye could stand it no longer.

"What can you possibly be writing? She hardly spoke to us."

"Really? She told us her husband worked at the lime-rock mine. She showed us that she's a loving mother—"

"But—" Faye had started to ask how Carmen could possibly make such a statement after observing the woman with her child for hardly thirty seconds, but she stopped herself. It was true. In the way Ronya Smiley had spoken to her son, in the uninhibited way he rushed up to her and grasped her leg, in the timbre of both their voices and the soft look in Ronya's eyes, it was apparent that mother and son enjoyed a special relationship.

"And," Carmen said, gesturing at a pole barn standing beside the house, "I think you can guess her profession."

Through the open sides of the pole barn, Faye could see a potter's wheel, a shovel, and buckets full of mud, or something very like it. "Looks like she throws pots. Are you sure that's her profession and not just a hobby?"

"Trust me, the Sujosa don't have the time and money to waste on hobbies," said Carmen. "More likely, she stays home with little Zack all week while Leo works at the mine, then she sells her pots at craft shows on Saturdays."

Faye conceded Carmen's point. Then, just to show that her powers of observation weren't completely overshadowed by Carmen's, she pointed at a satellite dish that stood in the Smileys' front yard like a metallic mushroom kicked on its side by a petulant kid. "Looks like somebody in this house likes television." Gesturing toward a brand-new box labeled *Satellite Dish—This End Up* she added, "And they just got real happy."

Leaving Carmen to her writing, Faye took a few steps to the side of the house. Looking deeper into the Smileys' backyard, she spied a large woodpile and, beyond that, a massive stack of mottled bricks. The pattern of mud on the lower bricks, splashed there by rainstorms, said that the brick pile had stood in the yard for quite some time.

"Reckon the Smileys were planning to build a new house when they bought that pile of bricks?" she asked Carmen. The idea made Faye sad, as if she were looking at an abandoned dream. Perhaps time and bad luck and the vagaries of low-wage employment had killed the Smileys' hopes for a modern home.

Carmen nodded and continued. "I also know the Smiley marriage is not a model of domestic bliss." Her head was still bowed over her work, but Faye caught her peeking mischievously through her bangs as if to see what Faye thought of her clairvoyance.

"She said nothing of the kind. You're making that up."

"Not exactly. Check your copy of the transcripts. I interviewed Leo Smiley last week and Ronya apparently knows nothing about it. That doesn't make them sound like one of those couples that sits at the supper table, chatting about every single minute of the time they were apart, now does it?" She grinned, picked up her briefcase, and headed for the next house.

RONYA SMILEY HAD heard that the Martinez woman never stopped working. Jenny Hanahan said that most evenings, while she was tallying up her cash register and locking her grocery store for the night, she saw the historian trudging out of her office, heading back to the house that the government people were renting from Amanda-Lynne Lavelle. And Jenny stayed open until nine.

Ronya respected hard work, but she didn't see how spending day after day just talking to people counted as hard work. Talking didn't earn any paycheck that she'd ever heard about, and it surely didn't buy groceries.

Elliott and Fred and Jorge had gotten good-paying jobs from those government people. They didn't have to do anything all day but dig some holes, and not many of them, and none of them very deep. They weren't clear on why they were digging. It wasn't like their old jobs at the mine where everybody knew what was supposed to come out of the ground.

Ronya had her own ideas about that Martinez woman, the one who was always asking people questions about their grandparents' stories, who wanted to know who was born in the settlement and who was an outsider. She'd even been known to ask who had slept with who. And now there was this new woman archaeologist, who was sure to be wanting to dig up everybody's old garbage pits and privies. No respect for privacy, there.

Well, everybody had secrets, and Ronya didn't know why these people thought the Sujosa should give up theirs. What would they gain from spilling their guts to these outsiders who asked so many questions?

Brent Harbison had promised the Sujosa that the project would be good for them, and she believed he'd meant it. He'd thought the government money would come rolling in, money to open a clinic, patch roofs, and buy groceries. That wasn't how it had turned out. The only jobs so far involved digging in the dirt, and the big money had gone to the outsiders, with their nosy questions that never helped anybody but themselves. Well, the little tutor girl was an exception, Ronya reflected. She was a sweet thing, and she seemed to be doing her best for the settlement kids.

The children needed her, no doubt about that. Children born to parents too tired and beaten down to even teach them their letters were doomed. Children like that started school too far behind to ever catch up. She'd made sure her own Zack heard the alphabet every day of his short life. Come fall, when he started school, his teacher would see that he could read all the letters and even some words. Zack's teachers would always know that he came from folk who valued learning. But not every child had that chance.

Ronya hadn't been surprised to see Carmen Martinez on the doorstep, but she hadn't expected to see the skinny little woman archaeologist, the one who came from outside but was as brown as a Sujosa. She'd heard about Faye Longchamp from Elliott and Fred and Jorge. They were pretty sure their work would be harder when the boss lady arrived. Ronya wondered at folks who would go around digging up other people's secrets, without first bothering to ask whether they cared.

Excerpt from an Interview with Mr. Leo Smiley, Wednesday, October 26

Interviewer: Carmen J. Martinez, Ph.D.

CJM: Mr. Smiley, I understand you and your wife both descend from very old Sujosa families.

Leo Smiley: If you mean it's been a long time since anybody in our families married an outsider, then you've got that right. My father's grandmother came from outside, and Ronya had an outsider great-great-grandmother, but neither of us can help that.

CJM: What kind of work does your wife do?

Leo Smiley: She's a potter. A ceramic artist, actually. And a good one. You won't find any pottery finer than what Ronya makes.

CJM: I don't know anything about pottery, except that it's a beautiful art form. Does she work in a particular style?

Leo Smiley: I don't know that her style has a name. She just adapts traditional Sujosa designs.

CJM: How wonderful! Are there galleries nearby where I can see some of her work?

Leo Smiley: Galleries like artists with lots of training. But teachers cost money, so Ronya's galleries are Hanahan's Grocery and the roadside flea market.

CJM: But if she's that good, she deserves the best training. I got all the way through the university on scholarships. She could—

Leo Smiley: Don't talk to me about scholarships. Don't even say the word. I know what art department scholarships are like. They pay your tuition, and that's about all. I spent two years at the university, carrying a full course load and working at a job that would almost feed me. All the time, I was trying like hell to find someone willing to offer Ronya a scholarship, too, so she could get the same education I was chasing. I don't know why I wanted that so bad. Maybe so we could both starve together.

CJM: You're an artist, too?

Leo Smiley: I was a sculptor.

CJM: Was? I don't think an artist ever stops being an artist.

Leo Smiley: (Interviewer's note: Mr. Smiley is about a foot taller than I am, but at this point in the conversation, he leaned down until we stood face-to-face at an uncomfortably close distance.) I work at the limerock mine. I take big pieces of limestone and make them into little bitty pieces of limestone. I guess you could say I'm still sculpting. I sculpt gravel, Dr. Martinez.

CJM: Is there a strong artistic tradition among the Sujosa? Did anyone teach you to sculpt?

Leo Smiley: I've always made things out of rock and wood. Sometimes even out of clay, though that's more Ronya's department. Nobody taught me. It's just something I have to do. Not that I have the time, lately.

CJM: But you said that your wife adapts traditional Sujosa designs, so I presume she's not self-taught.

Leo Smiley: Her mother taught her to throw pots. In fact, her mother always said their family wouldn't have survived the Civil War, if it hadn't been for their pots.

CJM: Did she mean they sold the pots for food money?

Leo Smiley: As my mother-in-law tells it, her great-great-grandmother only had one child live through childhood, and his health wasn't all that good. He had a limp. He had asthma. He needed glasses to read, and that was back when nobody in the settlement could spare money for glasses, nor time for reading. Since he was an only child, his parents scraped together enough money for little Junior's spectacles. After all that sacrifice, there was no way in hell that they were going to send him off to a war that they had no interest in.

CJM: Were they able to hide him for the whole duration of the war?

Leo Smiley: Are you kidding? Everybody in Alcaskaki knew which families in the settlement had sons old enough to serve. It wasn't long before the Confederates sent somebody out here to fetch Junior to the battlefield. Well, his mother knew he wouldn't live a month if she let the army take him. She met the officer at her door. If you've seen my wife, you know that she was probably a fearsome sight.

CJM: Yes, I've seen your wife. I understand.

Leo Smiley: She handed a paper to the officer and stood there like the Queen of England until he took it out of her hand. He read the first two lines and started laughing at her. She stared him down until he went back to reading. When he got to the bottom, he looked at her gape-mouthed, saying, "You can't be serious." But she was.

CJM: What did the paper say?

Leo Smiley: It was a document excusing her son and all the other Sujosa boys—the ones who hadn't already gone to war—from military service. She wanted him to sign it.

CJM: He couldn't possibly have agreed. The Confederacy was woefully short on men.

Leo Smiley: But it was even shorter on raw materials. She was offering to tell him where the Confederacy could mine tin, which they needed desperately to build weapons. After he stopped laughing, he thought about it, and eventually he realized that he held a very good deal in his hands. He signed her paper.

CJM: How did she know where they could find tin? It's not something most housewives use every day.

Leo Smiley: But potters use it all the time. There's not a lot of tin in Alabama, but the Sujosa potters have known where it was for centuries. Ronya's great-great-great-grandmother probably stretched that war out some by helping the rebels get raw materials for their weapons, but she insisted until the day she died that she didn't care. She said the United States government never did anything for her before or after the war, and the Confederate government never did anything for her while they had the chance, except leave her boy alone after she bought them off. She never cared who won, not one bit.

FIVE

DeWayne Montrose looked comfortable enough, resting in a faded recliner that seemed too big for the cluttered room, but his wife Kiki was a miserable thing. She sat in an old easy chair, swaddled in at least three blankets, her feet propped on a frayed ottoman. Illness had turned her naturally fair complexion to a gray-white, while failing to fade her lank hair from its original vibrant red. Withered skin clung to a set of patrician cheekbones that made Faye think of Katharine Hepburn. Carmen stood staring at Kiki, as if being in the same room with grave illness had wiped her mind clean. Faye wondered if Carmen was going to make it through this interview.

The Montroses' daughter, Irene, an eighteen-year-old with hair and skin the color of honey, hovered near her mother. It hurt Faye to watch her ply Kiki with drinks and snacks that the sick woman didn't want, while DeWayne sat there ignoring them both. Even the blare of the TV couldn't hide the soul-killing atmosphere that pervades any room full of unhappiness and disease.

The click-click-click sound of a recliner being kicked back to its maximum angle punctuated the silence. "This thing is so comfortable, you never want to get up," De-Wayne sighed. "A man could lose a crop sitting in one of these things."

Carmen roused herself into action. "As you know, I'm looking for stories from the early days of the Sujosa. Miss Dovey tells me that you come from some of the oldest

Sujosa families she knows about, Mr. Montrose," she said. "Most people in the settlement have at least one outsider on their family tree but we can't find any on yours. So you must have heard a lot of stories in your day."

"You can't believe everything Miss Dovey tells you," he said. "Sometimes she lets on that she remembers things that happened before she was born." He fussed with the lever controlling the chair's pitch. "Women's tales don't usually have much to do with the truth. If something happened before I was born, it don't mean nothing to me. I like to live in the right-now. I got my health. I got a roof over my head. I got no need to think about the past. Why don't you go bother somebody who cares about long-ago times? I got other things on my mind. Irene, turn up that volume. My show's on."

Irene glanced at Carmen, but did as her father asked. Then she returned to her mother's side and pulled the blankets tighter around her neck. Kiki's eyes slid closed and didn't open again, not even when Carmen and Faye rose to leave.

CARMEN MUTTERED, "CAN you believe that man?" for the fifth time since leaving the Montrose house.

"I thought a person in your profession would be used to the occasional snub," said Faye as they walked along the long path that cut through the woods to the river. "Either that, or it's me," she added, thinking of the previous day's adventure on the road. Maybe somebody had dropped a papier-mâché devil on her head on purpose, just because they knew they didn't like her before they'd even met her.

"Oh, I'm used to it—although two in one day is unusual. But I was thinking of Kiki."

"What's wrong with her?" Faye asked. "AIDS?" Brent Harbison's paper on disease resistance among the Sujosa had its roots in the AIDS epidemic, which had taken a heavy toll in the settlement during the 1990s. When Dr. Harbison recognized a pattern among the victims—people with mostly Sujosa ancestry were much less likely to contract AIDS than those with "outsider" blood—his future as a medical researcher was assured.

"She's got Hepatitis C, and the story is that Irene has nearly killed her young self taking care of her mama. She dropped out of high school and took over Kiki's old job at the dry cleaners in Alcaskaki to help make ends meet. From the looks of things, Irene's not going to be taking care of her mother too much longer. It's very sad."

Faye, who had cared for both her grandmother and her mother in their final illnesses, again ached for Irene, but she was less certain than Carmen that the girl's ordeal was nearly over. She knew that the human body could take a lot of punishment before it gave up its grasp on life. There had been no mistaking the shadow that fell on her loved ones' faces in their final days. Kiki was a desperately ill woman, but she didn't yet have the pinched features and sunken eyes of imminent death, and that wasn't necessarily a good thing. She and Irene could be heading for months or years of suffering. Faye walked in silence and tried not to think about that.

Looking for a way to change the subject, Faye said, "Did you see DeWayne Montrose's eyes? I've heard that some Sujosa have a distinctive eye color. Was that it?"

"Yeah. It's a really pretty color—I'd call it turquoise, I guess—except it's not so pretty when it's in the middle of a face as mean as DeWayne Montrose's. Could he have made it any plainer that he didn't give a damn about the woman who's dying in the chair right next to him? Can you believe—"

"Who else has eyes that color?"

"Well, even in the Sujosa, it's not all that common. You see a lot more of those scalp birthmarks that make light streaks in their hair. Every generation or so, the oldest Sujosa families produce one or two kids with those eyes. And they've been doing it for a very long time. The earliest recorded description of the Sujosa comes from an eighteenth-century traveler who described a people with 'nutt-browne Skynn and Eyes of blew-greene that put one in minde of Witchery.'"

"That description applies to DeWayne Montrose perfectly, although I'm pretty sure I wouldn't like his brand of witchery." Faye glanced back to the house. "Do you know anyone else with those eyes, maybe a high school kid?"

"Amanda-Lynne Lavelle's boy, Jimmie. Is he in his teens?" Carmen asked herself. After a second, she answered herself, "Yes. He's in his last year of high school. Amanda-Lynne's raised him by herself on just about no money since his daddy died of AIDS five or six years ago. She and DeWayne are related somehow. They're cousins, I think, but his parents raised her after her parents died. She's a little, well, eccentric, but what do you expect of a woman born to bluegrass musicians goofy enough to name her after her mother's mandolin? Amanda-Lynne's got those spooky eyes and a head full of dark hair just like DeWayne's to go with them. And she's passed her good looks down to Jimmie. If you want to see someone with classic Sujosa features, Amanda-Lynne's the one. Or her son."

"A boy with dark skin and turquoise eyes—I guess you're telling me that those are classic Sujosa looks—nearly killed me and Joe yesterday. He rigged up a life-sized dummy and dropped it out of a tree right in front of my windshield with a sign on it saying 'Devils go home.' A nice welcome that was—I damn near ran my car off the road and down into a canyon."

"Those roads are very dangerous, don't you think?"

Faye didn't think Carmen quite grasped the magnitude of Jimmie's crime. "He could have killed us."

"It must have been an accident. Jimmie is the sweetest boy you could ever hope to know. And so good to his mama. Jimmie wouldn't have set out to hurt anybody."

Carmen glanced at Faye, and she must have correctly read Faye's stormy expression, because she quickly added, "I'll talk to him. We're pretty good friends, considering that I'm nearly twice his age. I'll make sure he apologizes to you and Joe."

"Thanks."

"You want to talk about beautiful eyes that 'put one in minde of witchery'?" continued Carmen, who was apparently the president of Jimmie Lavelle's fan club. "Good Lord. When Jimmie looks you right in the face with those eyes, you'll be glad you're not a sixteen-year-old girl. That boy—"

Carmen was silenced by the sound of something large crashing through the underbrush behind them. A low growl told Faye that whatever was barreling in their direction was not friendly. Two more growling creatures topped the hill. The knowledge that she and Carmen were now outnumbered tripped something primitive in Faye. Grabbing Carmen by the hand, she dragged her down the path, looking for a safe harbor.

On her left, an army of ramrod-straight pines mocked her with branches that began thirty feet above her head. The pines sheltered spindly cedars that couldn't support the weight of a housecat. On her right, an eroded gully was shrouded in brittle stems left behind by kudzu vines that had shed their summer leaves. Venturing into that thicket would be like throwing herself into a vegetative net where she would wait, entangled, for her pursuers to descend.

Faye knew that the path's downward slope put them at a strategic disadvantage. With gravity on their side, the faceless beasts could pounce from far up the slope, using the momentum of their heavy and fast-moving bodies to roll their human prey downhill.

From fifty yards away, Faye spied a sycamore extending its lowest branch to offer shelter, and she focused on that single point. She knew only the pounding of her feet on the ground and the feel of Carmen's hand clutching hers and the beckoning sight of her chosen tree. Later, she would wonder whether some ancient part of her brain was always watching for escape routes, just in case a predator appeared, but for that moment she simply ran.

She nearly ran straight into the sycamore's solid trunk. "Climb!" she bellowed to Carmen, whose response to terror was not action, but paralysis. Faye jerked the hand she held upward, shaking it free of the heavy briefcase it clutched like a talisman. She forced Carmen to grab a branch, and was relieved to see her friend grasp it and haul herself up. Carmen continued climbing and Faye followed, one branch behind.

Their pursuers bounded out of the undergrowth that had concealed them, and Faye finally saw them for what they were. Hurling themselves at the trunk of the tree were three dogs, tremendous, barrel-chested dogs with dripping jowls and bared teeth. Their pelts were shiny, and their rounded flanks said that they were well-fed. Someone owned these dogs, yet they hadn't trained them not to treat humans as prey. Maybe it was worse than that. Maybe they had been trained to track human prey.

Rearing up on their hind legs, all three animals stood taller than a man. Their claws cut gashes in the sycamore's bark, and the largest one hooked a massive paw over the lowest branch. Faye knew that dogs couldn't climb trees, but these slavering beasts might be capable of shaking her out of this one. One at a time, each of them backed away a few paces, then hurled itself into the air, howling in frustration when it failed to clamp its jaws into the flesh of her leg. How long would they continue their onslaught? Faye reached around to the back pocket of her cargo pants.

"What are you doing?"

"Cell phone," said Faye.

"Don't bother. No coverage, too remote. They're building a tower but it won't be ready till the spring."

Faye put the phone away. "Let's hope we're not sitting in this tree until then."

The rhythmic slapping of small feet running down the hard-packed footpath caught Faye's ear. Someone small was running toward them. *Please, God, don't let it be a child,* Faye prayed.

Irene Montrose was no longer a child, but she was far too slightly built to overpower even one of the beasts baying for Faye's and Carmen's blood. "Go back," Faye yelled. "Get some help! These dogs will eat you alive!"

"Come, Bull!" Irene called. "You, too, Boss! Get away from that tree, Bruce! You boys should be ashamed of yourselves."

The three brutes turned shame-faced so quickly, whining and whinkering as they slinked toward the slender young woman, that Faye would have laughed had her adrenaline level been a shade lower. The hound Irene called Boss reared up on his hind legs, planted two ham-sized paws on her shoulders, and slobbered all over his mistress' face. "No kisses, Boss," she said, pushing him away roughly. "You've been very bad."

"Sometimes Daddy forgets to close the gate good," Irene said. "He forgets how scary the boys look to someone who doesn't know them."

"What are they? Pit bulls?" Carmen asked.

"Bull is half pit bull and half Rottweiler. Boss is mostly German shepherd and part bloodhound. Bruce is part Doberman and I don't know what else. Something big."

Well, yeah, Faye thought. Something big and mean.

Could anyone who owned dogs like Bull, Bruce, and Boss ever "forget" to keep them in their pen?

"You can come down," Irene said. "I won't let them hurt you."

"That's okay," Carmen said from her perch on the limb above Faye. "We like it here. We'll just hang out in this tree until you take the boys home. And don't forget to lock the gate good, okay?"

Irene smiled up at them and turned to go home. Walking along the woodland path among the huge animals, she looked like Red Riding Hood out for a stroll with three Big Bad Wolves.

Faye and Carmen gave Irene ample time to get the "boys" in their pen. The cold dry air carried the *clank* of a heavy gate being closed, but they waited a while longer, just in case, listening to the pitiable baying of three hunters deprived of their kill.

"The Sujosa sure have a peculiar way of saying, 'Welcome, stranger,'" said Faye, as she swung down from the tree.

SIX

FAYE CLIMBED THE porch steps of the women's bunkhouse and found Joe waiting there, whistling whippoorwill calls. She dropped into the rocker next to his, hoping that birdsong would chase DeWayne Montrose's dogs out of her head.

Carmen had recovered her good humor more quickly than Faye. She leapt onto the porch in a single stride and slid her briefcase through the house's open door into its broad central hall. Thrusting both arms out in front of her, she staggered past them, Frankenstein-style, bellowing, "Must. Have. Shower."

"I made beef stew," Joe offered as she passed.

"Shower. Then beef stew. Good." Carmen disappeared through the front door.

Faye looked up at the porch ceiling. It had once been painted blue.

"How you doing?"

"Okay, Joe," she said. "Ready to get to work."

"On Monday, you'll get your chance."

"Joe, what am I going to do? Raleigh's messed things up so badly."

"You'll figure something out. Raleigh may have a few more college degrees in back of his name, but you're worth ten of him. He couldn't dig up a dead skunk buried in a sandbox."

Faye laughed until she snorted. It was cool but pleasant there on the porch. Carmen must have showered quickly, because Faye could see her moving around the parlor, setting flatware and paper napkins and steaming bowls of stew on a card table. It was not yet six, but it was full dark outside, and the brightly lit window illuminated the porch and most of the front yard, but it didn't reach as far as the road. Only the crunching sound of tires on gravel announced the arrival of Faye's second housemate. It took a little time for the young woman to make her way from the darkened drive and into the light, but she moved well, considering her obstacles.

Laurel Cook had skipped the Friday night meeting to squeeze in a few extra tutoring sessions, and she'd been asleep when Faye had returned to the bunkhouse, so this was Faye's first sight of the education specialist. Laurel could have passed for a fifteen-year-old, but she was in reality a college graduate who merely *looked* like a child. She had waxy white skin, and her large dark eyes peered from beneath wispy bangs the color of ash. Her right leg was encased in a knee-high brace which, according to Carmen, had been part of Laurel's life since she was a child. Several weeks before, she'd had surgery intended to partially correct the congenital defect that had left her lame in both legs. Her new-and-improved left leg wore a walking cast that would support it while it healed and while Laurel relearned how to use it. Laurel's gait could best be described as a slow hobble, but her delicate movements had their own grace. She reminded Faye of a wren with an injured wing.

Faye rose to help Laurel navigate the porch steps, peering into the darkness to see who had driven her this far only to throw her out of the car and let her make her way without help.

Joe, who was quicker than Faye, reached Laurel in two huge steps. Standing behind her and cupping his hands under both elbows, he practically lifted her onto the porch.

Someone slammed a car door in the darkness. Faye knew

it was Dr. Brent Harbison before he stepped into the light, by the way his light hair reflected the moon.

He bellowed, "Joe," to get the younger man's attention. "She'll never get better if you pick her up and carry her over every obstacle she encounters."

"My mama would roll over in her grave if I didn't help a lady who needed me."

"Your mama," the doctor said, "is not here."

Joe just grinned at him. After brief introductions, he opened the front door and took hold of Laurel's nearest elbow to guide her over the threshold.

"Turn her loose and let her walk," Dr. Harbison barked in the general direction of the closing door.

He settled himself on the rocker that Joe had abandoned. "So, we get a chance to talk at last. You're Faye, the phantom archaeologist."

"I understand that I have you to thank for this job."

He cocked an eyebrow. "Do what?"

"You wrote the paper that started all this."

"Oh, that," he said. "Don't thank me. Thank Jimmie Lavelle for not getting chicken pox."

"Run that by me again?"

"Lean over here close to me," he said, taking Faye's chin in his hands and giving her skin more scrutiny than any woman over thirty should have to endure. "There," he said, pointing to a spot above her left eyebrow. He pointed to another spot beside her nose. "And there. Chicken pox scars. We've all got 'em. There's a vaccine now, but Jimmie Lavelle is too old to have gotten it as a child. When there was an outbreak at Alcaskaki High, I waited for him to break out in spots, but he never did."

"So he was your smoking gun? I wondered what set you on the trail."

"I started keeping track of how many Sujosa adults were free of chicken pox scars. There were quite a lot of them.

I know—it was a bizarre hobby, but I'm a dermatologist. Skin is my life."

He let go of her chin. Faye had a powerful urge to run her fingers over her face, looking for pockmarks. She willed herself to keep her hands in her lap. "I've known people who never got chicken pox."

"Yeah, me too, and who knows why? Usually, you can't predict who might have an unusually potent immune system. But if an isolated culture like the Sujosa is passing a trait like that along, then maybe we *can* find a genetic marker. I thought it might rate a short article in an insignificant journal."

"When did you know you had something more than that?" Faye asked, reflecting that *Health* was hardly an insignificant journal.

"You're really interested?"

"I wouldn't ask if I wasn't."

"I was sitting in my examining room, telling yet another married couple that one of them had AIDS. *One* of them. Somehow, the virus had failed to pass from husband to wife. And I realized that I'd delivered the same bad news before, more than once. On the day I gave Charles Lavelle the bad news about his HIV status, I looked into his wife Amanda-Lynne's beautiful blue-green eyes and watched her struggle with the fact that she was going to be a young widow."

He rocked his chair back and looked out at the night sky. "I flashed back to the day I looked into Jenny Hanahan's eyes, the same color as Amanda-Lynne's, and told her that her Barney was going to die. There's nobody in the settlement with more classic Sujosa looks than Jenny and Amanda-Lynne and their blood kin. They're healthy as horses. I thought of them, and I began to wonder."

"Your paper referenced an incredibly detailed sexual history of this community, tracing the path HIV traveled through the settlement," Faye said. "How on earth did you collect that data? I can't imagine, say, Ronya Smiley, whom I had the pleasure of meeting today, giving you an itemized list of every man she's slept with."

"Well…actually, she did. In her case, it's short. She started dating Leo when she was fourteen and married him a week after he got home from the university."

Faye eyed Brent Harbison with some respect. Only the most diplomatic of men could have extracted enough information on his patients' sexual histories to trace the couplings that had spread the virus and, more interestingly, the couplings that had not. She knew his genealogical information went back at least four generations for every family and, as with most things related to human relationships, the results were murky. Nevertheless, his evidence suggested that the more Sujosa ancestry a person had, the less likely that person was to contract HIV, even when exposed many times. This information had thrust the Sujosa, who had been shunned for generations, abruptly into the spotlight. If the secret to their resistance to HIV could be teased out of their DNA, scientists would be a big step closer to defeating AIDS. It had suddenly become incredibly important for the rest of the world to figure out who the Sujosa were and how they came to live in backwoods Alabama.

"I've read all the follow-up letters and articles to your paper, written by people who couldn't believe a rural doctor was doing such sophisticated epidemiology. I have to wonder why you aren't raking in the bucks in private practice some place where people have money. Or doing full-time research. That paper could be your ticket into academic medicine—if that's what you want."

"I grew up in Alcaskaki. I've known Ronya Smiley since we were in middle school. Hell. I didn't have to ask Ronya about her sex life. I already *knew* she'd never slept with anybody but Leo. And Leo, for all his other shortcomings, has always been faithful to her."

He ran his fingers through his short blonde hair. "I went to medical school because I wanted out of Alcaskaki. I wanted to see the world and I wanted to see it in style, with more money than a plain old family doctor would pull in." He spoke slowly, as if it were important that she understand the extent of his greed. "I was leery of a specialty like surgery. Can you imagine holding someone's life in your hands every blessed day? Dermatology was perfect. Acne and botox patients don't have emergencies. You just set your office hours, do your job, and go home. And people will pay a lot to be beautiful."

The light was too dim to make out his expression. Faye said, "Oh, come on. Dermatologists do more than that. They treat cancer. They cure disfiguring diseases."

"I had a partner for that. He loved challenging cases and he loved me, because I referred anything remotely challenging to him."

"Sounds…perfect, I guess."

"Yeah. Perfect."

"So why are you still around?" Faye asked for the second time.

"First, my father died. Then, a year later, my mother. And the house I'd bought them—the finest house in Alcaskaki—was empty. I was standing in the kitchen, listening to the Realtor tell me what she thought the place was worth, but I couldn't stop staring at the walls. Mama had hung family photos and some pretty plates and some pictures she'd cross-stitched. The head of a deer my father shot was still hanging over the TV. And it struck me that I'd bought my house in Birmingham at about the same time I bought them their house. Yet my parents' house looked like a home, and mine looked like a furniture store. There wasn't anything in my own home that proved I lived there.

There wasn't anybody in Birmingham who cared whether I ever came back—certainly not my patients and, as it turned out, not even my girlfriend. I couldn't make myself sell my parents' home. So I sold my house in Birmingham instead."

"You retired?"

Brent laughed. "No. It's better than that. Monday through Wednesday, most weeks, I'm in Birmingham, sleeping on my office sofa and seeing as many patients as my receptionist can squeeze into three days. Then, having made a disgusting wad of money, I drive back to Alcaskaki…to my home. On Thursdays and Fridays and sometimes on Saturdays and Sundays, I'm at my office in Alcaskaki, or here at my free clinic in the settlement, taking care of people who know me and like me. People who'll miss me when I'm gone."

"Supper's waiting," sang out Carmen from the front room. Through the window, Faye could see the other three gathering around the table. Carmen beckoned to them, while Joe helped Laurel into her seat. The aroma of Joe's beef stew wafted past her nose.

"So, Doctor," Faye said, rising. "Sounds like you have a busy life. When you're not saving the world, what do you do for fun?"

"How long's it been since you went to a high school football game?"

Faye tried to remember. "Not since I was in high school, I guess." She'd never missed a game in those days, though she'd been more interested in how Butch Sullivan looked in his hip pads than in whether he made a first down. Whatever a "first down" might be.

"Ordinarily, there's absolutely nothing to do in Alcaskaki on a Saturday night—trust me—but tonight's the big conference championship. Want to go to the game with me?"

"Sure," Faye said, hoping she could ditch Brent just long enough to find Joe and ask him precisely what a "down" was, and why it was important to get yours first.

SEVEN

JOE'S LAST-MINUTE coaching on the vagaries of football had been surprisingly effective. Faye was able to follow the game reasonably well. She found that it had a strong statistical basis. If a team hadn't achieved its goal of ten yards after three tries, the coach had to decide whether they had a reasonable chance of succeeding on the fourth try. Sadly, Alcaskaki's boys rarely covered the magic ten yards, so the home team punted an awful lot.

The Alcaskaki fans sitting around her found their enjoyment of the game further dimmed by the sheer skill of the opposing team's running back. Faye got a lot of pleasure from simply watching the graceful boy run, but she kept this pleasure to herself because she doubted the Alcaskakians would understand.

Turning off the statistical science part of her brain and focusing on a subject even closer to her heart, anthropology, she studied the crowd. Intentionally or not, the spectators had segregated themselves by color, and the grandstand was divided into one great swath of brown Sujosa faces alongside a second, bigger, splash of white Alcaskakians. Clumps of dark African-American faces punctuated the scene.

Faye had wondered where in hell she was supposed to park her brown-skinned, non-Sujosa self, but as Brent had settled in amongst the Alcaskaki folk, she'd sat beside him. Nobody had snubbed her or told her to go away, so she presumed the segregation was ruled by custom, not prejudice. Everybody sat where they'd always sat and never gave the matter another thought, except for those few people who, like Faye, didn't fit easily into any category.

She was nonetheless gratified to see that, unlike their parents, the high school kids mixed easily. Most of them never sat down, preferring to stand around with heads and hips cocked at very cool angles, so they never had to declare an ethnic category by sitting in, say, the Sujosa section.

Having grown up poor, Faye was all too aware that the Alcaskaki kids sported the kind of jeans that are fashionably worn out when brand-new, while the Sujosa kids' jeans had the unfashionable signs of wear-and-tear that show up on hand-me-downs. Several of the Alcaskaki teens were huddled over little teeny cell phones, whispering and laughing over messages being bounced off the nearest tower and beamed to kids standing three feet away. Alcaskaki apparently was a big enough town to rate cell coverage. She noticed that only two Sujosa kids had cell phones. These days, lack of money was more of a social kiss-of-death than skin color.

She eyed the two Sujosa teenagers who had somehow acquired the coveted phones, a possession made even more frivolous by the fact that the hilly terrain and remote location made them useless in the Sujosa's valley. Body language and pheromones advertised their love. Watching them stand hip-to-hip, the girl's head resting on the boy's collarbone, made Faye smile. The girl's honeyed hair was familiar. Faye finally recognized her as Irene Montrose.

Faye was glad to see Irene out of the house. The light in the girl's amber eyes said that her sad responsibilities as her mother's caregiver hadn't completely snuffed out her youth. Those eyes gazed upward at a tall slim young man with dark hair. When he turned his head to whisper in Irene's ear, Faye got her first good look at his face. His eyes were an impossible color of turquoise. And they were set in the dusky face that had watched Faye and her car skidding down a deserted gravel road the day before. This was Jimmie Lavelle.

There at the stadium, surrounded by people having a good time, she wondered if she could forgive him for nearly getting her killed with his devil dummy. In fact— With a start, Faye took another look at the opposing team—on the backs of their jerseys were written the words, "Blue Devils." She realized, with some relief, that Jimmie's stunt the day before had nothing to do with her; it was nothing more than a high school prank gone wrong. She looked back at Jimmie. The protective look in his lovely eyes showed that he returned Irene's love. For that, Faye was willing to cut him some slack.

But apparently someone else wasn't. Ronya Smiley was heading toward Jimmie and Irene, and she was wasting no time. Her long sturdy legs took the stadium stairs two at a time, and her voice boomed out over the stands.

"I thought you were supposed to be some kind of genius." She dropped a heavy hand on Jimmie's shoulder. "But now I see you're just an ignorant kid."

Irene started to speak, but Ronya silenced her by placing her other hand on Irene's shoulder. It was as large as the one restraining Jimmie, but a lot gentler.

"You say you want to take care of Irene. Well, how do you plan to do that when you don't appear to have good sense? Let me explain to you how this world works." Releasing Irene, she grabbed Jimmie's other shoulder and put her mouth right next to his ear.

Jimmie's air of teenage superiority evaporated, replaced by the vulnerable innocence of a young child shocked to learn that his actions have not pleased. When Ronya released him, he looked at her with turquoise eyes full of abject apology and muttered something inaudible.

"You want some more popcorn?" Brent asked.

Faye gave up trying to eavesdrop on Ronya's efforts to

jerk a knot in Jimmie's youthful cockiness. It wasn't nice
to ignore one's date by indulging one's snoopier instincts.
Still, she wished she could have heard Ronya's explanation
of how the world worked. She suspected the woman could
offer an original perspective on most issues.

IT SPOKE WELL for Brent that the Alcaskaki team's igno-
minious loss to the Blue Devils passed quickly for Faye.
He seemed to know everybody in the grandstand—whites,
blacks, and Sujosa alike—and if he didn't introduce her to
every last one of them, it wasn't because he didn't try. Early
in the evening, she'd mentioned that the soaring, spinning
trajectories of a flying football took her back to physics
class, and his eyes had lit up in recognition of another science geek. Brent's observations on a perfectly thrown football, spiraling along its parabolic path, were particularly
cogent, considering that he'd been a good physics student
and a quarterback.

All in all, it was hard to find fault with a handsome,
friendly, smart date who seemed to like her very much.

On the twenty-minute ride home, Brent provided an explanation of the mechanical advantage of tackling low, well
beneath the other guy's center-of-gravity, so that the longer
lever arm could help you knock him off his feet, at which
point Faye realized she'd been had.

"You're making fun of me," she said, twisting against
her seat belt to get a good look at his face.

Brent grinned. "I knew an evening watching small-town
football wouldn't change your life. You're more the foreign-
films-with-tiny-subtitles type, but we're a hundred miles
away from that kind of entertainment. Going to the game
is like—well, it's like being in high school again. You go to
see people and catch up with old friends. If you're a woman,
you check out what the other women are wearing, so you'll

have something to talk to your friends about all week. If you're a man, you check out the other guys' dates, so—"

"So you'll have something to talk to your friends about all week. Just like high school."

"Well, yeah." He reached for her hand. "Thanks for coming tonight. My social status is hugely enhanced because the pretty new archaeologist came to the game with me."

"Really?" Faye thought of the crowd in the football stadium. Sitting with Brent among his fellow Alcaskaki townspeople, she had felt like a dark smudge on a broad canvas of white faces. "Are you sure your Alcaskaki friends weren't wishing you'd picked a white girl for your date?"

"The twentieth century's dead, Faye, and good riddance. Nobody here cares what color you are. Although I'll admit, the grandstand did look a little segregated." He spoke as if he'd never noticed that his neighbors still maintained a color line, even while watching the big game. "I guess people just sit where they've always sat, but that doesn't make them bigots. I mean, did you get the impression from anybody that you weren't welcome?"

"No, I didn't," Faye said. She tactfully failed to mention the background reading she'd done while preparing for this project. She doubted that the citizens of Alcaskaki and the Sujosa settlement had dropped centuries of racial conflict merely because the millennium had changed. The fact that she thought her date was naive did not, however, dim her growing respect for his apparent color-blindness. She decided to put some effort into learning to enjoy football. Enjoying Brent's company required no effort at all.

"Do you think the Sujosa will lose themselves, now that the rest of the world knows they're here?" she said. "I mean, they've obviously mingled with the white folks from Alcaskaki for years, but the Rural Assistance Project should open up a million opportunities for them."

"You think so?" He shook his head. "I cannot believe

they're still calling themselves that. The Rural Assistance Project. There's the government for you."

"Why shouldn't we call the project that? It's paying for a lot more than the historical research I'm doing. It's funding home repairs. It's brought jobs—"

"Just some piddling low-paid temporary jobs. Jobs that will help put food on the table for a few months, then disappear."

Faye frowned. "That can't be right. I read—"

"I know what you read. But I'm telling you it's not happening. The Sujosa are getting shafted." Brent looked like he could taste his bitter words.

"What do you mean?"

"The draft budget I worked on had line items for Sujosa-owned businesses. There was money to help capitalize new firms. There were funds to train people to run their own businesses, but when the project was finally approved, all that money got slashed. Elliott Young has top-notch construction skills, and he's worked as a roofer. There is absolutely no reason for this project to hire outside roofing companies to repair the Sujosa's houses. Elliott could do it, and he could create jobs for a few other Sujosa while he was at it, but he doesn't have money for equipment and he doesn't know a thing about starting a company. So now he's going to get a new roof, built by somebody from outside the settlement. He's going to hate himself for accepting charity, and he's being robbed of a real chance to make a real livelihood."

Brent's eyes were on the road. His grim expression made him look less like a good ol' boy, and more like a man who'd left his small-town roots and made good, then found the guts to come back home.

Faye stated the obvious. "You're not happy with how the project is being handled."

"Hell, no. I don't care about all the high-and-mighty

research being done at the Sujosa's expense. Well, that's not true. Some far-off day, we'll find a cure for AIDS, and I like the idea of being part of that, so I stick around, but there are days I think it would've been better if I'd never published that paper. It's just that some people don't think the Sujosa are capable of taking care of themselves."

"People like Raleigh?"

"Raleigh, Bingham, Amory—they haven't given the Sujosa a thought, one way or another. They're just after a high-profile publication or two. But they don't harm the situation—not like some people."

Faye knew from his tone that Brent had someone specific in mind. He couldn't possibly be talking about Laurel, and she herself had only just arrived. Who was left?

"You mean Carmen?"

"Yes, Carmen. If you could hear the patronizing tone she uses in her talks and in her papers. As if she's talking about some other species—a lesser species. It's no wonder the bean-counters think the Sujosa needed to be treated like children; the government has no concept of giving them any real control over a project that is supposed to be to their benefit."

Brent's antagonism toward Carmen bothered Faye, because she liked Carmen. It wasn't the first time she'd found herself in this position; academia was rife with intriguing, intelligent people who couldn't stand half the other intriguing, intelligent people surrounding them. Faye generally chose to fly under the radar by being cordial to everybody and refusing to participate in the backbiting. Perhaps sensing her discomfort, Brent fell silent. Faye did too, for she was no good at small talk.

Brent, who was the world champion of small talk, managed to wrestle the conversation into submission, and Faye was glad. It wasn't good for a date to end on a downer.

"Maybe the Sujosa don't need anybody's help after

all," he said, forcing a smile. "Has anybody told you about Jimmie Lavelle's college plans?"

Faye shook her head.

"He'll start college next fall, and he's had multiple offers of full academic scholarships. His mama's so proud she can't see straight."

Faye thought of Irene's soft brown eyes gazing up at Jimmie. How would the young couple fare when he was a college graduate and she was a high school dropout with a dead-end job bagging up other people's dry-cleaning? She said only, "I hope Jimmie gets everything he wants."

"He's a good kid. He deserves it."

Irene's a good kid, Faye thought. *I hope she gets everything she wants, too.*

When they drove up to Faye's quarters, Brent's headlights raked across the front porch. There was no mistaking the big, lanky form of the man asleep in one of the rockers.

"Oh, I should have told Joe not to wait up," Faye said. "He worries. Especially since last year when I had a date that…um, didn't go well at all." She spared Brent the details of being chased with a gun after having half the life choked out of her.

"What is he to you, anyway? Your bodyguard?"

"No," Faye said, looking at the dark porch where Joe sat. "He's my very good friend, and everybody needs one of those. However," she said, and even she could hear the mischief in her own voice, "he *did* kill the last man I dated."

She leaned over and kissed him, lightly and just long enough to leave him thinking, then hopped out of the car. She would wait until he was safely out of sight before she woke Joe up and sent him home.

FAYE ENTERED THE parlor to find Carmen sitting at the table, reading the paper. She sat down opposite her.

Carmen nodded at the window, where Joe could be seen

ambling away. "There aren't many women lucky enough to have one good-looking man to take her out and show her a good time, and another one waiting at home to make sure her date brings her back safe."

"Did he sit out there all this time?"

"Do you think Laurel and I would let your studly friend sit alone on our porch? Oh, no. We invited him in. It was *such* a sacrifice on our part." Carmen laid the back of her hand across her forehead, trying for the dramatic pose of a silent-movie damsel. The winged pigs flying across the chest of her pajamas detracted from the effect.

"Did he talk?" Faye asked. "Joe can get a little tongue-tied around strangers."

"Did the man talk? Our friend Laurel could talk to a brick wall and get it to answer back. First, she told him she just *loved* his shoes. I've only seen him in his work boots, but he comes in here in these cute little leather shoes—"

"They're moccasins. He makes them himself."

"That's what he said. And leather pants—"

"He makes them, too."

"Well, neither of us wanted to talk about the pants, because he looked just a little too damn good in them, so Laurel asked him about the leather pouch hanging off his belt—"

Faye opened her mouth to speak, but Carmen waved the interruption away. "I know. He made that, too. And it was full of the coolest things. Arrowheads and stuff. Before I knew it, he'd spent two hours helping Laurel chip a little lopsided pointy thing. It doesn't look much like an arrowhead, but she's real proud of it."

"She should be," Faye said. "Flintknapping isn't easy."

"He was in the middle of telling us how he lived on an island with you—but not *with* you—when he realized how late it was. He got all flustered and said he had to hurry home, because Laurel needed to rest so her leg could heal.

And he pretended to go, but I saw him sneak back to the porch so he could wait up for you."

Faye knew Carmen was hoping she'd confess to being the apex of a budding romantic triangle with Joe and Brent at the other two corners. The truth was so prosaic—Joe had never been more nor less than her friend and, counting this evening with Brent, she'd had exactly three dates since Christmas. Christmas of 1997. Changing the subject was less humiliating than telling the truth.

"I believe I'm ready for bed," she said, retreating in the direction of her bedroom.

"Take an extra blanket," Carmen said, following her. "It's supposed to get cold tonight."

Faye, who'd been cold since she'd arrived, said, "I don't suppose there's central heating."

"Nope. Only the kerosene space heater here in the parlor. I'm sure it works fine, but I hate the smell of kerosene, so I've put off lighting it till I just couldn't stand the cold."

"That's okay. Blankets will do." Faye was freezing, but she was too proud to be the first one who lit the bad-smelling heater. Maybe her Florida-bred bones would be warmer once she got in bed.

Soon enough, Faye decided that maybe it wasn't all that cold. She curled up under thick blankets that smelled like they had been dried in the sun, and her sleep was full of gentle seaside winds and blood-warm gulf waters. For a few hours, she was home.

It was hot. Faye rolled over, throwing off her blankets and letting them slide to the floor. That was better; she'd be able to get back to sleep if she could just cool off a little, but shedding the blankets hadn't helped. She was still too hot. There was a ceiling fan in the room, but starting it would have required her to find the cord and yank it. And that would have meant opening her eyes and getting up.

The word "help" cut through her drowsiness.

A voice that wasn't Carmen's called out again. "Help! Wake up, somebody! The house is on fire!"

Laurel. The house was on fire and Laurel could barely walk. Faye opened her eyes to find the room flickering with a light that had nothing to do with dawn. The air above her was a smoky haze that reflected the light in a dark, ruddy glow. She rolled off the bed onto the floor, hoping to find some cooler, cleaner air that her lungs could tolerate. Where to go? There were two doors to her room and two windows. One of the doors led to the house's central hall, but it was part of a wall that was already on fire, so it was best to leave it closed. The windows appealed to her as the quickest and easiest way out, and Faye instinctively wanted to jump out the window and run, but she couldn't leave Laurel.

"Somebody help me! I can't reach my crutches."

On all fours, Faye lunged across the floor and reached up for the old-fashioned iron doorknob of the door that connected her room to Laurel's. It was hot, but not so hot that she couldn't turn it. The opening door revealed Laurel, cowering on the floor against the room's outside wall. Her crutches were propped against the wall on the far side of her bed, and that wall was on fire. Flames licked at the crutches and reached out for the bed where Laurel had been sleeping. The younger woman's hands scrabbled at the wall, trying to find something sturdy enough to help her pull herself onto her feet.

Faye crawled to the window nearest Laurel and tried to lift it. It was locked, and the locks were four feet above her head. She didn't dare stand up into the toxic smoke that might blind her or scald her lungs. Instead, she grabbed the bedside table with one hand, slinging a lamp and a paperback book to the floor. The table was old and crafted of solid walnut, so it had a satisfying heft as Faye hurled it at the window. It crashed easily through the old, rippled glass.

Using the base of the lamp, she knocked the broken glass out of the window frame, then dragged in a lungful of decent air and closed her eyes. Raising herself just enough to sit, crouched over, in the open window, she grasped Laurel under both armpits and lifted the younger woman to her lap. Then she let herself fall backward, and the two women toppled out.

Faye's head hit the ground with far more force than she would have preferred. The impact drove the air from her lungs and, as she struggled for breath, her field of vision collapsed into a narrow tunnel focused only on the hypnotic dance of the uncontrolled fire. It frightened her to watch the tunnel narrow, snuffing the orange and red flames, bit by bit. She needed to get them further away, but she was losing consciousness and there was nothing she could do about it.

Where was Carmen? Why wasn't she screaming for help? Had she escaped? Faye did her best to fight off the encroaching darkness, but she failed.

FAYE FELT TWO small hands grasp her under the arms, then pull her a yard or so in the proper direction, which was away from the burning house. She opened her eyes to see Laurel crawl another few feet, grab Faye under her arms, and pull her again. Laurel might not have the full use of her legs, but she was doggedly stubborn. While Faye was unconscious, Laurel had managed to drag her a safe distance from the house.

From Faye's flat-on-her-back viewpoint, the fire was spectacular. Flames burst out of the walls beneath a tin roof supported by rafters that must soon fail. The fire reached for them out of every window of the all-wood structure that had been seasoning for a hundred years or more. It would burn fast and hot, and it would leave almost nothing behind.

Her head clearing, Faye sat up. "Have you seen Carmen? Did she get out?"

The firelight illuminated Laurel's terrified eyes. "I don't know. Maybe she got out her window. She's on the other side of the house. I can't...."

"I'll go look," Faye said, rolling over onto all fours, shifting her weight onto her legs, then kneeling for a moment. She pushed off the ground and managed to stand up and take a wobbly step.

Staggering and weaving like a drunkard, she made her way around the house. Before she rounded the first corner, she was forced to drop to her knees. This was going to be hard. She tried to rise again but, instead, fell on her face and laid there. Maybe, if she rested a minute....

She heard Joe's voice crying her name and raised her torso, hoping to find enough breath to answer him. He was a shadow, silhouetted against the burning building, and he was charging the dragon's flaming breath to look for her.

"Joe." Her voice was barely a whisper against the fire's crackling roar. "Over here. I'm over here."

Joe could track wild animals by the sound of their paws hitting the ground as they fled through the forest, and his acute hearing picked up her faint voice.

"Who else is here?" he bellowed. "Is there anyone else in the house?" He stood ready to throw himself into the furnace and Faye couldn't answer him. She'd intended to take the same risk herself, but she couldn't make herself say the words that would spur Joe into the flames.

Laurel did it for her. She crept toward them, dragging her wounded foot. "Carmen's in there. She was sleeping in the back room on the other side of the house."

Joe bolted past them. Faye reached out to stop him, but she had no strength. Oblivion was sneaking up behind her, ready to throw his black hood over her head again, ready to make her sleep.

Before Joe had taken three steps, an earsplitting blast knocked him to the ground. "The LP tank," whispered Faye. "The fire got to the LP tank." She watched two of the exterior weight-bearing walls collapse, taking the tin roof to the ground with them. If Carmen was still under that roof, even Joe couldn't save her now.

EIGHT

FOR FAYE, WATCHING the fire was like taking a slide-show tour of hell. She slid in and out of awareness, watching flames rise out of the old house's windows. The tremendous updraft of hot air flung sparks so high that they blended with the stars in the sky and the stars in her dazzled eyes. Then her conscious mind flicked off completely and she slept for a time.

When she was aware of her surroundings again, firefighters—with the help of a steady drizzle of rain—were dousing the grass fires that had spread like cancers from the smoking heap that sat where a house had once been. She saw no sign of Carmen. Brent had arrived at some point, and he sat between her and Laurel. He seemed to be devoting all his efforts to tending their minor injuries, which struck Faye as an ill omen. If Carmen had been pulled from the flames, she surely would need a doctor's care more than Faye and Laurel. She tried to ask Brent about Carmen, but nothing escaped her lips but a sigh. Putting her hand up to touch the jangling ache on the back of her head, she found a lump that felt as big as her bony fist. The lump and the hair around it were crusted with something that could only be dried blood. She slept again.

SOMEONE STANDING VERY close to her was talking. "The place was a black hole before I got here. We're cooling things down now. I've called for an arson dog and handler. A couple of deputies, too. Should be able to retrieve the victim's body soon."

Faye tried to focus on the man's face. His voice was so calm and his words were so ugly. She would have thought that familiarity would have made him calloused to sudden death, but his face said something different. There were tears in his eyes and sweat in his reddish-blonde hair. His uniform told her that he was Fire Marshal Adam Strahan, but the tears said that he was a human being, too. Faye let sleep take her again, because it made her feel safe to know that someone like Adam Strahan was in charge.

NINE

"...SEEMS OBVIOUS. HAPPENS every year on the first cold night. Somebody puts an old space heater that worked just fine last year too close to their bedclothes. When it happens in a house this old, the whole thing goes up. Ain't nothing burns quicker than hundred-year-old heart pine."

The fire marshal was speaking to Brent. Faye's disoriented brain focused on the odd contrast between his ruddy, freckled complexion and Brent's smooth tan.

She was lying on a couch in a strange room. The light streaming through the window told her it was late morning. She could see the church through that window, which meant she must be in the house assigned to the men working on the Sujosa project. The church steeple pierced a sky that was the peculiar blue of an Alabama winter.

A neatly folded pile of someone else's clothes lay on the coffee table in front of her, topped with a new toothbrush, still in its wrapper. It took her a moment to realize that these things were for her. She turned her head away. The fire had taken everything but the pajamas on her back.

Seeing that she was awake, Brent came to her side. "Irene Montrose brought some of her mother's clothes to you, and some of her own clothes to Laurel. When you're up to it, I'll help you make a list of things you need, and we'll send someone to Alcaskaki to pick them up."

Faye found her voice. The smoke had left it raspy and faint. "Heater."

Fire Marshal Strahan's eyes were kind. "Dr. Martinez

must have been very sleepy when she lit it, because it was
way too close to her bed. Lord knows how old the thing
was. It set her bedclothes on fire, then…well, you know
what happened to the house."

"Carmen?" If only she could clean her mouth and throat
of a long night's worth of smoke and pent-up tears, she
would be able to manage sentences of more than one word.

"We found her. I'm sorry. She didn't make it."

The defeat in his voice set Faye's cleansing tears loose.
She found her voice. It was raspy, but it worked. "That was
the only heater we had. Carmen wouldn't have done that—
put it in her room." A shuddering cough and more tears interrupted her, but she pressed on. "She wouldn't have made
herself warm and left Laurel and me in the cold."

"People don't think straight when they're sleepy," Brent
offered.

A chill breeze brought the sound of tires on gravel and
slamming car doors through the open window. An old man
pushed open the church's double doors, welcoming men in
suits and women in sober dresses into the sanctuary.

Faye, overwhelmed, looked out the window and took
refuge in the vagaries of others. "It seems strange for people to be going about their business so soon," she said re-
proachfully.

"Death puts people in mind of prayer," Fire Marshal
Strahan said.

Faye picked Ronya Smiley out of the group, recognizing
her by her size. The defiant air was gone, and her jeans had
been replaced by a simple dress in a cobalt blue the color
of her eyes. Holding little Zack's hand, she walked quietly
beside a bearded man as big as she was.

"I thought I was going to have to fight Leo Smiley to
keep him from walking into that fire," the marshal said.
"Your friend Mr. Mantooth was just as bad. It was all I
could do to convince them that Dr. Martinez was already

dead by the time you hauled yourself and Laurel Cook out that window. Five more minutes, and you would've been dead, too."

The last of the Sujosa filed into the church—a young mother with her baby and an elderly man, his feeble steps steadied by a sturdy young boy.

"I feel like I should be in church today, too," said Faye, who wasn't sure whether she wanted to thank God for her deliverance or challenge Him to explain the mystical purpose behind Carmen's ugly death.

"We wouldn't be welcome," Brent said as the church's double doors swung shut and separated the Sujosa from the rest of the world.

AFTER SPENDING THE morning sleeping, Faye awakened at noon and headed out for the fire site. The fire marshal tolerated her kibitzing presence fairly well. She obediently stayed out of the way and outside the footprint of the ruined house. Her questions about the cause of the fire and the role of the kerosene heater were short, infrequent, and to the point. In return for her good behavior, she learned a great deal about how investigations into the origins and causes of fires were conducted. Also, she was invited to call the fire marshal by his given name, Adam. It was a productive Sunday afternoon, particularly for someone whose head had been banged hard on the ground about twelve hours before.

The bright afternoon sun belied the cold wind whipping through the valley. It numbed the neat, tiny stitches that Brent had embroidered across the back of her head. Pulling the hood of her borrowed parka over her head to leave as little of her face exposed as possible, she wished for a grown-up-sized pair of mittens like the ones her grandmother used to knit. Adam and his crew were working in their shirtsleeves. They must wonder why she was dressed for an Arctic expedition.

Let them wonder, she thought. *I'd like to see them survive a Florida summer. In cold weather, you can always put more clothes on. Hot weather's different. There's a limit to how much you can take off.*

Adam's deputies had removed the remains of the tin roof from the debris. There were so few standing walls left in the vicinity of Carmen's bedroom, she could observe them at work as easily as if they were standing outside. Watching an origin-and-cause investigation put her in mind of her own work.

"Fire leaves a trail of evidence, just like any other killer," Adam said. "It burns up and out, so you have to peel the debris back little by little, starting with the last thing to burn and working backward through time. If you get in a hurry, you can miss something important, and there's no way to get it back."

"Just like archaeology," Faye said. Adam nodded in assent, then went back to work.

The arson dog, however, was a remarkably useful tool with no analog in archaeology. The clues Faye uncovered in her work rarely retained enough odor to tickle even a dog's sensitive nose, which was probably a good thing, considering the amount of time she spent digging up garbage dumps and privies. Samson, a sleek black Labrador retriever, was trained to identify twenty common fuels used to set fires. These fuels, known to arson investigators as "accelerants," included gasoline, diesel, kerosene, and more than a dozen other esoteric chemicals. Samson could find them all.

"This fire may be a tough one for Samson," Adam said. "The tin roof held the heat in for a long time, so there won't be a whole lot of accelerant left behind for him to smell."

But Samson performed magnificently. He yanked his

handler across what was left of Carmen's bedroom, sniffed the remains of the kerosene heater immediately, and sat down.

Adam, who had stepped outside the charred footprint of the house to give Samson room to work, said, "That's how he tells us he's found something—he sits down. And let me tell you, Charlotte better be quick with the doggie treats, because Samson knows when he's been a good boy."

While Samson's handler, Charlotte, retrieved a handful of treats from the bag at her waist and doled them out to the happy dog, a deputy collected samples from the area around the heater.

"Your best bet in this kind of fire is to find accelerant residue in the cracks between the floorboards. It burns off the surface of the floor, but the stuff in the cracks is protected," Adam said as the deputy sealed his samples first in glass jars, then put the jars inside unused paint cans for transport.

Samson sniffed around the room for other fascinating smells, but he was unrewarded. He returned twice to the bed where Carmen had lain, sniffing what was left of her pillow, then looking at his handler for guidance.

"Do you smell something, Samson?" she said. "Make up your mind, boy."

Samson sniffed the pillow one more time, then moved on. In the end, the handler abandoned the search. Nothing in the whole house tickled Samson's arson-detecting nose except the area around the heater.

"Looks to me like she lit the heater and set it down at the foot of the bed on the bedspread, where it was dragging on the floor," Adam said. "Then she turned over in her sleep and knocked the heater on its side, spilling the kerosene. It wouldn't take much for a heater that old to light a fire."

Faye didn't like to think that such a simple mistake could end a life. Carmen deserved better.

As they turned to leave, Samson went back one more time to sniff what was left of Carmen's pillow.

"Okay," Adam said, "I'm going to collect a sample of that pillow Samson likes so well."

Having collected the sample and added it to the chain-of-custody form that would track it through the forensic lab's labyrinthine storage system, Adam shook the ashes from his boots, nodded goodbye to Faye, and walked away from the ruined house, saying, "Now I've got to go watch the damned autopsy. It's not my favorite way to spend a Sunday afternoon, but it's better than waiting for the coroner to send me a written report. The man's slower than Christmas."

A ROOM WAS found for Faye and Laurel in the tall green house where the men slept, so she had a place to lay her head. Brent had taken Laurel to Alcaskaki to shop for both of them, so Faye would soon have deodorant and all the other necessities of life. Feeling drained and sad, she wandered over to the office she had shared with Carmen and sat at her desk. Work would bring more solace than the questions and comments of her colleagues.

Using a magnifying glass, she studied a series of aerial photographs that dated back as far as the 1930s. She and Magda had spent the past month poring over these photos in search of the perfect spot to excavate, but that was before Faye had set foot on the site. Maybe she should spend some time ground-truthing the theories she and Magda had developed from afar.

There was remarkably little change from one photo to the next. Nearly every house in the settlement had been built before the first shot was taken in 1930. The photo series told her that a house trailer had stood behind DeWayne

Montrose's house in the 1970s and that the pole barn where
Ronya Smiley stored her pottery supplies was built after
2001. The grocery store was of recent construction—for
the Sujosa—having been built sometime in the late 1940s.
She could tell that the road into the settlement had first been
paved in the 1940s, but many of the peripheral roads that
meandered over the countryside weren't paved even yet.

From the pattern of footpaths that led into an open area
behind the grocery store, Faye and Magda had, at first
glance, judged that there was a good chance some kind of
a garbage dump had once been there. This had been Raleigh's stated rationale for beginning the archaeological
portion of the Sujosa project in that area, but he'd missed
the critical clues that had made Magda reject the notion of
excavating the supposed dump site. First, closer scrutiny
had failed to reveal the type of debris and disturbed soil
that should have been visible if someone had operated an
unauthorized dump of any size. Second, and more telling,
the site was situated on land that had been heavily treed in
1939, so it was doubtful that anything was dumped there
before World War II. Eyewitness accounts placed the Sujosa in this valley in the mid-1700s. Only God knew where
they had thrown their trash back then, but Faye was fairly
certain that this wasn't the spot.

To Faye's mind, there was only one way for an archaeologist to contribute to the search for the Sujosa's heritage.
She needed to uncover an artifact that was datable to the
earliest years of the Sujosa settlement, either by laboratory testing or archaeological context, *and* could be linked
to the material culture of a particular group of people. A
piece of Delftware, for instance, would fairly well scream
"Holland!" to a knowledgeable observer.

The remains of a very early Sujosa structure would be
helpful in much the same way. Even if she found only darkened soil and a few splinters of wood marking the site,

she could glean an amazing amount of useful information from the residue. The wood could be radiocarbon-dated, and information about the building's construction methods could be gleaned from patterns in the soil. These data points might point a finger at its builders and where they came from and when they lived.

Uncovering both a structure and, on the same stratum, implements that had survived the Sujosa's ocean crossing and centuries in the ground would be like winning the archaeological lottery. But she and her small crew could turn over only so many trowels full of soil in a day. Where should they dig?

The Broad River, named by a pioneer with no imagination, had carved the Sujosa's valley, and it dominated Faye's collection of photos. The river's breadth suggested that it had not been bridged until fairly recent times. The Sujosa had lived on the east bank of the river, self-sufficient, a hundred years or more before Alcaskaki, ten miles west, was founded, so they wouldn't have needed to travel there regularly. Once Alcaskaki was built, though, surely they would have visited on occasion to trade or to post mail, most likely crossing the river by ferry.

There were several hundred people in the Sujosa community now. How many had there been two hundred years ago? Three hundred years ago? No one knew. Faye couldn't even hazard a guess—yet. An abandoned ferry site, presumably at the current site of the bridge, where the banks were low and the river was shallow, would be a good place to look for signs of early settlement. She stood up to tack the photos up on the wall.

The door opened and Joe stuck his head in. "Playing with your pictures again?"

"Yeah," she said, trying to push a thumbtack into the rough wood that paneled the office's walls.

Joe set a package on her desk and brushed her puny

hand aside. His thumb, roughened and calloused by work and years of flintknapping, mashed the tack into submission. "You making plans for a dig? I thought Raleigh already picked the place."

"Well, he picked wrong."

"He seems like such a smart man," Joe said, running his fingers over a photo that showed a high river bluff upstream from the bridge.

"He certainly thinks so," Faye said.

"So, what do we do?"

"We'll need to backfill the area Raleigh already excavated. I want to make sure he trained my crew properly, or we'll be wasting our time, anyway. In the meantime, I'm trying to find a more likely spot to excavate."

"Laurel said she heard there was an Indian mound up here on Lester's Hill," Joe said, pointing to the upstream bluff that had first caught his attention. "I can't see it, but there's a lot of trees in the way."

Faye leaned over the photo Joe had picked out. There was, indeed, nothing much to see. Nothing of value, unless you found scrubby trees and meandering creeks valuable. "A mound would predate the arrival of the Sujosa in this area, so it wouldn't tell us anything we need to know for this project. But it would be interesting to get a look at it, anyway. But wait a minute. Did you say Lester's Hill? I saw "Lester" on the list of early Sujosa surnames. Sometimes settlers built their homesteads near, or even on top of, mounds. This is a real possibility."

Faye became aware that something wonderful was assaulting her nose, and her attention was drawn to the package Joe had set on her desk. The foil was not up to the job of holding in the aroma of Joe's pinto beans and rice. Peeking under the foil, she saw that he had loaded the beans with a goodly amount of smoked sausage. Praise the Lord.

She was suddenly hungry, but another knock on the

door prevented her from unwrapping the plate and looking for a fork.

Dr. Bingham peered in. "Are you—" Flustered, he fumbled a bit for what he intended to say. "You weren't at dinner, and I was concerned. After the events of last night."

"Oh, thank you, but I'm fine. I just had some things I wanted to do."

"She works when she's upset," Joe offered.

"Oh, I can understand that, since I'm so inclined myself," Bingham said, responding to Faye's welcoming gesture by coming into the office and shutting the door behind him.

"She works the rest of the time, too."

"Well, yes. I guess Ms. Longchamp and I do have a lot in common. Except my office is festooned with pedigrees and genetics reports, instead of these rather interesting photos." His eyes raked over the aerial photographs and Faye recognized a kindred soul: someone who was interested in everything, not just his own narrow area of specialty. It seemed natural to tell Bingham about her plans to change the focus of her investigation away from Raleigh's supposed dump site.

"Why would you do that?" Bingham asked, drawing back from the photo as if it were a snake. "You saw how Raleigh reacted when Carmen, God rest her soul, wanted to change the thrust of her project. And he hadn't had anything to do with her work. If you abandon his excavation, you won't just be dealing with him as a principal investigator. You'll be treading on his ego."

"His ego's the most substantial thing about him," Faye said. "Too bad he doesn't have the competence to go with it."

"Oh, you must be careful. Raleigh has the power to do your career a great deal of harm. And you're wrong about one thing. He's not incompetent."

"Well, what is he then? Stupid?"

Bingham winced, as if her rashness hurt him physically. "The project team is divided into two camps on that: those who think this project is too far outside Raleigh's field of expertise, and those who think he's sabotaging the project for political reasons."

"What could he possibly gain by doing that?"

"Maybe he's worried that the results will conflict with some of his earlier research. Or worse, from his point of view, maybe he's afraid they will confirm the views of one of his academic rivals. Maybe he's afraid of the truth."

Joe looked confused. "Professors don't build anything. They don't sell anything. They don't do things for people like waiters or housemaids or car mechanics. As far as I can see, they study things and find out the truth about them, then they teach other people about what they've learned. If Raleigh's not interested in finding out the truth, what good is he?"

Bingham looked like he wanted to find a hole and crawl into it.

Faye asked him, "Do you know why academic feuds are so bitter?" then she answered herself. "Because the stakes are so low."

A STOMACH FULL of comfort food—aided by the fact that her previous night's sleep had been disastrously interrupted—put Faye to bed by nine. Unfortunately, she was awake again at midnight with a splitting headache. She took a couple of the painkillers Brent had prescribed for her battered skull.

To free up a room for Faye and Laurel, Dr. Bingham let the two women share the room he had vacated by moving into Dr. Amory's room. Faye hated nothing worse than lying in bed, waiting for sleep, or for painkillers to work. Quietly, so she wouldn't wake Laurel, she groped around for her briefcase and slipped out into the hall. Padding in her bare feet on a floor so cold that her toes curled away from it, she paused to grab a quilt from the hallway linen closet. It was so big she could wrap her whole self in it with enough left at the bottom to cover her feet when she sat down. The quilt was soft, and it smelled just as good as the blanket she'd slept under in the house where Carmen had died. The Sujosa might not have welcomed the project crew with open arms, but someone had made sure their linens were freshly laundered.

She'd heard that this house belonged to Ronya Smiley and her four brothers, and that their parents had lived there until they grew so frail that their children insisted that they move in with the eldest brother. The other house had belonged to the unfortunate Amanda-Lynne Lavelle, who had first lost her parents and now the house her mother had grown up in. It was clear that Ronya and Amanda-Lynne could both use the rental income the project paid for the use of their property, but Faye saw real kindness in the women's efforts to make the old houses comfortable.

Wrapped in the quilt, she sat at the kitchen table and opened her briefcase to retrieve her notebook and some maps. When she set the briefcase down beside her chair, she misjudged the distance to the hardwood floor, and the aluminum case made a sharp thunk when it landed.

Try not to wake everybody in the house, she scolded herself, then she turned her head to look at the briefcase again. Aluminum. Carmen's briefcase had been aluminum, too, and she had brought it home with her on the night of the fire. Faye had spent all afternoon watching Adam Strahan's work crew excavate the remains of Carmen's bedroom, and she'd seen no sign of the briefcase. She couldn't conceive of a house fire hot enough to melt aluminum and then vaporize it, leaving no trace. When Adam arrived at work tomorrow to continue his investigation of the cause of the fire, Faye would be waiting for his explanation as to how Carmen's briefcase could have evaporated.

She returned to her slightly surreal occupation— "listening" to her dead friend's voice through the transcriptions of Carmen's interviews with Miss Dovey Murdock.

Excerpt from an Interview with Mrs. Dovey Murdock, October 27

Interviewer: Carmen J. Martinez, Ph.D.

CJM: I see you have some of the same lovely gray pottery I've seen in several other homes. Do you all get it from Ronya Smiley? **(Interviewer's note: Mrs. Murdock's mantel is crowded with a gray pottery tea set, old family photos, a couple of duck hunting decoys, and an interesting enameled brass platter decorated with the moon and a scattering of stars.)**

Dovey Murdock: No, dear, my mama made those pots, although I'd say that Ronya does even finer work than Mama did.

CJM: Mrs. Murdock—

Dovey Murdock: You can call me Miss Dovey, child. Everybody does, ever since I took the settlement school over from Addie Winstead in 1938. I was thirty years old and I'd been married to Taylor thirteen of those years. It was plain to anybody with good sense that if God had been thinking on giving us children, He would've done it by then, so Addie came to me. "Dovey, dear," she said, "you can only get so much satisfaction from keeping a nice house, and Lord knows you do that. Teaching children, even somebody else's children, lets you reach out and put your hands on the future."

Addie was right about that, but she didn't mention the best part. There is nothing so sweet as a hug from an eight-year-old with a snaggletooth smile and a dirty face. I taught school until I was seventy years old, because I couldn't get enough of the children. Would you like another cup of coffee, child? Or another egg or two?

CJM: Can you tell me about the oldest people you remember?

Dovey Murdock: Well, let's see. I was my mama's eleventh and last baby, the ninth one that lived. She was more than forty when I was born, so I reckon my grandparents were in their sixties by then. And I thought they were older than dirt! Well, why don't I quit guessing and just check the Good Book? **(Interviewer's note: Mrs. Murdock goes into her bedroom and returns with a large, worn copy of the King James Bible.)**

CJM: I'd appreciate the chance to copy any family history out of that Bible. I would be extremely careful with it.

Dovey Murdock: Of course you would, child, and you're welcome to copy anything out of it that you'd like. It belonged to my great-grandmother, and it has seen many years of careful reading. Let's see… Mama was born in 1866, after my grandfather came home from the war. My grandparents were married in 1860, and my grannie was born in 1842. That must have been when my great-grandmother got this Bible, when her first child was born.

CJM: Your grandmother was born in 1842—that was a very long time ago. Do you remember her?

Dovey Murdock: Lord, yes. She sewed my wedding dress. You're asking me the wrong question. You should ask me if I remember my *great*-grandmother. I don't know exactly when Mamaw was born, but Grannie wasn't her first baby. I reckon she was born sometime before 1820. **(Interviewer's note: Must remember to ask Brent Harbison if he has accurate longevity data on these people. Hell. Must remember to find a hydrogeologist to search this valley for the goddamn Fountain of Youth.)**

CJM: So she was in her nineties when you remember her. Did she ever tell you any stories about where the Sujosa came from? Do you remember any songs she used to sing?

Dovey Murdock: The old folks all used to say that God made us and put us right here in this valley. The Garden of Eden was no place for us—who'd want to live naked among the wild beasts with nothing to do all day? No, God molded us right here out of Alabama clay. He made us the same color as the dirt, so that when we died we could go right back where we came from, just as quickly as possible. And He gave us the dirt to make our living. 'Twould have been easier if He'd given us tractors right from the start, but I guess everybody has to earn their own way in this world.

CJM: So your great-grandmother—your Mamaw—

didn't tell you any stories or sing any old songs that might have originated somewhere else? As far as she was concerned, the Sujosa never lived anywhere but here?

Dovey Murdock: Sometimes she used to talk about the sea, though I know full well she never saw any water bigger than the Broad River. Nor have I. But when Mamaw talked, you could see the mast of a great ship high above you, brushing the sky. You could hear the ropes creak when the sailors tugged at the sails until they rose up and blotted out the sun. Even now, I believe I feel the floor rolling beneath us when I think about Mamaw and her old stories.

CJM: Did she tell you where the ship sailed from, or where it was going?

Dovey Murdock: I don't know the answer, but Mamaw said the sailors had hair as gold as the sunshine and eyes as blue as the deepest sea.

CJM: But she never saw the sea.

Dovey Murdock: Nope. But once, long ago, some Sujosa must have seen it, or we wouldn't be here. We don't exactly look like the folks that were here before Columbus came. And we don't have golden hair, either. Mamaw said that we weren't sailors on that ship, nor passengers, either. We were cargo.

CJM: Slaves.

Dovey Murdock: Not the kind you're thinking about. Not the kind people bought and sold. Mamaw said that we came from a group of women who had left home to walk to the nearest marketplace, carrying their water jars. The sailors were…lonely…so they kidnapped the women and hauled them away. They never saw their home again. I see the question on your face, dear. I wish I could tell you something about that home, but I can't. Probably someplace where no-body has blonde hair and blue eyes, I'd guess, or the women wouldn't have mentioned their looks when they passed the story down.

CJM: Yet they survived, and their story with them. I wonder how they did it.

Dovey Murdock: Mamaw said that one of the women was bigger than the others and bolder. After the sailors herded them all into the hold, she told the others to hang back and let her handle things. She waited at the foot of the ladder and when the ship's captain stuck his head through the hatch—he would have gotten the first turn with the women, you know—she busted her water jar over his head. Knocked him right out. Then she took the sharp pieces of it and passed them out among the women. The sailors didn't speak their language, but they figured things out right quick. The women showed that they were willing to slice the throat of any man that came close or, if need be, they'd slice their own throats before they would submit. So the sailors closed the hatch and locked it.

CJM: They left them without food or water?

Dovey Murdock: Yep. And let's not be prissy. They left them without so much as a slop jar. For days.

CJM: Good God.

Dovey Murdock: I don't know what God had to do with putting them in that situation, but He must have watched over them. I don't know anything else that could have turned the hearts of men like that. Because, soon enough, they started lowering plates of food through the hatch, which would have been a good thing, except the women refused to eat it.

CJM: Well, Miss Dovey, you've got me stumped. If those women starved themselves to death and rotted down in the hold of that ship, where did the Sujosa come from?

Miss Dovey: My Mamaw said that they laid there in the filth and tried to die, but it takes a lot to kill a young, strong body. One day, they heard a noise that they later learned was the sound of the anchor dropping. The ship was still, without the rolling and rocking that had made the days such a misery. It was their first taste of the calm of a safe harbor. Then the sailors crept down the ladder with bowls of water and plates piled with fruits the women had never seen before. They fed them with their own rough seafarers' hands, because the women were too weak by now to resist, and they sang to them in a language the women didn't know. The men had fallen in love with their captives' pride and spirit. In time, the sailors earned their love in return.

CJM: I wonder if that's where the Sujosa got the gene for blue eyes.

Dovey Murdock: It might well be. But that's hardly

the important part of the story. My Mamaw told me to mark her words well: In the darkest of times, our women had the good sense to hold on to everything they had with them. 'Twasn't nothing but their water jars and the clothes on their backs, but those jars held their salvation and their fortune. Mamaw said I should never go to a man empty-handed. A woman with property can't be ruled.

CJM (who doesn't want to be ruled and is thus sternly reminding herself to open up a retirement account): Do you remember your Mamaw's songs? Lord, I'd love to know what those sailors sang to your ancestors.

Dovey Murdock: Pshaw. Mamaw couldn't carry a tune in a bucket. But Papaw could. I should have told you about him, too. He was a year or two older than Mamaw. (Interviewer's note: Must remember to look for the Fountain of Youth, then funnel lots and lots of money into that retirement account.) By the time I came along, Papaw didn't do much but sit in a rocking chair and sing to himself. I just remember one of his songs, and only part of that. He called it Henry's Song, but his name was Henry, so that might not have been its real name. I'll sing it, if you like.

CJM: By all means.

Dovey Murdock (singing):

Pass time with good company
Grudge who will, but none deny
So God be pleased, this life will I.
I love and shall until I die.

I am black, Jerusalem
Just as the curtains of Salomon.
I am black, but comely, still
I love and shall until I die.

A jealous love, but comely, aye
I'll love thee best until I die
Grudge who will, but none deny
So God be pleased until I die.

Dovey Murdock (speaking): That's a nice song, isn't it, child? It gives a nice lesson, and there's nothing an old schoolteacher likes better than a lesson. The world would be a nicer place if all people lived to please God and loved each other, too, while they were at it. Can I get you a slice of pound cake?

TEN

FAYE'S NERVES WOKE her Monday morning before dawn. In two hours, she would be meeting her field crew. Ready or not, she would be the boss. She flopped over onto her back and sighed.

Not ready. No, you're clearly not ready, said the nasty little voice that lived inside her head. She'd tried to talk Magda out of putting her in charge of this project.

"Don't be ridiculous," Magda had said, in an authoritative voice that not even morning sickness could diminish. "The Sujosa project is going to look spectacular on your résumé."

It had been nearly two months since then, and Faye had spent most of that time with Magda, who'd taught her everything worth knowing about designing field surveys of inhabited sites in four easy lessons:

Lesson 1: You can't afford to dig up the entire site.

Lesson 2: Even if you *could* afford to dig the entire site down to bedrock, the site's inhabitants would be most unhappy if you did.

Lesson 3: Because of these constraints, you're bound to miss something.

Lesson 4: You'd really, really rather not miss a single thing so, in essence, you're screwed before you start.

Magda had emphasized repeatedly the importance of Phase I work—reviewing existing reports and maps and courthouse documents to glean site knowledge the cheap and easy way.

Making sure her crew was trained to work properly and watching them backfill the unproductive holes they'd dug under Raleigh's tutelage would keep them busy for a few days, while she located a better site. And she'd have to find time to wear out some shoe leather. There was no substitute for walking a potential site, but the Sujosa settlement was a big place. She'd have to choose carefully where she put her boots. The Lester's Hill mound would be an interesting place to start.

The sudden thrumming of raindrops on the tin roof over her head told her that she would not be walking anywhere that morning. She resisted the temptation to call Magda. This project was a chance for her to prove her professional worth, and she was going to succeed or fail on her own. Carmen's death was a blow of the sort she could not have prepared for, but it was her choice whether to give up before she had started, or to carry on. She got out of bed and got dressed.

After breakfast, she pulled the hood of her Army surplus rain gear far over her head to keep the November-cold drizzle off her face and slogged over to the church, where the archaeology crew met each morning to get their day's assignments. Joe was waiting for her just inside the door, dressed in rain gear, but the three Sujosa men sitting on the back pew barely looked up when she entered. Faye recognized them from the photos in their personnel files. Jorge was an olive-complexioned redhead in his twenties. Fred was stout and middle-aged. Elliott had a narrow face like the head of an axe. Their sullen expressions clearly said that they expected to be given the day off due to inclement weather.

"I'm sure we can find some work to do," Faye offered, in a tone of voice that suggested she thought her crew was champing at the bit for some productive work. "To start, I want to check over the artifacts you've found so far. You probably haven't had time to make sure they're clean and properly labeled—"

"They're clean," Jorge interrupted. "Cleaner than they need to be. Raleigh made sure of that. Go look in the shed."

So Raleigh *had* done a smidgen of crew training. That, at least, was good news. "Well, Jorge—" Faye said, taking care to give the name its proper Spanish pronunciation.

"Not '*Hor-hay*,'" Jorge said. "It's '*Zhor-zhay*,' but if that's too hard for you, why don't you try just regular old '*George*.' You never heard of the name 'George'? George Washington, George Bush, George W, King George, George Wallace.... It's a name for a man that's in charge. Presidents and governors and stuff."

For a half-second, Faye thought an incredulous "George Wallace?" was going to escape her lips. She settled for crisply dismissing Jorge's rant.

"Well, my name's not George, but I'm in charge at the moment," Faye said. "So let's go to the shed. Rainy days give us a chance to make sure our equipment is clean and that the artifacts we find are well-organized. You have the key?"

Elliott had the key and used it to open the door of the shed. From the looks of things, Raleigh hadn't been big on enforcing the cleaning techniques that had irked Jorge. Faye found three rain parkas pasted to the floor with a thin layer of dried mud. She handed them to Jorge and said, "You wanna be in charge of something? You're in charge of keeping our protective gear in order. Raincoats, safety glasses, rubber gloves—if I see somebody who's not dressed for work, I'm gonna look at you and ask why."

Gesturing at the spades, trowels, and machetes tossed into the rear corner of the work shed, she told Elliott, "You will keep our excavating equipment in good shape and in order. If I need anything—a screen, a bucket, a roll of duct tape, and I do mean anything—I will look to you."

She looked at her crew. Jorge and Fred had donned the filthy parkas. Elliott wasn't wearing his parka, apparently choosing to be cold and wet, but clean. Joe was standing three paces away from the others, as if to say he'd rather work alone than with such losers.

"Now," Faye said, "where have you stored the artifacts?" She stood in the shed and scanned the shelves for the acid-free cardboard storage boxes required by most government agencies.

Elliott pulled a single ratty shoe box out of the corner of the shed, and handed it to her. She lifted the lid and, remembering Magda's advice on keeping her temper, she twisted the corners of her mouth into a fake smile and took a few deliberate breaths. How could Raleigh have let this happen?

She selected a glass Coca-Cola bottle from the jumble of junk in the box. Its outside surfaces were slick-smooth, so these guys had at least taken a stab at the necessary cleanup. But its neck was full of dried red clay, as if someone had jammed it, neck-first, into the ground, about thirty-five years before. She could have dated the bottle fairly precisely by the raised lettering on the curved sides of the green glass bottle, but she didn't have to. Coke bottles of this design were older than Faye, but not by much. Poking at the bottle caps and aspirin bottles and spark plugs and broken plates thrown into the shoe box, she judged that the Coke bottle was the oldest thing they'd found in the month that they'd been on the job.

As she picked through the box of trash, her mouth fell open. "Not a single solitary thing is labeled," she barked in her crew's general direction.

"Aw, we know where we found it," Fred said. "We dug up the trash pit behind Hanahan's store and that's what we found. That's the only place where we found much of anything, so we just wrote 'Hanahan's' on the box and let it go at that."

Faye prayed that she had now uncovered the full extent of this debacle, and that no other ugly surprises awaited her. "Okay, Joe and Fred are going to haul every solitary item out of the interior of this shed. They're going to wipe the shelves down and mop the floor. Elliott, take the smaller equipment to the bunkhouse and wash every piece in the kitchen sink. Use soap, for heaven's sake, and dry everything good before you bring it back here to the shed. Rest assured that I will be here to make sure that you store it neatly. And you—" she said, looking at Jorge, "I want you to take these plastic garbage cans to the church and put them under the porch roof out of the rain. Any equipment that's too big to wash in a sink will get washed in those garbage cans. Joe will remind you how to properly clean your gear."

She pointed at the box. "This, gentlemen, is junk. It belongs in the Dumpster behind Hanahan's. We cannot forget to label any cultural materials we find and document them in our field notebooks. Not even the tiniest one. Nothing about this project is more important than that."

The men did not scuttle away to do their chores with the chastened expressions that Faye had hoped to see, but they did get the work done. By noon, the rain was gone, leaving behind it sunshine and a clammy breeze.

Faye's head prickled, and she would have sworn that she could feel every last suture holding the lips of her scalp wound together. The damp cold and her crew's insolence had taken their toll, leaving Faye drained by lunchtime. She couldn't help but wonder how she would manage to get through the rest of the day, and the day after that, and the day after that.

AFTER DISMISSING HER crew for lunch, Faye fled the scene of their archaeological crimes. Tired or not, she needed to talk with Adam. She found him supervising the removal of debris from the carcass of the burned house, taking notes and talking to the photographer, who was documenting the process from every angle.

Faye tried to catch his attention without bellowing. In the end, it was the photographer who tapped on Adam's shoulder and pointed her out.

"Take a water break," he told his team. "It's cool out here today, but you're working hard. You've gotta keep your fluids up."

He stepped away from what was left of the house, shaking ashes from his boots. "Are you back to watch again? The dog went home, so we're putting on a pretty boring show today."

"No, I'm working today, but I've been thinking about the fire. I may have remembered something important."

"Like what?"

She held up her shiny metal briefcase. "If I'd brought home a pile of work in this case, it would have still been in the house, wouldn't it?"

"Well, obviously, you didn't, but yeah, there would be a lot left of that briefcase after a fire. We would have found it."

"But Carmen *did* bring her briefcase home, and it was like mine, only bigger. I didn't see you find it yesterday."

Adam eyeballed the briefcase again. "You know, fighting fires is hands-on work. When you've got a house full of firefighters doing their jobs, things get kicked around."

"But you haven't found it yet?"

"No, and I think we would've found it by now, if it was anywhere in the house. But I promise I'll look for it. Are you sure she brought it home? I hear she worked door-to-door, asking the Sujosa folks questions they wouldn't answer. Maybe she left it at somebody's house."

"I don't *think* she brought it home. I *know* she brought it home. I saw her."

"So what are you saying?"

Faye swallowed, hesitant to say something that might make her sound paranoid, but determined to make her point. "I know you think otherwise, but I don't believe Carmen pulled that heater from the parlor into her own room, not after she told me she didn't need it. I'm saying maybe somebody else did it for her. And if her briefcase is missing, then maybe that same somebody took it."

"You're suggesting arson."

"I guess I am."

Adam sighed, but he refrained from calling her a paranoid nutcase, so Faye was encouraged. "Arson seems very unlikely in this case," he said. "The house wasn't insured, so Amanda-Lynne Lavelle suffered a total loss. I can't think of any way that anybody at all could profit financially from the loss of this house. That leaves us with only a couple of other possibilities. Either somebody wanted revenge on Amanda-Lynne or they wanted to hurt somebody asleep in the house. Or else somebody had a fire fetish. And yet, according to you, once they got finished moving the kerosene heater and setting the fire, they took Dr. Martinez's briefcase for a souvenir."

He had succinctly presented Faye's own suspicions, but they sounded far-fetched coming out of someone else's mouth. "If you don't think the idea's worth pursuing, never mind," she said in what she hoped was a meek little voice, as she turned to walk away.

"Go ahead and say it."

She looked back over her shoulder at him. "Say what?"

"Say what you're really thinking: 'If you don't think the idea's worth pursuing, never mind—I'll just pursue it myself.'"

Faye studied his face until she was sure she saw good humor in his brown eyes. "You're good. Do you read everybody that well?"

"I've got five sisters. I can damn near read the mind of anybody with two X chromosomes."

"And here I am, just an only child. When it comes to psychic ability, you've got me completely outgunned. I guess you don't want me to ask around the settlement to see if anybody's got Carmen's briefcase," she said, brandishing her own silvery case.

"Hell, no. Not even maybe. All right, I'll check it out. And stick close to your friends if you truly believe someone dislikes you enough to set fire to the roof over your head."

"I've thought that several times since I got here."

"What else has happened?" he asked, again reading her with alarming accuracy. "Something that put you on your guard?"

Faye hesitated, then shook her head. "Nothing as bad as the fire. Let's just say I'm not convinced that the project team is really welcome here."

"I'm going to tell you something," he said. "You'll have to keep it to yourself, but I want you to understand that it's not just male ego telling you to stay quiet and let me go around asking the questions. We found some footprints out back." He jerked his head in the direction of the wooded area behind the burned house.

The hair on the back of her neck rose. "Did the person walk from there to the house? Where did they go afterward?"

"Can't tell," Adam said. "The slow rain that started on the night Carmen died was a big help in putting the fire out, but it played havoc with any physical evidence an arsonist might have left outside the house. The fire—and the firefighters—made a holy mess inside the house, but we're used to that. We found prints that had been sheltered from the rain by some shade trees. They were made by boots that looked an awful lot like—those," he said, pointing at Faye's feet.

She looked at her feet as if she expected them to walk off and start another fire.

"—Except your boots are about four sizes too small to be the ones I'm looking for."

"You got any guesses about who's got those boots?"

"Nope, but if you see me watching somebody's feet, you'll know why."

A silence opened between them, filled only by a question that Faye was too chicken to ask. She decided to edge up on it sidewise. "You said yesterday that you were going to the autopsy," she began, then she paused, not knowing how to broach the issue that threatened to become a morbid preoccupation.

"It was smoke inhalation. She didn't suffer," Adam said, further enhancing Faye's opinion of his woman-reading skills. "A lot of times, house-fire victims wake up, realizing that something is wrong, and sit bolt upright in bed. They take one good breath of hot, toxic smoke, and it's more or less over."

Faye elected not to press him on what he meant by "more or less."

"In Carmen's case," he went on, "I couldn't say for sure that she ever woke up at all. If she did, you sure couldn't tell it from her position in the bed." He touched her gently on the elbow with the sturdy, dependable-looking hand of a fireman. "It could have happened to you. Instead, you kept yourself alive, and you saved Laurel, too. You said that Laurel's screams woke you up. Why didn't you hear Carmen call for help? Because Carmen was beyond your help. I know it's hard to let go of the notion that you should have saved her, but it wasn't possible."

"How easy would it be for you to let go of a notion like that? How soon could you forgive yourself?"

"I was a firefighter for ten years before I got this job."

It wasn't an answer to her question, but it was. Adam's simple declarative sentence held the despairing echo of other voices consumed by years of fires that couldn't be fought.

ELEVEN

FAYE STOOD WATCHING Fred, Elliott, Joe, and Jorge shovel soil like men who were serious about their work. She would have been happier if the soil had been traveling in the right direction—out of the excavation, rather than into it—but their work signified progress all the same.

Before they had begun backfilling the unproductive holes they'd dug under Dr. Raleigh's supervision, Faye had given them a refresher course on proper archaeological technique—the rudimentary knowledge Raleigh should have communicated before he let any of them near the excavation site. First, she'd demonstrated how to use the flat-bottomed trowel that would enable each of them to keep the walls of his unit absolutely vertical and the floor absolutely flat.

"What's a unit?" Fred had asked.

"The hole you're digging, dumbass," Elliott had said in his own tactful way.

She'd explained that they must clear away the soil in thin layers, each of them less than a centimeter thick.

"How big is that?" from Elliott.

"I don't know, smartass, but it looks like you don't, either," Fred said, enjoying his chance to retaliate.

Faye asked them to hold out their pinkie fingers. Jorge held up his middle one, grinning, until he saw the look on Joe's face. He quickly adjusted his hand to show the finger Faye had requested.

"Your pinkie fingernail is a little more than a centimeter

long. You will always check each layer you excavate with a ruler, but that fingernail is a handy rule-of-thumb—"

"You mean rule-of-pinkie," Elliott said, then doubled over with laughter, unable to resist his own wit.

She'd shown them how to pull back the tarps protecting the backdirt, in preparation for refilling the mud-lined units. Precisely why Raleigh had tarps protecting the backdirt, but none keeping the units dry, she couldn't say.

They'd watched with interest for a few minutes while she sifted a few trowels full of soil through a screen, looking for tiny bits of residue like bones left from long-ago dinners. She'd hoped to discuss the flotation techniques that were so useful for separating lightweight things like seeds from the surrounding soil, but it was obvious that their limited attention spans had been exceeded, so she set them to work backfilling the old excavations. As they had fairly well destroyed any information the patch of ground might once have held, there wasn't much more harm that they could do. By the time they'd put the site back the way they'd found it, Faye would have had several days to improve their field technique before they moved to the mound site and started doing some *real* archaeology.

As the late afternoon sun dipped low, Fred looked at his watch, as if to remind Faye that it was nearly quitting time. She let him stew while she walked past each worker one more time, since that seemed a supervisor-like thing to do.

As she stood watching Jorge, she noticed something that was too big in his pile of backdirt. If they'd used proper technique when they'd dug here in the first place, then the object would have been screened out of the soil. Whatever it was, she doubted it was pertinent to the goal of this dig, since it had come from a dump site that she believed to be less than seventy years old. Still, this was a teachable moment. She could show her crew how sizeable artifacts could be missed through sheer carelessness.

The palm-sized object had a pinkish-beige body, and Faye was certain it was man-made. Light-colored veins slashed across its surface, radiating from a single point. The sunlight reflected oddly off these radial imperfections, first red, then gold. Its surface had been coated with a glaze that probably owed its appealing white sheen to tin. Could it be made of enameled metal? Years in the ground would have been hard on an enamel coating; it was possible that the golden veins were simply areas where grains of sand had abraded the white coating, revealing the underlying metal.

Faye reached out a hand for the glimmery thing, but Jorge beat her to it. He snatched it out of the dirt and palmed it before she could get a good look at it.

"I'd like to see that, Jorge." She held out her hand.

"I thought you said you weren't interested in anything we found here. It's way too new."

"Nevertheless, I'd like to see it. Please hand it to me."

"No," he said, looking at her with his insubordinate eyes. She kept her gaze steady on his face and her hand stretched out toward his.

Jorge looked her square in the face and dropped the thing onto his trowel, where it broke into two pieces. Unsatisfied by that mutinous act, he used the heel of his boot to grind it into the ground.

There was nothing left but beige dust. Faye was at first struck dumb by the sheer, stupid destructiveness of his action, but she soon found her voice. "You're fired. Take your things and go, right this minute. You have no business here."

"You can't fire me."

"I'm sure I don't know why not," Faye said. "I can't think of many things that would get a field technician fired any faster than intentional, pointless destruction of an artifact. Any artifact."

"You can't fire me," Jorge repeated. "If you do, we'll

all leave, and nobody in the settlement will take our jobs.
You and the Indian can't get the work done without help."
Fred and Elliott walked over to stand shoulder-to-shoulder
with Jorge. All three were big men; if any of them were
to stretch his arm straight out at the shoulder, Faye could
have walked under that arm. If she lost her cool with these
guys, she would look like a Chihuahua throwing a tantrum.

Sarcasm was her tool of choice when dealing with large
people "That's true," she said in pleasant, even, measured
tones. "I couldn't afford to fire anybody who had been
any help whatsoever. Fortunately that doesn't apply to you.
You've been no help at all. Jorge, please leave and don't
return. Fred and Elliott, you may stay if you're willing to
learn to do your job correctly. But if you leave with Jorge,
you won't be coming back."

Jorge threw his trowel into the open excavation. Fred
and Elliott threw their trowels after his, and they landed
on it with two nerve-jangling clangs. "We quit," they said,
and they turned and walked away.

Elliott climbed into the passenger side of Jorge's shiny,
gunrack-adorned pickup, while Fred roared away on a
motorcycle that had the speed and throaty roar of a Har-
ley. Faye reflected that she may have been a failure as a
first-time manager, but she was still an archaeologist. She
grabbed a plastic bag from the shed and carefully gathered the tiny bits that remained of the artifact that Jorge
had crushed.

She rushed to the cardboard box in the equipment shed.
Grabbing one of the broken plates excavated before she arrived, she studied its glaze and the color of the clay that
had formed it. Gray. The body had been made of a clay
that turned gray when it was fired, and it had been given
a decorative gray salt-glaze. The vessel that had been broken into this sherd had looked very different from the sherd
that Jorge crushed.

She was most intrigued by the color-changing glimmer she'd noticed just before Jorge snatched the potsherd. It had looked like a lusterware finish of a type rarely made since machines had taken over the manufacture of everyday household ceramics—or since Columbus had crossed the ocean blue, for that matter. Finding a piece of pottery that had crossed the Atlantic with the earliest Sujosa would be an archaeologist's dream come true, but it was simply too much to hope for. What *was* this lovely artifact that Jorge had destroyed?

It would be hard to tease a date out of the crumbs that remained of the sherd. It was possible that thermoluminescence analysis would help. Still, even if the analysis proved that it was lusterware and that it was very old, there was the issue of where it was found. When it had been dug up and flung into a spoil pile, the potsherd had been completely divorced from its archaeological context. If she couldn't prove where it had been found, it would be hard to link it to the eighteenth-century Sujosa artifacts she needed to find.

She shook the bag and let the particles of the ruined potsherd sift around inside it. Surely it was her imagination that made some of the tiny grains sparkle. Lusterware owed its metallic glow to a layer of silver or copper only a few molecules thick. She wasn't sure any sheen could possibly be visible now that the sherd was pulverized.

Joe arrived, looking forlorn.

Pocketing the bag, she said, "We're done for the day, Joe."

"What are we going to do for help, Faye?"

"I reckon I'm going to have to hire a new team. Somebody will work for me, even if they're getting paid in dirty 'outsider's' money." She started to walk away, but a new idea stopped her in her tracks and she turned around. "Do you remember which units Jorge backfilled?"

Joe nodded.

"First thing tomorrow, I'd like you to empty all those units, then screen the soil before you put it back in. And keep it separate from that pile of soil he was using as back-fill, because I want you to screen that, too."

"Want me to do any flotation?"

Faye considered his question. "No. We'll do that at the mound site, but not here. Potsherds don't float, and I can't imagine we'll find anything else useful here. Even if some interesting stuff floated to the top, what would it tell us? Raleigh's scrambled the soil strata so badly that we've lost the archaeological context of anything we find here. The only useful artifacts he may have left us would be more pieces of that broken pot, so that's what we're going to look for. We could wind up screening the whole site."

"No problem. It'll take a while, though."

"Never mind that," Faye said. "I'm not making much headway on getting access to a new site, so we have the time."

IT HAD SEEMED politically wise to speak with Dr. Raleigh immediately. Far better for him to hear the story of how she lost her field team from her own lips rather than, say, from the lips of Jorge the mutineer. Unfortunately, she found that the Sujosa grapevine was faster than the Internet. In the time it had taken her to give Joe his assignment and walk over to the bunkhouse where Raleigh had his comfortable headquarters, the news had already reached her boss.

"You cannot fire those men," he said in his maddeningly complacent voice. "The grant that pays your salary requires you to hire local workers."

"Surely someone other than those three slackers needs a job."

"You tell me that you fired one of them—Jorge, I think it was—and the other two quit in protest. These people are all related to each other. What makes you think that you can find three Sujosa willing to work for the woman who canned Cousin Jorge?"

"Well, I can surely try."

"See that you do. You realize that I'll be monitoring the progress of your excavation closely, don't you?" These memorable words came from the lips of the man who had managed to work the crew for a solid month while accomplishing nothing. Faye didn't trust herself to give him a diplomatic answer, so she walked away, leaving Raleigh behind.

But, however far or fast she walked, she couldn't leave her frustration and uneasiness with him. Since the devil dummy had fallen from the trees in front of her car, everything that could go wrong had gone wrong. Without realizing where she was headed, she ended up standing in front of the few remaining timbers of the burned house. An acrid odor accosted her nose. How long would the burned-out house smell like charred wood, melted plastic, and death? Its presence was a scar on the small community, and the air was jittery with the unspoken words of people who craved resolution where none was to be had. The social codes governing behavior in the face of sudden accidental death were tenuous when the victim wasn't a friend of long standing. Carmen's parents lived far away, and they were strangers. Robbed of the chance to reach out to her bereft family, Carmen's new friends were left with no place to put their grief.

Raleigh had fed the team's uncertainty with his silence. He had hardly acknowledged Carmen's death to her co-workers upon his return that morning. Work had resumed as if nothing extraordinary had occurred over the weekend. He had announced at breakfast that Carmen's parents were planning a private memorial service in Miami after the coroner released the body. And that was all.

There was no eulogy planned for Carmen among the people who had worked with her for weeks. There hadn't even been an alcohol-soaked evening when everyone shared favorite memories of their departed friend. There had been no effort to acknowledge and heal the grief of people who must somehow learn to function as part of a team that was irrevocably changed.

The day's last red rays filtered through the bare branches and lingering seed pods of a sweet gum tree, and the dappled light glittered with reflected flames. Faye drew in a sharp breath full of fresh wood smoke, and panic wouldn't let her force it out again.

Something was on fire.

She sprang into action immediately, before her body reacted with adrenaline and a racing heart and trembling legs. Nobody was going to burn to death today. Not if Faye could help it.

Sprinting to the edge of the burn site, she checked the blackened timbers for evidence that the fire had rekindled after nearly forty-eight hours. It was a cold shell. There were no other houses close enough to be the source of the smoke she smelled. Perhaps there was a storage shed nearby? She didn't care if a storage shed burned slap to the ground, even if it were full of money, just so long as there was nobody inside.

Faye skirted the back of the house, covering the ground she had been too weak to cover the night Carmen died. She skidded to a stop near the place where Carmen's window had been, but wasn't anymore.

Joe was crouched there beside a campfire, feeding the flames with sticks and dry leaves. A faint plume of tobacco smoke rose from his pipe and drifted upward to join the campfire's heavy black wood smoke. A shallow basin full of water sat on the ground beside him. Varied leaves and berries had been scattered over the water's surface, floating in a pattern as spare and beautiful as Japanese calligraphy.

Faye wondered whether Carmen, who was probably

Catholic, would have liked the idea of a Creek-style send-off for her soul, because that's what Joe was giving her. He had built the fire to carry his good wishes to Carmen's everlasting spirit. She supposed that he had purified himself beforehand by washing his face and hands with water laced with ritual herbs, then drinking a cup of a purgative known as Black Drink, a noxious decoction made of water steeped in leaves of the *ilex vomitoria* species of holly. Joe was sending Carmen to her eternal rest in the only way he knew how.

She dropped to the ground beside him. "I wish some of the other field team members could be here. They would feel better."

Joe nodded, taking a deep drag of hot tobacco smoke into his lungs. Faye was pretty sure he only smoked on ritual occasions, and she wondered how he escaped addiction. He gestured to the basin. Faye responded to the wordless invitation and dipped a hand into it, anointing her hands and face with the good-smelling water. She understood almost nothing about Native American spiritual practices, but she would have given a lot to experience the kind of peace that Joe wore like a mantle.

"Is Carmen—" Faye hesitated. Her mind was so Western and analytical that she could hardly frame her question.

"Carmen is here," Joe said, relieving her of the burden of asking a question that her left brain said was ridiculous. "She doesn't know what happened to her. Most folks who die sudden or too young feel that way, but I think there's something else she wants us to know."

"What is it?"

Joe shrugged his broad shoulders. He took a long straight stick and poked at the fire. "I think Carmen's going to hang around here until we figure that out."

Since Faye knew Joe wouldn't be roasting a chicken over his ceremonial fire, she knew that supper would be sketchy and late. No one else on the project team seemed to have the time or inclination to cook. They were all accomplished eaters, though, so the odds that any of Joe's pinto beans had survived twenty-four hours in the communal refrigerator were negligible. Instead of looking for something to eat, Faye opted to try to salvage her day by finding out who owned the property around her two possible sites.

Jenny Hanahan, the woman who ran the grocery store which appeared to be the beating heart of the Sujosa settlement, was the obvious person to ask.

"DeWayne Montrose owns the property that the Indian mound sits on. He'll sprout wings and fly before he'll let you dig on any property that belongs to him," was Jenny's encouraging answer to Faye's first question. "What else do you want to know?"

"Who owns the property around the bridge?"

"Miss Dovey owns all that property, on both sides of the river and both sides of the road," said Jenny.

"Really?" said Faye. "Isn't her place in the other direction?"

"Her husband Taylor never had any brothers or sisters, so all the Murdock land passed to Miss Dovey when he died." She paused to ring up a six-pack for Jorge. "Miss Dovey's father left her a goodly chunk of the Miller land, too," she continued. "And of course she's got the property she and Taylor bought while they were married. Her land is scattered all over the place and most of it's worn out. The rest of it wasn't ever worth farming in the first place. That's the way land is in this settlement—it just sits there. Give me a store, now that's real property."

"Do you think Miss Dovey'd let me work down by the bridge?" Faye had asked.

"She's never been known to tell a young person no, and everybody's a young person to her, these days. Besides, the land's not worth a hill of beans. You couldn't hurt it if you tried. Ain't nothing underneath the briers and the kudzu but thin red dirt, and most of that's washed into the river. You could stand in some of those gullies and not even your head would poke out the top." Thrusting a phone into Faye's hand, Jenny said, "Give her a call. I bet she'll say, yes."

Age had rasped a jagged edge on Miss Dovey's voice, but it couldn't wear away the softness that revealed who the old woman really was. She would mother everyone within reach for as long as she drew breath.

"You spin an interesting tale, Ms. Longchamp. Do you really think you might find something important under my land?"

"It's very possible." Faye felt her Southern upbringing bubble up in her chest. She was incapable of speaking to a woman of Miss Dovey's age and experience without peppering her speech with terms of respect. She caved in to the urge to say "ma'am."

"Yes, ma'am, it's quite possible. May I have permission to excavate on your property?"

"I'm sure a few holes wouldn't hurt that worthless land, but why don't you come over here and let's talk about it? The old schoolteacher in me is right curious about what you and your scientist friends find so interesting about us Sujosa. I have some biscuits left over from supper that are still warm, and I'll put a pot of coffee on."

There was nothing for Faye to say but, "Yes, ma'am."

FAYE TOOK THE project's diesel pickup, a massive brute of a truck that was better suited to the settlement roads than her own ancient car. Before she'd traveled far, she realized that the trip might have been quicker and safer if she'd walked. Like most Sujosa homes, Miss Dovey's house was much closer to the settlement center when traveling by foot than it was by car. The route to Miss Dovey's crawled up a steep slope, one switchback at a time. The notion of streetlights was laughable, and neither Faye's headlights nor the cloud-obscured moon made much more than a dent in the inky night.

It was comforting to see that Miss Dovey had left the porch light on for her, until a shadowy figure that was too fleet-footed to be ninety-seven emerged from the house. The faceless person walked briskly toward the car where Faye waited and looked in through the open window. The car's dome light played dimly on Ronya Smiley's face.

"Miss Dovey's asleep," the Sujosa woman said.

"But I just spoke to her," Faye said, making a move to get out of her car by sticking her leg out the open door. Ronya didn't take the hint. "It couldn't have been thirty minutes ago. She invited me for biscuits and coffee."

"Miss Dovey's been feeding everything on two legs for seventy-five years, but she's old now. When she gets tired, she goes to sleep, whether she likes it or not. But she gave me a message for you."

"I hope so. We were going to discuss something very important—"

"Yeah. Well, she said, she'd had second thoughts about your question. She's not real sure she wants anybody digging on her land. What if somebody gets hurt?"

"Of course, she wouldn't be liable—"

The expression on Ronya's face moved past suspicion toward disdain. "A woman like Miss Dovey doesn't worry about legal things like 'liability.' She frets over what she'd do if someone was out-of-work because they hurt themselves on her property. What if they had medical bills they couldn't pay? She doesn't have any money, so she couldn't help them out, but she'd feel responsible forever. When you're that old, you've got a pretty good idea of how long forever is. Nobody around here would put up with anybody fretting Miss Dovey." Ronya helped Faye close her car door, then walked back into the house and shut the door.

As Faye was backing out of Miss Dovey's driveway, her headlights raked the front of the old woman's house. She could have sworn she saw a hand draw back the sheer curtains framing a window. A stooped figure stood silhouetted in the room's dim lamplight.

TWELVE

As Faye awoke on Tuesday morning, her newly conscious brain reminded her that Brent would be at his dermatology office through Wednesday, making sure the citizens of Birmingham were beautiful, so she likely wouldn't see him for another couple of days. She wondered if there would be another football game at Alcaskaki High the following weekend and whether he would be looking for company. When she came to full consciousness, she felt a trifle sheepish for daydreaming over a man she barely knew, but such silliness was healthier than dwelling on her work or on the question of Carmen's death and her own narrow escape.

Sitting up in bed, she hauled her briefcase into her lap and opened it. Her hands rested on the final work of Carmen's tragically abbreviated career. One advantage to waking up early was the extra reading time she gained before work.

Faye turned the pages over, one by one. It was a miracle that Carmen's work had survived. It could so easily have perished when the original copy was destroyed by fire. With that thought, she abruptly shut the binder and got out of bed, shucking her pajamas and throwing on her work clothes. She needed to get to a photocopier.

The original copy of Carmen's work hadn't perished in the fire. It had been in her briefcase, which had left no trace in the burned-out building. If Adam Strahan couldn't find Carmen's missing briefcase, he would have to agree with her suspicion that someone had stolen it. And he would be very glad to have a copy of material known to have been in that briefcase.

Jenny Hanahan had a photocopier in her store, and she'd agreed to let Raleigh's workers use it at a highly inflated per-copy cost. Faye had a feeling that when Adam Strahan saw Carmen's notes, he would be more than happy to let Jenny charge the Fire Marshal for the copying costs, inflated or not.

Faye loitered near the photocopier until the lone customer left in the store was standing at the checkout counter, chatting with Jenny. If someone had stolen Carmen's original notes while in the process of committing arson, it would be dimwitted indeed to let word get around that Faye had a bootlegged copy or two.

HAVING FINISHED HER furtive photocopying, Faye returned to the bunkhouse and went to the long row of trays in the parlor that served as mailboxes for the project's staff. Folding a piece of paper bearing the song Miss Dovey's Papaw had taught her, she slid it into Dr. Amory's in-box. Identifying an old folk song was not strictly within a linguist's job description, but it was possible that he would recognize something in the lyrics—a turn of a phrase or the archaic use of a particular word—that would shed some light on its origins. That mission accomplished, she headed for Raleigh's dig site, taking no pleasure in the prospect of the day's work. It was depressing to think that even though she only had one employee left, she really had nothing useful for him to do.

An ancient Ford was parked just off the road. Entering the clearing, she was surprised to find that Joe wasn't alone. As she approached, he and his helper grasped two corners of the tarp covering one pile of backdirt and folded it back neatly, accomplishing the task in a quarter of the time it would have taken Joe to do it by himself. Each of them began shoveling soil into a screen, pausing frequently to see what was left behind and working with efficient care. Joe must have cloned himself. There was no other explanation for what her eyes told her.

Then she came close enough to recognize Joe's helper. Elliott removed the cap that kept the sun out of his face and the sweat out of his eyes. He approached her, hat in hand.

"I'm sorry about the trouble yesterday, Ms. Longchamp. I need this job, and I don't go along with the things Jorge says when he's mad. I'll work hard for you, and I'll do the job the way you want it done. That is, if you'll take me back."

Though taking Elliott back would require her to reverse herself on her very plain statement that leaving the site with Jorge would mean never working for her again, Faye could not turn her back on a chance to salvage the situation, especially when Elliott had apologized with such sincerity. She reached out and shook his hand. "I can use a good worker. If you're ready to be one, you can work for me."

In the absence of Jorge and Fred, Elliott proved to be as tireless a worker as Joe, which meant that Faye didn't have to hound him every last second to keep working. This release from managerial hell allowed her the time to be productive herself. It was soothing to her soul to be working with good, honest dirt again. She plopped down on the ground and started running soil through an eighth-inch screen. The hypnotic repetition of scooping and sifting felt more like sandcastle construction than it did actual work, probably because she could do it with her brain turned off and her mind at rest.

The morning's clouds pulled back, allowing the sun to light up a perfect Indian summer day. Faye shed her jacket, working comfortably in a flannel shirt with the sleeves rolled up to her elbows. Elliott liked to talk more than she and Joe did, and he didn't seem to mind talking mostly to himself, with little response other than an occasional nod from Faye or grunt from Joe. Yes, Elliott was going to be all right.

"Don't know where Jorge and Fred get off," he said, "quitting this job when they ain't got another one to go to. Jorge has a little piddly part-time job driving a delivery van; he can't get by on that. Fred ain't even got that much money coming in. Margie and I can't live like that. We don't plan to live forever in her grandmother's old house. If we lose one more board to dry rot, the whole thing'll fall down around our ears. We're holding off on having kids, so she can get her R.N. from the community college and work a few years. Maybe we might be able to afford satellite TV before they think up something else more expensive. We were finally saving something when the limerock mine laid me off. If Jorge and Fred won't talk to me because I intend to work this job, with or without them, then they'll just have to talk to each other."

Excerpt from an Interview with Mr. Elliott Young and Mrs. Margie Young, November 2

Interviewer: Carmen J. Martinez, Ph.D.

CJM: You live on a beautiful piece of property, Mr. and Mrs. Young. Has it been in one of your families for a long time? **(Interviewer's note: The interview was conducted on the front porch of a home set on a high bluff over the Broad River. Tree cover obscures some of the view, but the river and a lower bluff on its far side are clearly visible far below. The Youngs live in a modest home, but they've inherited a million-dollar view.)**

Margie Young: This was my grandfather Lester's house, but I don't know if he built it. My parents

live in another old house on this same property, just
upriver, and I grew up there. They say the original
homestead was back in the woods away from the river
a piece, out back of Amanda-Lynne's place. Anyway, my roots are here, and Elliott's folks own the
next piece of land downriver from here, so his roots
are here, too.

Elliott Young: Yeah, we've both been looking at
this pretty country all our lives. Till they put the cell
phone tower in and ruined the view.

Margie Young: Hush, Elliott. You know you're looking forward to getting a cell phone. And that tower is
a blessing for the Montroses. How would they pay for
Kiki's medicine without the lease money?

Elliott Young: The cell company's not building that
tower so I can get a cell phone. They're building it
for the rich folks over yonder, but they'll be happy
to sell me a phone, too, if they can make a little bit
of money on it.

Margie Young: He's talking about the resort going
up east of here. It's on a big lake situated right between Birmingham and Atlanta, so rich people can
drive straight from their vacation homes to their big
city jobs.

Elliott Young: Yep. 'Course, we gotta go the long
way round to get to work, ourselves, since we've gotta
drive around Great Tiger Bluff to get anywhere. Margie has a long haul to get to the community college,
but she drives it anyway. I'll have to go farther than
that to find a decent job, but I plan to do whatever it

takes to get ahead without leaving my home. Margie and I—and our kids, when we can afford them—are going to live where we were born to live, but we plan to have the things that everybody else in Alabama takes for granted—right here on Donis Cliff.

CJM: Do you know why it's called Donis Cliff? I understand that the name "Donis" comes from the Cherokee. I've come across it several times in my research. It means "my daughter."

Margie Young: Oh, God. How sad.

CJM: I'm sorry. Did I say something wrong?

Elliott Young: It's okay. Margie always was a sucker for a good ghost story. I can't tell you how many times she's dragged me around the riverbank down at the bottom of that cliff, looking for Donis.

CJM: I'm a sucker for a good story, too. That's why I'm here. Why don't you tell me about Donis, Margie?

Margie Young: She lived a long time ago. Before the Civil War, for sure, because it was back in the slave times. Donis was a young Indian woman— maybe Cherokee, since you say that's where her name comes from—and she fell in love with a runaway slave. Before long, she was a runaway, too. I've never understood that part, because I remember reading that many tribes sheltered escaped slaves. Maybe hers wasn't one of them.

CJM: That's possible. Some Native Americans even owned slaves themselves—

Elliott Young: I didn't know that.

Margie Young: You need to get out more.

CJM: —So Donis and the young man might have been running from her own father. Or maybe his owner had discovered he was living with the Cherokee, and they had to run to protect her people.

Margie Young: That makes sense. Especially since she was pregnant. No mother would want her baby born to be a slave.

CJM: Do you know the name of the baby's father?

Elliott Young: I always thought maybe his name was "Tiger."

Margie Young: Why would you think— **(She begins to laugh.)**

Elliott Young: What's so funny? We've got two bluffs—Donis Cliff and Great Tiger Bluff. His name could have been "Tiger."

Margie Young: Have you ever looked at Great Tiger Bluff? It's got stripes—golden-red stripes and dark black gullies. It looks like a tiger. That's where it got its name.

Elliott Young: You were there when they named it? I still think the man's name was "Tiger," Dr. Martinez. You write that down. I have to put up with

Margie's foolishness, because I think she's cute, but you don't have to.

CJM: So what happened to Donis and...Tiger? **(Elliott Young grins in triumph.)** You said this was a ghost story, so I'm getting a bad feeling here.

Elliott Young (warming to the story): They were camping down at the bottom of Great Tiger Bluff. There's fresh water there, and at least a little shelter from the wind, but they were still afraid of getting caught. When Miss Dovey's grandmother climbed down the bluff one day to dig clay, they heard her coming.

Margie Young: They thought it was his master coming to take them away.

Elliott Young: *Tiger's* master. **(Margie rolls her eyes.)**

Margie Young: They ran all the way to the river, with Miss Dovey's grandma chasing them the whole time. They tried to swim it, but it was so cold and they were tired. They both went down. I guess Miss Dovey's grandma was as tough as she is, because she swam in after them and dragged Donis back to the riverbank, but her lover was gone.

CJM: You're right. That's really sad.

Margie Young: It gets worse. They brought her up here to one of these houses on Donis Cliff and took care of her. She was young and healthy, and her body bounced back, but her mind didn't. Time and again, they found her wandering the edge of the cliff, calling for her baby's father. Soon enough, the baby was born, and she seemed to rally, but it didn't last. As soon as the baby was weaned, she threw herself off the cliff right near where we're sitting.

CJM: And her ghost?

Margie Young: It wanders the riverbank below us. She calls for her lover, and the sound echoes over the water until it seems to come from every direction. Everyone in the settlement has heard her. Don't believe them if they say they haven't. Elliott and I have seen her, more than once.

CJM: You've truly seen a ghost? **(Elliott nods.)**

Margie Young: Donis doesn't look like a lady in a sheet. She's just a little ball of light like you could hold in your hand, bouncing through the air. Once, I thought I saw another glowing ball, but it was just the first one reflected in the water. I did so want it to be the baby's father, finally coming back to her. I think he will, someday.

CJM: What happened to the baby?

Margie Young: One of my ancestors raised her, and she married into a Sujosa family. So, in a way, Donis is still here.

CJM: Which family? What was the baby's name?

Margie Young: Oh, I can't tell you that. People won't talk about it, and they won't like it if I talk, either.

CJM: Because they don't want to admit to African ancestry?

Margie Young: Some of them, yes. I would be proud to claim Donis and…Tiger. **(She smiles.)** But it's not my place to make that decision for other people. The baby's name has been such a secret for so many years. Most people my age don't know she ever existed, much less whether or not they're related to her. I'll tell my children the story, so it won't die. Other than that, I'll let people keep their own secrets.

CJM: You know, Mrs. Young, you have a deep interest in history, and you seem to have read quite a bit on the subject. Have you ever thought of going back to school—maybe studying history?

Elliott Young: Margie's already in school. Come spring, she'll be a nurse.

CJM: Oh, good for you! Do you know what area of nursing you want to specialize in?

Margie Young: Right now, I'll take any job I can get, but one day I hope to be a nurse-midwife. I want to bring babies into this world and put them in their mothers' arms. It's just something I want to do for Donis.

THIRTEEN

AFTER HER CUSTOMARY bag lunch—peanut butter and honey on a hot dog bun, because it doesn't spoil on a hot day and because buns stand up to being banged around and because the combination tastes good—Faye felt fortified for an afternoon hiking the settlement hills. Joe and Elliott were working well together, and she knew she could trust Joe to make sure the job was done right. The sun was shining and the weather was mild. She'd assiduously studied maps and photographs of the Sujosa settlement, square inch by square inch, but there was no substitute for walking a site and looking it over, acre by acre. Even Raleigh had known that, according to Elliott.

Elliott had told her that the professor had seemed to spend most of the past month walking around the settlement, just staring at the ground. According to Elliott, Raleigh had called this activity "surveying the site for areas where artifacts were likely to be found." Joe, in his own terse yet eloquent way, had said, "You're saying he spent a lot of time dicking around?"

Which is why Joe was still chuckling when she left him in charge of Elliott and walked away. Elliott, the project's big talker, had asked, "Where you going?" and she'd answered, "Nowhere special. Just gonna do some dicking around." Elliott had watched her leave with the openmouthed gape of a hardshell Pentecostal who'd never heard gutter language slosh out of the mouth of a lady.

FAYE CHOSE THE footpath that branched off the main road to the north, which she knew led to the Smiley place. The path wound up a hillside so steep that she, in her flatlander ignorance, would have called it a mountain. Her goal was to get herself good and lost, looking for places that showed signs of human influence stretching back many years. The distinctions would be subtle—something as trivial as a grove of tremendous poplars edging into a forest of equally tremendous hemlocks could tell a tale to someone who spoke the trees' language.

Faye knew that, in some climates, poplars were the first trees to retake disturbed land. A homesteader who abandoned a farm might come back years later to find his pastures overtaken with poplars. Hemlocks grow more deliberately than poplars but, given time, they grow tall enough to shade the poplars out. If the homesteader lived long enough, he would eventually see hemlocks wrest his long-overgrown pasture from the poplars' grip.

Faye was also hoping to get a look at the built environment. Her aerial photographs told her that most of the Sujosa's buildings were already built in 1939, but her on-the-ground observations told her that the Montrose family lived in a Craftsman-style house probably built during the 1930s. This suggested a surprising degree of prosperity during the Depression that, unfortunately, must have been the family's last economic upturn in the twentieth century. Faye wondered whether they'd sent a son or two to work for the WPA, enjoying a brief influx of money into the cash-poor budget of a farming family.

When the footpath wound past a few Sujosa homes, she might get a look at outbuildings that pre-dated the houses they served. She had already glimpsed abandoned privies behind several homes. Often, an old homeplace was left standing to serve as a barn when a new farmhouse was built. If she got really lucky, she'd spy an old outbuilding that was just beginning to fall down, exposing all kinds of interesting construction methods.

Just past the Smiley house, a fainter path veered off to the left. Being Faye, she was irresistibly drawn to the route less taken.

Part of its attraction was the fact that it sloped steeply downward, so steeply that when her boot landed on a patch of slick mud, she landed on her rear and slid several feet downhill before she even knew she'd fallen. Gingerly patting the affected parts, Faye found that everything was undamaged, but that she was smeared from waist to heels with slick and sticky clay. Irrationally happy to be outdoors on a cool, sunny autumn afternoon, she ignored her ruined clothes and walked on.

The ground beneath her feet betrayed one of the origins of the Sujosa's poverty. It eroded easily. Any field plowed in such soil would lose some of its precious topsoil with every rain.

The Montrose house came into view on her right, set well back from the pathway. She saw no sign of activity. Even the dogs were silent. No doubt Irene was at work, and frail Kiki was asleep. DeWayne was probably kicked back in his easy chair, enjoying the rest of a man being supported by his teenage daughter. Faye was glad when the sight of that unhappy home receded behind her. The deserted forest was peaceful in a way that the Montrose home could never be.

She rounded a curve and stopped short. The pathway ended at the lip of a deep erosion gully. The chasm was too wide to step across and so deep that only a fool would have risked jumping and falling short. Fortunately, someone had constructed a bridge out of heavy rope, carefully knotted and fortified with wooden slats every few feet. The entire contraption was suspended from a pair of stout

trees on either side of the gorge, like a backwoods Golden
Gate Bridge.

The rope and slats had weathered to the same shade of
dull gray. Faye paused, wondering whether a critical component was rotten, but smears of fresh red mud told her
someone walked across within the past few hours. That
was good enough for Faye. Gingerly, she took a step onto
the bridge.

The gaps between the boards were uncomfortably wide,
and the bridge swayed with her first step. Faye stepped forward, putting both feet onto the rickety span, then made a
major error: She looked down—way down, to the bottom
of the gully, some thirty or forty feet away. Her stomach
flopped over. This was worse—much worse—than driving on the settlement's hilly roads. She gripped the supporting ropes until her knuckles turned white, but she had
too much sense to stop walking. Five more steps took her
safely across, where she paused to wipe the cold sweat off
her face before climbing up another steep incline.

Remembering her earlier fall, she kept her eyes on the
ground in front of her. A patch of slick clay here, near
the edge of the precipice, could send her on a dangerous
skid. Keeping her eyes prudently on her feet meant that
the Great Tiger Bluff of Alabama's Broad River caught
her by surprise.

Stepping into sunlight bright enough to cast sharp-edged
shadows of autumn's leafless trees, she was confronted
by a Technicolor abyss. Before her was a broad, sweeping
gorge that had carved away a section of hillside in a shape
that looked for all the world like God's own amphithe-
ater. The afternoon sun spread across the face of the bluff,
lighting up bands of soil in colors ranging from tangerine
to peachy yellow to buff white. She judged that the gorge
was at least two hundred feet deep. Danger and beauty intermingled here, as it does in the face of a predator. It was

a breathtaking sight, dramatic and lonely in a way that only nature can be.

But Faye was not alone. Someone was standing in the path that skirted the top of the bluff, perhaps two hundred yards ahead. She was only a silhouette, but she was an easily recognizable one: tall and broad, with heavy breasts and a small child perched on her hip. Ronya Smiley looked over her shoulder and caught sight of Faye, then stepped over the precipice and vanished.

Faye broke into a run. "Ronya! Can you hear me? Are you okay? Zack!" She reached the spot where the Sujosa woman had disappeared and looked into the yawning pit. The face of the bluff was etched with scores of vertical gullies where the eroding rain washed soil toward the river and toward the sea, one grain at a time. Ronya Smiley was standing in one of those gullies. It seemed to serve as her own personal stairway to the bottom of the bluff.

It was so deep that Ronya, once in it, could stand at her full height yet remain invisible to most passers-by, and it was broad enough to accommodate Ronya's considerable girth, leaving room for the bucket and curved wooden board that she carried. Zack was standing beside her, carrying a second bucket with the self-important air of someone who knew his help was indispensable.

Ronya looked up at Faye and said, "I don't suppose it would occur to you that a person might not want company."

Faye, relieved that she wasn't looking down at Ronya's broken and bloodied body, refused to be insulted. "I've spent most of my adult life living on an island, all by my lonesome. When you talk about somebody who doesn't want company, about ninety percent of the time you're talking about me."

She lowered herself into the gully. At regular intervals, the roots of long-gone trees extended across the floor and held the soil in place, resulting in a stair-step configuration that made it possible to descend quickly to an open treeless area at the bottom of the bluff. Climbing back up out of the tremendous hole might be a more difficult undertaking.

Without looking back, Ronya headed across the barren area toward a patch of trees marking the beginning of a forest that sloped gently downward toward the horizon. Faye followed her, craning her neck all the while to catch the contrast between the colorful face of the bluff with the dark shadows at the base of the erosion gullies.

As she passed into the first patch of trees, she realized why they grew there. The downward sloping ground intersected with the water table in this area, birthing a bevy of small springs that continuously oozed clear water into a shallow cleft in the sandy soil. Because water is made to flow downhill, this cleft captured all the springs' output. As it gained water and the water gained momentum, the newborn creek grew deeper and wider, swelling with every step Faye took along its banks. A few of summer's ferns clung to life in this place, where they were sheltered from wind by the banks of the gorge and from cold by the spring water emerging from the ground at a constant temperature year-round.

"I bet this place looks like a fairyland in springtime," Faye said to Ronya's back, since there was no one else nearby to share her delight. "Ferns and violets and wild azaleas—is it as wonderful as I think it must be?"

Ronya turned around slowly and said, "You are just not going to go away, are you?"

"Do I have to?" Faye asked. "I mean, if this is your property, I guess you can throw me off it."

"Well, it is my property."

"It's mine, too," Zack chimed in.

Faye leaned toward the little boy and whispered, "So— can I stay?"

Zack looked at his mother for guidance. She set her

burdens down and crossed her arms as if to think. Zack quickly did the same.

"Look at her all covered in mud, son."

"She's pretty dirty," Zack said gravely. "She's carrying half our property with her, stuck to her clothes."

"If we send her home now, she'll be taking it with her," Ronya pointed out. "We might as well let her help us with our work. Some of our dirt might fall off, if she gets busy enough."

"Good idea," Zack said. "Mama, I'm going to give her my bucket to carry."

Faye leaned down to take the bucket and whispered in his ear, "What kind of work will I have to do? Besides carrying this bucket."

In a low voice, he replied, "Oh, it's not all that hard, but it gets you mighty dirty. That's the fun part."

Hurrying after Ronya, who had resumed walking, apparently trusting her son to follow her, Faye said, "Well, I'm already dirty. I might as well have a little fun."

As they walked, the creek and the waterside path sloped ever downward, but the banks did not. Within a quarter-mile, even Joe couldn't have peered out of this miniature canyon carved into the floor of the tremendous one surrounding it. More springs seeped out of its banks and cascaded into the growing creek. Faye reached through the water of one of these springs, trying to figure out why it left a white streak through the colorful soil. She had thought that something white in the water had been deposited on the creek banks, but she found the truth to be the exact opposite. The water had washed loose sand and dirt from the soil's surface, leaving a bed of white clay exposed beneath the cascades.

She dug into the soft, plastic clay and looked at the bucket in her hand. There were two gardening trowels in it. "What will we be carrying back in these buckets? Are you looking for clay to use in your ceramics?"

Zack nodded vigorously, but Ronya just said, "Well, it's the wrong time of year to go blackberry picking, wouldn't you say?" The small canyon widened, leaving broad, flat banks on either side of the creek. Following close behind Ronya, Faye got a close look at the curved piece of wood she'd been carrying, which she now recognized to be a yoke shaped to fit the curves of a human's back. When the buckets were full, Ronya would attach them to either end of the yoke, then throw it over her shoulders for the long trip back home. The yoke had the look of a tool that had been used for generations.

"Who taught you to find natural clay that's suited for making pottery?" Faye asked, following where the antique yoke led.

"My mama."

"And where did you and your mama learn to work with clay?" Faye asked. The intuitive part of her was sure that the answer would take her to some of the earliest Sujosa. It had been a long, long time since dishes and vases had been so expensive that it was worthwhile to trudge out into the woods, dig up natural clay, haul it home, mold it into shape, and fire it with wood you'd cut yourself. Ronya didn't answer.

They rounded a bend in the creek and into view of a vista that reminded Faye of the pockmarked terrain left behind at Raleigh's mismanaged excavation. The sides of the canyon walls and the creek banks were studded with pits where clay had been mined by hand. Ronya and her mother couldn't possibly have dug them all.

"Who else digs clay here besides you and your mama?"

"No one. Not even Mama, not anymore. Her age is really catching up with her," Ronya said, surveying the area like someone who'd never really paid attention to the scope of this primitive mining operation. "Mama used to say that, before her time, there were usually three or four potters among the Sujosa, but her mama was the only one left by the time she was born. It's hard to live here. Whole families keep packing up and moving out. People can't afford a houseful of children anymore, and they can't afford the time to learn things like pottery that don't pay the bills."

"Pottery pays your bills, doesn't it?"

"Some of them. We couldn't get by without Leo's paycheck, but I make enough selling my pots and plates so that I don't have to work outside the settlement. I can stay home and raise Zack."

Faye reached into her bucket and pulled out the two trowels, handing one to Ronya. She felt an idea tickling her brain, but wasn't sure if she should speak yet. "Then let's quit wasting time. Show me where to dig." She looked at Zack, whose eyes were fastened on her. "But only if it's okay with Zack if I use his shovel."

Zack looked at his mother, who nodded her approval of Faye taking over his job. Within seconds, he had scrambled up the vertical creek bank, and slid down one of the clay-lined cascades, splashing into the shallow pool at its bottom.

"You should try that," Ronya told Faye. "It's a barrel of fun, and your clothes are already dirty, anyway."

"I just might—sometime next summer when it's warmer." Ronya set Faye to work digging white clay from the area dampened by one of the waterfalls, while she attacked a pocket of greenish clay.

"Does green pottery sell well?" Faye did not want to tell Ronya that she thought that particular shade of green was remarkably sickly.

"The green burns off, so it fires up grayish-white. I like to mix it with the white clay you're working on. The white stuff's a little chalky, but it's a pretty color and it takes a glaze real well. The green clay's easy to work with, but it's so plastic it'll hardly hold its shape. Together, they work just fine."

Faye squished a chunk of white clay in her left hand. It was stiff and gritty. Scooping up a clod of green clay, she found its texture almost greasy by comparison. "Did you figure out how to use the clays together by yourself?"

"No, Mama showed me how to do it when I was hardly bigger than Zack. Since then, I've done some reading about clay chemistry, so I know that the green clay turns white because it's got organics in it that burn off in the kiln. And I know that chalky clays shrink when they're fired, and that keeps the glaze from crazing. Mama didn't know any of those things. She just knew what worked and what didn't, and she taught it to me."

"And now you're teaching Zack?"

Ronya tested the weight of her half-loaded pail and decided that she could carry more. She hacked out another chunk of clay that reminded Faye of a peeled avocado. "I'm not just teaching Zack. It's too much of a risk to trust a whole family's wisdom to one person."

"Who else are you teaching?"

"Irene and Jimmie are learning to use a wheel, and Irene likes to paint," Ronya said. "Of course they both work in Alcaskaki, and then Jimmie's got his schoolwork and Irene has Kiki, but I give the lessons when they've got the time."

Ronya walked over and hefted Faye's bucket. "You can fill this thing up. I'm not going to make a little thing like you carry it all the way back to the settlement."

Faye hurriedly scooped a few more pounds of chalky clay into her pail, and Ronya hooked it to one side of the yoke and her own pail to the other. Crouching, she fitted the yoke's curve to her own shoulders and stood.

"Aw, Mama," Zack cried, looking up from his pile of

meticulously constructed mud pies. "I'm not ready to go home yet. Can't we stay a little bit longer?"

Ronya checked her watch and stood for a moment, considering his request. Faye noticed that her stance was relaxed beneath a considerable burden. The woman was as strong as Joe.

An idea had been forming since Faye followed Ronya down into Great Tiger Bluff. She'd spent the last hour looking for a fatal flaw, but there wasn't one. Turning to face Ronya, she asked, "Would you like a part-time job? I'm kinda shorthanded."

Ronya set down her burden and nodded at Zack, who happily resumed mucking about in the multi-colored mud. The crinkles at the corners of Ronya's eyes said that she knew all there was to know about Faye's newly acquired job openings. She scratched her jawbone, leaving an avocado-green smear behind. "I've got my pots to make and Zack to take care of, but I could use the money, and that's for sure. But tell me something—" She eyed Faye closely. "What do you want with me? I don't think you like me all that much."

Faye shrugged. "I don't know where you got that idea, so if that's what's stopping you, don't worry about it. I don't hire people based on their charming personalities, anyway. For the record, I thought it was you who didn't like me."

Ronya sized her up for a minute, which made Faye feel awfully puny, then she snorted. "Okay. I'll do it. You'll still be shorthanded, though. I won't be able to replace them both."

Ronya scooped up a fistful of red clay and rolled it between her palms like a snake. The muscles of her forearms contracted and relaxed as she worked, and Faye thought, *Nope, you'll replace Fred and Jorge, and then some.*

This was a very satisfactory move. Raleigh should be happy to hear that she was complying with project requirements by hiring Sujosa workers. And, despite her high-minded claim that personality didn't enter into her management decisions, she really did like Ronya.

Ronya broke off a few inches of her clay snake and shaped them into a ring. "See how it bends without breaking?" she asked. "I could work with this clay all by itself, if I liked the color."

"What color pot would this red clay make?"

"Um…red," Ronya said, in a tone of voice that suggested she'd heard dumber questions, but not many.

"Oh. Right," Faye said, trying and failing to duplicate Ronya's snake-and-ring test with a piece of white clay.

Ronya laughed. "I was just messing with you. It usually fires up red, but if you limit the oxygen in the kiln, it'll turn black."

Zack was using a stick to draw pictures in the damp sand at the water's edge. Faye leaned over to see what he was drawing, and he held up the stick in frustration. "It needs a sharper point."

"I can fix that," Faye said, pulling her father's pocketknife out of her pants pocket. It took only seconds to whittle a point on the end of Zack's stick. When he reached to take it from her, his muddy little hand touched hers, and she caught her breath. Faye had never in her life met anyone with skin the exact same color as hers.

She knew that the same could probably be said of everybody. Skin, after all, came in more than four shades, despite the "red and yellow, black and white" song of childhood. Still, Faye had never felt like she looked like anyone— not her practically Caucasian mother and grandmother, not the swamp-water-dark father that she'd never met, and certainly not the children at school who were always looking for a way to draw a line and shut someone out. Once, in an Indian restaurant, she'd been served a cup of chai with cream and she thought, *This is the color. This is my color.* She'd wanted to brew herself a bathtub full of the stuff and climb in, blending completely into her surroundings, just once. She was so mortally tired of standing out in every crowd.

But Zack didn't stand out. He'd been born into a settlement full of people who looked more or less like him. Faye swallowed the urge to tell Ronya to keep him there, to never take him out into a world where he'd always be different, just because of how he looked. She didn't need to say it, because Ronya already knew it.

Zack tentatively touched the sharpened end of his drawing stick to test it, then smiled his thanks at Faye. He still had all his baby teeth, small and even and white as pearls.

She looked over his shoulder as he drew in the sand. "Those are very nice tadpoles," she said. "When you come here in springtime, are there tadpoles in the creek?"

Zack didn't answer. He just made more tadpoles.

Ronya had been meditatively fiddling with her red clay snake, but Faye's question seemed to rouse her. "Honey, let's show Miss Faye how many letters you know." She wiped her hand across the dirt, consigning a whole herd of tadpoles to oblivion. "What's this letter?"

"A."

"And what's this one?"

"Q. I like Qs. They have funny tails."

"Like tadpoles?" Faye asked.

"Yeah, like tadpoles." Zack's laugh was silvery in the cool air. "Draw my name, Mama. Okay?"

Ronya inscribed "Zack" on the creek bank, making the "Z" oversized, with a tail that underscored the other three letters with a flourish. She rose and grasped her yoke. "Now it's really time to go, son," she said, balancing the load on her shoulders. She turned to Faye. "Miss Dovey can probably watch Zack most days, but could I bring him to work now and then, if she's busy? He'd entertain himself, just like today. I promise he won't get in the way."

"Oh, I'm sure he wouldn't be any trouble," Faye said, admiring the way the boy's neat haircut threatened to erupt into curls at the nape of his neck. Yes, she liked Ronya— very much—but she was halfway in love with Zack already. "Bring him any time you like." Zack took Faye's hand and the three of them headed up the path.

FOURTEEN

Ronya led the way back to the settlement by a different route, because even she couldn't haul a heavy load of clay up the nearly vertical bluff face. Their homeward route followed the stream running through the clay pits and beyond, until it reached the Broad River, where it swung south and paralleled the bank for a few hundred yards. Faye trusted that Ronya knew her way through the backwoods, even after her own sense of direction failed her. She was utterly lost, but she was enjoying pleasant company, and the woodland path was lovely, in its stark and wintry way.

At a spot marked only by a good-sized oak tree, Ronya turned away from the river. If there was a path through those untouched woods, it was hidden beneath leaves and pine needles. There was almost no underbrush, so the three of them could walk shoulder to shoulder, parting only to pass on either side of an obstructing tree. Faye scanned the area for any landmarks that might lead a traveler through this trackless thicket. There were a few—a lightning-scarred tree here, a copse of glossy-leafed magnolias there—but Faye decided that Ronya had traveled this route since she was Zack's size. It was part of her. Landmarks would have been superfluous.

When they emerged from the woods onto a well-traveled path, Faye tried to get her bearings. "Great Tiger Bluff is that way," she said, gesturing to her left. "So is the Montrose house." She pointed ahead. "Your house is that way."

"Not bad for a city girl."

Faye, who had abandoned Tallahassee (not exactly a tremendous metropolis) to live alone on a gulf island, was bemused to find that she seemed like a city girl to Ronya. "I started out this afternoon to get a look at the mound on Lester's Hill. Do I go that way," she said, pointing left, "and just follow the path I was on earlier, the one that skirts Great Tiger Bluff?"

"Yep. The mound is on some high ground past the bluff. Look for the first trail on your right past the rope bridge. If you see Elliott's house, you've gone too far."

"Can I get there and back before dark?"

"Probably. But that trail crosses DeWayne Montrose's land, and the Indian mound itself is on it, too. You don't want to walk DeWayne's land without permission. He'd shoot you as soon as look at you. If he saw you."

Faye heard the challenge in Ronya's last statement. "I'd heard he owned the land, but I thought the trails around here were treated like community property. Could he stop me from walking past the mound?"

"If he had a gun."

Faye saw her point. "I get the impression that Mr. Montrose doesn't stir far from his TV."

"The man hasn't ever walked his own property, I don't think. He doesn't even hunt." The tone of Ronya's voice said that DeWayne Montrose was the only man, and maybe the only human, that she knew who didn't hunt. The sporadic gunfire that Faye had heard every day since she first crossed the Broad River reinforced the impression Ronya gave: Practically everybody in the settlement hunted.

Faye affected a casual tone. "I believe I'll just take a walk past the bluff and see what I can see."

"As you like." Giving Faye a quick nod, Ronya led Zack home. Faye lowered her head against the late afternoon wind and walked in the other direction.

Skirting the lip of Great Tiger Bluff gave her another

chance to goggle at the multi-colored clays decorating its face. She kept an eye out for a trail that branched to the right.

The woods were denser in this area of the settlement, and she wondered if the land had ever been cleared. Not far past the bluff, she came unexpectedly on a fifty-five-gallon drum emitting a plume of smoke. The sight made her wonder whether the settlement had any garbage service at all. If not, then the woods surely hid garbage dumps, even if the clearing behind Hanahan's store hadn't turned out to be one.

There were two men hovering around the drum, as if hoping to warm themselves by the heat of the burning garbage. One of them was Leo Smiley and, when the other one raised a carrot-topped head, she recognized Jorge.

Jorge yelled, "Keep walking. Folks around here don't take kindly to people snooping in their backyards." Leo, content to let Jorge do the talking, fastened his eyes on hers.

A sudden flare of anger seized Faye. She was not the one who was stomping all over social boundaries. Her feet had never strayed from the footpath that everybody in the settlement treated like their own. She had not paused and goggled into someone else's private domain. Her eyes had made one casual sweep across an easily visible clearing.

She stopped to glare at them. The two men turned toward her and, in three long strides, they were standing shoulder to shoulder at the wire fence that defined the property's boundaries.

Leo bared his teeth in the perversion of a smile and said, "Hey, Jorge. Do you hear DeWayne's dogs barking? Reckon somebody forgot to shut the gate again?" Jorge threw his head and howled like a slavering hound.

"Better be careful. A little thing like you could disappear out here and nobody'd ever find you," Jorge said in a voice that had dropped the blustery edge she'd heard during her brief tenure as his supervisor. It was a voice that spoke facts and expected the hearer to understand and obey, or accept the consequences.

"Don't mess with me. Don't mess with anybody here. There are places in this settlement where even the law's afraid to go."

Faye backed away and kept backing until the wooded shadows absorbed every trace of Jorge's fiery hair. She still intended to visit the mound, despite DeWayne's contrariness and Jorge's threats, but prudence suggested that she wait for another day.

JOE'S HANDS SHOOK as he dipped chili from the Crock-Pot where it had been simmering all day. The afternoon had gone poorly. He'd screened a tremendous pile of soil, and there'd been a good handful of plain gray potsherds in it, but he hadn't found a single one with the glimmery finish that Faye had said was important. He dearly hated to disappoint her. Ordinarily, he would have kept working past quitting time, hoping to find what Faye wanted him to find, but he had an important appointment to keep. And he was nervous about it.

He wished he'd left the newspaper alone that morning, but he did like to know what was going on in the world. Reading, for Joe, was a slow, laborious process. That's why he'd never gotten his driver's license. How could he expect to read any road sign that came whooshing up at seventy miles an hour? Sometimes, when he tried to read a book, the letters seemed to squirm and flip themselves around. If he concentrated and took his time, he could make them put themselves back in order, but if he missed an important road sign because the letters wouldn't settle down and behave, he could kill somebody. That's why he liked piloting a boat. No signs to read.

It embarrassed him to know that his difficulties were so

obvious. After a few minutes of watching him squint at the newspaper, Laurel had limped across the room and handed him a sheet of notebook paper that she'd folded into a long, narrow shape, like a ruler.

"If you hold this underneath the line of text you're reading, it'll help you focus on just that line."

He'd tried it, and she was right. Then she'd said the words that had thrown him into a quandary that had lasted the whole day. "Would you like to come by my classroom this evening after work? I know some other little reading tricks that could help you a lot."

Joe had said, "Yes," because she was so nice to want to help him—and because he wasn't in the habit of saying no to ladies—but he felt shriveled inside when he thought about looking dumb in front of Laurel. He knew that tutors charged money and had offered to pay her, but she'd said, "Oh, no, no, let's just keep this between friends."

The walk from the bunkhouse to Laurel's schoolroom in the church basement seemed overlong, and he walked it slowly so that the chili wouldn't slop out of the bowls. She must have seen him coming, because she met him at the door.

"If you won't let me pay you, maybe I can at least make sure you get your supper on time," Joe said. He tried to hand her a bowl but, with a crutch in each hand, she could hardly be expected to reach for it, so he pulled it back and hurried over to her desk to set it down. He felt dumb again, and awkward, too, and he wished he could be anywhere else in the world. Anywhere.

"Oh, thank you, the chili smells so good," Laurel said, moving quickly back to sit at her desk and sliding her crutches under her chair. How could she be so graceful when he, who had a perfectly useable body, felt so clumsy?

She took a bite of her chili and said, "I thought we'd start with a few tests, just to see if you have some learning differences. Then we'll try to figure out what they might be."

At the word "test," Joe backed up a step toward the door. He remembered tests. They made smart kids feel smart, and dumb kids feel dumb. If a teacher wanted to teach somebody something, they should just do it, as far as Joe was concerned, and quit harassing people with their stupid tests.

Laurel's sweet voice cut through his panic. "Oh, don't leave. We don't have to do pencil-and-paper tests. My tests are almost like games." She jotted something on a piece of paper and held it up. "What letter comes before this one?"

Joe saw that she'd written down "C," and was relieved to know the answer. "'B' comes before 'C'," he said quickly.

"Great," Laurel said, scribbling something on another piece of paper and holding it up.

Joe recognized the letter "M," and was surprised that he couldn't come up with the answer quite so quickly. Chanting through the alphabet in his head, he got to "H," "I," "J," and "K," then triumphantly shouted, "'L' comes before 'M'!"

"Excellent," Laurel said, holding up a third card. "This is the last one. What comes before this letter?"

Joe knew the letter. It was "X", but he couldn't imagine what came before it. He tried to sing the alphabet to himself, but he was so nervous that he kept having to start over. This was taking too long. Laurel would give up on him when she saw how dimwitted he really was.

"It's okay, Joe," she said, rescuing him from the thing he dreaded worst—that he might cry from frustration. "You know a lot of things. You know how to read all your letters and you know the alphabet in order. Your brain just stores things in its own way, and that makes it hard for you to remember which letters come first unless you sing yourself the alphabet song. Big deal. Nobody in the real world ever needs to know that W comes before X. Knowing how your brain works just helps me help you. That's all."

Joe managed a smile.

"We'll start right now, if you like. And can you meet with me in the evenings after work? It won't take us long to make some real progress." She scooped up another spoonful of chili. "You don't have to bring food every time you come, but you can if you want to. This is really good."

FAYE DUMPED HER muddy clothes in the washer and headed for the kitchen. A few minutes in the shower had soothed her temper. Slightly. The fact that Joe was nowhere to be found didn't help matters.

It bugged her that she'd returned to the settlement without following through on her intent to get a look at the mound, but continuing along the path would have put Jorge and Leo between her and all of civilization. Too many things had happened since her arrival in the settlement for her to risk that. The situation irked her, nonetheless. Ronya had said that the mound was on DeWayne Montrose's property. Very well, she would beard the lion in his den. Remembering Adam's words of warning, she would not, however, do it alone.

Joe walked into the kitchen, set a couple of dirty bowls in the sink, and turned on the faucet.

"I've got to make a business call. Can you come with me?"

"Sure thing. Where are we going?" Joe said, swishing his hand in the soapy water to stir up some suds.

"I found out who owns that mound you told me about. DeWayne Montrose."

"Far as I can tell, nobody around here has much good to say about Mr. Montrose." He rinsed the bowls and set them on the drainboard. "You think he'll let us excavate up there?"

"Right now, all I want to do is look at it. He can't object to that." She pulled the keys to the truck out of her pocket.

Joe dried his hands and hung up the towel. "Then let's do it." As she pulled into the Montrose driveway, the blue light of a television lit up the house's front window. It seemed that DeWayne was home.

Not much had changed since the previous Saturday, when Faye had been there with Carmen. Kiki rested, eyes closed, in a threadbare armchair, with her long slim legs stretched out on an ottoman. DeWayne had risen to answer the door, but he'd been in his customary place only seconds before, because the seat of the recliner still showed indentations from his body. Irene, however, was nowhere to be seen.

DeWayne didn't say, "Welcome. Come on in." He didn't even say, "Hello." He just stood there and waited for Faye to speak. "Good evening," she began. "I wanted to speak to you about your property on the far side of Great Tiger Bluff. I've heard there was a mound there, and I'd like your permission to take a look at it."

His eyes narrowed. "I thought you people were here to look into the history of us Sujosa. I imagine that Indian mound was here waiting for us when we walked into this valley. Why would you want to waste your time there?"

Popular opinion may have been unanimous on the issue of DeWayne's laziness and his surly nature, but nobody, Faye realized, had ever said he was stupid.

"That's why I just want to take a look at it. Sometimes settlers built their homes near—or even on—old mounds. If that's not the case here, then I won't need to bother you about it anymore—"

"But if they did build there, you'll be back, wanting to trample over my land and tear it up, looking for something we both know you're not going to find." His voice rose to a bellow, and Faye suppressed the urge to take a step back, because that's what he wanted her to do.

The back door opened and Irene walked in with an armload of collard greens.

Jimmie followed her, carrying an empty feed sack. "Gonna need some more dog food," he said as he kicked off a dirty pair of boots and grabbed a clean pair waiting by the door. They both shrugged off their worn parkas.

Irene's lips were pursed, and Faye could tell that she'd overheard DeWayne's outburst.

"So," Faye went on in a pleasant tone, "will you give me permission to take a quick look at the mound?" *Make him say no,* she told herself. *Don't let him get away with cheap intimidation tactics.*

"No," he said quietly, switching to another tried-and-true bullying method. He spoke so softly that she had to hold her breath to hear him. "No, you may not set foot on my property. If you do, I will call the law. And don't come back here again."

The door slammed in Faye's face. They walked in silence back to the project truck. "So," said Joe as they got in. "When do we go take a look at that property?"

"Without the owner's permission?"

"I never noticed you asking for permission before."

Faye backed out of the driveway, venting some of her frustration by giving the truck more gas than was strictly necessary. "Things are different now. I'm working on a project funded by a government grant. I can't just run around ignoring the law. But that doesn't mean I'm giving up. I've got a few ideas I haven't tried yet."

"I'll bet you do."

FAYE AND JOE entered the bunkhouse through the back door, which brought them immediately into earshot of something Faye had heard before and would undoubtedly hear again:

two academics trashing a third one who was not present to defend himself.

"—Not much we can do about it. Raleigh's in charge," Bingham said.

"But our names will be on the final report and on every half-assed paper he publishes afterward!"

Faye had never heard Amory raise his voice before; he sounded like a man who was one step away from apoplexy.

"Don't be so naïve. Our names *may* be on those papers, if we're lucky. Raleigh doesn't have a history of being generous with publication credits."

Not liking the idea of being caught eavesdropping outside the kitchen door, Faye sauntered into the room and slid into a seat at the table beside Amory and Bingham. Joe, who tended to follow Faye's lead, took the fourth and last chair.

"So," she said, "I'm not the only one who's unhappy with the way Raleigh's running the project. Who's going to talk to him?" Bingham and Amory looked at her as if she'd proposed that one of them force Raleigh, at gunpoint, to abdicate his post. "I've been planning to talk to him myself," she continued, "so if there's anything either of you would like me to tell him...." She could tell that the idea of her speaking to Raleigh about their concerns gave both men visions of pink slips and unemployment lines.

"No," Amory interjected, "Bingham's the obvious person to represent our interests. He has tenure, so he's less vulnerable to Raleigh's...um...petulance."

"Well, then, let's make a list of things we want to bring to his attention. First, his archaeology work. So far, he shows no grasp for designing a field study of this type. I'd like him to use a more hands-off management style. I know Carmen felt the same way before she died. Do you gentlemen agree?"

"To a point—" Amory began.

Faye interrupted him. "And I sense that you're both con-

cerned about receiving credit for your work when Raleigh
publishes the results of this project."

Both men nodded.

"As a scientist of experience—not to mention tenure—
I'd think you could work with Raleigh to establish some
guidelines." She looked expectantly at Bingham.

"I should think so."

"Good," Faye said, pushing away from the table and
standing up. "Because if you can't work things out with
Raleigh, I'll give it a shot." Both men looked absolutely
terrified by the very thought.

LIGHT FILTERED THROUGH the screen door that separated the
merchandise inside Hanahan's Grocery from the moths
hovering outside. It was past closing time, but the heavy
door behind the screen was unlocked. Faye hurried through
it in search of shampoo. Brent and Laurel had replaced
her own shampoo, which had burned in the fire, with the
body-building brand Laurel used on her own fine locks.
Faye's coarse straight hair had quickly taken on the look
of black hay.

She was alone, as Joe, who probably made his own
shampoo out of slippery elm or something equally organic,
had elected to stay at the bunkhouse. Faye quickly learned
that finding shampoo in Hanahan's Grocery was not an intuitive process. It wasn't shelved near other toiletries like
toothpaste and aftershave. A quick trip down an aisle that
seemed to be reserved for "soapy" stuff—laundry deter-
gent, facial cleanser, and insecticidal soap—proved fruit-
less, so Faye tried the shelves lining the building's exterior
walls, where no pretense of organization was made. Picking
through the flotsam and jetsam scattered along the shelf
nearest the door, her attention was drawn to a display that
was distinctly uncluttered.

A yard-long section of shelving had been cleared out for

a teapot and six mugs sitting atop a large oval platter. Beside the platter were some salt-and-pepper shakers, a set of mixing bowls, and a collection of flower pots and vases. Each ceramic piece was finished with a gray salt-glaze that was unadorned except for the imperfections introduced by nature. The vessels' shapes were equally simple, but their grace caught Faye's attention in a way that gilded porcelain wouldn't have. The sweeping handles at the neck of one of the vases rose like wings. Faye could picture that vase sitting alone on a severe and sleek table, holding only a single white tulip, gracing the cover of *Architectural Digest*.

She picked up a mug and enjoyed the feel of its handle on her fingers. The subtle flare of its rim would feel good as it carried coffee to her lips. She wanted it.

The price wasn't marked, but she suspected she could afford it, which was too bad. Its maker deserved more. She turned the mug over and wasn't surprised to see "R. Smiley" scratched into its base.

Further along the shelf, she found several brands of shampoo. Having snagged one, she went to the cash register and found out why Jenny was still working when it was half an hour past closing time. A woman stood there, talking non-stop—a woman, who, Faye realized immediately, could only have been Amanda-Lynne Lavelle.

In addition to being a gifted talker, Amanda-Lynne Lavelle was as startlingly attractive as a middle-aged woman could be. Her shoulder-length brunette hair was curly and thick. The loss of pigmentation common to the Sujosa had given her a white streak of hair that framed her left cheek so boldly that any grays she might have weren't noticeable. Her blue-green eyes contrasted so strongly with her unwrinkled nut-brown skin and gleaming white teeth that Faye found herself focusing on the woman's face rather than her words.

"Do you think Jimmie will like these new energy bars?

He does like chocolate. I do believe he'd eat it for breakfast, but I make sure he gets something with vitamins in it
before he leaves for school. Lord knows what he eats for
lunch. This label here has a list of vitamins as long as my
right arm—"

"My customers seem to like them," Jenny broke in, taking the energy bar from Amanda-Lynne's hand and ring-
ing it up. "I ate one today for lunch, as a matter of fact. I
don't have anybody working here with me, so some days
get long. Mighty long."

"Oh, I do know about long days. I don't know how Jimmie does everything he has to do. I guess it helps to be
young. He leaves early every morning for school in Alcaskaki then he goes to school all day. And then he goes to
the library and works till they close at six. Some days, he
doesn't even leave at six, because he's picking out books
for himself. A library job is hardly even work for a child
like that, surrounded by the books he loves all the time."

Jenny reached under the counter. "That reminds me.
You haven't picked up your mail for a few days, and Jimmie's got a good little pile of college letters." She handed
Amanda-Lynne a double-handful of slick, brightly colored brochures.

The other woman caressed them, saying, "It's going to
happen. It's really going to happen. One of these colleges is
going to pay my boy a big lot of money to come and study
with them." She turned, fanning out the brochures, and
fastened her famous turquoise eyes on Faye's brown ones.
"Look at this! Ever since they got wind of Jimmie's SATs,
they've all been after him." She waved her son's mail in the
air like a lottery winner flashing her millions and cried,
"My son's going to college. Charles will be so proud!" as
she rushed out the door, leaving the energy bar behind.

Faye wordlessly pushed the ceramic mug and the bottle of shampoo across the counter toward Jenny, who rang

them up efficiently, took Faye's money, then locked the cash drawer up with a key. Faye stood silent for a moment, willing herself not to gossip, but finally she leaned toward Jenny and asked quietly, "Isn't Charles Lavelle dead?"

"Yep," Jenny said, shouldering her purse and herding Faye toward the door. "Six years now."

Faye opened her mouth to ask something else, but her gossip-hating self won out. She closed it again.

Jenny took pity on her. "You never can tell what's going to come out of Amanda-Lynne's mouth. She's the most entertaining customer I've got. But you know what? She's a real good mother. Jimmie Lavelle has nice manners, and he works hard, whether he's at school or at his library job. More than that, he's got a kind heart. He's good to his sweetheart, Irene. He spent most of the little bit he earns at the library to buy cell phones for the two of them, just so they can talk to each other when he's at school and she's at work. Now, it would be easy enough for anyone to be good to Irene, but Jimmie's good to her mother, too—which makes him a better Christian than me."

Faye didn't know how to respond. Jenny seemed so warm and gregarious that it was shocking to hear her speak so of a woman as ill as Kiki Montrose.

The look on Faye's face must have reflected what she was thinking. "Kiki never would've gotten sick if she'd stayed in her husband's bed," said Jenny. "She was always man-crazy. Why, she stole my boyfriend Ed, right before our senior prom. Now dear little Irene is suffering for Kiki's mistakes, sacrificing her whole life for her sorry mother. It's a crying shame. You wouldn't think it to look at her, but that girl's a genius when it comes to computers. But all she's got now is an old clunker of a machine just good enough so she can browse the Internet and see all the things she can't have. That cell phone lease would have paid for Irene's schooling and a few pretty things like young girls need.

Instead, the money's going for drugs to keep Kiki alive so she can torment everyone around her for a few more years."

Faye tried to imagine Kiki as a *femme fatale*. Perhaps when her lank orange hair had been lustrous and fiery, and her lined skin had been the pearly white of a natural redhead, maybe then Kiki could have had her pick of men. Or perhaps Jenny was biased because of the old rivalry. There were, after all, other ways to get Hepatitis C besides sexual contact.

Amanda-Lynne came fluttering back in the door, looking for the energy bar she had left on the counter.

"I mustn't forget this," she said.

Amanda-Lynne smiled sweetly at the two women, including Faye in her benevolent gaze as if she had known her all her life. It was impossible not to like her, quirks and all. Faye could hardly believe that she'd been reared in the same home as DeWayne Montrose.

Suddenly Faye had a brainstorm. DeWayne Montrose's mound wasn't the only early settlement site—not if Carmen's notes from the interview with Margie and Elliott were correct.

"Mrs. Lavelle?" began Faye.

"Amanda-Lynne," corrected the lady.

Faye smiled. "I'm Faye Longchamp, with the Rural Assistance Project."

"How nice to meet you," said Amanda-Lynne. "You're the new archaeologist, aren't you? That's such an interesting subject."

"Yes. And I'm hoping you can help me with something. Amanda-Lynne, Elliott's wife Margie mentioned the old Lester homestead." She neglected to mention that Margie hadn't actually mentioned it directly to her. "She said she didn't know exactly where it was or who owned the property, but I thought it might be you, because she said it was back of your place. Is that right?"

"Yes. Daddy showed me the place where his mama said the old house was. I can take you there. Well, I can get you close. I was real young at the time, and I might not remember the exact spot. There's nothing there now but trees, anyway, but I'll show it to you, if you like."

"Can I excavate there?"

"Sure. I'd be real interested to see if you can find something."

Faye wished she could see DeWayne Montrose's face when he found out that she was getting what she wanted, in spite of him. "You don't know how much I appreciate this, Amanda-Lynne."

Amanda-Lynne graced her with an angel's smile. "Charles will be so interested to hear this." She backed out the door, waving goodbye with Jimmie's energy bar.

"Reckon your work life is fixing to get more interesting?" Jenny looked at Faye.

The question was rhetorical, because Jenny clearly wanted to close the store and get herself some supper. As Faye gathered her purchases, she saw a mug like the one she just bought sitting on the far side of Jenny's cash register.

"I see you like Ronya's work, too."

Jenny picked up her own mug, wiping a drop of tea off its rim with her thumb. "Oh, you're talking about my coffee cup. This isn't Ronya's. Her mama made this for me, years ago. It's just plain old pottery like people around here have been making for years and years. Most of us have got a set of this stuff that used to be our grandma's. When somebody breaks something, Ronya's real good about making another piece so much like it that you don't miss the old one."

So that explained why Faye's crew kept digging up gray potsherds. People had been making the same pottery for generations here, handing their designs down like an inheritance.

Jenny was looking at her expectantly, as if she couldn't

understand why Faye didn't pack up her stuff and leave so she could go home, but she was too much of a business-woman to come out and say so.

"I guess I'll go make myself some coffee so I can try out my new cup," Faye said, awkwardly covering her retreat.

Jenny politely showed Faye the door, then locked it behind her.

As Faye walked across the parking lot, she saw that Amanda-Lynne hadn't finished her excited perusal of Jimmie's college mail. Faye would have walked over and spent a moment making polite conversation, except Amanda-Lynne was in no great need of a conversational partner. Bright and lively chatter streamed out of the open car window as Amanda-Lynne regaled the empty passenger seat with news of all the scholarships Jimmie was in line to receive.

Interview with Mrs. Amanda-Lynne Lavelle, November 5, 2004

Interviewer: Carmen J. Martinez, Ph.D.

CJM: Should I come back later? I don't want to disturb Mrs. Montrose. **(Interviewer's note: Mrs. Lavelle was caring for Mrs. Kiki Montrose on the evening of this interview. Mrs. Montrose is in ill health, and she was asleep on the couch when I arrived at the Lavelle house.)**

Amanda-Lynne Lavelle: Oh, heavens no! Don't you worry about Kiki. There's not much that can wake her up when she's having a good sleep.

CJM: I see you enjoy handwork. **(Interviewer's note: The walls of the Lavelle home are covered with**

**cross-stitch samplers, the furniture is cushioned
with crewel-work pillows, and every available
surface is covered with neat—extremely neat, in
fact—stacks of books. There is not an undecorated
spot nor a single mote of dust in the Lavelle home.)**

Amanda-Lynne Lavelle: I don't have much time
for my fancy work anymore, not since Charles died.
Charles wishes I had time to stitch, but when he says
so, I just remind him that I work all day in Alcaskaki
at the diner, now that he's gone and took his paycheck
with him. **(Interviewer's note: I feel compelled to
mention that Charles Lavelle passed away in 1999.)**

CJM: You and your cousin DeWayne are as pure Sujosa as two people can be. Our genealogists haven't
found an outsider on either of your family trees yet.
You two are walking, talking history.

Amanda-Lynne Lavelle: I'm not *that* old.

CJM: Oh, I didn't mean that you yourself were…I
just… Well, anything either of you have to say about
where the Sujosa come from would be so valuable.

Amanda-Lynne Lavelle: I was just messing with
you. I knew what you meant, but I don't think I'm
going to be any help to you. My mama always said
the Sujosa just grew up out of the dirt, right in this
spot. She wasn't much of a storyteller, except when
she was playing the mandolin and singing. I see that
light in your eye. No, she didn't sing any old Sujosa
songs and she didn't write any of her own, and neither did Daddy. They just played other people's tunes.

They were real partial to Bill Monroe and Roy Acuff.
But that doesn't help you out any, either.

CJM: Culture gets passed along in other ways. There
are other folk arts besides story and song. **(Interviewer's note: At this point, the significance of
Amanda-Lynne's décor strikes me. Sometimes, I
am exceedingly slow.)**

CJM: Did your mother teach you to do handcrafts?
What kind of "fancy work" did the women in your
family like to do?

Amanda-Lynne Lavelle: Oh, why didn't I think of
that? I have my great-great-grandmother's sampler.
It may be the oldest thing in the house, although I
guess all my stuff is getting old. There it is, hanging right behind you. Just look how finely she wove
the handspun cloth. You can tell she hand-dyed the
thread, too. And see the house?

Some girls just worked out a design of any old
house—four walls and a roof—but this house looks
real. You can see the grain in the cedar shingles. And
look at the brick foundation. She worked the mortar
in a different stitch, so every brick stands out. And
she put the house in a true-life landscape—see this
little hump in the backyard?

There's an Indian mound on my cousin DeWayne's
property, and Mary Alice's cross-stitched mound
looks just like the real one. I guess she exercised a
little creative license, since the Indian mound isn't
all that close to the old home site, but I'm inclined to
ignore a little mistake like that in the work of a child.
To think that she was only eleven years old when she
worked this picture.

CJM: Only eleven years old…you're right. That's amazing. **(Interviewer's note: The sampler is signed, "Mary Alice Lester's work, finished in her eleventh year, April 26, 1845." Beneath the signature is a list of her family members: Father—Sam Lester, Mother—May Lester, Sister—Edwina Lester. This is information that I know Dr. Bingham and his associates will be happy to have.)** I've heard the Lesters were among the first settlers, but nobody knows when they came to Alabama, and we lost most pre-Civil War records when the courthouse burned. If we can connect you to Mary Alice with this sampler, then somehow prove she lived here in the settlement—well, it would help a great deal.

Amanda-Lynne Lavelle: I don't know exactly where the house was, but I know she and her family lived in the settlement. I do recall my daddy saying there was a big hoo-ha when the Lester land was split up, sometime before the Civil War, so I guess we were here before 1860. Fortunately, Mary Alice and Edwina were not petty. They kept the trail hot between their houses, visiting back and forth like sisters do, while their children and grandchildren built up the biggest family feud that could be assembled without the help of the two injured parties. Feelings ran high, and there might have been killings, except it was mighty awkward to go shooting up your great-aunt's house when you weren't absolutely sure your grandmother wasn't inside having a cup of coffee.

CJM: Is the family still divided?

Amanda-Lynne Lavelle: Well, the day came when the sisters were too old to get themselves through

the woods to each other's houses. Mary Alice talked
one of her little grandsons—my grandfather—into
running notes back and forth between them, and that
worked for a little while, but she missed her sister.
And she was afraid the shooting would start for sure
now that she and Edwina were getting too old to keep
people in line.

CJM: What did she do?

Amanda-Lynne Lavelle: She called her children together and told them that she intended to walk to her
sister's house, and that they might better come with
her. If she collapsed and died of exposure, it would
look pretty bad for their side of the family. Then she
started walking. They didn't have much choice but
to trail after her.

Now, old women walk slow, so there was plenty of
time for word to get out in the settlement.

Mary Alice's grandchildren and great-grandchil-
dren and all their in-laws came out to walk with her,
until the woods were full of them. Edwina's kin all
rushed to her house to protect her, just in case shooting broke out. By the time Mary Alice dragged her
old carcass up to Edwina's front porch, there was
probably a hundred folks standing there looking at
each other.

The two doddering old ladies stood on the doorstep and faced the rest of them down. Mary Alice
said, "Daddy wrote his will a long time ago. Edwina
and I are perfectly happy with the way the land was
divvied up. It is time for you bunch of babies to grow
up." Then she turned to her oldest daughter and to
Edwina's—both of them well into their sixties by

this time—and said, "Do you think it's possible for you two girls to whip up a batch of tea cakes for this crowd?" And they did.

CJM: You know, that story sounds familiar. I've been reviewing an old will that divided up a big piece of property upriver from here. I'll show you—it's right here in my briefcase…well, no, it's not. I've got a pretty piece of a broken plate I picked up last week, though, and a couple of pens that don't work, but no will. Isn't that always the way? I must have left it on my desk. I don't remember the family's name, but it wasn't something down-home like Lester. It was a high-falutin name that made me think of British royalty or something. But never fear. Give me a little time and I'll find it. You were talking about the old feud?

Amanda-Lynne Lavelle: Those days are long over, I'm happy to say. These days, it's hard to understand why anyone would care about that patch of land—

(Mrs. Lavelle is interrupted by Mrs. Montrose, who is awakened by a fit of coughing.)

Kiki Montrose: Could you get me some water, please?

Amanda-Lynne Lavelle: Oh, certainly, sweetheart. Let me help you sit up, first. Maybe that will help.

CJM: I appreciate your time, and I don't want to overstay my welcome.

Kiki Montrose: Oh, please don't rush off on my account. I'll be fine. **(Another coughing spell says otherwise.)**

Amanda-Lynne Lavelle: I'm sorry…. Kiki needs me now.

FIFTEEN

FAYE BOLTED HER breakfast that Wednesday morning so that she could catch Raleigh before her work crew arrived. She wanted to get Ronya started early that morning, so Faye needed to get approval for her work plan—and for something else.

Raleigh fiddled with the plastic bag holding the ground-up remnants of the potsherd that Jorge had crushed. The professor lifted one hand and watched the tiny bits of fired pottery sift from one side of the bag to the other, running downhill like sand through an hourglass. Faye wondered if he'd forgotten that she'd asked him a question.

"So you'd like approval to run thermoluminescence testing on this…glorified dirt. Well, it won't come cheap," he said, proving that he was, on occasion, listening to her when she spoke. "You say there's some soil mixed in with the remnants of the potsherd? How will the lab distinguish the sample from its associated debris?"

"I feel sure they can use a microscope to distinguish crushed clay from dirt. I plan to speak with the analyst about the lab's preferred method of separating debris from artifacts, but I need your approval on the request form before anybody at the lab will give me the time of day."

Raleigh opened his file drawer and removed a laboratory request form. "I'll file the form and talk to the analyst. You have fieldwork to do. What is your work plan? And whom do you propose to use for field technicians, since you couldn't manage to get along with the men who worked quite well under my direction?"

"Elliott has returned to work. Joe never left. And I've found one Sujosa who *is* willing to work." Faye handed him the personnel form.

"And your work plan?" Raleigh asked.

It would not be wise to suggest that she planned to expend days of paid labor sifting through the spoil piles he'd left behind, looking for important artifacts that she suspected he'd overlooked. "I've received permission from Amanda-Lynne Lavelle to dig on the site of the original Lester homestead. From all accounts, the Lesters were among the first Sujosa settlers to come to this area."

He opened his mouth and she brazenly interrupted him before he could chastise her for abandoning his dig. "You've already excavated the areas behind Hanahan's Grocery most likely to show evidence of human activity." She mentally added, "because there *wasn't* any human activity there before 1940," but she kept that damning fact to herself. "For the next few days, I'll split my crew's time between completing your work behind the grocery, and surveying a sampling grid on Mrs. Lavelle's land."

"I'll want a full report on your week's activities at the Friday evening meeting. That gives you three days to accomplish something. I want you to understand that shutting down the archaeological portion of the project is within the realm of possibility."

Faye had been prepared for him to browbeat her. She had been prepared for him to criticize her work plan—the one that was, unlike his, actually based on logic and research. She had not been prepared for this.

"But archaeology is a critical component of the research. If we uncover the Lester homestead—"

"But you may not uncover anything. I wonder if you are aware of how I have built my career. I work in museums, carefully studying artifacts, and cataloging them in every detail. I build a case for their provenance through meticulous library research. It's not exciting, glamorous work, like your brand of archaeology, but it's a damn sight less wasteful. Not to mention that it avoids the danger of destroying irreplaceable information that exists every time you turn over a trowelful of soil. It is my position that excavation should be reserved for cases in which the project goals can be served in no other way. Our other scientists are making progress. I've seen no sign that you will be able to match them."

"I've only had two days."

"I've had a month, and I have found nothing worth pursuing." Raleigh filled out the request form and slid it, along with Faye's crushed potsherd, into a manila envelope and tossed the envelope into his out-box.

DURING HER BRIEF residence in the Sujosa settlement, Faye had been reminded time and again that Alabama geology differed from Florida geology in an important way: it was three-dimensional. The Florida islands where Faye had accumulated her professional experience were as flat as the paper her maps were printed on, but parts of Amanda-Lynne Lavelle's land might as well have been vertical. She knew that the crumbly sands and clays that blanketed the area surrounding the Sujosa settlement were highly susceptible to erosion—Great Tiger Bluff was ample evidence of that—and erosion gullies marred Amanda-Lynne's land all along the creek that tumbled toward the Broad River. As she stood—with the owner's permission—overlooking the area just south of DeWayne's mound, she realized that implementing a field survey for this site was going to be a bear.

The uphill side of the erosion gullies ended in the familiar tangle of winter-killed kudzu vines. Kudzu was as pernicious as a plant species could be, but it had apparently served its intended purpose here. It might have smothered any plant within its reach, but it had held the soil in place, just as the government had hoped when it sent the Civilian Conservation Corps across the South planting the Oriental vine now known as "the green cancer."

Leaving her team earlier that morning to continue the work at Raleigh's site, Faye had spent several hours walking the area south and east of Lester's Hill with Amanda-Lynne. Struggling with both gullies and kudzu, they had tried and failed to find the old Lester homesite. Unfortunately, Amanda-Lynne just couldn't be sure where her daddy had said it was.

"I remember that there were a few bricks lying around, but that was a long time ago. I do know that we couldn't see the river from the homesite, but we could see the creek."

It wasn't much information, but it was better than nothing, and Faye laid her plans accordingly. Faye dropped Amanda-Lynne off at her house so that she could get ready for her job at the Alcaskaki diner. Then Faye brought Elliott and Joe up to the new site, leaving Ronya, who had adapted to her new job like a duck to water, to continue the backfilling.

She'd set Elliott and Joe to work clearing out a manageable chunk of the kudzu-protected land within sight of the creek. When they finished, they would use the surveyor's benchmark she'd found beside the roadbed as a reference point to establish precise locations for the shovel test probes that would give her a feel for the level and intensity of human activity in the area. Meanwhile, Faye planned to walk every square inch of the eroded creek bank, searching the surface for exposed artifacts and cultural remains uncovered by rainwater runoff. The results of her walking survey and the test probes would help her to decide where and whether to begin full-scale excavations.

The hacking sound of two machetes slashing at recalcitrant vines was softened by the sibilant rush of water below her. In almost two hours of combing the bank, she'd found only a single Madison point lying near the bottom of an erosion channel. It had been discarded centuries before the Sujosa arrived in Alabama, and rushing water had forced it out of the archaeological context that might have told her more, but it was attractive to the eye and to the touch. If she didn't uncover anything else more interesting, she could always use it for show-and-tell at Raleigh's Friday meeting.

Faye checked her watch. She had left Ronya alone at Raleigh's site long enough. It was time to drive back and see how she was doing.

As Faye approached in the truck, she saw Ronya wave a trowel in her direction and then return to screening soil. The woman was a dogged worker. She had listened carefully earlier that morning when Faye had shown her how to use the screen apparatus and how to bag and document anything she found. Now, less than a full workday later, Ronya had made a noticeable dent in the pile of backdirt beside her.

"Did you find anything?"

"I found a silver dime, dated 1954, and some pull tabs from those old-fashioned soda cans, but that's it."

"That's okay. Joe and Elliott haven't turned over the first grain of dirt yet, so you're ahead of them. Let me see your field notebook and your sample bags."

Faye flipped through Ronya's detailed field notes, then approved her redundantly labeled artifacts—each of them placed in a bag with a form relating the details of its discovery, cross-referenced with the corresponding page in her field notes. No bumbling fool would be separating these artifacts from their provenance. It would take out-and-out sabotage to render Ronya's work unuseable. *Or another house fire,* whispered her paranoid side.

"The work's going fast today, because this soil's nice

and dry," Ronya said. "When I get to that clayey soil," she pointed to a reddish pile, "we'll probably have to wash it through the screens with a hose. We'd better cover up the spoil piles when we leave for the evening. If they get rained on, it'll take forever to get this job done."

"Bless your soul for thinking ahead."

Faye heard the sound of a passing vehicle, and looked up to see the truck belonging to the fire marshal pulling into the church parking lot. A familiar figure disembarked. Eager to hear what Adam might have learned about the fire, Faye headed toward him. He raised a hand and beckoned her to sit beside him on a bench on the little church's porch.

"Did you find Carmen's briefcase?" she asked before she bothered to sit down.

"Not yet."

Faye reached into her own case and pulled out the copy of Carmen's field notes that she'd made.

"Here's a copy of some of Carmen's notes. The originals were in the briefcase."

He took the binder and said, "Preliminary lab results are in, and I'm damned if I've ever seen anything like them."

He handed a stack of faxes to Faye. Most of the laboratory findings were marked "BDL," which the handy key at the bottom of each page said was an abbreviation for "below detection limits." Faye wasn't terribly experienced at reading lab reports but Adam had simplified matters considerably by highlighting everything *not* marked "BDL" with a yellow marker. Then he'd made a big bold "X" over most of the highlighted compounds, justifying each elimination with marginal notes that said things like "This compound's not volatile enough to be an accelerant," or "Common combustion product of polyurethane foam," or "Common cleaning residue." The numbers that remained told a story.

"They detected accelerants in the samples you took from the floorboards under Carmen's bed. Does that prove arson?"

Adam laughed and Faye knew that she was wrong, because he wasn't the kind of person to be amused by proof of a crime. "You do a good job of reading the numbers, but give another thought to what they mean. Why did I take the floorboard sample?"

"The kerosene heater."

"Right. And every compound we found in the floor sample is either found in kerosene or in one of its combustion products. The heater and its fuel are definitely the cause of our fire."

Faye felt foolish. Merely finding an accelerant didn't prove arson. Kerosene was an accelerant, but it was also a perfectly innocent heating fuel. "Then why do these results upset you so?"

"The results from the pillow sample are strange. I've seen every one of those compounds before in samples collected from a foam pillow. But some of the numbers are too high. I can't see any connection with the fire, because the chemicals that are out of whack aren't flammable enough to use for arson. But I can't explain them."

"Well, even if they weren't used to start the fire, we've still got to find out what they are and why they're there," said Faye. "Carmen's family is having a memorial service for her today in Miami. I try not to think about how they must be suffering, but I can't help it."

Adam nodded and riffled through the multi-page lab report. "Thank God for chemists. Their reports are long and confusing, and they usually manage to muddy up everything I think I've learned about a case. But ask them a question and they're like bloodhounds trying to sniff out a trail of—" He closed his eyes and jabbed a finger at a page of the report. Squinting down at the spot on the page where his finger had landed, he read, "—like bloodhounds trying to sniff out a trail of 1,1,1-trichloroethane. That's 1,1,1-TCA for us ordinary mortals. They found some of it in Carmen's pillow, along with—" his finger traced down the column of polysyllabic words, "—perchloroethylene, ethyl chloride, trichloroethylene, vinyl chloride, and a couple of dichloroethylenes. Also, formaldehyde and some urethanes."

Faye wrinkled her nose. "On her pillow? Sweet dreams. Where did it all come from?"

"Brace yourself. According to my chemist, all that stuff could be in the pillow you slept on last night. The urethanes are easy to explain when you realize that most pillows are made of polyurethane foam. Formaldehyde is released when kerosene burns—"

"That's a no-brainer. We know there was burning kerosene in the room."

"Yep." Adam flipped to the back of the report where there was a section labeled *Data Interpretation* and pointed to a paragraph labeled *Textile Treatments*. "And it says here that formaldehyde can be found in permanent press fabrics."

"Like the pillowcase."

"Yep. And the vinyl pillow cover underneath it could have decomposed into all those other things that have 'chloro-' and 'chloride' in their names. Or they could just be residuals from the last time the pillow was laundered."

Faye, who had been planning to rid her pillow of toxins by taking it to the cleaners, felt queasy. She must have looked queasy, too, because Adam said, "How do you think the people at the dry cleaners get the grease stains out of your favorite sweater? Soap and water won't do it, but a dab of 1,1,1-TCA or perchloroethylene—affectionately known as 'perk'—will work miracles. Some of the other nasty-sounding stuff on this list is helpful, too. Formaldehyde is used to fireproof fabrics. And some of the chlorinated compounds are used in medicine. Perk is an old general anesthetic. So is ethyl chloride."

"I'm on information overload here."

"Yeah, me too, and it's all the dog's fault."

Faye was opening her mouth to ask what dog when light dawned. "Oh, you mean Samson, the wonder dog. If he hadn't been sniffing around the pillow—"

"—I would never have taken this sample. He was acting funny, because he could smell all the chemicals in that pillow, but he wouldn't alert, because none of them were accelerants that he'd been trained to identify. If Samson had left well enough alone, I'd already be working on a report saying that the kerosene heater malfunctioned and lit poor Carmen's bedclothes. Do you know how long it takes a burning bed to reach a temperature hot enough to ignite everything in the room?"

Faye didn't speak, so he answered himself, "A hundred and twenty seconds. Two minutes after a candle—or a kerosene heater—gets knocked over onto your bedspread, everything flammable in your bedroom is on fire. It sounds so simple, doesn't it? Except that scenario doesn't gee-haw with your hunch that Carmen wouldn't have moved the heater. It also doesn't explain the absence of her briefcase. And this stuff in her pillow worries me to death."

Faye tried to think how she'd handle a situation like this in her own work. What if she dug into soil that just didn't look right, as if it had been brought in from somewhere else, maybe to fill a hole? She would take a background sample of soil that hadn't been tampered with, and she'd compare them.

"Do you still have my pillow, or Laurel's? Could you run the same tests on one of our pillows and see if those chemicals are there?"

"Consider it done." He didn't bother to hide his admiration. "That's why I like talking these things over with you, Faye. You think like a scientist."

Adam could hardly have said anything more likely to earn himself a warm spot in Faye's heart.

"Let's say somebody set the fire," she went on. "We

both think it. We might as well say it. If we're right, it was arson, but what if it was more than that? An arsonist could have set the fire in the parlor where the heater was, or anywhere that nobody was sleeping, and it would have been a lot less risky if they'd done that. Instead, they burned Carmen's bed, with her still in it."

"And they might have killed you and Laurel, while they were at it. It looks like Carmen was the arsonist's target, but I'm not going to feel good about the safety of anybody in the settlement until I get to the bottom of this."

Faye was still trying to digest the notion that someone might have killed Carmen on purpose. "I didn't know Carmen well, but she seemed like the nicest person in the world. Who would have wanted her dead?"

AFTER BIDDING A sober goodbye to Adam, whose parting words—"Be careful, Faye"—did nothing to settle her nerves, Faye went back to being an archaeologist. She helped Ronya finish up her work, then returned to the Lester site to help Joe and Elliott shut down for the day.

NEON ORANGE SURVEYOR'S flags danced in the cold wind, echoing the brilliant color of the setting sun. Even the creek, usually a sober chocolate color, shot tangerine glimmers from every ripple. Faye's day had been well spent, and she felt rewarded by the happy colors of sunset. Joe and Elliott had returned to the settlement to wash and store their equipment, and she was lingering at the site, enjoying the sense of having accomplished something that was her own. Squatting beside the neatly marked square of land where she hoped to strike archaeological gold, Faye perused Joe's filed notes, clumsily written out, but complete. She initialed each page.

Amanda-Lynne walked up to her and stood watching

the sunlit color of the creek darken until it was once again a lustrous brown that matched her hair. "I could never leave this place," she said as nighttime shadows crept over the gray and green hilltops and turned them black.

Faye rubbed at the line of stitches on her head. They were starting to itch. She zipped her jacket to ward off the evening chill. "I feel the same way about my own home."

Homesickness tugged at her, gentle but insistent, like a tide drawing its waters away from the shore. Her people had lived on Joyeuse Island for more than two hundred years. Whenever she strayed, the gravitational pull of home went with her. Yet all the evidence so far said that Amanda-Lynne's people had been established in this valley for generations before Faye's family ever laid eyes on her treasured island. What sort of homesickness would ripping up roots like the Sujosa's inspire?

"I'll live and die here," Amanda-Lynne continued, "but Jimmie won't. That's the only reason I'm glad of his outsider blood. One day, he'll be free to walk away. He won't have to dig limerock or try to grow something in this worn-out dirt, and he won't have to watch Irene get old and tired before she's thirty."

Faye studied Amanda-Lynne's smooth, taut facial skin. "You don't look old and tired."

"I feel it."

"You mentioned Irene."

"She and Jimmie plan to be married, and Miss Dovey has given her approval." Amanda-Lynne's blue-green eyes lit up at the prospect.

"Does everyone in the settlement have to ask Miss Dovey's permission to get married?"

"Lord, no, but sometimes it's a good idea. She knows who's related to who, and she's stopped more than one set of second cousins from marrying each other. But even Miss

Dovey can't make a body love somebody they don't. Why, she thought I should marry DeWayne, once upon a time." The idea made Amanda-Lynne giggle.

"I'd heard you were cousins, but Miss Dovey must think you're not close enough kin to worry over."

"She says we're fourth cousins, once removed, but De-Wayne seems closer than that to me. I went to live with his family when I was eight, after my parents' tour bus crashed. I just couldn't marry him. It would've been like kissing my brother. He felt the same way."

Faye thought of the dead Charles and the dying Kiki. Everyone concerned might have been happier if Amanda-Lynne had been persuaded to marry her "brother"—although she would not wish the unpleasant Mr. Montrose on sweet-tempered Amanda-Lynne, no matter what Miss Dovey said. She changed the subject to happier times. "When will Jimmie and Irene be married?"

"Lord knows. Irene would never leave Kiki for DeWayne to look after, because he's not up to it, but I don't think Kiki will be with us much longer. After she passes, the only thing keeping Irene and Jimmie apart will be money, but that shouldn't be a problem for long. Jimmie's scholarship money will cover his schooling and his living, and Irene's a hard worker. I'll be surprised if they're not married within a year."

Faye flashed back to the moment when she was skidding out of control down a deserted roadway, and a boy with magical eyes sat in a tree watching it happen. The events that had occurred since her football date had cast a new light on that near-tragedy. Had it been a football prank, or was it something more? "I'd like to meet Jimmie."

"Then you're in luck. I came up here to invite you to dinner tonight. I've had spaghetti sauce in the Crock-Pot since this morning. It should be good after cooking all day."

"I'll stop by Hanahan's and get a loaf of French bread to

go with it." Faye stood up and brushed the rusty red dust off her pants, and they headed for the truck.

"That will be lovely," Amanda-Lynne said. "Charles does love good bread."

SIXTEEN

FAYE WANTED TO talk with Joe about the next day's work, but he was nowhere to be found at the bunkhouse. She asked Amory to tell him that she'd be at Amanda-Lynne's house, then hopped in the truck and headed out to Hanahan's to pick up the bread.

Oversized tires raised the project pickup so high off the ground that Faye had to toss the loaf of bread onto its bench seat to free both hands for her assault on the vehicle. Grasping the steering wheel with her left hand and the driver's seat with her right, she planted a boot sole on the doorframe for leverage and yanked herself into the pickup.

"You do that well." The light from a gibbous moon glinted off hair that was silver-white, underlain with black. Faye was glad she'd showered away the grimy coating that characterized the working archaeologist, but she instantly regretted having accepted Amanda-Lynne's dinner invitation.

Brent didn't appear to detect her brief mental detour. He kicked a monstrous tire. "You'd think Raleigh would have rented you a vehicle your own size."

"I'm used to being small in a world designed for six-footers. It only bothers me when I'm sitting next to an air bag. They've been known to kill small women, you know."

Looking down on a man was an interesting experience she'd rarely had. It gave her a feeling of power that she knew was unearned. Still, having done time in the presence of men who were convinced that bigger was always better, she enjoyed it anyway.

"How's your head? Are those stitches starting to worry you?"

"Starting to, yes," she said. "I wish I had time to talk, but I've got dinner plans." She held up the loaf of bread as evidence.

The easy smile faltered for less than a heartbeat, but Faye liked him better for it, now that she knew his confidence wasn't completely imperturbable. She'd been purposely vague about her dinner plans, just to mess with his mind. As an act of kindness, she named his competition. "Amanda-Lynne Lavelle was kind enough to invite me."

"You did that on purpose," he said. Faye wondered exactly how much psychology he'd taken during his pre-med years. She allowed him a "whatever-do-you-mean?" shrug and cranked the truck. "If I don't hurry, I'll never make it to the Lavelle house before the spaghetti's gone. I've heard about how much teenaged boys eat."

She put her elbow on the back of the truck seat and twisted to look behind her so she could see to work her way out of Hanahan's cramped parking lot, but he spoke quickly before she could ease the truck into gear. "Would you like to have dinner with me tomorrow evening?"

She hesitated, not out of a calculated strategy that required her to play hard-to-get, but because her distracted brain was having trouble remembering what day it was. Wednesday. Yes, it was Wednesday, and she was indeed free for Thursday evening. "I'd love to have dinner with you tomorrow."

"What a relief. For a second there, I thought you were going to tell me you had a date with Raleigh."

Faye put the truck in gear, and said, "He dumped me for Miss Dovey. I'll see you tomorrow night," as she drove away. She had found that, whether the field be academics, politics, or romance, people held the warmest thoughts for the ones who left them laughing.

"Hello," Amanda-Lynne said as she opened her front door. She turned away without saying more, leaving Faye to come inside, uninvited, and close the door behind her. Faye thought this was unusually absent-minded, even for Amanda-Lynne.

After five minutes of small talk—"My, that smells good," and "I do hope it tastes good," and "I do like a hot plate of spaghetti on a cold evening"—Faye asked, "Will Jimmie be home soon?"

The panicked look on Amanda-Lynne's face told her that she'd stumbled onto the reason for the woman's uncharacteristic lack of hospitality. "He should be here now. I don't know where he is. His supervisor at the library in Alcaskaki called to check on him right before you got here. Jimmie got a call on his cell phone about five-thirty and left without saying a word. He never came back. It's just not like him. He loves that job so." She ripped the core out of a head of iceberg lettuce and thrust it under a stream of running water. "It's nearly eight. It's only twenty minutes from here to Alcaskaki. Even allowing time for him to do whatever was so all-fired important, he should be home by now. When I call his cell phone, I get a 'Client out-of-range' message, so he must be back in the settlement."

"Have you called Irene?"

"I called her at the dry cleaners a few minutes ago, but they said she didn't get any calls all afternoon and that she left at her regular time, seven-thirty. That means she's not home yet and her cell phone's out-of-range, too. DeWayne said he'd have her call me the second she walked in the door." She dropped the head of lettuce in the sink. "I can't stand it anymore, but I can't call all over the settlement looking for him, because it'll tie up my phone."

"Call a friend," suggested Faye, "and ask for help."

Amanda-Lynne nodded, and, hands still wet, dialed the phone. "Jenny? I'm so worried. It's way past time for Jimmie to come home. Will you call around and look for him, so I can keep my phone line open?"

Amanda-Lynne hung up the phone and silence descended. Faye had always imagined that a mother's worries would ease as her child grew up and began assuming responsibility for his own well-being. Now she knew she'd been wrong.

When the phone rang, Amanda-Lynne grabbed it with both hands.

"Irene, honey," she breathed into the receiver, "thank you for calling so quick." She listened for a few seconds, then her shoulders fell. "It's okay, honey, he's probably on his way home now and we'll all be laughing about this tomorrow. I'll call you when I hear something."

She set the phone on its cradle, but it immediately rang again. Amanda-Lynne answered with an abrupt "Hello? Jimmie?" Listening quietly, a tear crept down her brown cheek. "Thanks, Jenny. We'll be right there."

She hung up the phone again. "Jenny says that Elliott's found Jimmie's car in the woods near his house. She's calling everybody she can get ahold of, trying to organize a search party. I need to get there, and I'm not fit to drive. Can you take me?"

"Are you kidding? I've been sitting here, trying to think of a way to help. Let's go." Without thinking about it, Faye reached out and grasped Amanda-Lynne's elbow, as if she were an old woman who needed help to rise out of her chair. The distracted mother allowed herself to lean on Faye, and they hurried to the truck.

"Jenny said she could have a dozen people searching right away. That's what she said," Amanda-Lynne chanted as they barreled down a dark, curving road. "She said they'd have him found before I even got there. And she said his car looked fine, that he hadn't been in any wreck. He does love that car. It was his daddy's, and I would have sold it after Charles died, except Jimmie wanted it so bad. He'd go out and crank it every day. I got to where I'd let him drive down to the mailbox and back, just to keep that car in shape for the day when he was big enough to drive it."

Amanda-Lynne was shivering far more violently than the forty-degree evening warranted. Faye jammed the accelerator to the floorboard. Her rearview mirror showed a dense trail of dust tinted red by the tail lights. She took the curves smoothly, glad the deepening dusk hid the precipice dropping from the right side of the roadway.

"I'd give my firstborn for a cell phone that worked," she said, then she wanted to bite her tongue out.

The other woman didn't seem to notice Faye's ill-considered metaphor. She sat twisting a deep brown curl around every finger on her right hand.

The pickup continued its controlled plunge down the steep country road. Faye had only a vague idea where Elliott lived. Carmen's notes said that his house was on a high bluff overlooking the river, and Ronya had told her that his house was past Great Tiger Bluff. Unfortunately, Elliott had also said that you had to go "the long way round" to reach his property by car, so Faye knew she'd never find it unaided. Amanda-Lynne would have to hold herself together long enough to help. "Can you tell me the quickest way to get to Elliott's?"

Amanda-Lynne's head swiveled on her neck, and her bottomless and empty eyes moved toward Faye's face. Nothing else moved, except for her lips, which said, "I can get us there. First, you want to head for Miss Dovey's, only don't take the turnoff to her house. Just keep driving down the Alcaskaki-Gadsden road until I tell you different."

"I'm sure he's fine," said Faye. In other circumstances,

she would have believed it, too, but given her own experiences as the newest member of Raleigh's team, her words sounded hollow. She reminded herself that Jimmie was a local boy who had nothing to do with the Rural Assistance Project.

Faye stomped the gas, and her tires flung gravel skyward as the truck jumped into a higher gear.

THERE WERE SIX cars parked in Elliott's front yard, but the house was empty. Jenny had said that they'd found Jimmie's car in the woods. Elliott's house and yard were surrounded on all sides by trees and dense undergrowth, so "the woods" was not going to be sufficient information to take them to the car or to Jimmie.

Faye jumped out of the truck and clambered into the back to access the tool box. Groping blindly, she came up with a flashlight. She flipped it on and quickly located a second one for Amanda-Lynne. Slamming the box shut, she rushed to the passenger door and found Amanda-Lynne's seat empty.

Her flashlight beam caught Amanda-Lynne's back as she walked across Elliott's neatly mown lawn and onto a narrow footpath that led into the woods. Trusting Amanda-Lynne's local knowledge, Faye hurried after her. Soon the pale gleam of flashlight beams could be seen in the distance. The people searching for Jimmie were close by. She wondered why they weren't calling for the missing boy. The footpath led down a dry and ancient creekbed, then up the side of a hill.

The trees ended, and Faye took in the scene. There were dark figures ahead, gathered beside a behemoth that reached for the silent stars. It was the cell phone tower, standing on the flat crest of the hill.

Rising high above the trees that blanketed the hills around the Sujosa's valley, its modernity clashed with the softness of the natural world. A ladder crawled up its metallic flank, punctuated by landings that would provide rest for tiny humans who might climb it. High above the ground—A hundred feet up? Two? More?—metal arms reached out, ready to grab conversations out of the air.

The searchers were on the far side of the tower with all their flashlight beams focused on the ground. Some of them also held lanterns that added their own faint illumination to the moonlit scene. Amanda-Lynne was walking toward them slowly and with grace, almost gliding.

"Elliott!" Faye cried. "DeWayne! Amanda-Lynne is coming!" A large man detached himself from the silent watchers and ran toward Amanda-Lynne. He wrapped both arms around her and lifted her kicking feet off the ground.

"Where's Jimmie? What's everybody doing over there? Let go of me right this minute," she shrieked, but DeWayne hung on. "Somebody's got to tell me what's happening!" she screamed.

As Faye sprinted past the struggling pair, she heard DeWayne pleading, "Honey, you don't want to see this. I'm not going to let you see this."

The beam of Faye's flashlight combined with all the others as, together, they illuminated Jimmie Lavelle's body. He lay broken in a copse of trees near the base of the tower, arms outflung, boots twisted beneath him. At his side knelt Brent, who shook his head when he saw her.

The darkness surrounding Jimmie seemed opaque; the trees above him were enveloped by a strange shroud. Playing her flashlight over the scene, she saw that a vast mat of kudzu blanketed the area between the tower and the river. Its bare stems, leafless for the winter, hung in the air like a vegetal net that should have broken Jimmie's fall, but didn't.

Genetically programmed to reach up for the light, the

kudzu had killed tree after tree and was still reaching out for more. If the vines ever reached the monstrous tower looming over the scene, they need never know shade again. Turning her flashlight toward the tower, Faye shone its beam on one of the uprights. She saw that a metal ladder, which should have been locked into position out of reach, had been pulled down to within a few feet of the ground.

Amanda-Lynne's cry broke the silence, "My baby needs me! Let me see my baby!"

DeWayne was talking to her softly, but the silence of the night was so complete that Faye heard every word. "Honey, you can't help him, and he wouldn't want you to see him this way. Walk with me to Elliott's house, and Brent will give you something that'll help you through this."

Amanda-Lynne's laughter had a helpless edge, and it lasted too long. "You think something will help? Well, I'll tell you this. Nothing helps. I tried Brent's pills when Charles died, but you know what? The pills wore off and Charles was still dead. When I was little, I prayed to God every night, asking Him to send my parents back home to me. And every morning when I woke up, they were still dead."

"I know," DeWayne whispered. "I remember."

Her eyes narrowed and she studied DeWayne as if she'd just realized who he was. "Kiki's going to die. Did they tell you that?"

"Mandalyn, please!"

"Nothing helps. When it happens to you, you'll know. Nothing helps." Her eyes still narrowed, she studied De-Wayne. Then, like a zoo animal who has sat in its cage for years, learning its keepers' habits and waiting patiently for a chance to act, she twisted out of DeWayne's grip and ran.

Brent saved Amanda-Lynne from reaching the silent crowd and getting an unobstructed view of the sight no one wanted her to see. He stepped directly into her path and allowed her to slam into him, saying, "DeWayne and I are taking you to Elliott's house. You can walk, or DeWayne can carry you. I don't care. But you're not staying here."

Amanda-Lynne faked to the right, then ran hard to the left, trying to catch Brent off guard, but DeWayne reached out and grabbed her with a hand the size of a bear paw. He threw her over one shoulder, turned around, and headed toward Elliott's house, saying, "I wish to God I'd never heard about this tower. I'd pay back every cent of the lease money, if it would make this day go away for you, Mandalyn, baby." Faye hoped to God that Brent would drug her so completely that she never remembered this terrible night.

Leo Smiley waded into the tangled kudzu and began to gently disengage Jimmie's body from the broken vines that cradled it. It seemed that as Leo forced one tendril to release the boy, another one materialized to grip him more tightly.

"Shouldn't we wait for the coroner?" Faye said.

Leo finished freeing the body. He pulled Jimmie's limp arm around his neck and squatted slightly. Then with one arm under the dead boy's knees and the other supporting his back, he stood. He was even taller than Ronya, but without his wife's heavy build. The hollow cheeks beneath his beard were visible even in the moonlight, and heavy brow bones shaded his deep-set eyes. "If the coroner needs to be here," Leo said, "Brent will call him. What I want to know is this—why are *you* here?"

Taken aback by Leo's in-your-face question, she answered truthfully, "I just want to help."

"An outsider who wants to help. That's something I haven't heard before."

Leo took a step closer to her, Jimmie's broken body still resting in his arms. Faye's throat tightened. She had never met Jimmie, but she had heard so much about him, so many good things about such a young man.

He was so young. Her hand reached out of its own volition, to brush her fingers against Jimmie's dark hair, to smooth his ripped jacket into place so that it could keep him warm. Leo stepped back, snatching the boy in his arms away from Faye's caring gesture.

"Outsiders like to send our men to war. They sent my daddy to Vietnam. He never came home, and he was hardly older than Jimmie here. They like to collect taxes from us, but they don't like to spend the money on our roads or on our children. And what have they given us in return?" He bent his head over Jimmie's for a second. When he looked up, the glimmery moonlight reflected in every tear rolling down his cheeks, and nothing came out of his mouth but a faint choking noise.

Jorge stepped into the breach. He covered the ground between him and Faye in two steps, his face distorted by the faint light of the lantern in his hand. He stood a foot taller than Faye, but he leaned down close to her ear, so she couldn't miss what he had to say. "Outsiders ain't never brought us nothing but kudzu and AIDS and—" He looked up at the steel girders tracing a geometric outline against the sky. "—and goddamn cell phones. You need to go home. And you can take all the other outsiders and their so-called rural assistance with you when you go."

Faye had never in her life been lumped together with the powers-that-be who carelessly exploited anyone who was handy. Her first impulse was to say, "My great-great-grandmother was born a slave," as if that fact would set her apart from anyone who had ever oppressed the Sujosa. She surprised herself by saying something else entirely.

"My daddy died in Vietnam, too," she said. "I never met him." She met Leo's eyes, then Jorge's, then turned and walked away.

Excerpt from an Interview with Jimmie Lavelle, October 30, 2004

Interviewer: Carmen J. Martinez, Ph.D.

Jimmie Lavelle: I'm not that interested in the past. I'd rather think about the future. And I'm more interested in science than history.

CJM: What kind of science?

Jimmie Lavelle: Well, I like medicine. Dr. Harbison got out of the valley and got rich. But I also like astronomy. I've got a pretty decent telescope with a big honking mirror that I've put some mileage on, believe me.

CJM: I like astronomy, too. Have you ever heard the song *Stars Fell on Alabama*?

Jimmie Lavelle: Yes, I have! How did you know?

CJM: Actually, your mother mentioned it to me once; she said you liked it. There's also an old book by that title that I read while I was preparing for this job.

Jimmie Lavelle: My Great-aunt Lolly used to sing that song all the time, and every time she sang it, she had to tell me the same story about it. You know how old people are.

CJM (ridiculously pleased that this young man who is half her age doesn't lump her in with all the other "old people"): I interview old people all the time. I know exactly how they are. I love them, but they do tend to repeat themselves.

Jimmie Lavelle: Aunt Lolly said that her great-grandmother remembered the night the stars fell. I think she must have been talking about the meteor storm of 1833. Aunt Lolly told me her great-grandmother said it looked like someone had taken a million pins and scratched the black paint off the sky-dome. The sight marked her for life—she said she never saw anything to match it, not before nor after—but she would have missed it if it hadn't been for the Indians.

CJM: The Indian removals were going on in full force by that time. I've wondered whether the Sujosa had any conflict with local tribes.

Jimmie Lavelle: Aunt Lolly seemed to think the Indians—I guess they were Creek—kept to themselves in a settlement upriver from here. I've never heard that we Sujosa ever had any quarrel with them. We're probably lucky we weren't relocated ourselves.

CJM: Why did the Creeks come to your Aunt Lolly's great-grandmother on that particular night?

Jimmie Lavelle: They didn't exactly say. When the knock sounded, she was afraid, because her husband had just died and she was alone with a house full of children. She came to the door with her shotgun loaded and ready, but their leader waved it aside, saying nothing but, "Come and look." She said she was more embarrassed for them to see her with her hair unbraided than she was to go out into the night in her sleeping gown, but she got over it when she realized that all three of the Creek men standing outside her house had longer hair than hers. Then she saw the stars dropping out of the sky.

CJM: I've read eyewitness accounts of that meteor storm. Thousands of shooting stars fell every minute. People thought the world had come to an end.

Jimmie Lavelle: She stood there with her mouth open for a while, then the Creek leader said, "We woke our women and children. This is what men do." And she realized that he meant that she shouldn't let her children miss such a sight. She went inside to fetch them, and when she came back outside the men were gone.

CJM: Maybe they went to the other Sujosa homes, making sure nobody missed the spectacle.

Jimmie Lavelle: No. She was the only Sujosa they visited. Later, she said they must have known her husband was dead, because they didn't seem surprised when she came to the door herself. When she thought about it that way, their words made sense. They woke their women and children, then they came and woke her, because she had no husband to care for her. She reckoned they felt responsible for her.

CJM: Did she ever see them again?

Jimmie Lavelle: You don't see a Creek who doesn't want to be seen. But for the next couple of years, they left her little gifts at odd times. A slab of deer meat. A mess of fish. She was a damn fine gardener and her children never went hungry, before or after her husband died, but don't you know they were glad to have meat now and then? When their gifts stopped coming, she knew that the powers-that-be in Washington had finally gotten their way. Her friends had been taken to the Indian Territory, and there was nobody left in these parts but Sujosa and white folks and black folks.

CJM: Thank you for that story. It was a nice history.

Jimmie Lavelle: Hey! How did you do that?

CJM: Trick of the trade.

Jimmie Lavelle: Yeah, you don't give up.

CJM: Is that a nice way of calling me obstinate?

Jimmie Lavelle: No, but I like that word. I can think of a few other words like it. Contrary. Obstreperous. Tenacious.

CJM: I bet those words were on the SAT—which I understand that you aced.

Jimmie Lavelle: You know, I believe some of them were. If you want to understand the Sujosa and their history, you remember those words. We wore this land out, then we were too obstinate to leave. I've got to leave if I hope to make a decent living, just like Brent Harbison did, but you notice that he came home. One day, I hope to do the same. The stars are brighter here than they are anywhere else in the world.

SEVENTEEN

THE CORONER CAME and went before midnight, and Jimmie's body went with him. The security people hired by the cell phone company arrived nearly three hours after Jimmie tripped the tower's silent intruder alarm. The delay was hardly surprising, since the nearest security company was in Gadsden, down a hundred miles of bad road. Once there, they got busy and found the crowbar used to break the lock on the ladder.

Thursday morning, the sheriff and a couple of technicians from the medical examiner's office arrived in the settlement to interview Irene and every person present when Jimmie's body was found. Another team went out to the hilltop to lift prints from the metal ladder and scale the tower to see if they could determine where the boy had been standing when he took his fatal dive.

Faye, drawn back to the tower as she had been drawn back to the scene of Carmen's death, had driven out after them. Though the sheriff wasn't as forthcoming with information as Adam had been, he let her stand near the base of the tower and watch his team work. As far as she knew, no evidence had been gathered that could tell them whether Jimmie's death had been accident or foul play. The word "suicide" had been mentioned by the cell phone people, but nothing she had heard about Jimmie supported that thought. Indeed, the stunned Sujosa were as affronted by the word as Faye.

But what could have happened? The general consensus

was that it must have been an accident, just a drunken kid looking for excitement. Maybe Jimmie hadn't climbed the ladder alone. Maybe two or three drunken kids had climbed the tower and the survivors were afraid to talk. If so, then surely they would have left behind fingerprints or footprints, and alcohol would show up in Jimmie's bloodstream.

And if it had been foul play? The ladder was narrow and, though it occasionally widened into a landing as it crept up the tower, it was hard to imagine someone forcing Jimmie to climb the ladder, then pushing him off. Maybe they could have done it if they were holding a gun on him, but they would have to be very nimble on the ladder.

Faye knew that, if she'd been in that situation, she would have watched for an opportunity to stomp on the hand of the person forcing her up the ladder. She would have made her pursuer shoot her, or she would have grabbed the arm holding the gun and taken her assailant to the ground with her. Jimmie hadn't done either of those things.

All will be revealed in time, Faye's grandmother had always said, and she clung to that, though her more cynical side revised the old truism to say, All will be revealed in time—or it won't. It galled her to think that the truth about Jimmie's death might always remain a mystery. Her sense of justice demanded something, anything, that would explain what had happened to turn a gifted young man into the empty shell Leo had held in his arms the night before. Even a suicide note would have lifted the pall hanging over the community, if only a bit, by answering the question, "Why?"

She looked through the barren trees toward the hills on the other side of the Broad River. It was a beautiful view, lonely, yet serene, with one or two Alcaskaki farmsteads dotting the gray landscape beneath a blue sky. Was this the last thing Jimmie saw? She turned away.

Upon her return to the bunkhouse, Faye was surprised

to find Joe, Elliott, and Ronya waiting for her. Half the morning was already gone. She'd had no intention of asking her crew to work on the day after such a horrific event.

"You can't have gotten any sleep," said Faye.

"Working is better than thinking," Elliott said, and Joe nodded in agreement.

Ronya, gripping her son by the hand, said, "I can work all day, if you don't mind having Zack on the site. He's promised me that he'll be good while I'm working. I—" She looked Faye in the face, trying to communicate something she couldn't say in front of a four-year-old. "I just couldn't leave him. Not today."

Faye made a quick decision. She knew they were all too bleary to do any work that required conscious thought, so work on the Lester site was out. Instead, she had them set up their equipment at Raleigh's site, where they could sift soil looking for previously overlooked artifacts as long as they felt up to it. If lack of sleep caught up with them, they could go home and go to bed. Tomorrow, or Monday at the latest, they would all move over to the Lester site and start excavating for real.

Watching Ronya stoop over her work, Faye noticed that Zack hadn't budged from his seat on the ground about five feet behind his mother. His lips were set and his eyes were big. Zack might not know what had happened to upset his mother and every grownup he'd seen since dawn, but he was smart enough to know that it was something bad.

"Let me show you where you can play," Faye said, sticking out a hand and helping Zack to his feet. Pointing to a pile of screened soil that was waiting to be returned to one of the excavations, she said, "You can climb on that and dig in it and slide down the side of it. You can make mud pies with it, if you like. Just don't play on any of the other dirt piles, and don't go anywhere near any of the holes, okay?"

Zack responded by running to the top of the little pile

of dirt and rolling down it, pressing dark, loose soil into every fiber of his sweat suit. Faye looked at his mother and shrugged a wordless apology, but Ronya only smiled and kept working.

THE MORNING WORE away slowly. A couple of times, some-one turned up a fragment of the common gray pottery that the Sujosa had been making for generations, renewing Faye's consternation over how she could be expected to put a date on the stuff. For all Faye knew, they came from pots Ronya had thrown within the last year. When asked, Ronya said that she couldn't tell a broken sliver of her own work from a broken bit of one of her mother's pots, or her grandmother's, for that matter. The piles of unscreened soil dwindled, and Faye had to admit that finding something significant there had been an idea doomed from the start. As it often is, fate was poised to reward stubbornness. When Joe rose up from his screen, cradling something in his palm, and yelled, "Faye! Get over here," she knew what he'd found.

"You did it. Oh, Joe, look at this. You did it."

"You were the one that kept us looking for it when anybody with good sense would've quit." Joe's teeth showed white in his dark handsome face.

Ronya and Elliott gathered around for a glimpse of the tiny, broken thing that they had worked so hard to find.

The potsherd was tin-glazed and ornamented with luster painting, but Faye didn't think it came from the same piece of pottery as Jorge's sherd. It was shaped like a slice of pie, and one curved edge had been part of the rim of a plate or shallow bowl. The bottom surface was white, adorned with scattered blue flourishes, while the top had been under-painted in a deep blue pigment, probably cobalt. Luster in a reddish-gold hue had been painted on the rim and dotted in a random pattern across the blue background like stars in a midnight sky. Even broken, it was lovely. Faye hoped that the laboratory could tease a date out of it without marring its beauty too badly.

FAYE STOOD UNDER an ice-blue sky and watched her crew work. It was nearly eleven o'clock and she felt like spoiling a little boy's lunch. Walking over to a heavily trampled pile of soil, she noticed that it looked much smaller than it had when she left. Zack, who was practicing crawling like a snake, seemed to be wearing most of the missing dirt.

"Come with me," she said, extending her hand. "I need some help with my grocery shopping."

Zack grabbed her hand and looked over his shoulder at his mother. She waved them away, saying, "Go ahead. Miss Faye won't let anything happen to you."

Miss Faye. The nickname made her feel like she was on her way to Miss Dovey's stature. She'd be there in, oh, sixty years or so.

Zack ran toward Hanahan's so fast that Faye had to jog to keep up. A grimy little gentleman, he opened the screen door for her so she could enter first.

"Jenny," Faye called, walking down the candy aisle and snagging five Hershey bars, "do you by any chance sell cold Cokes?"

Jenny nodded. "Yeah. You're not the only idiot around here that likes cold drinks in the wintertime."

"In the bottle?"

"Do they come any other way?" Jenny pointed at a cooler, packed with ice, that sat near the checkout counter.

Faye fished five bottles out of the cooler and set them on the counter.

"You must be powerfully short on caffeine."

"And sugar," Faye said, piling the chocolate bars on the counter and laying a ten-dollar bill beside them.

Jenny gave Faye her change, then reached under the cash

register and pulled out a cardboard six-pack carrier. After opening each bottle, she loaded the Cokes into the carrier.

She handed Faye the carrier, then put the candy bars in a small paper bag. "Faye will need help carrying these." She dropped a piece of bubble gum in the bag and handed it to Zack. "There you go. Enjoy your nice nutritious lunch." Zack laughed until they walked out of the store, highly entertained by the notion that there might be vitamins in his candy.

FAYE'S CREW, POWERED by a late morning jolt of sugar, carbonation, caffeine, and cocoa butter, worked straight through the noon hour. Every few minutes, Joe or Elliott stood up and unconsciously started the field archaeologist's stretching routine—rolling his head, shrugging his shoulders, and twisting his back this way and that, trying to counteract a long morning of stooping over his work. Faye ached in all the same places they did, and her head hurt, too. She hoped Brent would take her stitches out soon.

When Adam's truck pulled into the parking lot behind Hanahan's, Faye rounded up the troops and barked, "Get some lunch. Those candy bars won't keep you going forever."

Elliott and Ronya headed to the concrete picnic table behind Jenny's grocery store while Faye hurried to greet Adam, with Joe on her heels. When they reached him, though, she found herself awkward and tongue-tied, unwilling to just blurt out, "What are the odds that two people would die in this tiny settlement within four days?" Joe, taciturn as always, was no help.

"I heard about Jimmie," were the first words out of Adam's mouth.

"Already?"

"I live in Alcaskaki, the gossip capital of the Southeast. I heard about Jimmie before the coroner left home. And

I heard that Leo and Jorge really laid into you last night, out by the cell phone tower. Do you think you could try to stay away from people who don't like you, just once? At least until we figure out what's going on here in the settlement to cause people to drop out of the sky or to burn to death? Have you had words with anybody else?" Adam leaned up against his truck's fender and drummed his fingers on the hood.

Faye followed his lead, leaning up against the truck while she considered his question. The hood was still warm, which was a nice antidote to the afternoon's chill wind. "Well, I fired Jorge and Fred and Elliott Monday afternoon. That wasn't a real cordial conversation."

"People don't appreciate getting fired, even when they deserve it."

Adam nodded to acknowledge the truth of Joe's observation. Feeling compelled to confess every unpleasant conversation, Faye added, "And a couple of days ago, Jorge and Leo talked like they might want to set DeWayne's dogs on me. Again."

"Woman, don't you have enough sense to get scared now and then?" Adam demanded.

Joe emitted a snicker.

"Will you please try to stay close to people you trust?" Adam went on. "People like Joe, here. He's big enough to look out for you. I don't want to find myself picking pieces of you out of DeWayne's dogs' teeth." Adam tried for a smile, but he didn't quite manage it. "Why does Jimmie's death make me think that somebody wanted Carmen dead?"

"Does it?" Faye asked. "I think so, too, but I couldn't tell you why."

"Then I'll tell you why. Two violent deaths in one week goes against the grain of the Sujosa's history: hundreds of

years of peaceful, uneventful poverty. Not that my boss will
be impressed by that as a rationale to keep this case active."

"Surely your boss won't take you off this case until
you're finished?" Faye was surprised at how abandoned
she felt by the thought of Adam driving his truck into the
sunset.

"Don't worry. I don't have to close the case, ever—
though I might get a nasty call from the state Fire Marshal
or the insurance commissioner, wanting to know when I'm
gonna get back to work on one of the multi-million-dollar
insurance fraud cases sitting on my desk. There's no stat-
ute of limitations on arson. I'm not about to walk away
and worry about leaving people at the mercy of a killer.
People like you."

"I've been wondering if Jimmie might have set the fire,"
she said, looking down at her feet. "I noticed he was wearing boots a lot like mine when he died."

"You have good eyes. We got a positive match on those
boot prints this morning. I think we can conclude that Jimmie was walking in the woods near the women's bunkhouse
when it caught fire Saturday night. But that doesn't mean
he set the fire."

"There's something else. I know from personal experience that Jimmie was capable of pulling pea-brained
stunts," Faye said. "He strung a life-sized dummy over
the road near his high school, with a sign on it saying 'Devils Go Home.' I nearly drove my car into a ravine. At first,
I assumed the message was aimed at me, since a lot of
folks in the settlement don't care for outsiders—particularly the Rural Assistance team. Then I thought the effigy
was probably one that he made for a pep rally, and I decided to give him a pass. But now...do you think he hung
that effigy, then set the fire the next night, thinking that he
could scare us outsiders away? Maybe he didn't consider
the possibility someone might actually die. Accidentally

killing Carmen might be enough to drive a conscientious young man to suicide."

"Nope." Adam pulled out a pack of gum and offered it to Faye and Joe. "You're contradicting your own theory. An act of arson that results in an unplanned death doesn't fit with your observations of the heater and the briefcase. In fact, the evidence coming in supports the notion that Carmen's bed was set on fire, with her still in it. Do you really think Jimmie did something that…well, evil is what I'd call it. Do you think someone who did something so evil would have such a drastic change of heart that he'd commit suicide a few days later?"

Faye shook her head, conceding his point. "So we don't know anything for sure, except that Jimmie was nearby on the night of the fire."

"We know more than that," Joe said. "We know he didn't tell anybody that he was there, or what he saw, if he saw anything. Anyone who's talking, I mean. And we know he got a phone call that upset him, but no one's come forward to say they were the one that placed the call."

Faye realized that, once again, she'd made a mistake that she'd vowed not to repeat—underestimating Joe's gifts of perception.

"The sheriff will be able to track down the call. It may take a day or two, but he'll get it done." Adam shot Joe an appraising look. "Joe, I notice that you look more than you talk. Have you seen anything lately that I might want to know about?"

"That's why I came over here with Faye. I wanted to tell you about something I heard. You see that pothole right near the bridge?" Joe said, pointing with his chin. "Can't nobody drive through here without hitting it. I've almost gotten to know who's coming into town just by the rattle of their car when they hit that pothole."

"You have the ears of a whitetail deer," Adam said. "Or

maybe the ears of a deer hunter. I'd like to hunt with you sometime, soon as gun season starts."

"From the sound of things," Joe said, "I'd say it's always gun season around here."

Adam chuckled. "Not for me. I like to play by the rules. So tell me why you're interested in the sound that pothole makes, before I get distracted and start talking about bow hunting."

"I heard Jorge's delivery van hit that pothole first thing yesterday morning, and again when he came home last night. The thing is, it was loaded different in the morning than it was in the evening."

"I'm surprised it's loaded at all. He only drives it two or three times a week, for his part-time delivery job. It wouldn't make sense for him to drive a loaded truck home and let the goods sit."

"No, it wouldn't. And that's not what he does. In the morning the truck was carrying a heavy load. In the evening, it was empty."

Adam rattled his keys in his pocket. "What in hell was he hauling out of the settlement?"

Joe shrugged.

Faye asked, "Can you get a warrant to search the truck?"

"Based on what? Nobody's reported anything missing. Is it a crime to clean out your truck?"

Faye and Joe were still puzzling over that observation when Brent walked past, carrying a box of books. Laurel walked beside him and she interrupted her slow progress to stop and raise a hand off one crutch to wave at Faye, Adam, and Joe. Brent, both hands occupied in carrying the large box, merely nodded in their direction as he and Laurel continued on their way.

Joe gave a disgusted grunt. "I told Laurel that I'd help her with those, but I slam forgot."

"Looks like Brent's taking care of things," Adam said.

Joe didn't answer. He stomped over to the picnic table and joined Ronya and Elliott.

"I guess I'm not the first person to underestimate Joe," Adam said.

"Neither was I," Faye admitted, "but I can't seem to quit doing it. I wonder what Jorge is hauling out of the settlement. Garbage?"

"People have been throwing their garbage in the woods around here for years. They're not going to suddenly start paying Jorge to haul it out of the settlement for them. It'd be too much trouble for lazy Jorge to be driving his own garbage to the dump two or three times a week. His employer can't be shipping things out of the valley. It's not exactly an industrial park, full of manufacturers. I don't have a clue what he might be hauling."

Adam reached in the truck window and grabbed a wrinkled fax off the passenger seat. "I don't have a clue about much of anything, not yet, but I do have this lab report on the chemicals found in Carmen's pillow. And I haven't found Carmen's briefcase yet. We're definitely investigating an arson, and possibly murder."

Faye nodded her head in silence. There was no real surprise. This was what she had feared; this was what her instincts had been telling her. Then she looked up at Adam. "Who's 'we'?"

"Walk with me. This wind is too cold to be standing still." They walked in a slow circle around the blackened timbers of the burned-out house. Adam's eyes roamed over the ruins as he talked, always looking for clues he might have missed during his first hundred tours of the site.

"I'm not so sure I'm doing the right thing—sharing information about this investigation with a layperson."

"Mama told me that Daddy always said that it's everybody's business when an innocent person is in danger. He was a soldier, so he would know."

"And what if the innocent person is you?"

"I've always tried to be strong, for him. I like to think that he's proud of me."

"I suspect he is. Look. I'm not so stupid that I haven't noticed that it was you who saw Jimmie doing something real strange a few days before he died. And it was you who noticed that Carmen's briefcase went missing on the day she passed. Two people are dead, and you're doing a better job of tracking down clues than I am. I just wonder how you do it."

"You think—" She stopped walking so suddenly that momentum carried Adam forward a couple of steps before he turned to face her. "Surely you don't think I had anything to do with causing the fire or the wreck or Jimmie's death."

Adam put a hand on the small of her back and nudged her forward. "Walk. I told you it was too cold to stand still. No, I don't think you're a mad arsonist. And you weren't anywhere near that tower when Jimmie fell. I just think your profession makes you a born investigator. I don't know anybody else who would have thought to ask where Carmen's briefcase was. Well, except maybe me, but I didn't know she'd brought her work home with her that night, so I couldn't ask the question. No, I think the Sujosa have trouble here in the settlement. Maybe you can help me find out what it is."

Faye looked at the stark contrast between Adam's fair skin and his reddish freckles and brows and lashes and hair. One of her grandmother's sayings leapt to mind. *That boy looks like he swallowed a silver dollar and broke out in pennies.* She looked at the ground until the urge to giggle passed. "Why do you assume that the Sujosa are at the root of all the trouble? I can hardly believe that the white folks in Alcaskaki have always gotten along with their brown neighbors. Maybe they see the Rural Assistance Project pouring money into the settlement, and they think the Sujosa are getting rich. Maybe they're trying to do something to stop it, or to get a piece of the action."

It was Adam's turn to look at the ground. "Honestly? I think racial relations in these parts improve all the time. Some of our older folks have rethought their attitudes, and we bury a few unreconstructed bigots every year. As for people our age and younger—we went to school with people of all colors. We've watched them on TV and idolized them on the playing field. I don't see how any of us could possibly judge people on the color of their skin, not anymore."

Having been brown in America all her life, Faye had no trouble seeing how people of her generation might still judge people by their race, but she admired Adam's good-heartedness. His lack of cynicism might hamper his effectiveness in law enforcement, but Faye could help him out in that respect. She had cynicism to spare.

"I was in junior high when the state finally closed the settlement school and bused the Sujosa to Alcaskaki," Adam continued. "It was hard at first, but kids will like each other if they're given a chance. I played baseball all the way through school. Brent pitched, I played shortstop, and Leo held down first base. Our team won the state championship twice during our high school years. We were like brothers."

Their winding route had taken them around the church, and the pale green of the bunkhouse showed through the bare branches of an oak tree. Laurel and Brent were standing at the front door, wiping their feet before entering the house.

Faye found her eyes drawn to the back of Brent's head. An inch or two of dark hair showed beneath the fashionable streaks that had made him into a blonde. She noted absently that he needed to touch up his roots—until her attention was caught by a swath of white hair that stood out clearly against his rather dark natural hair color. A depigmented area like those common to the Sujosa was clearly visible on the back of his head.

She tried to picture Brent without his artificially lightened hair. Suddenly, he didn't look like a brunette Caucasian who'd been playing in a peroxide bottle. He looked like a Sujosa who was trying to hide from who he was.

Adam, seeing the direction of her gaze and the shock on her face, said, "He didn't tell you, did he?"

"That son of a bitch."

Adam looked shocked by the vehemence of her response and, for a second, she was shocked herself. She and Brent had enjoyed a couple of conversations and one date. Why should she expect him to spill his life history to her when they were just getting acquainted?

Because he'd had more than one perfect opportunity and he'd blown them all, that's why. When she'd expressed discomfort at being the only non-white in a crowd of Alcaskakians, he'd kept his mouth shut. When he'd pontificated on how the twentieth century was dead, and racism with it, he'd neglected to share his personal experience of being brown in all-white Alcaskaki. And, worst of all, when he spoke of his work, he referred to the Sujosa in a sterile, scientific, third-person kind of way, never once admitting that he cared about the Sujosa's health and their future because they were his people. Faye fairly shook with rage.

"Brent—"

Faye interrupted him. "He said he grew up in Alcaskaki, but he's a Sujosa, isn't he?"

Brent and Laurel disappeared into the house before Adam spoke again. "His mother came from the settlement, but his father was a white man from Alcaskaki. Does it matter?"

"Of course not. But I don't enjoy being with people who are ashamed of what they are."

"Brent chose to come home to Alcaskaki. He gives the Sujosa settlement thousands of dollars in free work every month. Everybody that lives here knows who his mama was. Maybe he meant to tell you, but it slipped his mind."

"I don't buy that." She pointed to her own dark-skinned face. "Any fool would know that I, more than most people, would be interested in knowing about a heritage as rich as Brent's. And he had plenty of chances."

"His skin's almost as dark as yours. Maybe he thought his heritage was obvious."

His calm tone didn't do much to soothe her anger. "I thought he'd been hanging out in tanning booths." She allowed her anger to spill over onto Adam. "I notice that you're mighty quick to defend Brent. So you're good buddies?"

"Hell, no. More like good rivals. I didn't like it when he beat me out for valedictorian. I didn't like it when he made the All-State team and I didn't." He looked at the freckled backs of his clenched hands. "I damn sure didn't like having to compete with him for a pretty girl's attention. And I don't like having to do it now."

It took ten seconds of baffled silence for Faye to realize he was talking about her. "I spent one evening at a ballgame with the man."

"Women buzz around Brent like yellow jackets around a beer can. I've learned not to fight that."

"Well, listen up and take notes. I've got a string of stitches across the back of my head. I'm having nightmares about fires and smoke and dying friends. And, last night, I watched a mother cry over her dead son. I don't think it's possible to feel less romantic than I do right now. But when this is over, I'll be waiting to hear from you."

THERE WAS A time when a man could get away with saying, "You're cute when you're angry," but that time had passed before Adam was born. He might have said it anyway if Faye had stuck around instead of stalking off to watch her field team dig in the dirt, but God had saved him from his own honest mouth.

Son, there ain't no call to tell folks every last thought that runs through your head, his father had said more times than he could count. Maybe he had finally, at the venerable age of thirty-seven, learned to listen to the old man. His father had also warned him not to waste his time on stupid women, when the smart ones were so handy to have around.

Faye sure looked handy in those olive drab cargo pants, the kind with extra pockets sewn onto the legs at about knee level. All Faye's pockets looked to be full of things like tools and brushes and measuring tapes. You could go on a spur-of-the-moment picnic with a woman like that. Between the two of you, somebody would have a map or a roll of paper towels stashed in the glove compartment. And if you had need of a bottle opener or a corkscrew, one of you would have a pocketknife that sported the necessary tool.

He could see that she'd misinterpreted his frustration over having to compete with handsome, rich, and dashing Brent. He'd been trying to tell her that when she'd seen past Brent's façade, he would be there, but he'd pissed her off with his awkwardness. The lady had not dropped a dainty handkerchief; she had thrown down a gauntlet. When life returned to normal, she'd be waiting for him to ask her out. She had said as much. She didn't, he had noticed, say that her answer would be "Yes."

EIGHTEEN

Faye was used to the all-out fatigue born of physical labor. Hour after hour of stooping, digging, lifting, and hauling would sap anyone's endurance. Laboring until the large muscles in her arms and calves and thighs trembled with overwork, then forcing them to work some more, fed her fierce and competitive drive. Other archaeologists were bigger and stronger, but none of them were tougher.

She sat at the picnic table, digging through a pile of project paperwork and wishing it were a simple, uncomplicated pile of dirt. Keeping up with field notes and time sheets and triplicate acquisition forms made her weary in a way that physical labor never had.

Elliott, Joe, and Ronya were washing up a big pile of equipment. Their cleanup of Raleigh's site was, for practical purposes, complete. The backdirt was back in the excavations it had come from, so it technically wasn't backdirt anymore. The site had been restored to a safe condition—nobody would be breaking a leg by stepping in an open hole, and time would send a fresh layer of leaves to cover the disturbed soil.

Faye was cold sitting out in the open, where the afternoon wind could get at her. She should be working in her office, which had two conveniences that would make her work go easier: a heater and a phone. Some of the university forms required her to provide budget codes, but nobody had seen fit to give her a list of the codes, and she needed to track them down. The lack of cell phone service in the settlement made it impossible to communicate with the world while working in the field.

Suddenly, her busy hands stopped straightening papers and let them drop to the table. She stared blankly into the distance for a moment, then rose excitedly and looked around. Where was Adam?

His truck hadn't moved, but he was nowhere to be seen. She hurried toward the burned-out house. She knew he was drawn to it, despite all the hours he'd spent ferreting out its secrets, and she'd bet money that he was there. If anyone understood obsessive behavior, it was Faye. And there he was, walking up the path.

"What's wrong?" he asked, which told her that her consternation showed on her face.

"Jimmie's cell phone," she said. "We don't have to wait for the police to track down whoever it was that called him at the library yesterday afternoon. The answer is in the cell phone's memory. Was it found?"

Adam shook his head. "No, there was no phone on the body."

"You don't suppose it dropped out of his pocket when he fell? I remember that his jacket was torn."

"Could have. I'm sure the sheriff will send a deputy to look for it. Tell you what, though. It'll be a nice trick if anybody can find it in that mess of kudzu. I wonder if there's enough metal in that phone to—"

"I know somebody who can find it," Faye said. She took a few steps toward the shed where her crew was working and bellowed, "Joe!"

Joe's long-legged lope brought him to her side in seconds. Faye had seen him project the erratic flight of a fluttering bird accurately enough to drop that bird with a stone arrow shot from a handmade bow. Here was a twenty-first century use for his Neolithic talents.

"Joe, if Jimmie's cell phone dropped out of his pocket when he fell—"

"Might've dropped out if he hit the tower struts on the way down. Or a tree branch."

The thought made Faye cringe. "Either way. Do you think you could find it?"

"Well, there's only so many places it could be."

Faye looked first at Joe, then at Adam, and said, "Gentlemen. Shall we take a hunting trip?"

JOE STOOD HIGH on a bluff overlooking the Broad River, beneath a mammoth tower, looking for a needle in a kudzu patch. Faye hadn't said why she wanted him to fetch Jimmie's cell phone out of the wilderness it might have fallen into, but he'd told her he would try.

He began his search by standing at the base of the tower, looking toward the spot where Jimmie's body had landed. He looked up at the tower. It rose like a weapon into the sky, making nature's trees look squat and soft. In his mind's eye, he could clearly see the arc Jimmie must have taken, plunging downward like an eagle diving for sunfish. If the phone had fallen straight down, it was only a matter of hunting through the undergrowth around the base of the tower until they found it. But if the phone had bounced off the tower struts or a tree, the search area would be much broader.

Joe's chest tightened when he thought of Jimmie's fatal fall. It sickened him to think that the cell phone, and the information stored in it, was far more likely to have survived its flight. Its hard plastic shell had been designed to shrug off severe impacts in a way that the human body was not.

He walked to the thicket of loblolly pines where Jimmie was found, a haven of green in the gray winter landscape. He doubted that the phone would have nested in the pines' high flexible branches. The first branch it struck would have bent under its weight then, like a medieval catapult, flung it in an unpredictable direction, where it might have encountered a second tree limb, and even a third. It would eventually have hit the ground, but finding it would take some time. Having set in his own mind the most likely places where the phone might have landed, Joe divided the area to be canvassed between Faye, Adam, and himself. They began walking the ground, inch by inch.

Two hours later, dwindling daylight forced them to give up the search and head back to the bunkhouse.

THE PROMISE OF a damp, freezing night sent Faye to Hanahan's in hopes that Jenny stocked longjohns and flannel pajamas. Laurel went with her, and Faye was glad of the company, especially when the presence of Amanda-Lynne and Irene brought the evening chill right into the store. Faye felt her throat freeze shut. What could she possibly say to them?

As it turned out, any conversation that Faye or the other sympathetic souls in the store might have offered would have been extraneous, anyway. Amanda-Lynne talked enough for everyone. She chattered about how Charles had been cooped up in the house for weeks because the cold bothered his rheumatism. She confided that she'd be glad when spring came, because it surely was a trial to live with a man who never left the house. She said that she'd left a chicken stewing in the Crock-Pot, since Charles enjoyed chicken soup in the wintertime.

Faye knew that everyone in earshot was gritting their teeth in anticipation of hearing her speak of Jimmie in the same way. If Amanda-Lynne were to start musing over which of the colleges fighting over Jimmie should be the lucky one to win him as an entering freshman, Faye knew that her bottled-up tears would overflow. As it turned out, she was able to keep a solid grasp on her composure, because never—not once—did Amanda-Lynne mention her dead son.

Jenny stemmed the flow of words by turning to Irene, who had stood silent through Amanda-Lynne's torrent of nonsense. "Have you slept at all, honey?"

"No, but I'm used to that."

Amanda-Lynne chimed in with an explanation that no one needed. "Irene's mama is real sick, and it's scrambled her normal day-and-night rhythms. Sometimes she's up all the night long, and that means Irene's up, too. She has to be, because if Kiki wakes up and there's no one to stop her, she'll wander the woods in her nightgown."

"The whole settlement lives in fear that we'll find Kiki at the bottom of Great Tiger Bluff one morning," said Jenny with a sigh.

"Irene gave up her chance to go to college to take care of her mother, you know," Amanda-Lynne said, putting a hand on the girl's shoulder.

There was an awkward silence; even Jenny had nothing to say.

But Irene stepped smoothly in. "That's right," she said, taking Amanda-Lynne's hand and leading her toward the door, past the stricken bystanders. "I take care of her. And I'll take care of you now, too."

The door closed behind them, leaving the store under a pall of silence.

Excerpt from an Interview with Irene Montrose, October 30, 2004

Interviewer: Carmen J. Martinez, Ph.D.

CJM: I was looking through a stack of documents that our genealogist gave me, and I couldn't help noticing your middle name, because it's so similar to my given name. "Carmo" is beautiful, but I've never heard it before. Has it been in your family a long time?

Irene Montrose: It was my Grandmother Montrose's first name, and she told me it was her Grandmother Lester's first name. She said that there's been a Carmo in her family forever. When I was little, the other kids laughed at my funny middle name, but I've always kinda liked it.

CJM: I do, too. With a name that old, you've probably heard family stories about the Sujosa that will make this historian very happy.

Irene Montrose: I don't think so. (**Interviewer's note: She holds out her forearm next to mine.**) Anyone can see that my personal ancestry's a little murky. I'm hardly darker than you. Here's the bottom line: My mother's white and my father doesn't talk.

CJM: People are always surprised at how much they know, once they get started talking. Everyone has memories of their grandparents that are full of hidden treasures.

Irene Montrose: Grandma and Grandpa Montrose were both dead before I was five. I didn't know my mother's family in Alcaskaki either. They never spoke to my mother after she and Daddy ran off. They're dead now, too, and I'm not even sure when they passed.

CJM: It's sad to be cut off from your roots.

Irene Montrose: I'm not so sure. Seems to me that roots keep you stuck in one place.

CJM: So your father never talked about his youth?

Irene Montrose: He used to, before my mother got sick. He was different then. Sometimes, he'd just sit and look at her, like he couldn't believe how lucky he was. You can't tell it now, but she used to be so beautiful. When Dr. Harbison told Daddy she might die, it nearly killed him. Then he found out how Hepatitis C is transmitted. Mama only had one risk factor, and it wasn't something Daddy wanted to hear. When he found out her disease was sexually transmitted and she didn't get it from him, I think it did kill him. He just sits in front of the TV, leaving me to take care of my mother, while he waits for her funeral.

CJM: None of your relatives talked of the old days?

Irene Montrose: Well, Amanda-Lynne does. She's full of tall tales, though you never can tell whether to believe them or not. **(Interviewer's note: Irene finally smiles, and it is apparent that her mother must indeed have been a great beauty. Irene had to get it from somewhere.)**

CJM: Do you remember any of them?

Irene Montrose: Well, one story in particular comes to mind, since Amanda-Lynne says that it was my grandmother Carmo Montrose that told it to her. Apparently, people in these parts have always held Great Tiger Bluff as a special place. I guess you could even call it sacred. Maybe it goes back to the Indians. Lord knows I've found a pile of arrowheads in the woods around there.

CJM: That certainly suggests that it was an important place, perhaps the site of a town or a favorite place to hunt. But why would you say that the bluff is sacred?

Irene: Because they say that the whole earth was created right there, that's why. The story goes that the whole earth was flooded once, and the water stretched from horizon to horizon, unbroken, except for a single turtle. It was a small turtle, nothing special really, but a muskrat swimming in the water was drawn to it, because there was nothing else solid in sight. He tried to climb up on the turtle's back, and the turtle was okay with that, but the muskrat didn't like sitting on its hard, slick shell, so he dived back into the water as deep as he could go.

CJM: You may be right about this being a Native American tale. The earth diver myth is a famous creation story shared by many tribes.

Irene: I thought so. It just has the sound of a story told by someone who lived very close to the earth. Anyway, the muskrat scooped up a big pawful of mud off the bottom of the sea and slapped it on the turtle's shell, which made it a much more comfortable place for an animal to rest. Before long, he had a lot of company, because all the creatures of the land crawled out of the sea and joined him. They waited there until the water went down and the animals were free to scatter across the earth, but they weren't ready to go far. They were all drawn to the crater where the muskrat had clawed the mud that saved them right out of the ground.

CJM: That's different from any earth diver tale I've ever read. It may be original to the Sujosa.

Irene (shrugs): Maybe. The torn earth was striped brown and beige and red. As they watched, people walked out of the face of the bluff, and their skin reflected all the colors of the sacred soil. Each newborn human reached down into the green clay at the base of the bluff and they started molding all the trees and plants that bear food. The plant-eating animals were so hungry that they started eating the grasses and leaves as soon as they were made. The meat-eating animals watched them grow fat, then they got their first taste of meat. The people just kept making plants, because that was what they were born to do. Grandmother Carmo said that the Sujosa were meant to be farmers. Sometimes the work is a blessing, and sometimes it's a curse, but we Sujosa aren't happy unless our hands are in the dirt, and we aren't meant to stray far from Great Tiger Bluff.

CJM: Is that true? Do you think a Sujosa could be happy away from the land? Away from this valley?

Irene Montrose: I don't know. As far as I can tell, there aren't many folks around here happy, as it is. But I'd have liked to give it a try.

NINETEEN

As Faye approached the cash register with a set of turkey-red flannel pajamas, but, sadly, no longjohns, she found Dr. Amory waiting for her.

"I found the reference for the song you gave me," he said, drawing her aside so that they could talk out of earshot of the folks standing in the checkout line.

For a moment, she thought that some of her brain cells must already be frozen solid, because she had no idea what he was talking about. "Oh. Oh, yeah," she said as the memory slowly dawned. "Miss Dovey's song. You found out where it came from?"

He failed to suppress a very unprofessorial grin. "I know where it came from. I even know who wrote it, er, wrote them."

"What do you mean 'them'? I only gave you one song."

"But it's really two songs that the Sujosa, over the years, amalgamated into one. Look here." He drew a sheet of paper, folded together in quarters, from his pants pocket. "I put Miss Dovey's song alongside parts of the two old songs that her ballad was drawn from. Her words are on the right in italics."

**The Kynge's Ballad
Henry VIII, prior to
1547 C.E.**

Passe tyme with good
companye
I love, and shall until I dye;
Grugge who wyll, but
none deny,
So God be pleeyd, this lyfe
wyll I:

Miss Dovey's Song

*Pass time with good
company.
Grudge who will and none
deny.
So God be pleased, this life
will I.
I love and shall until I die.*

**Song of Songs 1:4
from the Geneva Bible,
1560 C.E.**

I am blacke, o daughters
of Ierusalem,
but comelie, as the frutes
of Kedar,
and as the curtines of
Salomon.

*I am black, Jerusalem,
Just as the curtains
of Salomon.
I am black, but comely, still,
I love and shall until I die.*

**Apparent amalgamation
of The Kynge's Ballad
and Song of Songs 1:4,
with original motif of
"a jealous love."**

*A jealous love, but comely,
aye.
I'll love thee best until I die.
Grudge who will, but none
deny.
So God be pleased until I die.*

"Henry the Eighth," Faye murmured. "I wouldn't have picked him as the writer of moralistic jingles. How could he possibly 'pass time with good company' when he had to live with himself?"

"Good question. But his ballad was apparently one of the greatest hits of the day. A book written in 1548, the year after the king met his maker—"

"I bet his maker sentenced him to an eternity of punishment at the hands of his poor wives."

"An interesting proposition. I have a feeling the Almighty specializes in poetic justice, so you may be right. But," Amory said, rattling his paper, "if you'll let me get to the point—"

"Sorry."

"Even back then, high moral standards were not a prerequisite for getting a song on the Top 40. A book written the year after Henry's death mentions that 'Pastance with gude companye' was quite popular in early sixteenth-century Scotland."

"Oh, my God. The Song of Songs. I cannot believe I missed a biblical quote," Faye said as she read further down the page. She wondered if it was time to go back to church before she forgot an important commandment or something. "Grandma made sure I got to church every Sunday when I was little. But I'm wondering why you picked the Geneva Bible as the source. Weren't there several English translations that were widely used in the sixteenth century? Didn't Henry himself commission Cranmer's 'Great Bible'?"

"Yes, he did. Your grandmother would be proud of your bible knowledge. But Miss Dovey used words that are specific to the Geneva Bible. I pulled this verse out of six bibles published in the century before the King James Version: the Coverdale, Matthew, 'Great,' Geneva, Bishops', and Rheims-Douay bibles. Only the Geneva and the King James describe the speaker as 'comelie.' The other versions use words like 'fayre' or 'welfauoured' or 'beautiful.' Only the Geneva and the King James compare her skin to 'curtines,' and the King James says those curtains belong to Solomon, not Salomon. I feel confident that the person who wrote new verses for King Henry's song was familiar with the Geneva Bible." Faye, ever-practical, moved from a word-by-word analysis straight to the point. "So, if we assume one of Miss Dovey's ancestors adapted 'The Kynge's Ballad'—"

"Or someone they knew," interjected the always accurate Dr. Amory.

"Right. An ancestor of the Sujosa, or someone they knew, probably lived in England or Scotland at least until the Geneva Bible was published in 1560."

"And I'd imagine that they composed their adaptation of Henry's ballad shortly after that, while it was still fresh in their minds."

"Right. But the combination of the two songs tells us even more than that," Faye pointed out. "Have you heard Miss Dovey's story about the yellow-haired sailors who kidnapped a group of women while they were gathering water? She specifically said that the men came to love their captives. Think about these lyrics: 'I am blacke, but comelie.' Can you name a bible verse or, come to think of it, any English poem of the time that would be as meaningful to a white man in love with a dark-skinned woman?"

"Not a one. So this song places some of the Sujosa's ancestors in present-day Britain through the middle of the sixteenth century, and it suggests that their dark-skinned ancestors entered their genealogy shortly thereafter."

"Yep." Faye read through the biblical passage again. Miss Dovey's ancestors had taken the words of Henry VIII and of Solomon's anonymous lover and made those words their own.

"I'm glad there's a team meeting tonight," Amory said. "I'll finally have something substantive to report. I mean *we'll* have something to report."

"Tonight?" It had been a long week, but Faye was pretty sure that it wasn't over yet. "It's only Thursday. Isn't the meeting tomorrow night?"

"Raleigh's going home a day early, so he moved the meeting up. It seems his wife misses him."

"Like Catherine of Aragon missed Henry the Eighth." Faye clapped her hand over her mouth after the undiplomatic comment escaped, but Amory seemed to enjoy it.

As Amory turned to go, she put a hand on his arm. "Wait. I've got another linguistics question. What is the etymology of the given name 'Carmo'?"

"How is it spelled?"

"C-A-R-M-O. It's Irene Montrose's middle name, and she says there's been a 'Carmo' in her family for generations."

"I've never heard of that name. At first blush, I'd guess it came from one of the Romance languages, but I could be dead wrong on that. Let me check the Internet and I'll get back to you." He nodded goodbye and headed for his office.

Faye purchased her pajamas and looked around for Laurel. She found her leaning on her crutches just inside the door. Her purchases were stuffed in a plastic bag that Jenny had tied with an extra-large loop to make it easier for her to handle.

"Let me carry that for you," Faye said.

Laurel slid the loop over her wrist and grasped the handles of her crutches. "Thanks, but I can manage."

Faye opened the door and followed Laurel through it, saying, "I'm glad we have this chance to spend a little time together. With work and the accident and the fire and now Jimmie's death, we've hardly had time to talk since—"

"Since we met."

"Yeah. I guess we've never had a chance to get acquainted, have we?"

"Part of that is my fault. I've made myself scarce on purpose."

"Whatever for?"

"I've been spending more time with Joe than I ever intended to." Laurel stretched one crutch forward and took a tentative step with her left leg. Then she reached out with the other crutch and dragged the right foot, encased in its heavy walking cast, forward. "I enjoy sitting at the kitchen table chopping onions while he cooks. And I'm really getting into flintknapping since Joe taught me how. It's something I can do sitting down that doesn't involve a needle. Knitting and cross-stitch are so tedious that they make me crazy, but chipping stone settles my mind."

"That's what Joe tells me. I mean, I don't know that he's ever tried needlework, but he says that flintknapping makes him feel peaceful."

Laurel picked her way slowly through the parking lot, making sure her crutch tips sat solidly on the uneven gravel surface before trusting them to bear her weight. After the rain ended, a cold front had swept through and sent the late afternoon temperature plummeting, yet Faye could have sworn she saw perspiration on Laurel's upper lip.

Looking up from the ground in front of her hobbled feet, Laurel said, "Maybe I'm being silly. I mean—I haven't known Joe a week, but I need to know now, not later, where you stand. When Joe started walking me to work and back, I was afraid you'd be mad at me, but you never said anything. When he gave me this," she said, reaching inside her jacket and pulling out a necklace fashioned from a bird point and a length of leather lacing, "I was sure you'd have something to say about it, but I was wrong. It looks like I'm going to have to come right out and ask you this. How do you feel about Joe?"

Faye was so busy trying to figure out why she'd never noticed Joe squiring Laurel around the settlement that she almost missed the real question. How did she feel about Joe, anyway?

"Joe's my friend," she said. This much, at least, was the truth. She was certain of Joe's friendship. "I'm happy that he's found someone who appreciates his gifts." She didn't add, *And who overlooks his shortcomings*.

"He helps me so much, without even trying. He tries to walk slow, so I can keep up with him, but I don't think it's possible for a man with legs that long to travel at my speed. After walking a quarter-mile with Joe, I'm worn out, but my feet are working better."

"He would die if he knew he was making you hurry."

"I know, so don't tell him." Faye watched Laurel creep slowly across a rocky patch of ground.

Even if Joe took baby steps, she could never keep up with him. "So?"

"So how do I feel about Joe?" Again Faye wished she hadn't been too oblivious to have seen this coming. There was no easy, obvious answer to Laurel's question, but Faye knew she must answer, and there was only one answer to give. "There's nothing between me and Joe. I wish you every happiness."

They neared the bunkhouse and saw Brent standing on the porch, wearing a Crimson Tide jacket and cap to ward off the growing cold. She wondered if he'd heard that Raleigh had rescheduled the team meeting, effectively canceling their dinner date, since Alcaskaki restaurants closed way too early to accommodate workaholic outsiders. And she wondered if he would realize she was angry at him. Faye had a hunch that, when it came to matters of the heart, Brent was as oblivious as she was.

Faye helped Laurel climb the porch steps. She noticed that Brent didn't scold her for interfering with the younger woman's progress. Perhaps he noticed the fatigue on Laurel's face.

As Laurel disappeared into the house, Brent said, "I hear we've got to work tonight. Could we set another date to have dinner?"

"Raleigh doesn't think the rest of us have social lives. He has no problem changing a meeting date at the last minute to suit his own schedule." She purposely didn't answer his question.

Too smart to let her reject him obliquely, he asked again. "Want to have dinner with me tomorrow night?"

Faye hated it when people sidestepped a simple question with a question of their own, but she did it anyway. "Why didn't you tell me you were part Sujosa?"

He actually took a step backward. "Did Adam tell you that?"

"No. You did. Your hairdresser blew your cover," Faye said, touching the back of her head, near where a line of stitches snaked across her scalp.

His hand crept up to touch the light streak on the back of his own head.

"What made you think Adam had given away your secret?" she asked.

"It's not a secret. Everybody in the settlement and in Alcaskaki knows who I am."

"I didn't."

He gestured toward the porch swing, as if he thought she'd be calmer and more rational if they had this argument while seated. She stayed on her feet.

"Was I supposed to announce it when we met? Should I have said 'Hello, my name is Brent, and I'm of indeterminate racial origin,' before I even asked your name?"

"No, but you could have mentioned it sometime. Like maybe when I was afraid I was out of place, being the only person of color sitting with your Alcaskaki friends. Or when you told me you'd decided to forgo a big pile of money, so you'd have time to do charity work in the Sujosa settlement. You could have said they were your people, instead of letting me think you were Mother Teresa, serving the poor just because they were there."

"I never said I was a saint. Why are you so angry over this?" Faye knew she couldn't explain what it was like to always—always—be set apart from everybody else because you didn't look like anybody else. Brent's bloodlines probably weren't so different from hers, but he didn't look multiracial. He looked like a white man with a tan. He was smart, he was good-looking, he was personable and, according to Adam, he was athletic. He was born for social success; it was his birthright.

It occurred to her that Adam, in his low-key way, might have tried to tell her about Brent, even before she realized the truth herself. When he'd said that he, Brent, and Leo had been like brothers when they were on the high school baseball team, she'd thought he was saying that proximity had broken down the racial barriers between Adam and Brent, two white Alcaskakians, and Leo, a brown Sujosa. If asked, Adam might have placed the racial barrier in a different place—with him on one side, and Brent and Leo on the other.

"Look," she said. "Maybe I'm overreacting and maybe I'm not. It's been a bad week. And my head really hurts. When are you going to take my stitches out?"

"Next week."

"Then let's talk about this next week."

She walked into the house before he had time to answer, and shut the door behind her.

She wanted to be alone for a while, but the bunkhouse provided few options for that luxury. Every horizontal surface in the parlor was festooned with Raleigh's budgetary paperwork. The kitchen, the only other public area, was chock-full of domestic bliss, for Joe was elbow-deep in the sink, washing grit out of a mess of collards, and Laurel was chopping pickles for the potato salad that would be accompanying Joe's greens. Faye might have given their relationship her blessing, but that didn't mean she wanted to give herself diabetes by watching it develop, step by sugary step.

Her bedroom offered certain attractions. She was assured of privacy, since her roommate was in the kitchen making cow eyes at Joe. Thanks to her recent purchase, she was assured of warmth, too. Though the thought of putting on those ugly pajamas and crawling into bed warmed her Florida-bred bones, it smacked of clinical depression.

Checking to make sure that Brent was out of sight, she slipped back outside. She would spend the hour before the meeting at her office. Jenny would sell her some Vienna sausages and saltines for supper. If the atmosphere at the bunkhouse didn't improve, Faye was pretty sure she could subsist on nothing but canned tubes of mystery meat for the duration of the project. Unless she got scurvy.

Interview with Brent Harbison, October 29, 2004

Interviewer: Carmen J. Martinez, Ph.D.

CJM: I understand that you're from Alcaskaki.

Brent Harbison: Born and raised.

CJM: And your parents?

Brent Harbison: My family goes back more than a hundred and fifty years in this county, on both sides.

CJM: They're both from Alcaskaki?

Brent Harbison: (Interviewer's note: Mr. Harbison took his time answering.) My father was born in Alcaskaki, and he never left, except to visit me in Tuscaloosa while I was in school there. My mother moved to Alcaskaki when she was nineteen and

stayed there all her life, except for those same trips
to Tuscaloosa.

CJM: And she was born elsewhere in the county?

Brent Harbison: My mother was born in the Sujosa
settlement, as you perfectly well know. That's why
we're talking, isn't it?

CJM: Well, if she ever told you anything about
Sujosa history, I'd love to hear it. That's why I'm
here, you know.

Brent Harbison: Is that why you're here? I helped
write the grant proposal, you know, and every day
I'm shocked by how far reality has strayed from our
original plan. There was supposed to be money for
another doctor to work in my clinic. Now I'm told
that I'll get a part-time nurse's aide sometime next
year. There were supposed to be four tutors for the
Sujosa's children: one for high school kids, one to
handle middle-schoolers, one for elementary kids,
and one to give preschoolers a good start on life.
Laurel Cook is a miracle-worker, but she can't do the
work of four people.

CJM: I'm concerned about those things, too, but I
can't do anything about it. You need to speak to Dr.
Raleigh, and I hope you do. He might listen to you.

Brent Harbison: Well, he sure as hell listens to you.

CJM: Pardon me?

Brent Harbison: I was there when you torpedoed Jorge Knight's proposal to do project-funded house repairs. The work went out of the settlement instead. It's being done by Alcaskaki's most prosperous contractor. That's not who we're here to help.

CJM: A portion of our grant money is earmarked to repair the Sujosa's homes, that's true, but have you met Jorge Knight? It would be irresponsible to trust him with public funds.

Brent Harbison: Jorge Knight only has one problem: he's got no place to put his brains and his ambition. If the vocational training budget hadn't been eliminated, Jorge would be a young man with a new home-repair business, instead of a troublemaker. But I don't expect you to understand that. I've read your work.

CJM: Pardon me?

Brent Harbison: You get your subjects to trust you. You flatter them, and pretend you care, so they'll like you and give you what you want. They play host to the parasite of your research.

CJM: I beg your—

Brent Harbison: You come off like Margaret Mead, describing the quaint customs of whatever primitive culture you've decided to grace with your presence. Then you marvel at what the "natives" have been able to accomplish with their limited resources and inadequate educations. Finally, you write your papers and get your fame and your dollars from their stories, while they get nothing.

CJM: Don't hold back, Brent. Tell me how you really feel.

Brent Harbison: I will. And I'll tell you about the Sujosa. Whether you want to hear it or not. You are well aware that the Sujosa were segregated into their own school until I was in my teens. Did anybody tell you about the time they finally got around to giving the settlement kids the SAT?

CJM: Nope.

Brent Harbison: Well, it was a small school, so there were probably only five Sujosa who took the test that year, compared to several dozen Alcaskaki kids. The smartest kid in Alcaskaki made the seventy-fifth percentile, which ain't bad for a poor, rural school.

CJM: And?

Brent Harbison: All five of the Sujosa—every last one of them—topped the seventy-fifth percentile. And don't forget that they'd had only one teacher, Miss Dovey, and she was working with out-of-date textbooks, when she had books at all. The settlement kids don't always do so well these days, without Miss Dovey on their butt day and night, but the intellectual raw material is there. Dammit, Carmen, we need those tutors here.

CJM: Brent, I agree with you. I had nothing to do with them being cut from the budget.

Brent Harbison: Maybe you had nothing *directly* to do with eliminating the tutors, but I'm talking about perception. Do you understand how important that is?

CJM: I'd like to think so.

Brent Harbison: Then listen to this. More than a hundred years ago, a Sujosa man shot an eagle that was flying with a rabbit in its talons. Now, don't go getting environmental on me. The woods were full of eagles in those days. Anyway, this man weighed the rabbit. He weighed the eagle and he measured its wingspan. After he did some figuring, he built wings and something kinda like a tail, then he attached them to his bicycle. When he got finished, he wheeled the contraption to the top of a hill on the far side of the river.

CJM: You're not telling me—

Brent Harbison: I am. He hopped on that bicycle and pedaled down the hill. About halfway down, he took off, so his calculations must have been accurate. Later, he said he'd planned to steer by shifting his weight, and that he'd hoped to be able to land by leaning forward. Instead, he flipped the thing endover-end, nearly killing himself. This was ten years before the Wright brothers went to Kitty Hawk.

CJM: Everybody was experimenting with air flight in those days. They say that "In steamboat times, men build steamboats." Those were airplane times.

Brent Harbison: Yes, but not everybody has the brains and the mechanical ability to give flying a try. That young man survived his adventure and lived long enough to father Jorge Knight's grandfather. Jorge could run a home-repair business in his sleep. He deserves that chance, and so do all the Sujosa. It's people like you who aren't perceptive enough to want to give it to them.

TWENTY

THE SUJOSA CHURCH was of a spare and unadorned design. Simple beams supported the vaulted roof, and clear windows let in dim moonlight that stained glass would have obscured. Pendant light fixtures that put Faye in mind of 1950s schoolrooms radiated brightness throughout the sanctuary, as if to make sure that God's truth never languished, unseen, in an unlit corner. There were worse places to conduct a meeting of academics who were, as always, torn between their pursuit of pure truth and their need to build their reputations and their careers.

Faye's presentation of the lustered potsherd received a quiet response from her peers. They agreed that the sherd was aesthetically interesting, but even Faye had to admit that its historical value was questionable, at least until the laboratory put a date on it.

Then Faye and Dr. Amory presented their interpretation of Miss Dovey's song, with remarkable success, considering that they hadn't rehearsed the presentation. Faye began by briefing the group on the transcript of Carmen's work that had survived the fire, then Dr. Amory stepped in with his interpretation of the origin of the song and with a cogent explanation of what could be inferred from the dates of the two verses that had served as source material.

"So, as you can see," he concluded, "Miss Dovey's songs and stories give us a direct connection between the Sujosa's oral history and datable European texts. If our interpretation of the texts is correct, the Sujosa are descended from

seamen who left England shortly after the reign of Henry
VIII, in the mid-1500s. Oral tradition, buttressed by these
texts, suggests that they kidnapped a group of dark-skinned
women—maybe from the Mediterranean region or from
Africa—whom they later came to love, perhaps even considering them their wives. So far, we have no information
on how they came to Alabama."

Faye was gratified to see one or two of the support staff
taking notes on Amory's interpretation of the song's text.

"Interesting," Raleigh said in a tone that dampened her
gratification considerably. "Of course, a huge percentage
of people of all races now living in North America have
at least one ancestor who was living in England in the
1500s. And it's a pretty good assumption that the Sujosa's forebears didn't leave for the Americas until sometime after 1492. So you've narrowed our time frame by,
oh, fifty years or so."

Somehow, Raleigh had managed to make their exciting
news—the first evidence connecting the Sujosa with their
Old World roots—sound puny.

"Good work," he added, relegating his faint praise to
an afterthought.

"Now, Ms. Longchamp," said Raleigh. His change in
tone signaled a new topic for which he felt more enthusiasm,
"there is the question of Dr. Martinez's notes. She passed
away five days ago. Her notes were not found among the
papers in her office, so I had assumed that they perished
with her. How is it possible that you failed to tell me that
you had them?"

Faye felt the edge of the pew bite into her thighs. Its hard
seat pressed against her legs, effectively preventing her
from sinking through the floor and away from the accusing
eyes of Raleigh, who was finally right.

There was no excuse for her failure to bring him
Carmen's notes.

Her negligence made perfect sense when considered in the context in which Carmen had given them to her. Raleigh had belittled her choice to do in-depth interviews with Miss Dovey, so she'd arranged with Faye to look her notes over while she altered her work plan to suit him. Eventually, she would have incorporated all her work into her final report, but her raw notes were never meant for Raleigh's eyes.

But Carmen's death had changed that. Raleigh had every right to expect Faye to help him gather any surviving remnants of data that his project had paid to gather, and she had simply forgotten to do it. There was only one possible response. She stood up and handed him the sheaf of papers in her lap and said, "You're right. I'm sorry for my oversight."

Silence settled into the old church. Her coworkers sat quiet and still, like soldiers unwilling to peek out of their foxholes for fear of attracting enemy fire.

In the silence of Faye's defeat, Joe unfolded his lanky frame from the pew beside her and stood, his muscled arms relaxed at his sides.

Raleigh glared at him, as if wondering what on earth a mere assistant might be able to add to the discussion.

Joe waited a moment, then appeared to interpret Raleigh's silence as permission to speak. "We haven't been together like this since Carmen passed," he said quietly. "Some of us knew her better than others, but we all liked her. She was friendly and generous, and she was too young to die. None of us knew Jimmie Lavelle, but he was too young to die, too. We would have done anything to help them, if we could. This seems like a good place to remember them." He gestured at the old church's hand-wrought beams. "Would anybody like to join me in a moment of silence?"

The pews creaked as the project team rose as one to honor Joe's request. Everyone present, except Joe, knew that his usurpation of Raleigh's role was unforgivably presumptuous, but their quick response spoke their relief that this uneducated technician had done what needed doing.

FAYE WENT BACK to her office to call Magda after the meeting, despite the fact that a pregnant woman should be asleep at that hour. Magda sounded tired, but stronger; it was good to hear her voice. They talked for an hour about Faye's work plan for the Lester excavation, and Magda's enthusiasm shored up Faye's flagging confidence. Focusing on science and nothing else cleared Faye's mind until, finally, she thought she might be able to sleep. The bunkhouse lights were out when Faye walked home in the weak moonlight and climbed wearily onto the porch.

She paused, one hand on the front doorknob, to wipe her boots on the welcome mat. The sound of the sisal mat rubbing against her rubber boot soles brushed loud against the evening's cool silence. When Amory spoke, his whisper rising from the dark in the direction of the porch swing, she was as startled as if he'd hailed her with a full-voiced shout.

"Faye. I've been waiting for you."

"Dr. Amory?"

"Come sit with me. I have some interesting news."

Faye reflected that it had been a week for interesting news—none of it good. She made her way toward Amory's silhouette and settled herself beside him on the swing.

"I found the origin of the name 'Carmo,'" he said with an excitement most people would have reserved for statements like, *My rich uncle died and left me his 1953 Corvette.*

"It's Portuguese. And you know what else?" he continued. The excitement in his voice escalated, as if he were preparing to tell her that his uncle's Corvette had 30,000 original miles.

"Portuguese?" Faye's heartbeat quickened, reminding her that she, like Amory, was just geeky enough to prefer unraveling a knotty historical question to owning a low-mileage sports car. "What else did you find out?"

"You know how Jorge pronounces his name? He doesn't pronounce it the Spanish way, 'HOR-hay,' even though he spells it like the Spanish do. But he doesn't pronounce it like the English 'George,' either. His pronunciation is very distinct: 'ZHOR-zhay.'"

"And he's very ticky about having people pronounce it right, too," Faye said.

"Guess who else pronounces 'Jorge' his way?"

"The Portuguese."

"Yes, indeed."

Faye did a little historical math. Moors from northern African had occupied the Iberian Peninsula, including Spain and Portugal, for more than seven hundred years before their final stronghold fell in 1492. Miss Dovey's song and stories suggested that British sailors had kidnapped a group of dark-skinned women about a half-century later. Could they have stolen Portuguese women who were descended from African Moors?

She smiled at Amory, though she couldn't be sure he could see that smile in the dark. "We can work with this," she said. "We'll have to get Bingham to check Jorge's genealogy, to see how far back the name goes in his family."

"Trust me. I'll sic him on this lead before he's finished with his breakfast cereal."

"'Sic'? Aren't you from Massachusetts? I never heard a Bostonian use that particular colloquialism."

"Maybe I've been in Alabama too long."

LEAVING AMORY ON the front porch to savor the results of his research, Faye groped her way through the bunkhouse. After four days' residence, she was familiar enough with the floor plan to find the way to her bedroom and into her nightclothes without flipping on a light that might awaken

Laurel. Sliding under the chilly bedcovers, she curled up into a tight ball.

But sleep didn't come easily. She couldn't quit sifting through her questions about the two deaths. Shoving those questions aside, she found that her nervous anticipation of starting the Lester excavation, compounded by the damp cold slowly penetrating her bones, threatened to keep her up all night. Had she chosen the right site? Were her workers sufficiently trained to get the job done?

Having exhausted the possibilities of her job worries, Faye's mind looped back to the mysterious deaths. Was there a reason they hadn't found Jimmie's cell phone? Was Carmen's death related to her professional work? What was to be done about the decision to keep the much-needed project money out of the pockets of the land-poor Sujosa? Was Carmen really part of that ill-conceived plan?

Faye frowned at the ceiling. Years of living on a pittance had honed her financial skills to the point that she had an instinctive feel for balancing income and outgo. Now that she had a moment to think about it, she realized that something was seriously out of balance in the settlement. The signs of poverty were everywhere, but...some people seemed to be doing better than others, for no reason that was obvious to Faye. Her eyes widened in the dark. That was it!

How had the Smileys been able to afford a new satellite dish? Leo worked at the limerock mine, where there had been a recent round of layoffs. She doubted he'd had a raise, and Ronya had said she made very little from her pottery. Yet they'd paid an upfront fee for the dish and assumed a monthly satellite service bill that would go on forever. And, she remembered, there was that pole barn, which hadn't been there four years before.

How had Jorge managed to buy that brand-new delivery van—when he already had a late-model pickup? And how

could she explain Fred's souped-up motorcycle? Even Jimmie—where had he gotten the cash to buy near-useless cell
phones for himself and Irene, not to mention a "pretty decent telescope"? In teenager-speak, "pretty decent" meant
top-of-the-line.

The Sujosa's income didn't meet their outgo. Faye knew
she was going to waste the rest of a night's sleep trying to
figure out where they were getting all that extra money.

TWENTY-ONE

ADAM DROPPED A folder onto the red-checked table of the Alcaskaki Diner and slid into the seat opposite Faye. "You gonna tell me why you had to ask me for a copy of the very same interviews you gave me two days ago?"

"Would you believe me if I told you I lost my copy?"

"Nope."

"Okay," sighed Faye. "I had to give it to Raleigh. I should have done so sooner, but I screwed up. Big time."

"I think with what's been going on around here, not to mention the fact that you almost died in a fire, you're entitled to a slip or two."

Faye glanced around the diner, bustling with Friday-morning breakfasters. "Maybe. Why don't you tell Raleigh that? Listen, let's order. This cold climate has fired up my appetite, and we don't have that much time. Does this place serve quick?"

Adam smiled and beckoned the waitress. Their "Rise-and-Shine Specials" arrived quickly.

Faye had always believed that calories consumed in diners didn't count, but she saw ample evidence around her, in the form of broad rears and rounded bellies jammed under dining tables, that those calories did indeed count. Ignoring the likelihood of added poundage, she tucked into her fried eggs and buttered grits.

"Why aren't you working? I thought you archaeologists were at it before the crack of dawn," said Adam through a mouthful of cheese-scrambled eggs.

"That's fishermen," said Faye. "Archaeologists need sunlight to work in." She peered out the window at the gray sky. "Anyway, I'll be back at the site by nine. Not that anyone will notice. With everything that's happened, I can't see that anybody will be doing much work today."

"I see Amanda-Lynne isn't working here today," said Adam. "I'll admit I'm relieved."

"I know. It's awful to see her. Everybody's worried she'll completely lose her grip on reality, but Jenny says she's coping by making plans for Jimmie's funeral."

"It's going to be a tough winter for her," said Adam. "Who knows when she'll be able to work again, and how much can she make here anyway? You don't rake in a lot of tips when the all-you-can-eat special goes for seven bucks. She's got no other skills, and she's lost her husband and now her son. I don't know how she'll get by."

"That's what I wanted to talk to you about," said Faye. "You know this community better than I do." She ran her thumb over the chipped rim on her coffee cup. "How did Jimmie, who worked part-time in a municipal library, and whose mother waitresses part-time, afford to buy a pair of cell phones and a telescope? How did Jorge pay for that new delivery van? How did Ronya and Leo afford that very nice pole barn and the satellite dish?"

Adam buttered his toast with care and deliberation. "When people don't have a lot, Faye, it means a lot to them to have the big TV and the fancy car. They stretch every cent to get all the things that advertising companies tell them they need. It isn't until the car blows a hose or they need a root canal that they see their mistake. I wish human nature was different, but that's the way it is."

"Maybe," said Faye, "but if that's so, why doesn't Miss Dovey have a convection oven with all the bells and whistles? Why are Elliott and Margie driving a thirty-year-old Ford and only dreaming about a satellite dish?"

"What are you suggesting?" asked Adam.

"That there are people in the settlement who have more money than they should have. That they're hiding something. And whatever it is, it could be a motive for murder."

Adam ruminated a moment. "I talked to Jenny Hanahan, and I managed to bring up the subject of that pothole Joe mentioned. She lives by the bridge. She says Jorge always comes back late on Wednesday nights, and she always hears his truck bang through that pothole."

"Every Wednesday?" Faye's eyes widened. "That's got to be it, then."

"Not necessarily. It's Jorge's job to drive that truck, and every driver hates to run empty. It may be that somebody's taking advantage of Jorge's schedule to save on shipping for a legitimate product they're selling."

"Like what?" asked Faye.

"Well, Ronya Smiley has her flea market pottery sales. Maybe Jorge takes her stock out every week, so she won't have to lug it around."

Faye shook her head. "What Ronya can get from her pottery doesn't come close to explaining the amount of money I'm talking about." She picked up her coffee cup. The chip in its brown rim inexplicably made her think of riches. *Real money.... Something the right person would pay a fortune for...*.

"Well, I'll check it out," Adam said. "I suppose you're suggesting that if Carmen found out this secret, she might have been murdered to keep her quiet."

Faye nodded wordlessly, still too deep in her own moment of revelation to speak.

Adam, apparently not noticing that his breakfast partner had left the building, finished his coffee in silence, then nodded to the window. "There goes Brent Harbison. Looks like he's working, anyway."

Faye roused herself to watch Brent's red sports car crawl

past the diner and disappear around a corner. "Did you know Brent didn't like Carmen?"

"Why, because it took her about two minutes to blow him off?" Adam joked.

"No," said Faye coolly.

Adam's freckled face reddened. "Then why?"

"He said she didn't care enough for the people she worked with. He accused her of only being interested in using them to further her own career and offering nothing in return. I believe the exact word he used for her was 'parasite.'"

"Parasite? Ouch." He drained his coffee and looked around for the waitress. "Why didn't you tell me this before?"

"I thought it was just normal antagonism between two hard-charging professionals...until I read Carmen's transcript of her interview with Brent. When he called her a parasite, he meant it."

The waitress brought the check and Adam rose. "Well, it's a quarter to nine. You're going to be late."

"I think the odds of my doing any useful archaeology today are exceedingly slim," said Faye. She followed Adam out without telling him that she might have figured out what Jorge was hauling out of the settlement. More than that, she knew precisely what he was hauling back home in his nearly empty truck.

Money didn't weigh much.

TWENTY-TWO

RETURNING FROM ALCASKAKI, Faye went first to the bunk-house to look for Joe, but she had no luck. Laurel was missing, too, and it didn't take a rocket scientist to guess where Joe might be. He had picked a fine time to discover the pleasures of romance.

Elliott was waiting for her at the excavation. Faye found it a pleasure to work with someone who was anxious to be on the time clock, but she didn't have time to brief him on the full details of the new work plan. She just sent him off to the Lester site, telling him to carry on with the work they'd begun Wednesday and promising to join him as soon as she could.

Joe's absence was unfortunate. She did not really want to do what must be done alone, but it wasn't safe to delay the upcoming confrontation any longer. Two people were dead. She couldn't live with herself if someone else died and she could have prevented it. Making up her mind, she headed out again into the cold on foot, stopping first at her office.

In her desk was the sample bag holding the cobalt blue lusterware potsherd Joe had uncovered the day before. She retrieved it and cradled the lovely thing in the palm of her hand. The making of useful things—plates, cups, jars—was a worthy craft. In the right hands, even the most utilitarian pottery rose to the level of high art. Faye would put the artist who had made this artifact into that category.

The decorative painting on this lustered fragment looked nothing like the plain glaze on the gray sherds her team had found all week. Still, in the end, they had all been made from dirt using skills handed down through the generations.

Light from the overhead bulb played over the fragment's luminous surface. She rocked her hand back and forth, admiring the way the luster ornamentation changed color. Collectors loved medieval lusterware for its luminous color and its great age. Luster painters of the time, typically Islamic, had incorporated eastern designs into their work, giving it an exotic flair that made present-day rich people happy to part with piles of money just to own something so beautiful. Why was a piece of something so old and so valuable buried in a vacant lot behind a country store in a poor, remote, American village?

One of the stars on the potsherd glittered at her, giving away its secret.

There was no longer any doubt in Faye's mind how the Sujosa were earning their extra money. She wouldn't grieve much to see Jorge and his poisonous attitude headed for jail, but Ronya was her friend. She deserved a chance to explain herself.

Pocketing the lusterware fragment, Faye stepped out of the store into a world where her Army-surplus camouflage jacket utterly failed to fulfill its design parameters. She was the only green thing in a sea of winter-gray. Raising her hood to fight off the chill winds that had begun stirring with the sunrise, she cuddled her face deeper into her hood and started walking.

JOE STOOD AGAIN under the shadow of the tower. Faye and Adam had assumed that, since they hadn't found Jimmie's phone after two hours of looking, they never would. That was a silly attitude. Even Joe, who was not a whiz at math, knew that there was a big difference between two hours and forever. Somebody needed to take those two people fishing. A day spent watching a bobber fail to bob was an exercise in patience.

He paid heed to all of his senses as he canvassed the winter-blighted vegetation. He would continue looking until he found the phone, or until he was sure it had never been near that tower.

FAYE STOOD ON the Smiley doorstep, the potsherd in her closed hand. Ronya opened the door and took a step forward, trying to herd Faye away and obscure her vision into the house. Faye stood her ground.

"Tell me how to make lusterware the old way, Ronya," she said, looking up into the silent face of a woman twice her size. She opened her hand and held the potsherd up. "And tell me how you found buyers stupid enough to believe your brand-new pots are hundreds of years old."

Ronya said nothing.

"This sherd hasn't been buried long. It couldn't have been; the luster wouldn't have survived those conditions. That doesn't mean it isn't old, just that it was buried recently, but I think you know exactly how old it is."

Ronya ran her eyes over the sherd in Faye's hand. She held her silence.

"If you won't talk to me, I'm going to have to take this to Adam Strahan."

"You're going to take it to him anyway."

"Carmen Martinez is dead."

Dusky eyelids flickered over luminous blue eyes. "I know."

"Somebody set the fire that killed her. The vessel this came from would be worth a lot in the collector's market. Maybe enough money to justify murder."

"I said I know!" Ronya's low voice broke. "After the fire, I wanted to go to Adam and tell him everything. But people will be ruined, innocent people, when this comes out."

"Innocent?" challenged Faye.

"I think so. I wanted to take as few people down with me as I possibly could. But it's hopeless." She stepped aside and let Faye into her parlor. "I decided last night that I was going to have to tell somebody what I've done. I have to say I'm glad that you'll be the one. With all the trouble haunting the settlement, I have to speak."

"All the trouble? You mean Jimmie's death, too?"

Ronya nodded. "We've never had anything of our own here in the settlement, nothing but land. And peace—but now we've lost that." Tears spilled out of her deep blue eyes. "I babysat Jimmie when he was a tiny thing. There was no reason in this world for that child to die. I can't figure out how his death is connected to the things I've done, but dishonesty is like a cancer. I've dragged the whole settlement into a lie that's eating us alive. It's got to stop and I'm the one that's got to stop it. Even if it takes me to the penitentiary for a long time."

It was impossible not to believe her. "Oh, Ronya. Is it that bad?"

Ronya led Faye toward a door at the back of the parlor with a ponderous grace that made Faye think of Demeter leading Persephone to her annual date with Hades. She threw open the door, and Faye walked into a room filled with glitter and earth.

Platters and bowls and tureens in all stages of completion were scattered around the room, but dominating the scene was a winged vase nearly as tall as Faye. It had been coated in luminescent white, and an intricate pattern in a dull brown was being painted over the fired glaze. Faye knew that the dull brown decorative design was deceiving. When the vase was properly fired a second time, the clay paste could be rubbed away to reveal ornamentation with the iridescent sheen of gold or ruby or bronze that gave it the name "lusterware." Shaped in the style of the great vases that had adorned Spain's Alhambra Palace in medieval times, the vessel's slender neck swelled into a graceful belly like a wine jar.

Or a water jar.

'Twasn't nothing but their water jars and the clothes on their backs, but those jars held their fortunes.

"Miss Dovey's stories aren't talking about just any old water jars, are they?"

Ronya dragged a finger over the vase's sweeping wing. "It's hard to say. I've been reading a lot about pottery in Moorish Spain and Portugal. I'm guessing my people descended from the Islamic potters that brought luster painting to Iberia from the Middle East. They probably left for the Americas sometime after the Christians overthrew the Moors, maybe during the 1500s."

"Based on the dates of one of Miss Dovey's songs, I think you're right."

"Well, the Alhambra vases that survive are more than a hundred years older than that, so I'd say that the women who left were descendants of Alhambra potters who had passed their knowledge down to them," Ronya said. "I'm thinking that after they got kidnapped by the English sailors, they kept passing the techniques down to their children and, eventually, to me."

The tiny arabesques and stylized floral decorations on a completed platter caught Faye's eye. The patterns had been made by incising the pigment with a sharp stick while it was still wet, leaving a distinctive comma-shaped design that Faye found oddly familiar.

"Zack's tadpoles!" she cried.

"Did you ever once think I wouldn't pass on what I know—every bit of it—to Zack?"

Faye circled the unfinished vase. It was magnificent enough to fool the eye, if not the analytical laboratory. "Only eight jars from the Alhambra are known to have survived. It wouldn't be too hard to convince a wealthy collector that this was the ninth."

"Tenth. I've already sold one."

Faye had no idea how much a collector would pay for a lustered vase from the Alhambra, but it would be a fortune. Selling a modern forgery for that much money was serious fraud. Ronya was right to worry about going to the pen. "That other jar must have brought in a big pile of money. I noticed you were doing okay, but you don't look rich."

"I pay Jorge to truck the merchandise out of here. I don't let anybody touch the big vases but me, but I'm teaching Irene to dig clay and make pots and to do simple glazing and painting.

Jimmie, too, when he was still with us. I pay them for their time. I pay Jorge and Fred to help with the drum kilns that I use for less important pieces."

"And I thought they were burning trash in the drum behind Jorge's house."

"Irene helps with grinding pigments and processing clay," Ronya continued. "Leo cuts the wood for my big kiln, but I fire the good stuff myself. The money goes fast. I learned early on that we couldn't make enough really fine reproductions—"

Faye cocked an eyebrow. "You mean forgeries?"

"Yeah. The good stuff takes too long to make. I couldn't keep everybody busy with it, so while I'm doing this—" she said, gesturing at her own artwork, "they're making cartloads of tiles and nun's bowls that we sell for cheap."

"Do you let people think they're old, too?"

"Sure. I know you've seen ads for our work. You know how some popular archaeology magazines are full of advertisements that say things like, 'Own an oil lamp from the time of Christ!'?"

"I've seen them."

"Well, now you can own a tile that comes straight from Moorish Spain."

"By way of Alabama."

"Yep."

"And Jorge trucks a load of that stuff out of here every week. It never occurred to me that it was you paying him to drive his truck. How do you stand working with that bastard?"

"It's not fun, but I need help, and Jorge needs the money. They all do. My business lets my crew make enough money to put food on the table and buy a few luxuries for themselves and their families. But that's all. The middleman skims off a lot of the profit."

Faye nodded. She had her own stories to tell about dealing with the black market.

Ronya had created a ninth Alhambra vase. The authentic ones graced some of the world's great museums, and collectors would have been waiting in line when word got out that a ninth one had turned up on the black market. Even accounting for all Ronya's business expenses, Faye guessed that the middleman was keeping ninety percent of the profit, maybe more.

"Zack's college fund is doing well, too," Ronya continued. "I thought it was worth the risk—until people started to die."

"Have you ever met your customers?" Faye asked. It could be dangerous to deal with wealthy people doing illegal things. She'd learned that the hard way.

"I've never even met my middleman." She turned her back on Faye, looking out the window at the backyard kiln that Faye had thought was a simple pile of bricks. "Leo takes care of sales." Her brittle tone did not speak of marital bliss.

"How on earth did Leo find somebody who had connections with this much money?"

"It's somebody he met while he was away at the university. He took some of my pieces to show around to people who might be able to get me a scholarship to art school. Nobody came up with any scholarship money, but one of Leo's connections was happy to ask me to make fake antiques. He came home all lit up like a Christmas tree. 'This is it, Ronya,' he said. 'We can both go to school, then we can come back here, where we belong. We'll able to afford a nice house and nice things for our kids. And we'll be able to afford a lot of kids.'"

Faye was doing the math. "It's been fifteen years since Leo went away to school. I don't think you've been doing this that long."

"Fifteen years ago, I told Leo, no. I told him I wouldn't lie and I wouldn't steal. Even if it meant we lived here in his parents' old house for the rest of our lives."

"But you changed your mind." Faye could hear Zack rattling around in his room, making piles of blocks and knocking them onto the worn wooden floor of his grandparents' home. "I bet you started your business sometime within the past four years."

Ronya actually cracked a bitter grin. "You got it. You're a woman, so you understand. I would kill somebody for that child without blinking an eye. Of course I'm gonna grab the chance to make sure I'll always be able to give him the things he needs." The grin faded when she realized what she'd said. "I didn't mean that. I didn't kill anybody. Truly, Faye."

"Who did?"

"No one on my payroll, I swear. I may be able to swallow being a forger, but I couldn't live with being an accessory to murder. Look, it's true we've all been on edge since the project came in and we heard there was an archaeologist on board. The last thing we wanted was someone with knowledge of artifacts wandering around—evidence of our

operation is all over the place. As you see." She gestured
to the fragment in Faye's hand. "We were relieved when
Dr. Raleigh started his dig in the last place on earth he'd
find anything, and when the original archaeologist wasn't
available after all. But then we heard you were coming. We
did what we could to discourage you."

"I noticed," said Faye. "Then the dummy in the tree was
meant for me, after all."

"It wasn't my idea," said Ronya. "You could have been
killed. Jimmie did a stupid teenager thing on the spur of the
moment—he was capable of that. He'd made that dummy
for the game, but when he heard you were coming, he
thought putting it to another use was an absolutely brilliant idea. I told him how wrong he'd been. After the fact."

"At the football game."

"You saw that? Then you saw how contrite he was. He
was scared witless when he saw your car start to skid. It
had never occurred to him that he might hurt somebody.
Teenagers aren't big on thinking things through—they're
deep-down certain that they'll live forever."

Ronya's dark skin blanched as her words reminded them
both that Jimmie had been dead wrong about his own im-
mortality. She shook her head abruptly, as if frustrated with
herself for yielding to weakness, then continued. "What
I'm trying to say is that young people can't always fathom
the possibility of dire consequences for themselves or for
anybody else, until they see life's realities up-close. For a
few seconds, Jimmie thought he'd killed you and Joe. Trust
me. That was the end of his pranks." Faye remembered the
look on Jimmie's face as Ronya had told him off. Was it
enough to remove him as an arson suspect? She wasn't big
on eliminating possibilities, just on somebody else's word.
She needed hard evidence to be sure. "What about the others?" she asked.

"They all have pretty good alibis," said Ronya. "Leo

was with me, in bed. Fred and Jorge were playing poker all night with three other men at Jorge's house. Irene was in bed. She sleeps in the same room as her mother. I managed to find out from Kiki, who was awake off and on, as usual, that Irene was sleeping like a lamb. For once, poor kid... ."

"And Jimmie?" asked Faye casually. Jimmie's footprints placed him at the crime scene. If Ronya came up with an alibi for him, it would be proof that she was lying.

"I asked him." Ronya hesitated. "He had his own room, and he was alone. He admitted he was up in the middle of the night. He's always done most of his studying while Amanda-Lynne was asleep. You've heard her talk, so I know you can understand why. I pressed—after all he did put up that dummy—but he was adamant. When he said he couldn't comprehend how anyone could do such a thing, he looked so betrayed. I guess we all look that way when we first find out that people can be evil. I believed him. Jimmie adored Carmen. I can't believe he did anything to hurt her."

"No. But he might have died because he knew who did." Faye closed her eyes briefly. "If only he had told you, when you asked."

"Well, I'm not going to make Jimmie's mistake," said Ronya. "I'm not planning to die, and I don't plan to see anybody else die, either. I can't leave the authorities in the dark about something this big."

"I'll call Adam Strahan. Can I use your phone?" Ronya gave her the phone, and she tried his cell, in case he was back in Alcaskaki. The goddamn tower that killed Jimmie was a hateful thing, but it would be a boon when it was finished and the Sujosa finally had cell phone reception. No luck.

"What's the number for Hanahan's?"

Ronya took the phone, poked in the number, and handed it back.

"Jenny, it's Faye. Is Adam around? Damn. Well, tell him I need to talk with him. He can call me at—"

"Tell him to call you at Miss Dovey's."

Faye raised an eyebrow, but she did as Ronya said. "We're going to Miss Dovey's?" she asked when she had concluded her call. "Three days ago you did everything but stand on your head to keep me from going into her house. There must be some interesting secrets in that house. Care to tell me what they are?"

"Come with me and I'll show you. Pottery lasts a real long time."

TWENTY-THREE

"HOW LONG DID you think you could keep this thing going?" Faye asked as Ronya wrapped Zack in a coat and hustled him out the back door. The morning's clouds seemed to have settled to earth. Faye stepped out into a gray mist that wormed its way into her clothes, leaving them damp and useless as a barrier against the winter air.

"A month ago, I'd have said forever. Until Zack was grown and educated. Until I was absolutely certain that he'd never be hungry when payday rolled around because his check wasn't big enough to feed his children and still leave enough money to feed him all month, too." She was silent for a few paces. "But we're all profiting from a lie. We're stealing from people who trust that the art they're buying is hundreds of years old. Nothing good can come from that, but I never expected people to die."

Faye knew something of collectors. She was well aware of the sins they would commit to hoard treasures that by rights belonged to no one, and she knew they would happily buy stolen goods, so long as they weren't required to do the stealing. She would shed no tears over the collectors Ronya had duped. But she was deeply concerned over the price Ronya would pay if her crimes came to light.

"Does Miss Dovey know about your forgery business?"

"Lord, no."

Faye's lips had already begun forming the word, "Why not?" when she swallowed the question and delivered the answer herself. "Because everybody does things that they just don't want their mama to know about."

"Exactly. It's been hard to keep it from her. I've used a lot of Miss Dovey's old pieces as models for my work, and I gave her a lot of lame excuses about why I was spending all that time and money on individual pieces of pottery when nobody at the flea market will pay what they're worth. Like most mamas, Miss Dovey's smarter than her kids give her credit for. She knows something is wrong, but nobody will tell her what. Isn't that an awful way to spend your last years—believing that your children can't trust you with the truth?"

"But if Miss Dovey doesn't know there's a secret to be kept, it would be easy for her to say too much without realizing it. I wonder who knew that she'd been talking to Carmen."

They stepped onto the back doorstep of a house that had been well built, but had suffered in the twenty years since its builder died and left an old woman to care for it alone. Its window screens were torn, and green mold clung to its wooden siding. The porch floor beneath Faye's feet was mildewed. Ronya knocked on an unpainted door that was soft with rot.

The elderly woman responded quickly to her knock, dispelling Faye's mental image of her as slow-moving and frail. Even with a slight dowager's hump, Dovey Murdock was significantly taller than Faye, and she didn't move like a woman who was approaching the end of her first century. Her golden-brown facial skin was heavily marked with age spots, and there were very few black strands left in her thin gray hair, but her alert brown eyes had not grown old.

The old woman flung the screen door open, and Ronya caught it before its spring-loaded action banged it shut again.

"Have you come to explain to me why my friend Carmen

burned to death? And to tell me who's responsible for young
Jimmie's death? Because, Ronya, if you haven't, you can
go away and stay gone."

"I don't know the answers to your questions, ma'am, but
I promise you I'll help find them out."

"Well, then, come in. And bring your archaeologist
friend. The one who never showed up when I invited her
for biscuits and coffee."

Ronya hung her head like a child caught swearing in
Sunday School.

FAYE AND RONYA left Zack in the kitchen eating cookies and
sat on the floor of Miss Dovey's bedroom, surrounded by
relics. One by one, Ronya hauled treasures from beneath
the bed. Miss Dovey sat to one side in a worn easy chair,
while Faye fondled the merchandise.

"This is why we call ourselves the Sujosa," Ronya said,
stretching out her arms as if to gather every piece of pottery into her arms. "Look what we can make out of dirt."

"And here I thought your Spanish ancestors got the name
from some Portuguese-speaking neighbors who enjoyed
calling someone else 'dirty.'"

"I don't know about any neighbors giving us our name.
Some of our ancestors could have *been* Portuguese, for all
I know. There were Islamic potters in Portugal, too. I think
we earned the name 'Sujosa' ourselves." Ronya held up an
intricately molded tureen.

"How old is this stuff?" Faye asked, holding a lustered
apothecary jar up to the light.

"That one's worthless to anybody but us. Miss Dovey's
mother made it in the late nineteenth century."

Faye admired the jar's delicate design. "I understand
that certain Sujosa families like Ronya's handed their skills
down to their children. Did your mother teach you how to
make pottery, Miss Dovey?"

"My mother was sick with the consumption from the time I was a little girl, and she died young. She never had the energy to teach any of us what she knew. That's why Ronya's the only potter we've got left."

"Did your mother make all these things?"

"Lord, no, child," Miss Dovey said, and the instincts of an old teacher overrode the grief of a mother whose children have strayed from the righteous path. "Ronya, show her the oldest pieces. What's left of them."

Ronya lay on her belly and reached far up under the bed. Faye noticed that no dust bunnies clung to the small bundle. Unfolding the protective rags, Ronya revealed a collection of sizeable potsherds.

"May I?" Faye asked, reaching for the broken pots. The clay exposed along their broken edges was a much lighter buff than the potsherd she'd found the night before. "These were made from different clay. Was it dug somewhere else?"

"They were made in Spain," Ronya said, and her quiet pride told Faye the rest of the story. Goose bumps prickled her forearms.

"These are the water bottles from Miss Dovey's story?"

"What's left of them. Ship travel was hard on pottery in those days, and I've heard tell those jars went on more than one long sea journey," Miss Dovey said. "If the old stories are to be believed, at least one of those pots was broken over the head of a ship's captain."

"There used to be more," Ronya said, and the brittleness Faye had heard in her voice earlier was back.

"You never told me why you wanted to hide these here," Miss Dovey said. "Why didn't you trust Leo not to take them? Did you have a fight? Sometimes men do awful things when they're drinking."

"Leo doesn't drink, and he knew exactly what he was

doing." Zack came in and ran straight to Miss Dovey, climbing into her lap. She began to sing to him, rocking slowly.

Ronya distractedly straightened the potsherds, grouping them by age and style. After a minute, she was ready to address the question of why she'd been hiding things from her husband. "Our buyer told him to bring the oldest pots we had, and Leo took him all he could find. He would've taken them all, but I was trying to copy these, so I had them in my shop. I don't understand exactly why they needed old, broken pottery, but it has something to do with faking out the lab tests."

Faye rifled through her memory for an article she'd read about antiquities forgers in Mali. The native potters took broken pieces of ancient clay figurines, crushed the smaller pieces into powder, then mixed this powder with newly dug clay to fashion modern reproductions out of larger ancient fragments. It had proven very difficult to distinguish these fakes from authentic antiquities, even for analytical laboratories.

Based on Faye's understanding of thermoluminescence analysis, she believed Ronya's pottery could be made almost completely from modern materials, as long as the laboratory collected its sample from an area made from the old potsherds. Thermoluminescence testing would give the date of the last time the clay was exposed to high heat—in the case of the first Sujosa's Spanish potsherds, sometime in the mid-1500s, maybe earlier.

"The buyer pulverized the sherds Leo stole from me and sent the powder back," continued Ronya, "telling me to use it in the bases of my best pieces—the ones that cost so much that the buyer might pay to have them tested."

Ronya's explanation made sense. If the base of each plate or jar or vase—the spot where the laboratory would surely take its sample to avoid diminishing the piece's aesthetic value—contained significant amounts of clay dug in Spain and fired in late medieval times, then the most sophisticated analyst could be fooled into thinking the whole piece was old. It wouldn't take a particularly large volume of truly old artifacts to pull it off, but the thought of grinding up potsherds like the ones she held in her hands broke her heart.

"I'm so sorry," Faye whispered, caressing the old things. Faye looked at the other pots on the floor around her, like a landscape in blue and white and gold. "You brought these here to keep them safe because even Leo doesn't have balls enough to mess with Miss Dovey?"

"Yep."

"Who made all the others?"

"You're looking at centuries of Sujosa art," Ronya said. "I made some of these, trying to copy the older pieces. My mother and Miss Dovey's mother made some of the others. I don't know who made the rest, but some of them might be nearly as old as the water jars," she said, gesturing at the sherds in Faye's hands.

"Wait," Ronya said, jumping to her feet and hurrying Faye into Miss Dovey's parlor. "You're an archaeologist. Maybe you can tell me what this is. It's not like any of the others."

On Miss Dovey's mantel sat the gray tea set Carmen had described in her notes and, with it, something that Carmen had not had the skills to recognize. The object that she had described as a brass platter enameled in blue was something else entirely. It was a ceramic platter underpainted in blue, then adorned with a brassy gold luster.

Faye pulled the potsherd she'd found that morning out of her pocket. The patterns were remarkably similar, but the platter was graced with a bigger splash of gold in an unmistakable shape. The flames of the sun's fiery crown surrounded a dark disk in a perfect depiction of a total eclipse of the sun. This once-in-a-lifetime event had clearly made an impression on some long-ago potter.

Ronya, looking at the sherd in Faye's hand, unbuttoned a pocket near the knee of her cargo pants and pulled out a half-dozen similar ones, holding them next to the one in Faye's hand. They matched. "Goddamn Jorge for his laziness—"

Miss Dovey cleared her throat.

"Excuse my language, ma'am." Holding the eclipse platter up, Ronya said, "I was trying to copy this piece, but the new one broke in the kiln. I gave Jorge a pile of waster pots, mostly plain grayware with a couple of broken luster pieces mixed in and I told him to take them to the dump. Instead, he drove over to Jenny's store and threw them out back. I'd gathered up everything I could find before Raleigh started digging, and Jorge and Fred did a pretty good job of hiding the pieces they found from Raleigh."

"Who wasn't all that interested in finding anything anyway."

"He sure didn't seem to be. That man is no archaeologist, but you sure are. You terrified me from the start."

"I did? Then why did you come to work for me?"

"Well, with Jorge and Fred out of the picture, we needed some way to keep you off the track. I went home from work Wednesday with my pockets full of lustered potsherds I didn't want you to see."

Faye's ego shouted at her for letting her employee outsmart her, but there were more important things at hand. "I notice that some of these pieces are decorated in blue," she said, walking back into the bedroom and surveying Ronya's treasures. "Why didn't you use blue on any of the reproductions I saw at your house?"

"The Alhambra potters had access to blue pigment, but you can't just go out and dig up cobalt in Alabama. Mama used to buy commercial pigment when she could afford it, because she just thought blue was pretty. That's what you're looking at here. And here."

She held up two potsherds, one in each hand.

"I let Irene use store-bought blue pigment on the cheap stuff," she continued, "because it sells and because we don't try to use authentic materials in those pieces. Who's going to spend a lot of money on laboratory testing of something they didn't pay a hundred dollars for? Sometimes I buy blue for my own work, when I'm copying a Spanish piece made with cobalt pigments. On the good stuff, though, I only use primitive materials. I dig the clay. I make the tin glaze. I—"

"Where do you get the tin?" Faye interrupted. Then she interrupted herself. "Wait, I remember. The Confederacy had tin mines in Alabama, thanks to your great-great-great-grandmother."

"You can find tin here if you know where to look, and I guess she must have told the Confederates where the right spots were. And I can get silver and copper ore here, too, for the luster pigments, but I can't get cobalt or anything else that will give me a decent blue. So I don't use blue. My work is still authentic, though. The Spanish didn't always use blue, even after they got cobalt pigments. Leo's buyer can't get that through his head. He's always pestering for blue and gold pieces."

"Blue-and-gold *is* the classic Hispano-Moresque color scheme," Faye said, bending down to study a cracked platter decorated with a golden ship sailing across a deep blue sea. Looking back at the eclipse platter to compare the color of the cobalt ornamentation, she was struck by the precise pattern of stars scattered around the sun's corona. "I don't think this one is as old as the water jars—"

"I'm pretty sure it's not," Ronya said, rubbing a thumb over the painted surface.

"—but I think it may be really important. Almost as significant as the oldest pieces. It almost—"

The old-fashioned ring of a dial phone interrupted her

train of thought. Miss Dovey set Zack aside and rose to answer it.

That would be Adam, thought Faye. The knowledge dampened her spirits in the midst of her excitement about the pottery finds. She would have to tell him about Ronya, and that would give her no pleasure at all. She was halfway to the bedroom when Miss Dovey called to her.

"It's for you, Faye," she said.

Faye took the receiver reluctantly. "Hello?"

Adam, usually the soul of good manners, didn't even bother with hello. "I got a preliminary lab report on the sample I collected from the second pillow for comparison."

"And?"

"In both pillows, there was a wide spectrum of the chemicals produced when you burn kerosene or heat up a foam pillow, but at fairly low levels. But there were some fairly hefty spikes of chlorinated chemicals that only showed up in Carmen's pillow—"

"I remember," Faye said. "You said they could have been leftover cleaning compounds."

"Yeah, but I talked to the lab director about that. She said the levels were too high to be cleaning residuals. She says someone must have put those chlorinated hydrocarbons on that pillow."

"Were they used to set the fire?"

"They aren't flammable enough. But they would do a good job of anesthetizing anyone who put her head on the pillow."

Faye felt something crawling at the base of her skull. This changed everything. A missing briefcase and mysterious chemicals on a pillow had been interesting clues. They had intrigued her mentally, without making her think too much about the reality of Carmen's death. But this…someone had made sure Carmen was unconscious so that she couldn't possibly survive the fire. Faye hesitated, uncertain of what to say.

"Look, I've gotta go," said Adam. "I've got a meeting with the sheriff. All hell is about to break loose. Stay safe. I'll talk to you later." With a click, the line went dead.

"Did you tell him?" asked Ronya, standing in the doorway.

"No," said Faye.

"You'll have to, sooner or later," said Ronya. "We should go. I need to tell the others, and you've got things you have to do. I'd rather not be standing there when you tell Adam."

Faye nodded and went to retrieve her coat. Adam wasn't going to be happy when he found out how his high school buddies had been spending their time.

TWENTY-FOUR

THE MOTION OF the pale sun through a cold, sodden sky told Joe that hours had gone, but he'd paid no attention to their passing. Woodcraft required a man to remain in the moment. Otherwise, he would never smell the odor of a broken limb or a crushed leaf. The slight change in color of a dirt clod that had been scuffed by a hoof or a shoe or a hurtling phone would pass unnoticed.

The search had been easier without the distracting sounds and smells of Faye and Adam, both of whom were very smart and very well-intentioned but were more or less clueless when it came to woodcraft.

The phone eventually showed itself. He squatted down beside it and rested his elbows on his knees. It had struck three pine limbs on its way to earth, then bounced off a bare patch of ground and crash-landed on a fragrant sassafras seedling. A physicist would have said that each of the first three collisions had transferred some of its energy into a flexible branch, slowing its velocity to the point that the final collision with the soft clay soil had been survivable. Joe couldn't have communicated such a thought in words or through mathematics, but he understood intuitively why the cell phone was still whole and functional. He wished Jimmie's fall had ended so well.

Joe stood and put Jimmie's cell phone in his pocket without much looking at it. He'd seen the innards of electronic gadgets before and he knew what this one looked like on the inside. It was chock-a-block full of many-legged rectangular chips crawling across a rectangular wafer, but it felt empty to Joe, filled with nothing but pain.

LEO SMILEY WASN'T proud of what he was doing, but he was doing it. That was the problem that had confounded his life for four years now. He had found a way to get Ronya's art into the hands of people who saw her for the genius she was and were willing to pay princely sums for her work. Except they didn't actually know who she was. And the princely sums dwindled down to pennies before they reached rural Alabama.

The fact that people were being deceived into believing Ronya's work was very old nagged at him some, but not much. On any given day, he could use a different technique to rationalize that problem away. For example, he truly believed that one of her pots was just as intrinsically valuable as one that was five hundred years old. Also, he held a certain degree of contempt for people willing to part with all that money for an antique when they couldn't actually tell the difference when somebody sent them a modern reproduction instead. On one of his more resentful days, he could work up a lather of indignation over the prejudice the Sujosa had endured through history. Every dollar Ronya's fakes brought in could be seen as a single reparation for segregated schools, biased courts, and poll taxes, if you looked at things the right way.

All of which meant nothing on that particular day, when his buyer had sent him word to stop next week's shipment, and maybe the one after that, too. Leo felt sure that this was the beginning of the end. The news only compounded the soul-sickness he felt over the deaths of Carmen and Jimmie. He headed out into the chill morning to find Jorge. He didn't know what he would say to Ronya.

He headed along the path to the clearing where Jorge ran his drum kiln, hoping to find him there. But the clearing was empty, and the fire was cold. *Just as well*, he thought, and turned down the path to Jorge's house. He hadn't gone far when something caught his eye a few feet into the woods: an orangey-red patch of disturbed soil. Something had been buried there, and it was the work of five minutes for Leo's long arms and big hands to unearth it.

It took a moment for him to recognize the misshapen hunk of metal. It had been an aluminum briefcase before Jorge had crammed it in his kiln and tried to obliterate it. Leo knew that Adam Strahan had been looking for the dead woman's briefcase ever since the fire. The whole settlement knew it. And anyone with half a brain knew that if Adam was looking for something stolen from a dead woman, then the odds were good that the thief was the one who had made her dead. Leo stalked through the woods and across Jorge's backyard without troubling himself to use the footpath. Jorge met him in the driveway.

Leo hefted the chunk of aluminum and threw it at Jorge's prized pickup. It bounced off, leaving a sizeable scrape in the metallic red paint job. Then he wrapped one raw-boned hand around Jorge's neck and used the other hand to grab him under an armpit, lifting him up to his own eye level. "I would have never pegged you for evil, Jorge, but you killed a woman. You burned her to death, then you took… that. Why?"

Jorge's red head sagged onto Leo's hand. "I didn't kill her, Leo. I didn't do it."

"Why should I believe that? Adam says somebody started that fire. He's smart and he ain't never learned how to lie. If somebody did it, then it might as well have been you." He lifted Jorge higher, so that even the toes of his dangling boots didn't touch the ground.

"I took the briefcase out of the burned-out building the day after the fire. I waited until the firemen went home, then I slipped under the yellow tape and took it."

Leo dropped him to his feet, but he didn't release his grip. "Tell me why you'd do something that stupid."

"She had some potsherds in there. I saw them when she opened her briefcase at Hanahan's the day before she died. I don't know where she got 'em. Probably picked 'em up off the ground back behind the store. Some of them sherds were lustered. I just wanted to get rid of them, like the others. I didn't think anybody'd notice."

"Looks like you didn't think at all."

"I can't risk losing the money! Can you?"

A shadow, tall and broad, spread its coolness on Leo's back. He looked over his shoulder and saw Ronya standing behind him, her fists on her hips.

"The money's already gone. They've found us out. It's over—for better or worse, I'm not sure which. I'm sorry, Leo."

"Don't be," said Leo, releasing Jorge's throat. "In a way, I already knew." In a few words, he told them about the buyer's decision to pull out. Ronya, in her turn, told them how Faye Longchamp had put the pieces together—literally.

"Has she told anyone yet?" asked Leo, when she was finished.

"Not yet. She's a good woman. I'm sorry I ever tried to cross her. We should have been friends."

"Then we've got to get rid of the drum kiln and the merchandise we have on hand," said Leo.

"Look what's in front of your eyes!" Ronya pointed at the briefcase, lying by the truck. "We've been interfering with a murder investigation. Faye will tell them, and if she doesn't, I will."

"You'll do no such thing. There's got to be another way. Think of Zack!" Leo hardly recognized the woman in front of him. He had never noticed the frown lines running from her nostrils to her jaws. The circles under her eyes were dark as bruises. "Who'll take care of him if we both go to jail?"

"I guess we should've thought of that before," she said as she turned to walk away.

"No," said Leo, determination showing in every inch of his weathered face. "We'll think about it now. Jorge, get that truck of yours started up."

BACK AT HER office, Faye had only her unsettling thoughts for company. Joe was still nowhere to be found. Laurel was at the church, working with a student. And the other members of the project team were ensconced in their offices, doing whatever it is academics do.

She tried to cipher out who would have wanted Carmen dead. Was it one of Ronya's co-conspirators, worried that Carmen would reveal their crime? Had Carmen uncovered the forgery ring? Or did she stumble onto something else? She had bounced around the settlement, talking to just about everybody.

What else might she have discovered? What was worth murdering for?

Faye turned to the interviews for guidance. Carmen had been in contact with all the conspirators shortly before her death, with the exception of Jorge. In her notes were documented conversations with Leo on October 26 and with both Jimmie and Irene on October 30. Also on November 5, the day of the fire, Carmen and Faye had gone together to talk to Ronya, before their uncomfortable visit to DeWayne and Kiki Montrose's house. At the time, Ronya's surliness had surprised her. Now she understood it. But what was DeWayne's excuse? Ronya hadn't mentioned him as one of her conspirators. DeWayne made an attractive suspect, but she could see no evidence pointing his way, other than his general bad attitude.

She wondered what Carmen's colleagues knew about

her last days. Bingham and Amory used another of Jenny's converted storage rooms for office space, so Faye knocked on their door.

"I've been reviewing Carmen's notes one last time," she said. "Trying to get an idea of what she was doing in her last days. Do either of you know of any research she might have done, other than her interviews?"

Amory shook his head, but Bingham yanked open a file drawer and shuffled through his folders. "Yes. Yes, she and I talked the day before you arrived. I gave her a document that I found intriguing. It looked like an ordinary enough deed, but the marginal notes were fascinating."

Faye went to his side. "I saw a mention of that in her interviews."

"Yes. It seemed that two branches of a family were scuffling over a tract of land, and I wondered whether any stories about the conflict had survived in the oral tradition. She said she'd try and find out. I made her a photocopy, but here's my original. Of course, it's not *the* original. That's in the library where I found it. But this is a very good copy."

He handed her a legal-sized sheaf of paper. It was obvious that larger pieces of paper had been reduced in photocopying to fit the modern size. The first page was a will, with all the traditional declarations of the maker's soundness of mind, that distributed the maker's personal items between his two children. The second page was a map and a hand-written property description. Notes apparently written by several different people were scribbled in the margins. They had been faded and blurred by time and the limitations of the photocopier, but the gist seemed to be that everybody thought they'd gotten the short end of the stick when the property was divided.

The name of the will's maker jangled in Faye's head. Sam Leicester. There were no Leicesters in the settlement now. "Why does the name Leicester make me think of Queen Elizabeth? The first one," she mused aloud.

"Because she gave one of her favorite courtiers that particular earldom," Bingham said. "Except you're pronouncing it wrong, like an American—Lye-chester. The queen would have called her sweetheart the Earl of 'Lester.'"

Faye hands tensed, nearly tearing the paper in two. The Lesters—also known as the Leicesters, apparently—had first settled in this valley when people didn't trouble themselves much with spelling anything consistently, even including their own names. Regaining her composure, she carefully smoothed the deed out, squinting in an effort to make out the details of the map. Amory handed her a magnifying glass.

"It's dated 1845," she said. "And take a look at this property description. The life of a property owner must have gotten a lot simpler when someone finally opened a land surveying business in these parts."

She scanned the description quickly. *Beginning on Leicester's Hill at the source of Leicester's Creek, travel downstream along the creekbed past the Leicester homestead until reaching the Injun mound that stands alongside said creek. Skirting the mound and the homestead so that they are contained within the property being surveyed, along with a fifty-foot right-of-way, travel due south until reaching Raccoon Branch and follow said branch upstream to the southeast corner of the fence marking the Leicester family cemetery. The source of Leicester's Creek is visible by line-of-sight from this fencepost and the final boundary of the property deeded to Edwina traces this straight line. The remainder of my property shall pass to my daughter Mary Alice.*

The map included the area of her new dig site, which was discouragingly far away from all the important landmarks like the family cemetery and the homestead, not to mention the mound she had heard so much about. Still, something didn't add up. The description seemed to say that the mound and the homestead were both on the same property, but she knew from Amanda-Lynne and DeWayne that they were not. And if there was one discrepancy, there might be more. Wills were a good place to look to find out if there was money to be had anywhere, and, if so, where it had gone. And money was always a good motive for murder.

"Well, this'll give me something to do with the rest of my day," she told the two doctors. "I think I'll take a trip to the property assessor's office in Alcaskaki."

JOE PROWLED FROM one of Faye's haunts to another—from office to bunkhouse to Hanahan's to excavation and back. He had something to tell her.

Adam had been so pleased when Joe brought him Jimmie's cell phone. He would surely tell Faye the good news as soon as he saw her, but Joe wanted to get there first. Faye had been the one who knew that Joe could find it, and he planned to be the one who told her she was right.

Maybe she was with Brent, talking about medicine or genetics or world politics. Joe didn't feel like interrupting such an intellectually high-powered discussion, so he decided to just lurk in the basement of the church where Brent ran his free clinic.

Twenty minutes passed with no sign of Faye, but the door to the left of Brent's clinic opened and Laurel stepped out. She was leaning far forward, struggling to balance a torso weighted with an overstuffed backpack over her crutch tips.

Joe was incapable of letting this situation continue. He rushed to Laurel and stood in front of her, blocking her path. "You're not going anywhere until you give me that backpack," he said, holding out both hands.

Too smart to argue with him, Laurel leaned first on one crutch, then another, as she slipped the pack off her shoulders. "Come inside," she said, turning back toward her office door. "I finished scoring your diagnostic tests and I want to show you the results."

Joe would have preferred for her to say, "Come in here and wrestle this gator for me," but he followed her, because she asked him so sweetly.

They sat beside each other at the table where she taught the children. Joe didn't even try to force his knees under it. He just scooted his chair away from the table and cocked it back on two legs, like he did when he was nervous. Laurel spread several papers out in front of them, and every one of them was covered with tiny type that spelled out words like "auditory processing" and "dysgraphia" and "language-based learning disability." This didn't look good.

Laurel squinted her eyes at his face and swept the papers into a folder, tucking it into a desk drawer. "Never mind these," she said. "What they tell me is that you are a very smart man whose brain is wired differently from other people's brains."

He let the chair's front legs drop to the floor. "I don't know much about the 'very smart' part, but I sure do know I'm wired different from regular people. Tell me something I don't already know."

"Your eyes and ears don't communicate with your brain the same way mine do. I'd guess you use a whole different part of your brain to do some things. Maybe that's why you're more aware of things like birdsong and weather signs than the rest of us, but letters and numbers make you nuts. We can work with that, Joe."

"Sometimes I just feel so stupid." Hell. He hadn't really meant to speak of the hateful thing that nested so close to his heart.

"That word—'stupid'—makes me angry. You're an intelligent man with a fine mind. You can't help being put together differently."

"I can read quicker since you gave me this," he said, reaching in his pocket for the piece of paper he used to cover the line of type underneath the one he was trying to read.

"I know some tricks that will help you with math, too."

"I thought of you this morning when I was making biscuits," he blurted.

She looked at him with a question on her calm little face, but she didn't ask him what in the world he was blathering about. "I needed to make a lot of biscuits to feed all those people, but I didn't have quite four cups of flour," he explained, "so I couldn't multiply the other ingredients by four. I had to figure out how much shortening to use with three-and-two-thirds cups of flour, and how much milk. I'm not sure I did the math quite by the book, but the biscuits turned out all right."

She smiled. "They were delicious. They didn't even need butter. Would you show me how to make them sometime?"

"If you'll let me take you to a movie." Joe was flabbergasted to hear the words come out of his mouth. He didn't even know if Alcaskaki *had* a movie theater.

"I'd love that. Tomorrow's Saturday. Is that good for you?" Joe had been thinking of that very night, but he could probably use the extra twenty-four hours to locate the nearest theater. It had also occurred to him that neither he nor Laurel had a car and that he, himself, didn't even have a driver's license. Perhaps the extra day would give him time to figure out a way to get them both to Alcaskaki while still retaining his dignity. There was no way he was going to ask Faye for a ride.

Laurel put her left palm on the table, pushing herself toward a standing position as she reached for her crutches. She kept her eyes on Joe, rather than looking at what she was doing, and her fingertips barely brushed their metal shafts. Both crutches clattered to the floor. Laurel, thrown off-balance, nearly went with them, but Joe stretched out a hand and grasped her by the waist.

She clenched her fists. "Oh, what a stupid thing to do. I—"

"I thought that word 'stupid' made you angry. You can't help it if your feet are crooked, and I can't help it if my brain's wired up wrong. We do the best we can."

She looked up at him with eyes as innocent as a fawn's. He had no choice but to lean down and kiss her. Her breath was as fresh as a sea breeze playing through the trees of his island home on Joyeuse.

TWENTY-FIVE

IT WASN'T THE first time that Faye had found a treasure buried in public records, and it wasn't the first time that she'd looked around a shabby county office and wondered what skeletons would turn up if somebody took the time to go through every last file, page by page. But she had a specific task at hand that afternoon.

The clerk had located what she was looking for with only the usual amount of talk and flourish. Faye sat now at a small desk alone with her findings. Attached to the deeds for Amanda-Lynne's and DeWayne's properties were identical photocopies of Sam Leicester's will. At the bottom of both copies was a gorgeous nineteenth-century signature. Today's stylishly illegible signatures would not have gone over well in those days, when the ability to write was a mark of breeding.

The distinctive curl of Mr. Leicester's capital "L" caught her eye. Patting herself on the back for remembering to bring a magnifying glass, she admired the man's penmanship for a moment before recognizing the obvious. This signature didn't match the one on the will she'd gotten from Dr. Bingham.

She laid the three wills side by side: Bingham's version, Amanda-Lynne's copy, and DeWayne's copy. The differences were subtle but real. Bingham's photocopy was different from the other two, but that wasn't so surprising for a document written by a man without access to a photocopier or carbon paper. He had probably written out several copies of his will—one for his records, one for each of the children, and one for the court that would settle his estate. Faye steeled herself to do a line-by-line comparison.

The first page tracked perfectly. The same words were on the same lines. At first glance, they were nearly as alike as photostatic copies, until Faye's magnifying glass teased out the inconsistencies that were the hallmark of anything made by a human hand.

The second page, however, was a different matter. The handwriting on Bingham's copy took up more of the page, which seemed unlikely since it said the same thing, word for word. Or it should have. Shifting her magnifier back and forth between the pages, she quickly determined what part of the text was missing. All references to the "Injun" mound, the homestead, and the cemetery had been removed. Instead, the reader was instructed to *Begin at the source of Leicester's Creek, travel downstream three hundred feet, then travel due south until reaching Raccoon Branch.*

Faye pondered the consequences of removing all references to landmarks other than bodies of running water, which were notorious for changing their course. This could explain why Amanda-Lynne and DeWayne both thought that the property line ran between the homestead site and the mound, when one of the original wills clearly stated that it didn't. The current property boundaries were almost certainly wrong.

A professional thrill went through her when she realized that Amanda-Lynne owned the mound as well as the homestead site and the cemetery. She was going to be able to excavate where she had intended, after all. DeWayne might fuss, but what did it matter, really, which piece of worthless property was his? All of the Sujosa were land-poor, paying taxes on land they couldn't farm and couldn't sell. And Faye's romantic side liked the idea of restoring the property boundaries to the places Sam Leicester/Lester intended all those years ago.

But as she ran through the rest of the document comparison, her ardor cooled. There was nothing else of interest—no lost inheritance, no buried treasure—no motive for the murders of Carmen Martinez and Jimmie Lavelle.

BACK AT THE SETTLEMENT, Faye whistled tunelessly as she threw her coat on the back of her desk chair. Despite her lack of success, she had enjoyed her time digging through historical photographs, looking for cool stuff like old homesteads and older mounds. It was probably a form of mental illness, but it was a cheaper and healthier addiction than, say, alcohol or nicotine. When Adam spoke, she nearly jumped out of her skin.

"Sorry to scare you. You might want to think about putting a lock on that door."

"Jenny says the lock on the outside door is good enough, thank you very much. She also says that she keeps an eye on everybody in her store, which cuts down the shoplifting problem significantly, and she'd know the second anybody opened my office door."

"Well, here I am."

"Jenny probably thought you were safe, being a lawman and all."

"Maybe so." He sank into the desk chair that had been Carmen's and looked at her with a face that said *I have news. Ask me.*

She cooperated. "What's up?"

"Joe and his superhuman talents found the phone. He looked for you, but came to me when he couldn't find you."

"I knew he could do it. He was probably just too polite to ask us to get out of his way yesterday. Was there anything useful on it?"

Adam rocked the chair backward. "Useful? Only a text

message saying, 'Meet me at the cell phone tower.'" He let the chair flop back to its default position. "Well, that's not exactly what it said. It was something more like, 'I can't go on like this. Meet me at the tower to say good-bye.' Signed—"

"Irene?" Adam nodded, and Faye's mouth went dry. "Have you talked to her?"

"The sheriff and I went over there straight away. She says she didn't send it, but when we asked her to produce her cell phone, she couldn't find it."

"Do you believe her?"

"Maybe. The poor kid seems torn up with honest grief. But she has admitted that sometimes she and Jimmie went up to the tower—to be alone together, she said. She says they stopped it months ago, when their parents found out and raised holy hell. Maybe she was overwhelmed—God knows she doesn't have an easy life—and sent the message. Then maybe she chickened out and Jimmie fell by accident. Or maybe someone stole her cell phone and she was never there at all." He ran a hand through his ruddy hair. "I do know one thing: whoever used Irene's cell to send a text message to Jimmie's cell wasn't here in the settlement at the time."

Faye nodded. "Because it'll be months before they get cell coverage here." She knew what he was thinking—she was thinking it herself. Who had been in Alcaskaki Wednesday afternoon? Irene was there, working at the dry cleaners. Jorge was God-knew-where, driving his delivery van. Brent could have been in his Alcaskaki office or his settlement clinic. Then there were DeWayne and Fred to consider, and a host of others. There were more people who didn't have alibis than there were people who did.

"I'm going to have a chat with Jorge," said Adam casually.

"Is it okay if I talk to Irene?"

"She's not officially a suspect. I don't see how it could hurt the case."

Faye wasn't thinking about the case. She was thinking about Irene. The poor girl had been through so much, and now she'd found out that a message purportedly from her had led to Jimmie's death.... If Irene was able to talk, Faye would listen. The girl might need to talk to someone who knew what it was like to have a sick mother and nobody to turn to. If she couldn't talk, then Faye would simply be there with her.

"Anything else?" asked Adam.

Faye hesitated, then shook her head and turned away.

FAYE HAD NOT intended to have her womanly chat with Irene while standing in the Montrose driveway, but she was lucky to get a chance to speak with the girl at all. Irene was on her way to work. Grief and loneliness didn't stop the bills from coming.

"Irene," Faye began, "are you sure you want to go to work?"

"I'm sure," she said.

The tears were gathering on the rims of the girl's eyes, poised as if they needed to spill over. Faye didn't want to be the one who made them fall. "Do you know that Jimmie was the first Sujosa I laid eyes on? He was perched in a tree over the road the day I arrived."

"He told me what he did. He was so scared when he thought you were going to crash. Then, when he saw that you were going to be okay, he got more scared that he was going to be in real trouble. He ran away, but he lost sleep over what might have happened to you. He didn't mean anything...."

"I have to wonder, would he have done anything else really stupid? Like maybe set a fire?"

"No. Oh, no." The horror on Irene's face said that she'd

never even considered that possibility. "Jimmie was a gentle, gentle soul. He was just...." She hesitated, so Faye helped her out.

"Irene, I know what Ronya is doing, and I know that you and Jimmie were involved."

Irene looked more relieved than surprised. "He was just worried that Ronya might have to shut her business down, that's all. If that happened, his friends would have lost out. It was them that he was worried about—and me—more than himself."

"Did he ever talk to you about the fire?"

"No. I tried to talk to him about it. I guess I just wanted to make sense of what happened. I never understood why Carmen would want a heater in her room, anyway. It wasn't so cold. But he wouldn't listen to me. He said it would only make things worse to talk about it, and he didn't like to see me upset. That's the way he was...." The tears in the girl's eyes finally overflowed.

Faye had never been a physically affectionate person, but she'd been brought up by her mother and grandmother, two women with powerful arms and shoulders made to be leaned against.

She could think of nothing to do for Irene but to throw her arms wide and let the young woman walk into them.

As IRENE DROVE AWAY, Faye stood, irresolute, in the Montrose driveway, eyeing the house. The new information she'd gained at the property assessor's affected her professional relationship with DeWayne Montrose. DeWayne might not like it, but he wasn't going to be able to stop her from excavating the mound he'd been so adamant about protecting from her dirty archaeologist's hands.

She climbed the porch steps and knocked on the door. Kiki opened it and stood leaning weakly against the doorframe. Lank curls the color of flame framed her pallid face.

"Is DeWayne home?" Faye asked.

"He went to Hanahan's for groceries. Can I help you?"

Faye considered. It might be good to have DeWayne's wife on her side during the inevitably tense discussion with the man himself. She decided to present her case to Kiki—quickly, before the frail woman collapsed. "Yes, I think you can. Should we sit down?"

Kiki sank right down on the doorstep, clearly intending to have this conversation on the front porch, so Faye did the same. "I asked DeWayne for permission to dig on his land when I stopped by the other day."

"I bet he said no. DeWayne is funny about his possessions."

"You know your husband well."

"We've been married a long, long time."

Faye pulled copies of both versions of Sam Leicester's will from her briefcase, telling the story in as few words as possible. "These documents show that there's some question about who actually owns some of the land up on the river bluff. I'm pretty sure that Amanda-Lynne really owns the piece near the old mound, and that's the part I'm interested in. Now, I'm not a lawyer, but I imagine DeWayne and Amanda-Lynne can work this problem out without going to a lot of legal expense. I'm hoping I can get permission to dig while they sort things out. I won't do any harm to the land, Mrs. Montrose. I promise. Will you talk to your husband?"

Kiki nodded, then looked over Faye's shoulder.

Faye turned, expecting to see DeWayne approaching, as fierce and frightening as his bloodthirsty dogs. Instead, she saw Brent striding up the front walk, an uncomfortable smile fixed on his face.

Kiki rose so quickly that Faye feared she might fall. "I don't want to talk to you," she cried, with more vim than Faye would have thought possible. "I don't have anything to say to you. You know that." The sick woman slipped through the front door, closed it, and shot the deadbolt home.

Faye and Brent looked at each other.

"Guess she doesn't want to see you," said Faye. "Can't imagine why."

"She's refusing treatment," said Brent. "Spending all her money buying miracle drugs over the Internet, hoping against hope. She doesn't realize those quacks are robbing her blind. Lately, she won't even let me see her."

"Too bad she's not Sujosa. She might never have gotten sick at all."

Brent shook his head. "I thought I had her in remission—I thought she was getting better. But then she began to slip away. I keep coming by, hoping she'll let me help her before it's too late."

"Would that make you feel better about yourself? Money didn't do it. A big house didn't do it. My guess is that it's going to take you a long time to find what you're looking for—simple pride in who you are."

Brent turned away without a word and headed to his car.

TWENTY-SIX

FAYE FOUND JOE back at the bunkhouse, having exchanged his role as woodsman extraordinaire for one as chief cook and bottle washer. They sat together at the table, and discussed the finding of the cell phone as they ate.

Faye couldn't explain why Joe's bologna sandwiches tasted better than anybody else's. The lettuce was juicier and crisper. The white bread was softer. If someone had told her that his mayonnaise-spreading technique was the secret, she would have believed them. Of course, they were enjoying a very late lunch, so hunger might be part of the answer, but only a small part.

Joe was on his third sandwich when Ronya and Zack arrived. Ever the perfect gentleman, he offered to make them sandwiches, an offer they accepted gratefully.

"I tried to find you earlier," said Ronya. "To ask if you had…" she glanced at Zack, "you know."

"I told Joe, but not Adam. Not yet. Anyway, you couldn't find me because I went into Alcaskaki," said Faye. "And I had a very enjoyable but pointless time puzzling over some old Sujosa deeds. Not wholly pointless," she corrected. "I found out that DeWayne doesn't really own the mound site."

"Who does?" asked Ronya.

"Amanda-Lynne, I believe. And since she has no problem with me working on her land, this means I'll be able to excavate the entire site as soon as possible. That's something."

"Don't be so sure," said Ronya. "Once the lawyers get involved, it could take a while."

"I don't think it will involve a lot of litigation. There's nothing but scrubland between the creek and Great Tiger Bluff. One tract is worth no more than the next."

"Faye," Joe said. "Are you talking about the property where you want to dig?"

"Yeah," Faye said.

"It's not all worthless, Faye. The cell tower's up there."

"No, it isn't," said Faye. "It must be—I don't know, a mile away at least."

"You only think that because the road is so roundabout it takes forever to get there. It's only a few hundred yards north of the Indian mound."

Faye blinked. The cell tower. The one that brought with it a monthly lease payment that would, presumably, go on forever. Someone who had lived on the hard cold line of poverty for a lifetime might do anything to hang on to a gold mine like that.

Faye thought out loud. "Carmen knew about Sam Leicester's will. I know she did, because her interview transcription shows that she told Amanda-Lynne about it. Kiki was there, too. If she or Amanda-Lynne told DeWayne what Carmen knew, he might have killed her to keep the property dispute quiet. If Jimmie saw him doing it, DeWayne might have killed him, too. It wouldn't have been hard for him to steal Irene's cell phone. And...listen to this...Irene just told me that Jimmie said it would only hurt her more if they talked about the fire. Maybe he was thinking of how it would hurt her if she knew what her father had done."

"It can't be true," said Ronya. "DeWayne? He's turned into a real slacker these past few years, but he's not a bad man."

"He set his dogs on me and Carmen the first time I met him," said Faye.

Ronya backed down at that, but not all the way. "That could have been an accident. Let's at least check this out before we start making accusations. There may have been a property transaction that you missed. Talk to Amanda-Lynne."

"Do you think we can get reliable information from her?" asked Faye. "Especially now?"

Ronya shrugged to acknowledge Faye's point. "Then talk to Miss Dovey. She might know the details."

"Okay, I can do that," said Faye. "But let's take some precautions. Joe? Can you find DeWayne, and keep an eye on him? Make sure—well, make sure he doesn't try anything. If we're right, he may think he's silenced anyone who could hurt him, but I don't want to take any chances."

"I won't let him out of my sight, Faye."

"Okay. Do we walk or ride?" she asked Ronya. "Always quicker in this settlement to walk."

"Let's go."

THE SCENT OF fruit and cinnamon greeted them at Miss Dovey's door. "Hello, ladies. And hello to you, too, Zack. You'll have to excuse me, I need to spread the custard before it separates." She headed for the kitchen, saying over her shoulder, "Just amuse yourselves while you wait."

Faye crossed the parlor and picked up the eclipse platter from its spot on Miss Dovey's mantel. Even in the midst of the hunt for a murderer, she was glad for another chance to study the star pattern adorning its slick surface.

Ronya stepped aside as Miss Dovey emerged from the kitchen, a triple layer cake in her outstretched hands. Its un-iced sides were nut-brown and speckled with spices, and a rich golden custard oozed from between the layers. A dollop of deep blue huckleberry jam, as glossy as the platter in Faye's hands, adorned the top. Even Miss Dovey's cake was a blue-and-gold work of art.

The truth finally dawned. Faye heard again the words

that she'd spoken herself earlier in the day. *Blue-and-gold is the classic Hispano-Moresque color scheme.*

"I'll get us some tea," said Miss Dovey, heading back to the kitchen.

"What is it?" asked Ronya, coming to Faye's side.

Faye jerked her head upward. "Your ancestors were probably potters in Moorish Spain or Portugal?"

Ronya nodded.

"Did Leo go to school in Tuscaloosa?"

Ronya's eyes widened. "How did you know?"

"Damn," Faye said, hurriedly setting the fragile treasure down so she could concentrate without breaking something irreplaceable. "You remember you told me Leo got the idea for selling your pottery, made by techniques that originated in Moorish Spain, while he was away at school? Well, one of the world's top experts in Hispano-Moresque pottery teaches in Tuscaloosa. His name is Dr. Andrews Raleigh."

"You're saying that you think Raleigh is Leo's buyer? But he's…he's a scholar, a professional with a reputation to keep up."

"That's what's been bothering me. I couldn't figure out how a man with his reputation could have bungled this project so completely, but now I understand. He did it on purpose. He underbid the Rural Assistance Project, not caring that he cut out most of the actual rural assistance to the Sujosa, so that nobody else could possibly win the contract. And now I understand why. As long as he was in charge of the project, he had a shot at keeping the truth about the Sujosa's history as potters quiet."

"Because if somebody—like you—published a paper on medieval lusterware in modern Alabama, his collectors might put two and two together," Ronya said.

"You got it. He sabotaged my work because he *wanted* me to fail. It's no coincidence he's away from the project on the day it's all going to come out. He knew there was no way you'd be able to keep your forgery business a secret now, with fire marshals and sheriffs and all their helpers crawling over the valley, looking for a killer."

Ronya stared at her. "You're right. You have to be. Leo told me he got a call from his buyer, calling off next week's shipment. More than that, Leo got the impression it was all over. He assumed the man knew we were in trouble, and we both wondered how he knew."

"Raleigh knew. Or guessed. Or...." Faye gripped Ronya's arm. "He's not coming back. How far would he have gone to protect the racket he had going?"

"Or to keep himself out of the pen." Ronya pursed her lips. "Would he do murder? I think he might. My impression of Raleigh is that he does whatever it takes to cover his tail. He must have already made a fortune off my work. That money could take him anywhere in the world."

It seemed that Raleigh had gotten away with murder, not to mention a large heap of money. The notion rankled Faye to her very core.

Miss Dovey reappeared with a tray of tea things. "Now," she said, "what was it you ladies wanted to talk to me about?"

Faye dragged her mind back to the reason for her visit. Why was she here? Oh, yeah—to talk to Miss Dovey about whether there was any possibility that DeWayne had acquired the mound property legally.

But she was no longer certain that DeWayne had anything to do with the murders. After all, he wasn't actually seeing any of the lease money. It was all going to buy Kiki's medicines. Whereas Raleigh had probably been making a fortune. Nevertheless, she still needed to find out the truth about the property lines. "Remember the old story about the feud between the branches of the Lester family?" she began.

"We think there may be a problem with the property line between Amanda-Lynne and DeWayne," cut in Ronya.

"Do you know if it's been changed in any way since the days of the feud?"

Miss Dovey looked bewildered. "Why, no, not to my knowledge. Why would it be?"

"Are you sure—" began Ronya, then stopped as the telephone rang.

Miss Dovey answered the phone. She listened for a moment, a look of concern growing on her face. Looking at the two women, she held the receiver out to Ronya. "It's Kiki. I think you'd better talk to her."

Ronya took the phone. She listened for a moment, then spoke. "Stay right where you are. Yes, I know I'll need help. Faye's here with me, and you're not that big. We can manage." She paused to listen to Kiki. "Okay. Lock the doors and windows if you can. We'll be right there." She hung up.

Faye and Miss Dovey looked at her expectantly. "De-Wayne's just beat the crap out of Kiki—I'm guessing he's drunk—then he busted up the TV and left in his truck. She wants to get out of there before he comes back and does it again, but she can't even get up off the floor."

"Let's go," said Faye, rising.

Ronya held up a hand. "DeWayne is out there, drunk. Are you sure?"

"Joe will be on his tail soon, if he isn't already. We'll be all right. You can't count on everybody, but you can always count on Joe."

"Okay," Ronya said, grabbing her coat and throwing Faye's at her. "I hope you don't mind watching Zack, Miss Dovey."

The old woman pulled the boy to her so that he could rest comfortably against her hip. "Of course not. But, Ronya—"

Miss Dovey might as well not have spoken, for all the notice Ronya took. Once she was assured that Zack would be looked after, her attention shifted to the task at hand: helping Kiki.

Miss Dovey hobbled along behind them, trying to say something, but they were in too much of a hurry to stop and listen to an old woman.

TWENTY-SEVEN

RONYA AND FAYE took a narrow footpath back through woods to the north of Miss Dovey's house, coming out on the trail about half a mile from the Montrose place. As they hurried along the final leg, Faye wished for home. A cold mist, not quite a rain, hung in the air. On her island, the temperature never plummeted in mid-day, turning puddles to slush. She couldn't remember the last time her teeth had chattered or her breath had condensed like a white ghost in front of her mouth.

The Montrose house came into view about two hundred yards ahead. Faye could see the fence that kept De-Wayne's dogs and their fangs contained. She couldn't see the dogs themselves, but she imagined she could hear their bays echoing in the frigid air. The thought made her shiver even harder than the weather did. "Can you imagine what it was like for Kiki, living with DeWayne all these years?" she asked.

"Marriage ain't always fun and games," Ronya said. "We'll find somebody willing to take Kiki in until...well, for as long as she's got. Irene, too. They'll be okay, and DeWayne can rot out here with nobody to beat. Nobody to put food on his table, either."

Faye could hear the dogs for real, now. "Do you hear—"

Ronya stood straight up and bellowed, "Sweet Jesus! De-Wayne's set the dogs on us." Wrapping a big hand around Faye's forearm, she yanked her practically off her feet.

"Don't look back," she said, and veered off the path and into the woods at a dead run.

Faye, struggling simply to keep up, couldn't have looked back if she'd tried.

The sound of baying dogs echoing through the frigid air had left Faye's imagination and become her reality. Faye followed Ronya blindly, with no idea where they were headed—until they burst out onto a footpath. Autumn's final leaves had dropped, obscuring the ground and covering the slick patches of mud that had knocked Faye off her feet on her first trip down this trail. She ran on faith, trusting that each footfall would land on solid ground.

The blood throbbed in her almost-healed scalp wound. Ronya's speed put the lie to any notion she might have had that heavy people were slow-moving. Ronya must be built of nothing but skin, bones, and muscles, with every fiber of those muscles pulling toward a single goal: getting them out of danger. They plunged deeper into the colorless winter forest, each step taking them further away from civilization.

DeWayne and his pet monsters remained out of sight behind them, but their sounds told Faye that they were still there. Strange echoes of barking dogs bounced through the swells and hollows of the wooded countryside until Faye couldn't have pointed in any one direction and known, with certainty, that their pursuers were there. There was no question in her mind that the dogs would catch them, sooner or later. She couldn't think about what they would do to her flesh, and Ronya's, so she found herself dwelling on one particularly maddening thing: DeWayne might get away with this.

A jury drawn from this county, where dogs were seen as working beasts necessary for hunting and security, might well believe a story that his dogs had escaped their pen and run two defenseless women to ground. They might believe his remorseful tears over their grisly deaths. Perhaps he would serve some time for negligent homicide, perhaps not, but it would be nothing compared to his rightful punishment for two counts of first-degree murder. No, make that four.

The erosion channel came into view, and Faye began again to harbor hope.

"The dogs?"

"I ain't never seen a dog outside the circus that could get across this," Ronya said, leading the way across the rope bridge that Faye had crossed on her first trip to Great Tiger Bluff. Ronya was right; the slats were too narrow and too far apart for any dog to cross. Faye prayed that the gap was too wide for them to jump.

Faye grasped the supporting cables and stepped onto the bridge. The misty rain was crystallizing into ice, and falling pieces of sleet, dagger-cold, pelted her scalp. She felt suddenly lost and frightened. She was too high up—too high. Her step faltered and she swayed; her cold fingers clutched at the icy ropes.

Ronya's face appeared in the mist. "Come on!"

Faye felt Ronya's strong hand on her shoulder, and she staggered forward onto solid ground.

"That should take care of the dogs. DeWayne's not man enough to come after us on his own," said Ronya. "We'll be all right now."

Then the sound of a rifle being fired echoed through the misty hills, and a white scar appeared in the trunk of the tree from which the rope bridge extended.

Ronya looked at Faye and started running again. Faye had no choice but to follow, but her thoughts turned to Joe. She'd sent him to trail a violent man. Alone.

MISS DOVEY WISHED young people could be made to be quiet and listen to their elders. She'd tried to tell Ronya and Faye to wait while she fetched something that would help them, but they'd been too busy to listen to what she had to say. Little Zack probably felt the same way sometimes.

It had almost been too much for her, slithering on her belly up under the bed and hauling out Taylor's old hunting rifle. When he was first dead, this gun had been her security. On dark nights when her imagination insisted that criminals and wild beasts waited outside in the darkness, aware that she was alone, she'd whiled away the hours by cleaning it. On dark days when she wasn't sure she had the money to feed herself, it had represented her last bastion against starvation. If need be, she had told herself, she could always learn to hunt.

Taylor's rifle was useless to her now; she could hardly lift it. Old age had robbed her of the muscles that had once roped her forearms. Her body wasn't strong enough to defend her friends against DeWayne and his temper, but her mind and her will were still under her control.

A gunshot echoed through the woods north of her house, way too close to the settlement for her to be able to explain it away as the work of a hunter. Her hands played over the barrel of Taylor's rifle. She wished she could give it to someone who knew how to use it, someone who would do what had to be done. Now she could just wait and pray that things turned out as they should.

Miss Dovey barred her door, then picked up the phone to call for help for Kiki, and maybe for Faye and Ronya, too. Zack sat at her feet. He couldn't comprehend what was happening around him, but his company was comforting, all the same.

FAYE TEETERED ON the edge of Great Tiger Bluff for a second, then followed Ronya over the edge. The steep path lay at the bottom of a gully that was flanked on both sides by thick buttresses of clay—ideal protection against gunfire.

As slick, cold slopes of mud go, the path looked incredibly appealing.

Ronya took the moment of relative safety as an opportunity to share her plan. "We're gonna get to the bottom of the bluff. Then we're gonna run for the trees at the source of the creek—you remember it?"

Faye thought of the lovely afternoon she and Ronya and Zack had spent digging clay along its banks. "Yeah. I do."

"Okay. We follow it to the river, walk downriver—in the water, so we don't leave tracks—"

Faye cringed. The temperature was well below thirty degrees Fahrenheit, and dropping fast. Slogging through the river was going to be brutal.

"Then," Ronya continued, panting as she continued toward the bottom of the bluff, "we take the back way home, like I showed you. There's no trail. DeWayne doesn't know the woods. If we stay at least this far ahead of him, where he can't see us, we can lose him."

"Sounds good," said Faye.

The two women kept moving.

ICE RAINED INTO the deep brown creek, and circular ripples expanded from each point of impact. White mist rose from the surface of water that was still the temperature of the groundwater it had been mere minutes ago, before it poured out of the ground. Standing on the damp sand at the water's edge, the creek looked to Faye as if it were boiling. There was no bank here, just sheer bluffs rising up higher than their heads, so she and Ronya waded in, jogging as fast as the water would let them. Trying not to think of the ever-warm waters of her Gulf island home, Faye slogged downstream toward the river.

She was wet from the thighs down. She hoped that the exertion of running through the resisting water was forcing her heart to pump warm blood to her cold-numbed hands and feet and legs and arms. From the time they had stepped into the water, Ronya hadn't spoken. Faye just kept following her. What choice did she have, so deep into an unfamiliar and hostile country?

They rounded a curve in the creek and Faye found herself in a familiar place, where the creek banks on both sides were wet and clay-slick and pocked with holes. There was room to run here, so Ronya left the creekbed, traveling as fast as her heart would let her through the clay pits dug by her mother and Miss Dovey's mother and all the Sujosa potters in all the years since their people came to Alabama. Once through this obstacle course, they would be damn close to the river and, maybe, to escape or rescue.

Ronya was breathing hard. Faye had been pushing the limits of her own endurance for so long that she'd begun to believe that Ronya's body had no limits.

People watching accidents over which they have no control often report that the world seems to shift into slow-motion. Faye saw her friend lose her footing with complete clarity. She lengthened her own strides to try to reach Ronya in time to break her fall, but she herself had shifted into slow-motion, too. When Ronya's right foot slipped on the wet clay, Faye watched, impotent, as the larger woman's ankle twisted and her knee buckled and she pitched over into a five-foot-deep clay pit.

"Are you okay?" Faye hollered over her pounding footsteps, heedless of the possibility that their pursuer might be near. "Are you okay?"

After a long silent moment, a soft voice rose out of the depths. "I'm okay, but my leg isn't."

Faye flung herself onto her belly in the mud and reached a hand down to help Ronya up. Her friend shook her head. "Nobody your size is going to be able to get me back to town."

A livid lump was rising on Ronya's temple. Her leg,

twisted in the mud beneath her, was bent in several places, as if she had more than one knee.

"Go ahead, Faye. I'll wait here for you. Bring somebody big to haul me, okay?"

"I can't leave you here. You left a string of big muddy footprints behind you. He'd have to be blind to miss the mudslide you rode to the bottom of this pit. Maybe I could go back upstream and leave a false trail that'll draw him away from here...."

But she knew that wouldn't work. She'd have to scale a fifteen-foot bluff to get out of the creekbed, then she'd have to find her way out of the woods without Ronya's help. Even if she abandoned Ronya to DeWayne, she'd still have to make her way down the creek to the river, then strike out overland. How many landmarks did she remember from that faraway afternoon with Ronya and Zack? There had been a tree with a lightning scar and a copse of magnolias and a whole lot of land that looked a whole lot alike.

The gray sky had begun to look even darker, and Faye realized that night was coming. The odds of Faye finding her way back before dark were vanishingly small and, all that time, Ronya would be vulnerable to a killer and to the growing cold.

She was going to have to make a stand.

"I'm going back," Faye said, gesturing toward the creek they had just left. "I have to stop him before he gets this far."

"He's got a—" Ronya swallowed. "He's armed."

"So am I," Faye said, fishing her pocketknife out of her pocket. "Don't worry. And stay warm." She loped back down the creek bank toward the bluff.

FAYE WAS A WARRIOR. She was under attack by an enemy who wanted her dead. She'd had no quarrel with him before he started this battle, but she was willing to kill to save her own life, and she was more than willing to kill to preserve the life of her friend. She intended to bring Zack's mother home. It was her duty.

She ran to the confrontation, dressed in olive drab pants and heavy boots and an Army surplus field jacket. She'd always pretended that she chose her routine field garb for the simple reason that she looked good in green. Like hell. Her military clothing bound her to the hazy image of her father, who had died wearing clothing issued to him by the Department of Defense.

Her father had died in Vietnam, where the oppressive heat and stifling humidity might actually have felt like home to a Florida boy, but he'd had a whole army shooting at him. Dripping wet with creek water and melted sleet, she faced only two enemies— DeWayne Montrose and hypothermia—and she had her father on her side. His open pocketknife was warm in her hand.

Ahead, a venerable laurel oak reached a long branch over the creek and the clay pits that lined its banks. With a running leap, Faye grabbed the branch and hauled herself up onto it. She pushed her hood back, exposing her bare head to the icy water dripping from the branches above her, because she needed her peripheral vision. From her cantilevered perch, Faye could see the pit that sheltered Ronya, and she'd be able to see DeWayne long before he reached her. The footprints she and Ronya had made went right past the tree, and, with any luck, he would pass directly beneath her. Dressed in mossy green and nestled in the limbs of a laurel oak, which would keep its leaves all winter just like live oaks did in more southerly climes, she was well-camouflaged from a pursuer who had no reason to look up.

Faye watched for her adversary to approach. She tested the pocketknife's edge, running a finger over its blade while she listened for the sound of her pursuer's footsteps.

She heard DeWayne before she saw him. Over the faint

noises of the flowing creek, she could pick up the quiet but unmistakable sound of boots on muddy ground. She readied herself, knowing she would only have one chance. Her eyes searched the woods, until she caught her first glimpse of him, bundled in his great gray coat. She caught a glimpse of red, the only spot of color in the winter wood, like the last autumn leaf clinging to a bare branch.

Her heart froze in her chest: DeWayne didn't have red hair.

TWENTY-EIGHT

JOE, PERCHED IN a sycamore tree just off the Alcaskaki-Gadsden road to the east of the settlement, rubbed his eyes. He had been watching for signs of movement around the old pickup truck among the trees for the better part of an hour. All had been quiet. No cars had passed. Nobody had walked down the footpath that crossed the road a few yards from Joe's tree. The only evidence of human life had been the sound of a hunter's gun, just a single sharp blast. Joe respected anyone who could bag his prey with a single shot.

It was getting to be time to do something. Joe was a patient man, but he drew the line at sitting in a tree in an icy rain for no good reason.

After Faye and Ronya had hurried off to Miss Dovey's, he'd set out to find DeWayne Montrose, as Faye had asked. He'd checked Hanahan's first, then, being a practical soul, headed for DeWayne's house. His practicality had been rewarded, for as he had approached by the footpath in back, DeWayne had slammed out the front door, an open bottle sloshing in one hand and a white rag in the other, and stumbled to his truck. Joe watched through the shrubbery as DeWayne fairly threw himself into the driver's seat, burying his head in his hands. Joe raised his eyebrows when he saw his chest shudder, again and again. The man was weeping.

Once he regained his composure, DeWayne had taken a swig and put the truck in gear. Staying barely within sight of the truck, Joe paced it at a dogtrot. As long as DeWayne kept to the dirt roads and narrow lanes of the settlement, and as long as he traveled at the deliberate pace of a drunk trying to keep his vehicle between the ditches, Joe would have no problem tracking him. And if he took the bridge out of the settlement, he would stop being an immediate threat to Faye's safety and, thus, cease being an immediate concern to Joe.

But DeWayne hadn't headed for the bridge. At the end of the road, he'd turned left onto the Alcaskaki-Gadsden road. Joe looked at the smooth pavement with dismay. There was no way he could keep up with DeWayne on this road. He'd watched as the truck sped away, then veered off the road, across the strip of grass at its side, and right into a stand of trees, where it narrowly avoided a pine as it rolled to a stop. Joe's instructions had been clear. He had climbed up into his sycamore and commenced keeping an eye on DeWayne, who had cooperated by passing out, dead drunk.

But enough was enough. The time had come to fish or cut bait. Joe figured Faye'd had time to get Kiki out of harm's way. It only made sense for Joe to go back to Miss Dovey's and let people know where DeWayne was. But first, he wanted to eyeball DeWayne, just to make sure he wasn't fixing to sober up and drive away. Joe dropped down to the ground and approached the truck in a crouch. Raising his head slowly, he peered in the window.

DeWayne had fallen over onto the seat and lay there breathing heavily, his eyes glazed and his mouth open.

The window was open a crack. The fumes that escaped stunk something awful of sweat, alcohol, and something else—a chemical smell, like paint thinner or cleaning fluid. In a flash, he pulled DeWayne out of the truck and onto the ground. DeWayne groaned and rolled over onto his side. On the passenger seat was a terrycloth towel soaked in something that was the source of the evil smell permeating the truck's cabin.

Holding his breath, Joe reached in and grabbed the

towel. Something told him that Adam would want to have his lab people take a look at this.

DeWayne groaned again, and Joe knelt at his side. "Mr. Montrose?" Joe shook the man's shoulders. "DeWayne?"

The man's eyelids fluttered, and he reached out to touch Joe's shirt.

"Kiki," he said.

"She's not here," said Joe. "I'm Joe Wolf Mantooth."

DeWayne shook his head and moaned. "How can I live without her?"

"She's dead?" asked Joe in some alarm.

DeWayne, even in the midst of his stupor, looked at Joe like he was crazy. "No, you idiot. She threw me out." His eyes rolled and he vomited onto the wet grass.

Bewildered, Joe looked around. He needed to get De-Wayne some help. Miss Dovey's house wasn't far away. If he was lucky, Faye would still be there, lingering over the Sujosa treasures she had told him about. Faye would know what to do.

THE SIGHT OF Kiki's red hair filled Faye with hope. Despite her injuries, she had come to help them. Maybe she could talk some sense into DeWayne. At the very least, maybe she could go for help—if, that is, she was strong enough to get back to the settlement.

Faye almost shouted out to their rescuer. She came within a single word of giving her position away. Then she saw the rifle in Kiki's right hand and the look on her face. It was the look of a hunter. Kiki, not DeWayne, had tracked her and treed her. It had been Kiki driving the dogs to kill for her, while wearing DeWayne's coat and boots. No wonder Joe had not come. He was still doing what Faye asked him to do; he was watching DeWayne. She was on her own.

Despite her fear, Faye felt a bitter admiration for Kiki's game. It's hard to keep yourself in good physical condition when you're faking a serious illness, but Kiki had found a way. She'd been wandering these woods in her nightgown for months, maybe years. No wonder she'd been able to match Faye and Ronya, step for step.

The whole settlement lives in fear that we'll find Kiki at the bottom of Great Tiger Bluff one morning, Jenny had said. Maybe it wasn't so hard to convince good-hearted people that you were sick, if you tugged on their sympathies hard enough. You could even fool a gifted doctor whose treatments had put you into remission, if you suddenly refused to let him examine you. And she, Faye, had been clueless enough to tell Kiki the very thing that Carmen had been killed for knowing.

Kiki approached deliberately, each step slowed by the mud sucking at her boot soles. For Faye, crouched in the branch above, there was no time to think, no time to wonder why. She waited for the step that would take her enemy beneath her and, her warrior nerves on edge, she waited for one step more. Then she dropped.

She aimed the pocketknife at Kiki's right arm. Its short blade couldn't be expected to inflict grievous harm, but her foremost intent was to neutralize the gun.

The knife missed Kiki's bicep and struck her assailant's shoulder. Its blade penetrated the thin skin over her collarbone, then broke as it struck the bone itself. Handle and broken blade dropped into the muck beneath them.

The momentum of Faye's falling body carried both of them to the ground and into an open pit. Faye kept her foot on the rifle as they went down, trying to use her body weight to wrest it from Kiki's grip. Even then, so ingrained was her image of Kiki the invalid that she didn't expect much resistance, and so was wholly surprised when Kiki fought back, agile and strong. Faye reached for the rifle with one hand and tried to hold Kiki off with the other.

Still hanging on to the gun, Kiki scrambled to her feet.

She slammed Faye down so hard that Faye lost her one-handed grip and dropped into the mud.

Faye reached out and grasped the rifle again, this time with both hands, and regained her footing. Looking her adversary in the eyes, she did the unexpected. Rather than try to wrest the weapon from Kiki's hands, she yanked it sideways, jamming its muzzle into the muddy wall of the pit. Maybe she had succeeded in plugging it with stiff clay, and maybe she hadn't, but only an idiot would risk pulling its trigger now. Kiki responded by kicking Faye hard in her undefended abdomen.

Faye's grip loosened reflexively and Kiki seized the opportunity to swing the rifle like a baseball bat, clipping Faye hard on the head. When the stock made contact, Faye felt blood flow over her ear and down her neck, and she knew that her stitches and the wound they protected had burst open. Her legs buckled and she went down on her knees, but she was a warrior. She was her father's daughter.

Kiki's belly was the only vulnerable target she could reach, but she could by God pummel it for all she was worth. She landed a solid blow to her assailant's diaphragm and heard Kiki's breath leave her in a whoosh, but it wasn't enough to knock her to the ground, where Faye could fight her on her own level.

Faye saw Kiki raise the gun, preparing to strike again. She feared that another blow to the head would leave her senseless, so she threw herself down, hoping to roll away from the point of impact.

Someone behind them barked, "Hit that woman again and die."

Joe stood on the creek bluff above them, an antique rifle at his shoulder.

Kiki looked at him. A wild smile spread over her face as she pointed her rifle at Faye's head. "You don't want me to hit her?" she asked. "Okay. I'll shoot her, instead."

Faye lay as still as she could. If the barrel of the rifle was plugged, anything could happen when Kiki pulled the trigger. She could wind up with a bullet in her brain. The plug could force the bullet out the opposite end of the chamber and into Kiki's face. Or the barrel could disintegrate into shrapnel. No one in their right mind wanted to be near that rifle when its trigger was pulled. But then, Faye saw no evidence whatsoever that Kiki Montrose was in her right mind.

Faye had never seen Joe fire a gun, but he was a master at shooting a hand-made bow. His eye-hand coordination was perfect, and he had an instinctual understanding of ballistics. She was sure he could hit Kiki if he aimed at her.

She was not, however, completely sure that Joe was capable of shooting a woman.

"Drop the gun. I'm not bluffing," said Joe.

Kiki smiled at him, and touched the barrel of the rifle to Faye's forehead.

As the shot echoed down the canyon, Faye closed her eyes and waited for death.

THE ECHOES OF the gunshot died, and Faye found that she was still alive. She opened her eyes.

Kiki loomed above Faye, but the rifle was no longer pointed at her head. And a bright red stain was spreading down Kiki's right arm.

Faye's eyes swiveled to Joe. She should have known he'd find a way to save her without doing irreparable damage to Kiki. Then she blinked. DeWayne Montrose had appeared at Joe's side.

"Oh, God, woman, what have you done?" He started down the creek bank, but Joe stopped him with a twitch of his rifle.

"Drop it," Joe repeated, to Kiki.

Kiki's right arm hung limp, immobilized by Joe's bullet, but her left arm was in perfect condition. Moving smoothly for someone with a gunshot wound, she tucked the rifle's stock under her left armpit and reached for the trigger with her good hand.

"If I'm going, I'm taking you with me, you son-of-a-bitch," snarled Kiki, pointing the rifle at DeWayne.

The rifle's barrel was still jammed full of mud, and Kiki was still hell-bent on firing it. Faye rolled, covering her head with her arms against the expected explosion.

A shot rang out, clear and true. As the echoes reverberated down the canyon, Kiki slumped to the ground, her lifeless body coming to rest on top of Faye.

FAYE'S HAIR WAS matted with blood and muck. Her whole head hurt, not just the torn skin of her scalp. It hurt on the inside, within her skull, as if Kiki's attack had bruised her very brain. It probably had.

"Are you all right?" Joe demanded, squatting beside Faye on the ground. Laying aside the rifle, his big hands gently lifted Kiki off Faye. "Where's Ronya?"

"She's okay, but her leg's broken." She waved toward the pit where Ronya lay.

DeWayne walked toward the body of his wife. He dropped to her side, his head weaving from side to side. "What will I tell Irene?"

Faye turned her eyes away, staring at the gray sky, and then looked back at Joe. "Are you gonna be okay?"

Joe looked at Kiki's body and sat down heavily, overcome by the realization that he had pulled a trigger on a woman. Faye reached out her icy hand. Slipping it into his big warm one, she squeezed as tight as she could.

TWENTY-NINE

DeWayne sat with his wife's body while Joe went to the nearest house, Elliott's, for help. In a surprisingly short time, the sheriff and a team of investigators arrived, as well as those Sujosa who, having heard about the third violent death to strike their community in a single week, felt compelled to venture out into the freezing dusk.

Adam and Brent arrived with the police. Together with Joe, they lifted Ronya out of the clay pit that trapped her. While Brent stabilized her leg for transport, Adam approached Faye with a bucket full of icy creek water, several sponges, a towel, and a bottle of disinfectant. He was wearing goggles and rubber gloves that reached his elbows.

"Are you afraid of me or something?" she asked, but the joke fell flat. Kiki had been suffering from a lifelong and often-fatal blood-borne infection, and here Faye sat, covered in blood. Some of it was hers and some of it was Kiki's. This wasn't good.

Adam made her remove her blood-soaked jacket. They were both relieved to see that her clothes were clean underneath. Then he told her to lean over and put her head between her knees. It wasn't pleasant having a bucket of ice water poured over her head, but by the time Adam was finished, the blood dripping from her hair ran clear.

"This is what you call 'seat-of-the-pants' first aid," he said, gently drying her wounded head. "You go with what you've got." Then he daubed disinfectant all over her scalp

wound and checked her over for other wounds. He found
bruises, not cuts, which was a good thing, contagion-wise.

"I think Kiki was cured," Faye said, hoping it was true.
"That's why she wouldn't let Brent examine her."

"I don't think doctors are ever willing to say that a virus
like that is cured, but Kiki was obviously in remission.
Maybe that meant she didn't have so many viruses swimming around in her blood to pass to you. Let's hope so."

An ambulance was waiting to take Ronya to the hospital
in Gadsden, and Brent climbed into it with her. A police
car arrived to take Adam and Faye back to the settlement.
In the confusion, no one realized that they were taking her
to a place where there would be no doctor to stitch up the
open wound on her head. Faye didn't care. Brent would
come back eventually, and he could do it then.

The officer at the wheel gave Faye his jacket and cranked
up the heater. All the way to the settlement, she rested with
her wounded head in Adam's lap.

FAYE SAT IN an easy chair in the bunkhouse parlor. She had
wrapped herself in two quilts, and she was still cold.

"You should get to bed, Faye," said Laurel.

Faye knew she should be in bed, too. If she didn't rest
soon, her body would simply quit on her. But her mind
wouldn't let her stop worrying over what she knew she
had to do.

"I'll rest soon, but I need to find Adam first. It's important. Do you think he's still here in the settlement?"

Laurel nodded. "He's over at Hanahan's. You can bor-
row my coat."

Oh, yeah. Adam had decreed that her coat had too much
tainted blood on it, then thrown it in a Dumpster. "Thanks.
I think a coat will be mighty handy on an icy night like

this." Faye stood slowly. The last thing she wanted to do
was to go back out into the cold.

THE RAIN, AT LEAST, had stopped, but she lingered on the
porch, reluctant to step into that blasting wind.

Brent and Adam were walking up the street. Between
them walked Leo, his head bowed. They stopped at one of
the sheriff's cruisers in the church parking lot, and spoke
to one of the officers. But she hadn't ever told Adam about
the forgery ring. How did he know?

When Faye noticed that Leo stood tall for a man being
hauled into jail, she knew. He had confessed. There was a
tiny shred of dignity to be had in facing your sins, and Leo
was hanging onto that dignity.

Faye remembered Brent talking about the years the three
of them—Brent, Leo, Adam—had anchored their high
school baseball team. Time could wreak grievous changes.

"ADAM," SHE CALLED, as the cruiser drove away with Leo
in back.

Adam came to her side.

"I need to talk to you," she said. "Now."

"Let's go inside," he said. "You've had enough cold for
one day. Or one lifetime."

They went back into the bunkhouse and sat on the parlor sofa. The space heater was running, as it had been all
evening, but Faye was still chilled through.

"From the looks of things, I'm guessing you know about
Leo and the forgeries?" she asked.

Adam nodded. "He's not saying much, other than that
nobody else knew that Ronya's pottery was being passed
off as valuable antiques. Well, he did say one thing: he's the
one who took Carmen's briefcase from the burned house.
Seems there were some pieces of pottery in it that he was
afraid would give his game away. It's a damned good thing

he's told us that—we'd have been searching high and low for that briefcase, thinking that Kiki took it so that nobody would get a look at Carmen's interviews. It would have put a crimp in our case if that clue were left dangling. I'm having trouble believing that Leo brokered Ronya's work all by himself, but he's keeping his mouth shut."

"That's what I needed to tell you," said Faye. "Our friend Raleigh was his buyer. Since he left town this morning, he is probably, right this very minute, skipping the country with his ill-gotten dollars."

Adam stared at her. "Are you sure?"

"Pretty sure," said Faye. She told him how she had put it together.

Adam let out a disgusted laugh. "The hell of it is that I waved goodbye to him about lunchtime while you were busy solving this case. 'Have a nice trip, Dr. Raleigh,' I said. Christ. If the man hasn't driven to the Birmingham airport and departed for parts unknown, then he's an idiot."

"He's an arrogant ass, but don't be fooled into thinking he's an idiot. That was my mistake."

"Care to take a guess where he would go?"

Faye didn't know Raleigh well enough to answer that question, but she knew plenty of people like him. "Raleigh's one of those academics whose work and personal life are completely intermingled. He's married to a Spanish woman from Manises, where some of the finest Hispano-Moresque ceramics were produced in the 1400s. In fact, if I had to guess right now where the Sujosa came from, it would be either Manises or Malaga. Anyway, somebody should check flights to Spain. Though he's probably already in the air. He's had all day."

"I doubt it," said Adam, hope audible in his voice. "They call the Birmingham airport 'international,' but there are only a couple of flights a day that actually leave the country from there. He had to drive to Birmingham and wait for a flight to a real international airport. Flights to Spain don't leave all that often, so he had to wait for one of those, too. Factor in time for getting through security, and I'll bet Raleigh's cooling his heels in the Atlanta airport right now, waiting for a red-eye to Spain. I'd better go find the sheriff. Luckily, he's in Hanahan's, drinking coffee and tearing his hair out." He rose from his chair, and eyed her. "Are you done?"

Faye nodded. "I'm going to bed."

"Good." He put a hand on her arm as she headed for the stairs. "Your daddy would be proud of you."

THIRTY

IT WAS LATE Saturday morning. Faye, feeling better than she had thought she would, but still far from her best, wandered around the bunkhouse with a cup of coffee, looking for Joe, who was certainly still suffering over killing Kiki. She didn't want to intrude, but she did want him to know she was there for him. Probably he had gone outside—Joe never felt entirely comfortable indoors. She gazed out the frosted window in the kitchen; she had no desire to go out into that cold—ever.

In the parlor, she found Bingham and Amory in quiet conversation with a couple of the technicians who had remained in the settlement for the weekend.

"Faye," said Bingham, standing up. "You're looking well, considering the events of yesterday. We're trying to make sense of all this, as you can guess. Why don't you join us?"

Faye was glad to comply. A dose of rational academic chatter sounded like a fine remedy for the surreal week she'd just survived. "Any news?" she asked, settling into a cozy chair.

"The sheriff's people have been all over the settlement since midnight. They've set up shop in Hanahan's."

"That must please Jenny," said Faye. "I hope they eat a lot. Does she carry doughnuts?"

They heard the front door open. Brent and Elliott entered, hesitating when they saw the group in the parlor.

"Come on in," said Bingham. "We're just having a little Rural Assistance Project get-together."

"Not hard to guess what you're talking about," said Brent as he sat on the sofa. He gave Faye a critical look. "I'm not happy about how long your wound was open. Any pain?"

"No," she said, her eyes on Elliott. The man's facial expression was flat, and his eyes were blank. He moved like a sleepwalker.

"How are you and Margie doing?" Faye asked.

"Margie's over with Amanda-Lynne and Irene. I'm... still trying to understand." His face showed a bit of life as he peered intently at Faye. "I need to hear it from you—is it true? Kiki tried to kill you?"

"Yes," said Faye.

"But why?" he asked, as if he thought that understanding what happened would make the tragedy go away.

"Because, like an idiot, I told her that I knew she and De-Wayne didn't own the land the cell phone tower was on—the very land that she killed Carmen and Jimmie to keep."

"But she must have known she couldn't get away with it!" argued Elliott.

"My guess is that Kiki planned to kill me, and Ronya if she had to, and put the blame on DeWayne."

"Dangerous for her to turn on DeWayne," said Bingham. "He might have been able to prove he was somewhere else."

"Not if she got rid of him, too," said Faye. "Joe found him unconscious in his truck, alongside a rag soaked with a cleaning solvent that can also be used to knock folks out—the same stuff Adam thinks she used to keep Carmen from escaping the fire. DeWayne remembers Kiki holding the rag over his face, but he got away from her before he passed out. I'm sure she planned for people to think he set his dogs on me and Ronya. I also think it's a pretty good bet she intended to give him a fatal dose and make it look like he committed suicide out of remorse. Nobody would have thought to accuse a sick woman. She'd be free of DeWayne, and the tower lease money would just keep rolling in."

"That's a lot of ifs for a scientist," said Amory.

Faye shrugged. "I admit it's just speculation, but it fits the facts. Kiki was already running on a knife edge. She'd killed two people, and I was getting ready to tell the whole world about her motive."

Elliott ran a hand over his face. "Poor Jimmie. How did he get involved in this?"

"Adam and I think he saw Kiki the night of the fire," said Faye. "Maybe he knew she set it, or maybe he was just suspicious. Either way, he must have approached Kiki about it. If he'd approached Adam, instead, he'd still be alive." Faye shook her head. "It would have been Jimmie's word against hers—she would have claimed to be out on one of her midnight rambles—but she couldn't afford to take the chance that he could prove she did it. So she snitched Irene's cell phone and sent him a text message to lure him to the tower."

"Wait a minute, Faye," said Brent. "That can't be right. Irene's cell wouldn't have worked here in the settlement. Kiki would have had to get halfway to Alcaskaki somehow, driving DeWayne's truck—presuming he wasn't off somewhere in it. She would have had to drive right past Jenny's. Surely someone would have seen her."

Doubt shadowed the faces around Faye. Could she be wrong? Was a killer still among them?

Faye shook her head grimly. "There's one place in the settlement where a cell phone *will* work—up on the tower itself. It's the only clear line-of-sight from anywhere in the settlement to the Alcaskaki tower. Standing on the ground, you'd never get a clear signal, but high up the tower? It would work, and no one would ever suspect Kiki—or anyone else who was in the settlement at the time. All she had to do was sit tight and wait for Jimmie to come, thinking he was meeting Irene."

"Um, Faye?" Elliott interrupted. "Irene doesn't look much like her mother."

"If Kiki were sitting high in the tower, dressed in one of Irene's old parkas with the hood pulled up, there's no way Jimmie would recognize her, not until he climbed almost up high enough to see her face-to-face. Right before that happened, I think she just raised a boot sole, put it on his chest, and shoved him off the ladder. And the boots she was wearing were Jimmie's gardening boots. That's why all the footprints Adam found at the tower were his."

"Incredible," said Bingham. "I mean—credible! Extraordinary work, Faye."

Faye shook her head. "I just wish I'd put things together sooner."

"Poor Irene," sighed Elliott. "I can't believe Kiki'd do that to her own daughter. One thing, though, Faye. Kiki and Irene slept in the same room. How could Kiki get out to set the fire with Irene right there?"

"She worked at the dry cleaner for a long time, long enough to bring home all the spot remover a housewife could ever need. She had more than enough perk to make sure Irene and Carmen slept soundly that night, and enough left over to nearly kill DeWayne."

The room fell silent, as everyone tried to take it all in. "What about the deed we were talking about yesterday?" asked Bingham.

"I reckon the confusion over the boundary line must have started when Lester's Creek changed course. I don't know if it was an honest mistake that Kiki took advantage of, or if she went out of her way to change the deed. Either way, she knew she would lose that cell phone lease, and the money that came with it, if the discrepancy were uncovered."

"But the money was going for her drugs...." Elliott's

voice drifted off. "She wasn't spending it on medicine, was she?"

"She stopped seeing Brent just when he thought his treatments were helping her—because they were. She just didn't want him to know about it. A computer expert got into Kiki's computer early this morning. She had a couple of good-sized accounts with an on-line brokerage, where she was taking advantage of her remission to squirrel away the money that DeWayne thought was going for medications. She'd even made a down payment on a condo in California."

"I wonder how much longer she would have kept it up before taking off," said Amory.

"If DeWayne were dead, she'd get the money anyway, no matter where she lived," said Brent.

"Bad luck for her that a bunch of eggheads came to town and started poking around," said Bingham.

Amory pointed a finger at his colleague. "I think you've had a lucky break, Bingham. You were the one who found the deed. You might have been next, after Faye."

Bingham's pale face went paler.

"How did she ever find out that Carmen had the deed?" asked Brent.

"Dumb luck," said Faye. "Kiki was there when Carmen interviewed Amanda-Lynne, and the subject came up. Carmen told her flat out that the deed was in her office. Adam thinks that Kiki drugged Irene. Then she went to Carmen's office—which doesn't even have a lock on the door—and stole the will. After she was sure everyone in the bunkhouse was asleep, she knocked Carmen out, using a rag soaked with cleaning fluid. Adam's chemist found traces of it on Carmen's pillow, where it dripped off the rag. Once Carmen was asleep, Kiki used the kerosene heater to set Carmen's bedclothes on fire."

"My God," said Elliott.

"What I don't understand," said Amory, "is how Kiki knew you were at Miss Dovey's yesterday."

"Jenny told her. I'd been on the phone with Jenny, looking for Adam, so when Kiki called her looking for me, she didn't think twice about telling her I was there with Ronya. Kiki must have been planning to use the dogs to get rid of me ever since I told her about the property mistake," continued Faye. "She called us, claiming that DeWayne had beaten her up. Trust me, she was ready with the dogs when Ronya and I came to her rescue. She had tried to get De-Wayne out of the way—getting him drunk and trying to knock him out just like she did Carmen—but he got away. Kiki knew she had to eliminate me as soon as possible, before I blabbed about the property dispute, so she went ahead with her plan, hoping to catch up with DeWayne after his dogs had eaten me and Ronya."

"If Joe hadn't found DeWayne…" Brent said.

"Then he might not have gotten back to Miss Dovey's in time for her to give him her rifle and send him to our rescue. Miss Dovey knew that gunshot didn't come from any hunter. The settlement men don't hunt so close to people's houses. Running in the direction of the gunshot got Joe close enough to pick up our trail. Joe can track anything."

Faye put aside her empty coffee cup and rose. She really needed to find Joe.

"Has anyone tried to contact Raleigh?" Bingham asked. "It would be a good idea to have a staff meeting first thing Monday morning and agree on how all of this affects our relationship with the community."

Faye paused on her way to the hall. "I think you should take the lead on that, Dr. Bingham. You have a good relationship with the Sujosa, and, well, it may be a while before we hear from Raleigh."

"I second that," said Amory.

Faye went to the entryway and located the coat that Laurel had lent her.

"Where do you think you're going?" asked Brent in his doctor's voice.

"I need to find Joe," she said. "He's—this has hit him hard."

A peculiar expression came over Brent's face. "He's with Laurel. I saw them out walking about an hour ago."

"Oh." Faye nodded. "That's good. I'm glad he's not alone. Thanks." She hung the coat back on the rack and headed to the kitchen, wondering how much coffee she was going to have to drink before she felt human again.

THIRTY-ONE

ON SUNDAY AFTERNOON, Faye finally got the chance to enjoy a slice of Miss Dovey's jam cake. Adam, who had suggested the visit to her after Jimmie's funeral service, attacked his piece with the intensity of a man who had tasted this particular delicacy before. The cake was flavored with a liberal dose of cinnamon that warmed Faye from the inside, and the cold spot in her chest that had lingered since her ordeal was threatening to thaw. Miss Dovey, who had lived a long time on this earth, had shown the good sense to withdraw into the kitchen, ostensibly to wash the dishes, but probably just to give the two of them a chance to be alone. Faye suspected that she had thrown more than one couple together in this room, only to leave and let them find their own way to each other.

Faye needed to find a way to fill the silence. "I guess you want to see Miss Dovey's treasures."

"Yes," said Adam, "I do."

Miss Dovey had given Faye permission to handle her treasures as much as she liked. *You're a professional, child. You know how to take care of them.* Faye went into the bedroom, reached under the bed and retrieved the package of Spanish fragments and some of the loveliest later pieces. She took them into the parlor and set them carefully on the coffee table in front of Adam, then she fetched the eclipse platter off the mantel and displayed it, too, like a child showing off her colorful toys.

"Aren't these gorgeous?" she asked, flinging her arms

out to encompass the Sujosa's glorious past. "And this is the prize of the collection," she said, pointing to the eclipse platter. She lowered herself to the floor, so she could get closer to the beautiful artifacts.

"I reckon that means it's the oldest one?"

It was a reasonable guess, but in this case, Adam was wrong. She held the platter up where he could see it better. "Look here in the middle. The artist obviously witnessed a total eclipse of the sun. Here's the corona and the eclipsed disk. And these," she said, pointing to dabs of lustrous gold adorning the blue surface, "would be the planets and brightest stars. They're visible in the daytime during an eclipse. See these stars over here? If that's not the Southern Cross, I'll eat my telescope."

"And that makes it valuable?"

"Don't you see? It tells us that the Sujosa's kidnapped ancestors and their English sailors didn't come straight to Alabama. They were living in the Southern Hemisphere when this potter saw an eclipse. Considering that the word "Sujosa" seems to come from a Portuguese word but their pottery looks Spanish to me, I'll wager they sailed from Spain, then spent time in Brazil. They probably lived near a port where they could trade for cobalt pigments," Faye continued, "or the platter wouldn't be blue."

Adam shook his head, saying, "That's a lot of information for one little plate to carry."

"Wait. It gets better. I've got an astronomer friend whose computer can use the star and planet patterns to tell me the day and place that this eclipse occurred. We know from Miss Dovey's song that the Sujosa left Spain after 1560. Jimmie told Carmen that the Sujosa were already here in time for the great meteor storm of 1833. And now we'll be able to get a precise date when they were in Brazil. This is why I came here in the first place—to find out who the Sujosa are and where they come from."

Faye wanted to hug the platter, but she was afraid she'd
scratch it with a shirt button, so she refrained. She continued her ecstatic monologue. "And look at this one," she
said, holding up a white platter ornamented by fine golden
brushstrokes radiating from a single point, a color combination that reminded her of the lone glimpse she got of
the potsherd that Jorge crushed. "This has to be a repre-
sentation of the meteor storm of 1833, but the sky is white
because the painter couldn't get cobalt pigments here in
Alabama."

"This is all real interesting, Faye, but—"

"Adam, you don't understand. All these little pieces of
evidence tell us so much. Now we know that the Sujosa's
ancestors came from Britain and Spain, probably Manises or Malaga. They likely intermarried with Brazilians
of European descent, and possibly also with native North
and South Americans. And they may have African blood
from Moorish Spaniards, or from slaves held in Brazil or
the United States."

"Impressive," Adam said. "I'm sure you'll get a publication out of it. I know how important that is to you academics." His tone was cool.

"Yeah, publications are important and all, but solving
puzzles about people and how they live is the exciting part
of my work."

"Yeah. That's what I do every day. Solve puzzles. Why
did this building burn? Did somebody set that fire on purpose? Why would they do such a thing? I like getting those
kinds of answers."

The platter in her hands felt heavy, cold, fragile. She
put it down carefully, and sat in silence. What did he want
her to say?

"We got Raleigh," he said, with less enthusiasm than
the arrest of a criminal should have merited. "He was in

Atlanta, waiting for a plane to Spain, just like we thought. He's talking, but he insists he had no contact with anyone other than Leo. They're both in big trouble."

Faye said only, "I'm glad you got Raleigh." She let the silence deepen.

Adam broke it. "Faye, I cannot believe that Leo conned Ronya and the others into making those pots for him without them realizing that his business was illegal. They're smarter than that. Leo says he was taking orders from Raleigh and giving them to Ronya, but everybody knows that she's smarter than he is. If I had to guess who was the mastermind of this operation, I'd say it was her. And I think you know it."

Faye said nothing.

"Faye, it would be Ronya's first offense. The judge probably won't come down too hard on her and all the others, but it's not my call to make. It's not yours, either. You need to tell me what you know. It's the right thing to do. It's the law."

Faye thought of the laws that had barred Sujosa children from attending school with their peers. She thought of poll taxes. She thought of her great-great-grandmother Cally, who was born a slave. There had been a time when the law smiled on all of these things. By what logic should she trust the future of Zack's mother to the tender protection of the law?

Faye thought of Raleigh, raking in a fortune from Ronya's work and paying her a pittance. She thought of Ronya, sharing with her community the outrageously small sum he gave her for museum-quality work. She thought of Leo, who was accepting the full blame for all their crimes, deliberately shielding Ronya and his friends from the punishment in store for him. She thought of little Zack.

She didn't say a thing.

There was disappointment in Adam's eyes, and judgment, and anger. He said, "I have work to do," and left her sitting on the floor alone.

THIRTY-TWO

Friday, December 16

FAYE WAS EAGER to get home. Christmas on Joyeuse was a quiet and comforting thing. Joe would cut a small tree from her own island and they'd hang her mother's ornaments on its branches. The gulf and the sky would be winter-gray, but the breeze would be gentle and warm. This year, it appeared that there was a possibility they might enjoy company for the holidays. She sat on her suitcase, forcing it to close, then wheeled it outside and put it in the trunk of the Bonneville.

A heavy white frost covered the ground, the nearest thing to snow that Faye had ever seen. It softened the hard edges of human encroachment on the lovely river valley, adorning the shabby houses of the Sujosa like a light blanket of diamonds. She reflected that time had begun to cover the scars of Kiki's crimes in much the same way. The people who suffered at her hands could never be completely whole again, but time had already begun to soften their pain.

Brent was underwriting Ronya's new business, doing the work that the Rural Assistance Project should have done. She had apologized to him for questioning his motives for helping the Sujosa, and he'd had the good grace to accept.

With Brent's financial backing, Ronya and her workers were creating signed reproductions of famous Hispano-Moresque pieces, and demand was brisk. Leo's lawyer was encouraging, saying that his sentence would be shorter than it might have been, since he had come forward with evidence related to Carmen's and Jimmie's murders. Ronya would be waiting for him when he came home, and they were both determined to make a new beginning.

Amanda-Lynne was dealing with her loss by lavishing her abundant mothering skills on Irene, whose own mother had never had any love to give. Irene's pain had managed to rouse DeWayne from his twenty-years' sleep, and Irene now had a father, too. Plans were afoot for her to go to college to study computer science the following fall, with all her expenses paid out of Kiki's secret accounts. Rather than battle each other in court, Amanda-Lynne and DeWayne had had a lawyer draw up an agreement by which they shared the tract of land leased to the cell phone company. The income would make neither of them wealthy, but it had already softened the edges of their poverty. And Faye saw a real likelihood that the marriage between DeWayne and Amanda-Lynne that Miss Dovey had blessed all those years ago might someday take place.

Faye's personal life had been on hold in favor of intoxicating professional possibilities. She had closed the door on a relationship with Brent when she accused him of being ashamed of his Sujosa heritage, and Adam had closed the door on her when he realized that he couldn't live with her shades-of-gray perception of justice.

She'd had little time to dwell on her romantic failures, though, because her professional victories had been so sweet. Clue by clue, she had put together a history of the Sujosa. The eclipse platter, Miss Dovey's song, the buried remnants of the Lester homestead—all these things were giving life to the past. Under the gentle hand of Dr. Bingham, who was taking over as the new head of the project, her spring and summer would be split between the study of the old homestead and of an evocative rectangle of mortared stones—the foundation of a gristmill from the mid-1700s—that she and her crew had uncovered on a tract of Miss Dovey's property. ("I did tell you that my maiden name was Miller, didn't I, child?" had been the old woman's response when Faye told her what they'd unearthed.) One day soon, there would be a published paper documenting what she'd learned among the Sujosa, and Carmen Martinez would be listed as co-author.

She stuck her head in the door at Hanahan's, asking Jenny if she'd seen Joe. It was odd that he wasn't around when there were suitcases to be toted.

"I saw him telling Laurel goodbye," Jenny said. She glanced around the store, then added in a low voice, "I don't think it went well."

Faye said nothing, not wanting to betray Joe by gossiping over his pain. She needed to find him, but where would he go? On instinct, she headed toward the burned-out ruins where Carmen had died.

Joe was there, sitting in the corner of a roofless room on a floor burned to the color of charcoal. He was weeping.

"Faye, all I did was invite Laurel to come spend Christmas with us at Joyeuse. She started talking about how it hurt her to watch me walk slow so she could keep up with me on her crutches. She said she'd be a useless burden on a wild island like Joyeuse, that she didn't think she could even haul herself off a dock and into a boat."

Faye pictured a tall dock and a heaving boat and a rough sea. She thought of the main living area of Joyeuse's big house, only reachable by stairs. She remembered the sheer vitality of Joe striding through the muck and the sand of Joyeuse Island, just happy to be alive in such a beautiful place. Sweet little Laurel could never be a burden, but life on Joyeuse would be a minute-to-minute struggle for her.

"I told her I'd help her, that I could tote her when the going was too hard, but she said no. She said I needed a woman who could keep up with me. She said she was letting me go."

Faye sat down beside Joe and he rested his tear-stained face in her lap. Her palm, splayed across his muscled back, felt his breathing settle and slow until she knew that he was asleep.

Joe had come a long way in the time they'd known each other. Laurel, by helping him with his reading, had finally convinced him that he was in no way stupid, that his path to an education was simply strewn with boulders in the form of severe learning disabilities. He had even spoken of studying for his GED and his driver's exam.

What had Faye done for him? She had given him a place to live, and she had patronized him. And what had Joe done for her? He'd saved her life, twice, and never asked her for a thing.

His hair had slipped loose from its customary binding and spread itself over her legs. It was lustrous and strong, with the lovely rough texture of raw silk. Faye stroked his hair as she watched him sleep and wondered what she was going to do about Joe.

* * * * *

Author's Notes

THE SUJOSA AND their valley settlement are completely fictional, but there are many "triracial isolate" ethnic groups like them in the United States. This is hardly surprising, considering that the collision of the world's diverse peoples in the Americas happened so recently, in historical terms. For *Relics,* I researched quite a number of real groups like the Melungeons of Appalachia, the Redbones of Louisiana, and the Cajans of Alabama, who are not related to the Cajuns of Louisiana.

Establishing a history for any of these people is difficult. Time is quick to obscure anyone's ancestry. How many of us know the names of all of our great-great grandparents? By creating the Sujosa out of whole cloth, I avoided this problem. They have the history I want them to have.

I am a writer who loves my research, and I found that establishing a realistic background for the Sujosa was particularly illuminating. In my reading, I discovered a collection of common Melungeon surnames and quickly noticed two familiar names on the list—White and Roberson. My great-great-great-grandmother, Susan Mariah White Beasley, was born to William White and Sarah Roberson. (Many of these names will be familiar to those of you who read *Artifacts.*) The Whites and Robersons on my family tree lived in North Carolina, which is home to many Melungeons. Even more interesting is the fact that family lore says that Susan Mariah White was Native American, probably Cherokee. Many people claimed to be "Indian" or "Black

Irish," rather than admitting to Melungeon ancestry. I will probably never know any more than this about my great-great-grandmother, but the questions make me feel closer to her and to my imaginary friends, the Sujosa.